For bulk orders and wholesale prices for your
bookstore or local library, please contact the publisher at
legendarybooksllc@gmail.com

Other books by Mary Ann:

Into the Mind of Mary Ann Gouze

Table of Contents:

PROLOGUE

Fourteen miles south of Pittsburgh, St. Luke's Hospital looks down into Warrenvale, one of the many mill towns in Pennsylvania's legendary Steel Valley. Here, for over a century, thousands of immigrants eked out their lives in the brutal world of the early steel industry. These men—mostly laborers and many illiterate—stoically endured the horribly hard labor, the fiery explosions of the open-hearth furnaces, and the stench of sulfur that remained with them long after the blare of the quitting whistle.

In the bars along tavern row, many drowned their frustrations in alcohol. But some, like Walter Lipinski and his father before him, could not extinguish their hatred of the working conditions they were forced to accept. And these deplorable few...would go home drunk, and abusive.

CHAPTER ONE

February 11, 1951, Monday

Walter Lipinski, third generation steelworker, was stuck in the waiting room of old St. Luke's. Occasionally he paced, leaving dirty footprints on the green shag carpet. Walter hated hospitals. He hated waiting. But most of all he hated his mother-in-law, Maggie McBride, who was dying in room 303.

With stumpy fingers, he fumbled into his pocket to retrieve his cigarettes. He stuck a crumpled Chesterfield between his teeth, glanced briefly at the naked woman faded into the side of his Zippo lighter and clicked. A flash of orange sent pungent smoke upward, stinging his eyes. When his vision cleared, he saw his wife, Sarah, who had finally returned from her mother's room. Glancing at his watch, Walter realized she had kept him waiting for almost an hour. It seemed like two. "Well?" he asked in the raspy voice of a heavy smoker. "Did you tell her?"

Sarah, a small woman with a round face and a thick waist, avoided his eyes. She pushed a few strands of dull, brown hair from her forehead. Walter grabbed her by the shoulders. "Damnit! You didn't tell her?!"

Sarah paled as his meaty hands tightened their grip. "I'm sorry," she said. "I tried to tell her. But she keeps insisting that my sister will come home. Could we just keep the baby until she does?"

"Becky ain't comin' home! You go back and tell your mother we ain't keepin' that baby."

With the veins in his neck now standing out, Walter turned and walked to the window. His breath fogged the icy pane as he looked into the distance, where the blazing open-hearth furnace was little more than an orange glow. He took a long drag on his Chesterfield, blew out the smoke and waited. Finally, he spun around, stubbed out the cigarette in a nearby ashtray and pushed his wife out of his way. "Then I'll tell her!"

"Please," Sarah cried grabbing his sleeve. "Don't!" she pleaded, stepping in front of him to block his path. "Don't you understand? My mother is dying!"

"Big deal," he hissed into her face.

A nurse entered the room and asked them to go with her. They glanced at each other then followed the nurse down the hall and into the conference room.

*　　*　　*

Two minutes later, Sarah shot out of the conference room and ran down the hall to room 303. She stopped at the doorway, stunned and disbelieving. Her mother's sunken blue-gray eyes were fixed upon the far wall. Sarah took a deep breath and walked over to the bed. With a trembling hand, she smoothed the sparse gray hair that lay tangled over the pillow like a damaged spider web.

"Mother . . . it's me . . . Sarah," she said, cupping her mother's face in her hands and turning it toward her. Maggie's skin was ashen and etched with a thousand lines. Her opaque eyes stared at Sarah. From the corners of her mother's cracked lips, blood-streaked spittle dripped to the pillow.

"No!" Sarah cried. "Good God—no! Mother?" Her breath coming in huge gulps, she begged, "Don't die now!" She dropped to her knees and buried her face in the sheet, her muffled voice pleading, "I want you to understand. I'm twenty-five years old. I know Walter married me just to take care of his kid. I always knew that."

Blinded by tears, Sarah continued to beg her dead mother. "Please don't make me keep Becky's baby. Walter doesn't want her. He'll leave me. Tell me it's okay to give her away. She's only four months old. She won't remember. Tell me!"

Sarah stood up, grabbed her mother's lifeless body and began shaking it. "Tell me!" she screamed. "Wake up and tell ..."

Two hands broke Sarah's hold on her mother's body, and two more pulled Sarah away from the bed. They dragged her out into the hallway. The nurse stood by as Walter stiffly held Sarah against his chest until her sobs reduced to whimpers.

An hour later, Sarah and Walter Lipinski stepped out into the frigid air of late afternoon and descended the hospital's wide stone steps. Although salted, there were still icy spots as they made their way carefully down to the sidewalk. When they reached Walter's dark blue 1949 Buick, he got in and started the engine. While the car was running, he got out to brush snow from the windshield. Sarah tugged at her frozen door handle. He pushed her aside and yanked the door open.

Third Street, cobble stoned and winding precariously around steep drop-offs, had been sprinkled with black ash. Walter clutched the wheel, maneuvering the car to the bottom of the hill. In the small city of Warrenvale, the streets were clear, with snow piled into dirty heaps along the sidewalks. After driving a few blocks, Walter stopped the car at the bottom of Vickroy Street hill. He grunted for Sarah to get out. It was understood. He would go to the bar. She would have a cold walk home. She said nothing as she stepped out of the car and around a mound of snow. Walter reached across the empty front seat, slammed the door, and drove away.

CHAPTER TWO

Sarah stopped to catch her breath before ascending the four wooden steps to the front door. Though the house was warm, she still shivered as she removed her coat and walked down the short hall to the kitchen. Sitting at the table in a flowery red house-dress, her neighbor, Olga Nikovich, held a sleeping baby. "Vell?" asked the older woman in the thick accent of her Russian homeland.

"Mother's dead," said Sarah. "And," she added, pouring herself a cup of steaming black coffee, "Walter said we can't keep little Anna Mae."

"You husband is wrong." Olga pulled the pink blanket back, and the infant stretched out her legs until her tiny toes parted. The baby yawned and when she closed her mouth, a little bubble popped at the bow of her tiny pink lips

Sarah stepped closer. "Such a sweetie-pie."

"You haf to do what's right. It ain't Annie's fault she is born."

Sarah's eyes met Olga's in uncomfortable silence. While returning the coffeepot to the stove, Sarah said, "Walter won't let me."

Olga stood up, walked to the stove, and placed the baby into Sarah's arms. As little Anna Mae was moved from one woman to the other, her bright blue eyes opened. "Now you tell me," Olga said, sitting back down at the table, "that those eyes ain't—God rest her soul—you mother's eyes."

"They are. But they're my sister's eyes too. I can't keep her."

"So, little Anna Mae—you just throw her away?"

Holding the baby close to her chest, Sarah sat down and began to cry. Olga was silent. Several minutes passed with one woman weeping, the other just sitting. Finally Sarah sighed, "Olga," she said as she coaxed the cover over the baby's energetic little legs, "I had hoped that with mother dying, he might change his mind. But he didn't. He said no, and he really meant it."

Olga frowned. "You take care of Valter's son, right?"

Sarah nodded.

"So now he takes you sister's baby! And that's fair!"

Sarah shook her head. "She stole money from him."

"Your sister? Becky? When?"

"Before she left. I don't know how much but it was a lot. Walter hates my sister and he hates this baby."

"The baby—she stole nothing. You keep her." Olga reached for the frayed cotton coat hanging on the back of her chair. "That vas you mother's last vish!"

"Tomorrow, I have to call the adoption agency," said Sarah.

"You better not," Olga warned. "You take the baby an' do just like you promise. You gif the baby away, you gonna be sorry!"

As Olga let herself out the kitchen door, a gust of freezing air let itself in and Sarah bundled the baby against the cold.

"When's Aunt Becky coming home?" said a small voice. With his blond cowlick sticking straight up, five-year-old Stanley rubbed his eyes against the bright light of the kitchen. "I want Aunt Becky to take that baby home," he whined.

"Go back to bed!" Sarah snapped.

"She doesn't have to go to bed." He grabbed the corner of the blanket and pulled so hard the baby almost slipped out of Sarah's arms. Clenching a small fist, he aimed it at the baby. Sarah jumped from the chair, sending her half-full coffee cup smashing to the floor. She snatched a long-handled, wooden spoon from the dish drainer and swung, aiming at Stanley's buttocks. But the spoon hit him across the back. The boy cried out, then ran to a far corner where he slid down into a crouch. Tears streamed down his reddened cheeks and he wiped his nose on the sleeve of his pajamas.

Suddenly, the front door banged open and a wave of cold air carried the stench of whisky into the kitchen. Walter's heavy jacket thumped on the dining room table. "I should have known!"

She stood, frozen, his foul breath in her face.

"What's he doing up?" Walter pointed to Stanley, still cowering in the corner

Stanley lifted his pajama top and turned enough to display a red mark on his back "She hit me!"

"Get out of here!" Walter ordered.

Stanley scrambled to his feet, crossed the kitchen, squeezed by Walter who was almost blocking the doorway, and ran down the hall and up the steps to his bedroom.

Walter took a step towards Sarah. She backed away. With the baby in her arms, she was unable to protect herself when her husband's hand slammed across her face. She stumbled backward against the kitchen counter. Regaining her balance, she pointed to the broken cups and splattered coffee. "Look what your son did!"

"I don't care what Stanley did," Walter raged. "You keep your hands off my son."

Sarah held tight to the infant as Walter pushed her out of the kitchen, through the dining room and into the dark living room where a bassinet sat in the corner. "Put that bastard down. Now!"

A faint glow from a streetlight cast a soft illumination across the room. Sarah placed the baby into the bassinet. Her eyes were striking even in the dark. As Sarah tucked in the edges of the blanket, Anna Mae's tiny hand found Sarah's finger and gripped it tightly.

Walter, already back in the kitchen, yelled, "Get in here!" The baby turned her head in the direction of the sound. Sarah pulled her finger from the baby's grip. Walter's fury shook the house. "You ain't keepin' that whore's kid!"

Ignoring the frightened cries from the bassinet, Sarah went back to the kitchen. "I'm not asking to keep her. I'm just asking—wait until the funeral. Becky will come home for the funeral."

"The thieving bitch ain't comin' back. She didn't care when her mother was alive and she sure as hell ain't gonna' care now that she's dead."

"She does care!" Sarah cried.

Walter shoved Sarah backward. She tripped over a chair and landed on the floor. She scrambled under the table to get away from him. Her hand landed on the sharp edge of the broken cup. Looking at her bloody palm, she wailed, "Don't you have any feelings? My mother just died!"

When he couldn't get to her, he pounded his fist on the table. "Don't tell me that shit," he yelled. "You're mother drove you nuts. Always bossing you around— always complaining. You ought to be happy she can't bother you anymore."

The cut on Sarah's hand was bleeding down her arm and she wiped it on her blouse. *Dear God. What am I going to do? What in the world am I going to do?*

CHAPTER THREE

The next morning the thermometer on the Lipinskis' porch said thirty-two degrees. By noon the snow was melting and the gutters on the Vickroy Street Hill overflowed with dirty water. In town, Trinity Church's bell tower emerged with dignity above the grimy shops along Washington Avenue. People in dark clothes scurried about, energetic with the break in the weather.

Walter, knuckles white on the steering wheel, waited for the jaywalkers to clear a path. Sarah had done it again; taken advantage of his guilty conscience to trick him into doing what she wanted him to do. And Father John! What the hell did he know about being stuck with a baby?

Walter looked over at his wife who gazed down into the bundle of blankets, while Stanley squirmed around in the back seat. "Why couldn't you leave the kids with your Russian friend?"

Sarah said nothing. She held the infant tighter and looked straight ahead. Walter looked back at the road. He'd better not push her. If he made her too mad she might be stupid enough to tell Father John about last night. Before they left the house he made her take off the big bandage covering the mere scratch from the broken cup. She had a way of making things worse than they really were.

Inching the car forward, he looked into the rearview mirror at his son. "Damn it! Quit kicking the seat!"

"Where're we goin'?" Stanley whined.

"To the church," said Sarah.

"Are we going to leave the baby in the church?"

"Don't I wish," said Walter.

Eight minutes later, Walter parked the car at the bottom of the wide stone steps, leading up to the church's huge, red, double doors. Walter and Stanley waited on the curb while Sarah carefully carried the baby over the gutter that was running like a small, dirty river.

The strong scent of incense hit Walter as soon as he entered the church. He looked at Sarah who didn't seem concerned so he just brushed it off as another weird thing about churches. Walter wasn't raised in a church-going family. As a kid he had somehow got the idea that if he ever stepped foot inside a church he would find an angry God waiting to punish him. He didn't want to go inside then, and he didn't need to go in now. He could solve his own problems.

The door leading to the church office was near the altar. With Sarah in the lead, they walked along the rows of pews as sunlight streamed through the lavish stained glass windows, casting a mellow light throughout the nave. Halfway up the aisle, Sarah shifted the baby so that the infant's head was resting on her shoulder. The baby was now facing a bank of candles. Her eyes, wide with fascination, reflected the flickering flames. This was the first time Walter noticed the baby's eyes. They were an odd crystal blue. Sarah's now dead mother had eyes like that. He found it unsettling.

At the end of the hall, the door to the church office was open. Father John, a small, pleasant looking man, was sitting at his big mahogany desk, shuffling through a pile of papers. When they walked in, the priest stood up, fastened his white collar and put on his jacket. Walter was surprised that the priest was so young.

"You must be the Lipinskis. I'm Father Falkowski." He offered his hand while walking around to the front of the desk. "But everyone calls me Father John."

Sarah shook his hand while Walter seated himself in the leather armchair. Walter caught a flash of disdain in Father John's face as he went to the wall to retrieve two wooden chairs for Sarah and Stanley. Walter smiled to himself. *It ain't going to take me long to show this wimp who's in charge.*

Avoiding Walter's challenging stare, Father John leaned against the edge of his desk and asked, "What can I do for you today?"

"My daddy don't want that baby," Stanley announced.

"Shut up," said Walter.

"Yes sir," Stanley mumbled, kicking the chair legs.

"It's like this," Walter said, "This here baby my wife's holding ain't ours. It's her kid sister's. When the baby was born, Sarah's sister, Becky, was only sixteen. She took off leaving it with Maggie, my mother-in-law. Then the old lady got sick. My wife went ahead without even asking me and told her mother we'd keep it. And then Maggie died."

"Mrs. McBride passed away? The funeral— Wednesday?"

"Yeah. That one. Anyway, like I said, my wife promised..."

"My mother made me promise," Sarah interrupted.

Walter looked at Sarah. *She better not turn this meeting into a battle.* Still looking at his wife, Walter told the priest that they had come for some advice about what to do with Becky's baby. He turned back to the priest. "Sarah's mother always got her way. She forced—no, she tricked my wife into making that promise. And that don't count. Right, Father?"

While Walter was talking, Stanley slid off the chair and was trying to squeeze himself between the bottom rungs. He managed to get one little leg through then bumped his head, almost toppling the chair. Walter held the seat of the chair steady with one hand, and with the other he grabbed his son by the back of his overalls and yanked him out. Father John went to his desk, found paper and crayons in a drawer, took Stanley by the hand and led him to a small table at the back of the room where the boy could stay busy.

When the priest was back at his desk, he asked Sarah, "What about you? Do you feel the same as your husband?"

"No, I don't. I think we better keep the baby until my sister comes back."

The heat of anger surged through Walter's body. He lit a cigarette, blew the smoke in Sarah's direction, and said, "Show Father that letter!"

Father John gave Walter an ashtray while Sarah fumbled with her oversized, black purse.

"Give me that!" Walter yanked the purse out of her hands. An ash from his cigarette fell to the floor and he slid his shoe over it, rubbing it into the carpet. "Look at this," he said pulling out a crumpled piece of paper and handing it to the priest. "What does this sound like to you?"

The priest took his reading glasses from his shirt pocket and put them on. As the priest read the letter, Walter mentally recited it word by word.

Mother,

I'm sorry I brought you so much shame. I have some money. I'm going away. Please don't try to find me. I'll be OK.

Becky

Father John slid his glasses back into his shirt pocket. "She doesn't mention her baby."

"Because she don't care about it!" Walter said. "She ain't coming back!"

"Do you know who the father is?"

"She slept around," Walter said. "Could be anyone. The girl was a slut."

"Walter!" Sarah's face reddened. "How could you!"

Walter resisted putting Sarah in her place but he couldn't keep the sarcasm out of his voice. "I could say that, dear wife, because I won't raise someone else's bastard." And to the priest he said, "Excuse my language, but my wife don't know her sister as much as she thinks she does."

"So there's no father in the picture," the priest said rubbing his forehead. "Have you talked to Children's Services?"

Ignoring the question, Walter said, "The kid should be adopted."

"That'll be a long way down the road," Father John said. "First Children's Services will place the baby in foster care while they try to locate Miss McBride. If they can't find her, they'll look for the baby's father.

"I don't know how long case workers have to wait before they can put a child up for adoption. I think it's at least—at the very least—five years. During that time they'll do everything they can to locate the parents."

Father John stood up and walked to the small table where Stanley was busy with the crayons. The priest picked up a paper scribbled in red and green and began complimenting Stanley. Sarah kept fussing with the baby. Walter wished she'd lay the kid down before it woke up.

"Is there somewhere I can change the baby's diaper?" she asked.

"Just down the hall," said the priest returning to his desk. "There's a changing table in the Ladies' Room."

Tapping his fingers on the arm of the leather chair, Walter waited until Sarah was out of the room. "Let me tell you something, Father," he said, leaning forward. "Sarah don't have no backbone. I know a little something about how it was before I met her because I worked with her brother, Joe.

"When Sarah was ten, her father died. And ever since then, her mother made her do all the things she should have been doing herself; like cleaning the house and stuff like that. Her mother, Maggie, walked all over Sarah, and she was dumb enough to let her. But I didn't know her then. I met her when her brother Joe got his head crushed. At the mill a crane hook snapped and dropped a chunk of hot steel on him. That's when I met Sarah, at Joe's funeral.

"She hardly knew me when she came right out and told me that now that Joe wasn't there her mother would treat her worse than ever. Sarah was too spineless to stick up for herself. She's so damn pathetic! Now she wants to let that old bitch—her mother—boss her from the grave. It ain't right, Father. I already got Stanley. He's enough. I don't want no more kids. Becky's baby is not my wife's responsibility. Or mine either. Especially not mine!"

"Your wife is struggling with her conscience," said the priest, in a tone that was gentle yet firm. "However manipulative her mother may have been, Sarah did make that promise. Your wife's feelings on this matter must be considered."

Walter ground his cigarette into the ashtray. He needed a drink.

*   *   *

In the Ladies' Room, Sarah placed the squirming baby on the padded table. The baby didn't need a fresh diaper. That was only an excuse to get away and think. She must have been crazy to drag Walter to see Father John. It clearly wouldn't make any difference. Walter didn't want the baby and he didn't want her talking about any promises. *Worse yet, he's about to blow up.*

She went to the sink, threw some cold water on her face and wiped it with a paper towel from the dispenser, then walked back to the changing table. There were times, many times, when she wondered why she had married Walter. Before she even met him the gossip was enough to send a sensible woman running. Was it true he had driven his first wife to suicide?

Too distracted by her thoughts to remember that the baby wasn't wet, Sarah took a dry cloth diaper from her big black purse, laid it beside the baby, then pulled the receiving blanket aside. Unsnapping the little pink overalls, she removed the plastic pants and ran her hand over a dry diaper. She shoved the unused diaper back into her purse and re-dressed the baby as her mind drifted back to three years ago when her brother was killed. At that time all she wanted was to get away from her demanding mother. So she convinced herself that if Walter had a good and faithful wife and someone to take care of his son, he'd be the kind, considerate man she wanted to believe he was. If she hadn't been so desperate, she would have taken a closer look at Walter.

It had taken one year and two black eyes to realize her mistake. Then three months ago her sixteen-year-old sister dumped her illegitimate baby in her mother's lap. At that time Sarah was glad she was away from home and married to Walter. Little Anna Mae would not be her problem. But then her mother died.

Surely someone out there would be glad to have the baby—someone who didn't have to deal with the likes of Walter. She certainly didn't need the extra work—feedings four to five times a day...

Making a quick decision, she bundled the baby into the blanket, scooped her up and left the Ladies' Room. To hell with what her mother wanted. If her husband didn't want this baby, so be it!

As she entered the office, she was aware of two things. The room reeked of cigarette smoke and Walter abruptly stopped talking. Father John nodded for Sarah to sit down. She kept standing. The priest said something to her but it went right by because she was watching her disgruntled husband crush out another cigarette. He then stood up, placed the full ashtray on the gleaming mahogany desk, went over to where Stanley was still coloring and grabbed him by the arm.

While Walter was pulling Stanley away from the table, the priest walked around to where Sarah was standing. He looked at her with kind gray eyes. "Mrs. Lipinski—Sarah—did you hear what I said? Your husband has changed his mind. You can keep little Anna Mae until Becky comes home. Your husband agrees it's the right thing to do."

Sarah was stunned.

With Stanley in tow, Walter walked to the door. "Com' on Stanley. We're leavin.'"

CHAPTER FOUR

March 1954

"Rain, rain go away. . . "

Cold pellets of rain poured from the churning sky, pounding the bare boards of the back steps and splashing three inches high from the puddles in the yard. Three-year-old Anna Mae peered out, her nose pressed against the dirty screen door.

"Shut up! And close that damn door."

Her little body stiffened at the sound of her Uncle Walter's harsh words. She turned and looked up—way up—until her head was so far back she almost lost her balance.

Walter shoved her aside and slammed the main door. "Go wash your face!"

She ran across the kitchen, down the hall, up to the second floor and into her bedroom. She had run so fast her little legs hurt. She scampered onto her bed and picked up her baby doll, Susie. She wrapped the doll in a tattered, pink receiving blanket and held it close to her heart.

*   *   *

Sarah was sitting on the living room couch with an open cookbook on her lap. She called out to Walter. "What would you like for supper?"

Ignoring his wife, Walter went into the dining room where eight-year-old Stanley was on the floor, cutting pictures of heavyweight boxers from a pile of Sports Illustrated. Walter leaned over, grabbed a handful of scraps and shoved them under Stanley's nose. "Who said you could do this?"

"No one."

"No one?"

"No."

Still holding the scraps, Walter straightened up and yelled at Sarah. "Aren't you watching these kids?"

She yelled back. "How about Swedish meatballs? Or do you just want hamburgers?"

Walter threw the scraps at Stanley, walked into the living room and knocked the cookbook on the floor. "Did you hear me? Do you see what he's doing?"

She picked up her cookbook. "He's just cutting stuff out of those old magazines."

Suddenly there was a loud bang as the wind blew the back door open, crashing it against the kitchen wall. Sarah put her cookbook aside and went to the kitchen, intending to close the door. Cutouts in hand, Stanley followed his stepmother. Walter came up behind Stanley and grabbed him by the arm. "You'll learn, boy, to keep your hands off what don't belong to you." He then shot Sarah a warning look that told her not to interfere. He then dragged Stanley across the kitchen. The boy stumbled over his stocking feet, towards the rush of wet air. His father shoved him outside and slammed the door.

"Daddy!" Stanley's screams could barely be heard above the storm. "Daddy, let me in. Daddy, it's raining!"

Walter slid the latch, locking the door. He walked across the kitchen, opened the refrigerator and took out a beer.

Horrified, Sarah watched her husband casually rummage around in the kitchen drawer and retrieve a bottle opener. "Walter!" she snapped, "are you going to make him stay out there?"

"Yep."

"Why?"

He popped off the beer cap, took a long drink, and then wiped his mouth on his sleeve. "To teach him a lesson," he said, walking out of the kitchen.

Sarah stood by the sink wondering what to do. Stanley's cries had stopped. She went to the window beside the door and pulled the curtain aside. Her stepson was crouched in a corner of the small porch, stuffing the cutouts under his shirt. "Walter!" she yelled.

"What?"

She walked to the living room where her husband was slumped in his chair, eyes closed, cigarette in hand, beer on the end table, and feet propped up on the hassock. "Walter, open your eyes!"

"What?"

"You're not going to just leave your son out there, are you?"

"Woman," he said, with his eyes still closed, "leave me alone."

"Walter!"

He opened his eyes.

"You can't leave him out there. It's cold. And it's raining."

Walter's eyes flashed. She thought he was going to jump up and hit her. But he just sat there staring at her until the hot cigarette stub burned his fingers. He dropped the butt into the ashtray, took his feet down from the hassock, stood up, and walked out of the room.

She heard him open the kitchen cabinet above the sink. When he came back he was holding a pint of bourbon. "So?" he said defensively.

"I didn't say anything."

She never said anything about his drinking. She didn't dare. She wondered why he felt he had to drink so much anyway. "I didn't mean to upset you. But he's just a little boy and ..."

Walter was standing in the middle of the room, unscrewing the bottle cap. When she saw the look in his eyes, she stopped talking. He took a long drink of the whiskey, wiped his mouth on his sleeve and mumbled something.

"What did you say?" she asked.

"My grandmother used to tell my father that. ' Joseph! On jest naly chlopiec!'"

Sarah stared at him. She didn't understand.

"On jest naly chlopiec." It means, 'He's just a little boy.' That's what it means."

Walter sat down in a straight back chair, his jaw clenched, and his breathing heavy. Sarah slid the hassock near the chair to sit in front of him. "Did your father make you stay out in the rain?"

Walter looked at his wife as though the question didn't make any sense. "My grandmother raised me," he said. "Bubka." He smiled to himself. "I killed my mother, ya know. When I was born my mother died." He took another gulp of whiskey. "I killed her."

He leaned forward, placing the pint of whiskey next to an empty beer bottle. "What did you ask me?" he looked at his wife. "Oh, yes. Did my father make me stay out in the rain? No! Absolutely not!" He laughed. "It was snowing." Shaking his head, he frowned. "No, it wasn't snowing. It was cold. Below zero. Way below zero. Freezing! Bubka tried to sneak out and give me my coat—my mittens..."

He looked down at his huge callused hands and laughed again.

Sarah reached out to touch her husband.

He pushed her away saying, "He hit her! My father hit my grandmother."

"Because she wanted to give you the coat? Is that why he hit her?"

"I don't want to talk about it."

"Sometimes it's good to talk about things. Was that your mother's mother?"

He nodded. "My grandmother said I didn't kill my mother. She said it was the doctor's fault. She said my father was crazy. She said my father should have sued the doctor."

"Why didn't your grandmother sue the doctor?"

"Woman! You don't know when to shut up! My grandmother could hardly speak English. She was afraid."

Sarah was silent. Walter lit a cigarette. He got up and walked to the front door. With the cigarette dangling from the corner of his mouth, he put on his coat and walked out.

Sarah followed him out to the porch, then began to follow him down the steps. The rain had eased but the wind was still strong. It blew into her face, sending her back to the protection of the doorway.

*   *   *

Upstairs in the front bedroom, little Anna Mae sat on the floor, her face still smudged. With one hand, she held her doll, Susie, close to her cheek. She sucked the thumb of her other hand, her index finger hooked over her nose. She had done something wrong. She felt that. But she didn't understand what she had done wrong or why her Uncle Walter had sent her upstairs. She heard

Aunt Sarah out on the porch. A moment later she heard her come in and shut the door.

Anna Mae went to the window. Standing on tiptoes, she could see down to the street. She watched the Buick pull away from the curb and coast down the hill.

CHAPTER FIVE

Once inside his car, Walter wiped the rain from his face and ran his fingers through his wet hair. He had worked all day and so he was hungry. But he had to leave the house and Sarah's infuriating questions. He turned the ignition key. There was no way to control his anger—no way except to drown it in bourbon.

The windshield wipers smeared grime into black semi-circles and even with the headlights on, he strained to see the road clearly. Months of street ash and mill soot made Warrenvale indecently filthy. A polluted black puddle at the bottom of the hill glittered as it reflected the street light. Walter lit a cigarette and leaned back in his seat until he reached Tavern Row. The sewers were backed up. When he stopped the car, it was up to the hubcaps in sludge.

A red Ford truck was parked in front of Mickey's Pub. It looked like his brother Nick's truck. Walter drummed his stumpy fingers on the steering wheel. Nick lived in Pittsburgh. So, what was he doing in Warrenvale?

Nick was ten years old when Walter was born. As Walter grew older it became obvious that Nick had bought into his father's twisted reasoning. He really believed that his younger brother's birth had killed his mother.

Walter was barely walking when he knew instinctively that out of four older siblings, three boys and a girl, Nick was his father's favorite. When Walter was six, Nick stole money from his father's wallet. He blamed it on Walter. "I saw him do it. Look in his pocket."

His father had reached into Walter's pocket and pulled out three crunched up dollar bills.

"I didn't take it!"

"You lyin' little son-of-a-bitch! I'll teach you to steal!"

Sixteen-year-old Nick gloated in the background.

Walter's eighteen-year-old sister, Mary, rushed into the room. "Daddy! Stop! He didn't do it. He was with me all morning. We cleaned out the basement. Honest, Daddy. He didn't take that money."

Walter thought his little arm was being pulled from its socket when his father dragged him through the house. "So you cleaned the basement, huh? Well live in it!"

By the time young Walter hit the dirt floor at the bottom of the basement steps, he was unconscious. In what seemed like only a second, he awakened terrified. He crawled into a dark corner near the coal bin. The next day, when his father was at work, Mary dared to bring him upstairs. She tried to comfort him. He wouldn't talk. For two days he vomited most of his food.

Looking again at the red truck, he thought that maybe he should go to another pub. He put his hand on the ignition key, but didn't turn it. Instead, he opened the car door, stepped into black muck up to his shoelaces and went into Mickey's Pub. If his brother was looking for trouble, Walter was ready. The last time they had seen each other, at least six years ago, a few punches were thrown. Nick, had backed off so Walter quit swinging and just laughed at him. Walter no longer feared Nick. And after what just went on at home, he was more than ready for a good fight.

Walter entered the pub immediately spotting not one but two of his brothers seated at the far end of the bar, each with a mug of draft beer. Andy was five years older than Nick, with a bald head and huge gray mustache. Walter had no quarrel with Andy. However, Mickey's Pub was Walter's territory and he felt invaded.

"What're you doin' here?" Walter asked.

"Lookin' for you," said Nick who was now permanently bronze from years in a Pittsburgh foundry and had wrinkles so deep it looked like cats had attacked him. Nick's blue work shirt seemed several sizes too big.

Walter wanted to ask him if he had been sick. Instead, he asked, "So why not call?"

Andy ran a finger over his sweaty beer mug. "We don't have your number."

Walter slid onto a barstool next to Nick. The bartender poured a double Jim Beam. Walter drank the shot in one swallow. "Are you gonna tell me why you're here?" Walter's brothers exchanged glances. "Come on! Don't waste my time."

Andy spoke. "Mary's dead."

"What?"

"Mary's dead."

Walter raised a second shot to his lips as the room shifted out of focus. No. Not my sister. Not Mary. Mary—the only one in the family to ever show him any kindness. Mary, who smelled so good, like Sweetheart Soap. "Don't pay attention to Dad," she would tell him. "He doesn't really hate you. He just misses Mom."

According to Mary, if their father hadn't been such a stupid, cheap bastard, if he had taken his wife to the hospital instead of leaving her to bleed to death on the bed, she might have lived.

Walter had not seen his sister Mary since his first wife died.

He downed the second shot. A stream of heat traveled down his chest as the room went back into focus. "What are you telling me?"

"Mary had cancer," said Nick. "She died last week."

Walter felt the pulsating veins in his forehead. "Last week?" He jumped from the barstool. "What d' ya mean last week?"

"Settle down," said Andy.

"Settle down? Settle down? You come in here tellin' me my sister died last week. Where the fuck was you last week? Why didn't you come down last week? I didn't even know she was sick!"

Nick took a sip of beer. "Would you have cared?"

Walter lunged at Nick, knocking him off the stool then pinned his scrawny body to the floor. Someone pulled at Walter's jacket. Others grabbed his arms. Walter was breathless by the time three mammoth steelworkers pulled him off his brother. Andy told the men to take Nick out to the truck and make sure he stayed there. Walter slid back onto his barstool to catch his breath.

Andy put his arm around Walter's shoulder. "We wanted to tell you sooner. There was so much confusion and we weren't even sure where you lived."

Walter looked across the bar, past the liquor bottles and into the foggy mirror. He should have been there for his sister. He should have called her. Why hadn't she called him? Memories flooded his mind like film clips. Mary holding him when he cried. Mary taking his side when everyone was against him. Mary—the gentle one in a family of brutes. Why? Why had he cut himself off from the family? From his sister? From Mary?

Andy had been talking but Walter wasn't listening.

". . . and all the neighbors were there. So many flowers! Mary would have loved all those flowers..."

"Flowers?"

"At the funeral."

"Oh. Mary's funeral," Walter said casually. He looked at his empty whiskey glass, past the bottles and into the mirror again. His mind was now closed down, as though he had just received a shot of anesthetic. "Oh, yeah. Mary's funeral," he mumbled. The bartender poured him another shot. He took his eyes off the mirror just long enough to toss it down his throat. "Thanks for coming all the way from Pittsburgh," he said. "I appreciate it."

A few moments later Walter turned to say something to Andy. The barstool beside him was empty.

*　　*　　*

Sarah waited until Walter's car was out of sight then she hurried to the back door. Stanley was not on the porch. Ducking her head against the rain, she ran across the yard to Olga's, quickly letting herself in.

In the tidy yellow kitchen, a big pot of ham and cabbage simmered on the stove, sending its pungent aroma throughout the house. As Sarah wiped the rain from her face, Olga looked up from the counter where she was shaping dark brown dough into bread. Stanley, his wet cutouts spread over the kitchen table to dry, was drinking hot chocolate and eating a cookie.

"Thank you for taking him in," said Sarah. "I hope he wasn't a problem."

Olga covered the dough with a clean white cloth and placed it beside the warm stove. "The boy is not the problem," she said. "Who puts him out in the rain is the problem."

With hands dusty with flour, Olga guided Sarah into the living room. Peter Nikovich, a brawny man with a huge, black handlebar mustache and thick half-glasses sat in his easy chair with the Russian newspaper, Izvestia, on his lap.

"Go sit with the boy," Olga ordered.

Newspaper in hand, Peter marched to the kitchen.

As soon as the women were alone, Sarah explained in a whisper: "There was nothing I could do."

"You should stop you husband. A mother is supposed to stand up for her children."

"But Stanley's not my..."

"No different. You the mama now."

Sarah sat down on the overstuffed sofa and ran her fingers over the handmade doily covering the arm. "You don't understand. Walter's had a hard life."

"You tell me one person who works in that mill who don't have a hard life."

"But Walter's mother..."

Olga stood over Sarah with her hands on her hips. "I don't want to hear about no mothers. You make it your business Walter don't hurt that boy. And little Annie too!"

Together the women heard a loud sizzle and hiss. Olga exclaimed, "Da cabbage!"

Sarah followed Olga back to the kitchen. While Olga adjusted the flame under the cabbage pot, Sarah took Stanley by the hand, led him out the door, and went home.

Walter did not come home for supper. Sarah washed the dishes, wiped them, and put them away. She then went into the living room to watch television. Anna Mae was on the floor near the couch cuddling her doll. Stanley was upstairs with his cutouts. Sarah heard a car out front. She hurried to the door.

CHAPTER SIX

It was dark when Walter struggled out of the driver's seat, unaware of the substantial space between his car and the curb. Once out, he slammed the door. He stumbled on the curb but didn't fall. After a few more steps, his feet seemed to tangle. He landed hard in the middle of the wet sidewalk. His left knee stung and he pulled aside the ripped pant-leg, revealing blood mixed with cinders. Again on his feet, he reached for the handrail and climbed up onto the porch. He took out his house key. His body swayed. He could not put the key into the lock.

He pounded on the door. It opened. He lurched forward into the hall. Sarah tried to catch him but he landed in a heap at her feet. His eyes adjusted to the dim light as he waited for the hallway to stop spinning.

Sarah knelt beside him. "What happened, Walter? You're a mess."

"My sh-sh-shister died."

"Mary? Mary died?"

Bracing himself on the banister, Walter struggled to his feet. "My brothers—Nick—Andy. They were at the bar. Mary had..." The word 'cancer' stuck in his throat.

"Oh, Walter. I'm so sorry."

"Sorry shit!" He lunged at her. "You knew, didn't you?!"

The blow to her face was off-center but he had swung hard enough to knock her off balance. If she hadn't backed into the banister, she would have fallen.

*   *   *

Stanley gathered his boxing pictures then sat near his bedroom door listening. His father was yelling. His words were slurred.

"Sorry shit! You knew, didn't you?"

He should never have cut his dad's magazines. It was all his fault. He wanted to go down and tell his dad he was sorry. But he was afraid.

"How come that bastard's up?" his father bellowed.

Stanley looked across the room. Anna Mae was not in her bed.

"It's early, Walter," Sarah explained.

Alarmed, Stanley realized that his three-year-old cousin was still downstairs. His heart pounded. There was nothing he could do to help her. The voices grew muffled. Were they in the living room? He heard a scuffle. Someone ran through the house. The back door slammed shut. His father yelled, "Go ahead! Run away bitch!"

Stanley picked up a handful of scraps. Good! Sarah probably took little Anna Mae next door to Mrs. Nikovich's. She would be safe there. His fear turned into anger and he found a target in the things he believed had caused all the trouble. "Take that!" He ripped Rocky Marciano in half. "And that! And that! And that!" When he threw the last piece down, he was sitting in a pile of shredded paper.

Walter was yelling again. "We ain't never gonna' be rid of you!" Who was he talking to? Anna Mae? Did Sarah forget Anna Mae? Stanley could never understand why his father hated her so much. What did she ever do to him? He didn't want to believe his father would hurt little Anna Mae.

He went to the top of the stairs then crept down a few steps so he could see into the living room. His father was standing over Anna Mae. She was sitting, motionless, holding her doll.

"Get the hell out of here!"

Anna Mae looked terrified. Why didn't she run away? She looked up at her uncle. Her eyes were so big. There was something strange about her expression. His father grabbed her doll and threw it into the dining doom. Anna Mae cried out. "Susie!"

"I said, get out!"

Stanley watched in horror as his father reached down for the little girl. When Anna Mae screamed, Stanley ran back up the steps, scurried across the room then dived under his bed.

*   *   *

When Sarah had fled from Walter, she had gone next door to Olga's house. She came home an hour later. Her husband lay passed out on the couch. The angry lines in his face had softened. For the first time she noticed his torn pant leg, the scraped knee. She also saw traces of the innocent boy beneath the harsh exterior he had acquired over the years.

Confident that nothing could wake him now, she picked up the receiving blanket at the foot of the couch. Walter grunted. She watched as he struggled to turn over and face the back of the couch. His breathing was slow and even once more.

She righted a lamp and looked around for its shade. There it was, in the shadows of the dining room. She shoved Walter's favorite chair back into place then went to get the shade. Her anguish, her shame was now pushed to the back of her mind. You just do what you have to do to survive.

She stepped on something soft. "Oh my God!" Trembling, she picked up the doll. Its little nightie was pulled off at one shoulder. Its face was cracked.

"Anna Mae," she whispered.

In her panic to get away from Walter, she had forgotten that Anna Mae was in the living room. Fear and guilt turned like a brick in the pit of her stomach as she ran up the steps to the second floor. The light in the hallway shone dimly into the children's bedroom. Stepping over the pile of scraps, she went to Anna Mae's bedside. Under the covers and curled in a fetal position, Anna Mae faced the wall, her short blond hair a mass of tangles. Sarah placed the doll beside the sleeping child.

Anna Mae stirred. She reached out, touched the doll, gathered it into her arms, and sat up. "Auntie Sarah, you found Susie!"

Sarah sat on the bed. "Are you okay?"

"Susie has a boo-boo." Anna Mae ran her finger down the crack in the doll's cheek.

"I know," said Sarah. "But are you okay, Sweetie?"

Her lower lip quivered. She pulled the nightie over the doll's shoulder. "My Susie is crying. Poor little Susie."

Sarah drew back the covers. Anna Mae was still in her play clothes. Her shirt was torn and she wore only one shoe. There were big, ugly red marks on Anna Mae's arms. A small cut on her scalp had bled into the little girl's hair.

Anna Mae pointed across the room. "Lookie, Auntie Sarah! Stanley's sleeping under the bed."

Sarah saw one foot sticking out. She got down on her knees. He seemed to be sleeping so she shook him. Unable to get a response, she took hold of both feet and tried to pull him out. In reflex he kicked her away. Deciding to leave Stanley where he was, Sarah got up and resumed her seat on Anna Mae's bed.

With her tiny finger, Anna Mae touched Sarah's face and Sarah flinched.

"My Auntie has boo-boos!"

"I'm okay." She stroked Anna Mae's tangled hair. "What about you? Oh God. Look what he did to you!"

Anna Mae appeared puzzled.

Sarah touched the bruises on the little arms. "I'm so sorry he hurt you."

"Uncle Walter didn't hurt me! Only Susie."

Sarah pushed back the intense guilt of leaving this baby alone with her drunk and enraged husband.

"Why Auntie sad?"

Sarah was confused. Didn't the child remember?

"Auntie Sarah?"

"What, Baby?"

"Uncle made a booboo on your face."

Sarah had all but forgotten Walter's blow that had sent her hurtling into the banister. She touched the side of her face. It was sore. But why was her little niece so concerned? Wasn't she upset about her own injuries? "Don't worry, Sweetie," Sarah said. "It was an accident."

Anna Mae, clutching Susie to her chest, lay back down. Sad as it was, the child would be okay. Sarah pulled the blankets up and around her little niece. She leaned over and kissed her. "Go back to sleep."

Later, in the kitchen, Sarah's hand trembled as she measured coffee into the percolator basket. Why? For what reason? Why would Anna Mae deny anything had happened? It was obvious that Walter had hit her. Yet Anna Mae insisted he hadn't. How could that little girl be so unaware of her injuries?

Sarah sat up all night nursing one cup of coffee after another. The red mark around her left eye gradually became black and blue as the window above the sink grew lighter. At five-thirty she called the mill and told the foreman that Walter wouldn't be at work because his sister had died. She replaced the receiver and dropped her head in her hands. "God help us

CHAPTER SEVEN

Seven years later

She was sitting in the pew near the votive candles—the little girl with the long blond hair. With her head hardly reaching the top of the pew, she sat motionless, schoolbooks beside her. She was ten years old, too young to sit alone in an empty church. She should have been outside playing with other children.

Anna Mae moved forward, putting one foot on the kneeler. She frowned and put her hands up to her face. There it was again: that same strange, confused feeling. She became aware of the rise and fall of her chest, the labored rhythm of her own breathing. In the dim lights she saw the tall wooden cross, the pulpit, the red carpet, and the candles.

She took her foot off the kneeler, turned around, and looked behind her. Empty. She ran her fingers across her schoolbooks then picked one up. The last thing she remembered was sitting at her desk, watching her third grade teacher writing a long division problem on the blackboard. Then suddenly the air had exploded with a deafening siren. Her teacher dropped the chalk and turned to the class. "Oh God! There's been an accident at the mill!"

Anna Mae vaguely remembered her classmates running to the windows, trying to see the half a mile to the mill. During the chaos, Anna Mae was bumped and pushed until she fell between the desks. She remembered feeling dizzy, her hands tingling. That's all she remembered.

Anna Mae put the book down and slid forward to kneel. She placed the palms of her small hands together. "Dear God," she whispered. "Please help me to understand why I don't remember. It makes me scared, God. Please! Help me!"

She heard footsteps at the back of the church. Moments later a figure genuflected at the end of the pew. Her heart skipped as her uncle sidestepped his way over to where she was kneeling.

"You little bitch!" He grabbed the back of her coat. "What the hell' re you doin' here? We've been looking for you everywhere."

Anna Mae scooped up her books as her Uncle Walter dragged her out of the pew. Her steps faltered as he pushed her toward the door. With her feet barely touching the ground, he dragged her down the church steps then shoved her into the car.

Sarah was waiting at the front door with her coat on. She snapped at Anna Mae. "I was ready to go next door and ask Olga to watch Davie. You know I hate to ask her for favors. Where were you?"

"Never mind where she was," said Walter, pushing Anna Mae inside.

"How many times have I told you," Sarah scolded. "You come straight home from school!"

"Come on, Woman!" Walter yelled from the curb.

Anna Mae didn't know where her aunt and uncle were going but she was relieved. At least for now she would not be punished. As she hung up her coat, three-year-old David charged through the hallway, holding a toy airplane over his head and roaring, jet-like, to the curves and dips of the plane. When he saw Anna Mae, he squealed with delight. She knelt down to hug him. He dropped the plane and threw himself into her arms. How she loved this little boy with his curly brown hair and eyelashes as thick as brooms.

Anna Mae had been seven when David was born. Sarah had had a long labor and a painful delivery. When it was over Sarah seemed depressed. She didn't even want to hold her new baby boy. To make matters worse, because of her age, it took her a good six months to recover. All the baby's care-giving duties fell to Anna Mae. Sarah told her young niece over and over again, "I wasn't much older than you when my sister—your mother—was born. My mother, your grandmother Maggie, made me take care of her. If I can do it, you can do it."

Anna Mae hated when her aunt mentioned her mother. Because that's all she ever did—just mention her. If Anna Mae asked questions, she was immediately told to shut up. The subject of her mother was taboo.

In the months that followed David's birth, Anna Mae fed, diapered, and bathed the infant. She did it cheerfully. Anna Mae didn't think of little Davie as a cousin. He was her brother.

Now, three-year-old David nuzzled into her shoulder. "Daddy's mad. My Annie not home. All gone!"

"I wasn't gone," she assured him. "I came home, didn't I?"

Stanley, who was almost fifteen, yelled from the dining room, "You're lucky you didn't get a beaten!'"

Ignoring Stanley, she kissed David on the cheek. He picked up his airplane and with a loud sonic boom and a shrill errrrrr, flew it—roaring and sputtering into the kitchen, through the dining room, into the living room and back to the front hall.

"Stop running or you'll break your neck," Anna Mae shouted on her way up to the second floor.

In the bedroom she shared with little David, she placed her books on her nightstand and walked to the window. The Lipinski house, like so many others, was built on a hillside overlooking the Monongahela River. From her window she could see across town to the steel mill. The yellow-red glow of the open-hearth furnaces stretched for three miles along the river bank. Eighty-foot smokestacks spewed enough ash to blot out the sun. Pipelines flushed their poisonous waste into the river, turning it an ugly brown.

Anna Mae thought that it was because her uncle worked in that terrible mill that he had to drink a lot of whiskey. Once he had spent all the grocery money on what Aunt Sarah called booze. Her aunt had run out of the house yelling that she was never coming back. She went next door to Olga's. Later she came home because Uncle Walter wanted his supper.

Last summer her Uncle Walter and some other men walked around with big white signs and didn't go to work. Her uncle said that the bosses at the mill were unfair. But he didn't say it like that. He used a lot of bad words.

When Uncle Walter's friends stopped marching around with the signs, she heard Aunt Sarah reading the newspaper to Olga. The strike had lasted for 116 days. Olga got mad when Sarah told her that Uncle Walter had been drunk for over half of them. Anna Mae vowed that when she grew up she would not let David work in that mill. Stanley could. She didn't much care about Stanley.

Squinting, she looked to the west where the setting sun sprinkled golden flecks across the murky river.

Anna Mae liked to think there were angels in the clouds casting sparkles over the water.

Frowning, she turned away from the window. Today it had happened again. She started out in one place, ended up in another, and didn't know how she got there. When she was little she thought it happened to everyone. Once Aunt Sarah accused her of lying about not remembering. She said Anna Mae made it all up so she could get out of trouble. Sometimes she wasn't even in trouble and her Aunt Sarah would still accuse her.

Sometimes Aunt Sarah forgot to buy something at Vinko's. Stanley was always forgetting about his homework. But that wasn't the same. Eventually she realized other people usually knew where they had been and what they had been doing. She knew now that her kind of 'not remembering' was a very bad thing. That must be why her real mother didn't want her.

She asked God about it. However, everyone knows that God does not always answer questions. She promised God she would study hard and make good grades if He would help her remember. Although she received an A or B on every test, nothing changed. Maybe that wasn't good enough for God. Or maybe He was just too busy.

"Anna Mae!" Stanley's shrill voice made her jump. "Hey, dog face," he called up the steps. "The rug rat is hungry. Get down here and feed him."

She wanted to yell back at Stanley, but she was afraid of him. He was bigger and stronger and sometimes he hit her. She'd be a little fuzzy afterward. Most of the time she would remember what happened.

She yelled back. "I'll be down in a minute."

She changed out of her school clothes and pulled her long, blond hair into a ponytail. On her way down the steps she laughed as David, complete with sound effects, taxied his plane into its hanger under the living room couch.

"Come on, Davie," she said, reaching for his hand. "I'll fix you some supper."

"Peanut budder. Pweaseeee! Peanut budder an' jellwee!"

"I ain't eatin' thupper," Stanley mocked from the dining room.

He was sitting with his feet propped on the dining room table, eating potato chips and drinking Coke. In fourteen years, Stanley's hair had changed from light blond to buff and finally to brown. The sickly shine of too much Brylcreem failed to control his cowlick.

"That goofy George's father got hurt at the mill," he said. "You know George Siminoski. He's a freshman."

Anna Mae hardly knew George. He was one grade ahead of Stanley and the smartest kid in school. He was also fat, wore the thickest glasses in the whole world and had a big nose. The other students tormented him constantly and George would yell back at them in the same language her uncle used when he was mad.

Sometimes the other kids would tease her, saying George had a crush on her. The very thought made her shudder.

"What happened to George's father?" she asked.

"Almost got burned to death," Stanley said through a mouthful of potato chips.

"When?" she asked on her way to the kitchen.

"Today. I was with George when he found out."

"What happened?" she asked from the kitchen, convinced that Stanley was exaggerating.

"His father got splashed with hot steel," he explained as her head popped back through the doorway. "It was something about the ladle. It was crooked or something.'"

Anna Mae stepped back into the dining room where Stanley was guzzling his Coke. He put the bottle on the dining room table saying, "Two other guys jumped away just in time. They could have been burnt to a crisp!" He stuffed his mouth with chips and mumbled, "Guess who saved George's father?"

Anna Mae stared at Stanley. How could he eat while he was telling her stuff like this?

He swallowed. "Guess!"

She shook her head.

"My dad saved Dobie's life. The man was on fire and my dad ran straight into the flames and threw his jacket over him. And Dad doesn't even like him! Can you believe that? Huh?"

Anna Mae could not imagine Walter helping anyone, let alone risking his own safety.

Stanley threw his head back to shake the last of the chips into his mouth. He wiped his face on his sleeve. "Anyway, Dad went back to the hospital to see if Dobie was still alive. That's why they were looking for you." He shrugged. "I guess they don't trust me to watch Davie."

"You're not supposed to call Mr. Siminoski 'Dobie,'" she said. "Aunt Sarah says not to call older people by their first names. And you're not supposed to put your feet on the table either."

"Dobie! Schmobi! What's the difference?" He blew up the empty chip bag. "He is probably dead anyway." He whacked the inflated bag. "Pow! Just like that. Gone!"

"You're a creep!" she said and went back to the kitchen. She pulled a chair to the cupboard above the counter and stepped up to reach the peanut butter. Suddenly Stan was in the kitchen, shaking the chair so violently that she had to hold onto the shelf to keep from falling.

"Who you callin' a creep?" Stanley shouted.

"Quit it!" she yelled.

"Say you're sorry!"

"I'm SORRY!"

He let go of the chair and went back to the dining room.

Anna Mae climbed down and began fixing David's sandwich. The older Stanley got, the meaner he became. He was becoming just like his father, who never seemed to care about anyone else's feelings. Why did her uncle rush off to the hospital anyway? Why would he care about Mr. Siminoski?

She put the sandwich on a plate, set it in front of David then sat down across from him. She hoped that by the time Aunt Sarah and Uncle Walter came home they would have forgotten about being mad at her.

CHAPTER EIGHT

Walter and Sarah arrived at St. Luke's Burn Unit twenty minutes after Dobie's coworkers had gone. Across the hall from swinging doors that said Hospital Personnel Only, Irene Siminoski sat on a corner chair in the waiting room, her auburn hair pulled carelessly back from her wrinkled, tear-streaked face. Her fifteen-year-old son, George, sat next to her, wiping his thick glasses on the tail of his white shirt. Respectfully quiet, Sarah sat next to him. Walter stayed in the hall, pacing around with his hands in his pockets.

"Who's that?" George asked, squinting into the hall.

"That's my husband," said Sarah.

"What's he doing here?" George asked.

"He—ah—he's your father's friend."

George put on his glasses. "No, he isn't."

The double doors to the treatment room swung open, sending the acrid smell of antiseptic into the hallway. A doctor in a yellow gown, splattered with orange betadine, snapped off his gloves and walked over to Walter. "I'm Doctor Heiss," he said, pulling down his facemask. "Are you here for Mr. Siminoski?"

"I am," said Walter. "But I'm only a friend. His wife is in the waiting room."

George rushed out of the waiting room and pushed between the doctor and Walter, saying, "I'm his son. You talk to me."

Doctor Heiss brushed aside the teenager who followed him into the waiting room. Mrs. Siminoski jumped to her feet. "How is he? How's my husband?"

Dr. Heiss thoughtfully placed his soiled surgical gloves into a swing top wastebasket. George, a head taller than his mother, stood behind her. Walter and Sarah were a respectful distance away.

The doctor was talking so low that Walter couldn't hear so he moved closer. ". . . and the burns on his arms and face are extensive. However, the chances of your husband making it through this, barring complications. . ."

"What complications?" Walter interrupted.

George shot Walter a hostile glance.

"The most likely complication in third degree burns is infection. That's why sterility is vital. As a matter-of-fact, I can only permit one person to see him now. And you need to be prepared. At this stage, well, it looks bad—very bad."

Irene stepped forward. "I'll go."

When the doctor and his mother were gone, George turned to Walter. "Go home, Lipinski. We don't need you here."

Sarah placed her hand on the boy's shoulder. "If there's anything we can do . . ."

"Go home!" said George. "That's what you can do!"

*   *   *

Twenty minutes later, Walter dropped his wife off in front of their house. He turned the car around and coasted back down the hill.

Except for the yellow glow of the furnaces, the sky was black and the chilly October air was heavy with the choking stench of sulfur. Company railroad cars rumbled and clanked northward along the embankment above Tavern Row. Except for the train and the usual din of the mill, the street was quiet. On the corner across from the mill's main gate, the red neon Iron City Beer sign above Mickey's Pub glowed eerily in the night.

Walter opened the pub door to the familiar blend of smoke, sweat, and stale beer. At the thirty-foot bar, elbow to elbow mill workers sat in front of their drinks with their heads down. Along the wall, more laborers sat at small tables, some still wearing their mill-hunk jackets and hard-hats. A young man with pink cheeks and blond hair quickly slid off his barstool so Walter could sit down.

The cigar-chewing bartender, in a thin T-shirt, put a double shot of Jim Beam on the bar in front of Walter. Then, with the skill of experience, he filled three mugs with perfectly foamed beer, sliding one to Walter and the others to the men on either side.

Walter reached into his jacket for his lighter. Before he retrieved the lighter a hand reached from behind with a ready flame. Walter lit the cigarette, parked it in an ashtray, and tossed the jigger of whiskey down his throat. He then placed a five-dollar bill on the bar and picked up his beer. The young blond man, who had given Walter his seat, asked politely, "How is Mr. Siminoski?"

"Alive," said Walter.

To the left of Walter a hard-hat foundry worker, his entire face covered with black dust, looked at Walter through eyes circled in white. "Ain't that the way your old man got killed?" he asked. "By a tipped ladle?"

"Nope," Walter replied. "The bastard drank himself to death."

The hard-hat shrugged and turned back to his beer. At a nearby table, Mike, a lanky Irishman, stood up raising his beer mug. With foam spilling over his callused hand, he looked around the room. One by one the mill workers rose to their feet and lifted their glasses. "To our hero, Walter Lipinski." A gray haired pensioner removed his baseball cap and bowed his head, adding "And may God help poor Dobie." The workers murmured a solemn Amen and seated themselves.

Walter tossed down another double. He pushed the five-dollar bill toward the bartender. The bartender pushed it back.

From the far end of the bar someone called out, "Lipinski! Hey! Lipinski! You just come out from tha hospital?"

Walter leaned forward to look down the bar to the brawny Italian, who, in order to keep a mass of jet-black curls off his forehead, wore his blue striped railroad cap backwards. Droplets of foam edged his full mustache and he wiped them away with the back of his hand. Walter took a long drink of cold beer and burped.

"What' a you go back to hospital for?" the Italian called out as railroad men at that end of the bar gathered around him.

"Who wants to know?" Walter asked, although he already knew. What he didn't know was what Salvador Tamero and his railroad friends were doing in Mickey's Pub. Tamero, an engineer on a company train, very rarely went to any bar. Mostly he was known for being a family man. He was also Dobie Siminoski's neighbor.

"You blind?" yelled the Italian. "You know damn-a-well who wants to know! Why'd ya go back to St. Luke's? What you hope to find there? A dead compadre?"

Walter leaned back on his barstool and studied his own blurred image in the murky mirror, behind the row

70

of whiskey bottles. He tightened his fist on the mug handle. "That's none of your business."

Salvador Tamero's dark eyes radiated anger. "It is my business."

Tamero's railroad sidekicks were getting nervous. Some had backed away. Some avoided looking at either Salvador or Walter. A short, husky railroad man put his hand on Tamero's shoulder saying, "That's enough, Sal. The bastard ain't worth it. When the doctor told us to go, Lipinski left with everyone else. I saw him!"

"So? My wife went back to the hospital to give Dobie's wife her heart pills. She saw Lipinski and his wife going through Emergency." Louder and directed straight at Walter, he added, "And they ain't never been friends with Irene and Dobie!"

A wave of fear gripped Walter in the gut. Did Tamero know something? No. He couldn't. Nobody was around when that ladle slipped. He drummed his meaty fingers on the bar.

"Calm down, Lipinski," said the pensioner.

"Che voi anascondere?" shouted Salvador.

"What'd he say?" Walter asked leaning to his right.

"Nothing. Nothing important," said the pensioner.

"Come on," Walter nudged the older man. "What'd he say?"

"It's nothing."

"Tell me!"

The old man's face paled as he reluctantly gave in. "He asked what you're hiding."

Walter slammed his mug on the bar, so hard that the beer splashed onto his jacket. He slid off his barstool. At the other end, Salvador Tamero also slid from his stool, his enormous size a fair match for Walter Lipinski.

"Knock it off," warned the bartender.

Tamero sat back down. Walter, still standing, yelled, "Kurze gowna!"

Tamero ignored it.

"Wanna know what it means, Dago?"

Tamero remained silent.

"Chicken'a shit! Chicken'a shit!" Walter shouted, mimicking Tamero's broken English.

The huge Italian stood up and quickly began elbowing his way through the crowd.

"Hey, you guys!" the bartender yelled, "Take it outside!"

The foundry worker with the black face and white eyes jumped in front of Walter in an attempt to shield him from the oncoming Italian. However, when the engineer emerged from the mass of sweaty laborers, Walter's would-be protector vanished.

Tamero's thick arms bulged against his uniform sleeves. "You need you head kicked in," he growled, reaching for Walter. Two railroad workers stepped forward, each grabbing a muscular arm, saying, "It's not worth it, Sal."

As the railroad men held Tamero, Walter swung, his fist making solid contact, snapping Tamero's head back and sending his cap flying. His black curls now in his face, he staggered sideways. Tamero's two sidekicks lunged forward as Walter grabbed a chair, knocking a table over in the process. Walter threw the chair, sending glasses of beer and whiskey crashing to the floor. One railroad man managed to jump away. The other was caught in the side and he doubled over, gagging.

"Fuckin' coward!" yelled the man who had dodged the chair. He then catapulted across the room and grabbed Walter by the throat. With tremendous force, Walter brought up his knee. The man fell and rolled around on the floor in agony. Tamero leaped over his friend and punched Walter square in the face. Walter reeled backward, his nose spurting blood. Three mill workers jumped Tamero, sending both themselves and

Tamero smashing through a table. His hand gushing blood from having landed on a broken beer mug, Tamero lunged at the nearest leg and pulled down another hard-hat.

As Tamero struggled to his feet, a monster railroad track-man lifted the young blond kid and propelled him up and over the bar, shattering the row of whiskey bottles and clearing the mirror to reflect the free-for-all.

After six minutes of chaos, the brawl was beginning to wind down. Suddenly, the bartender, his white T-shirt splattered with Southern Comfort, climbed on top of the bar and yelled, "Cops!"

Everything stopped. The sirens grew louder—closer. Tables were up-righted, chairs shoved into place, jackets and hats retrieved from wherever they had landed. When the overhead light went on, a resounding groan filled the room. Men, shielding their eyes from the harsh glare, hollered, "Shut those damn lights off!"

The bartender, down from the bar and holding a mop, ignored them. The police arrived, decided that nobody was seriously hurt, had free drinks and left. Salvador Tamero, his cut hand wrapped in a bar rag, followed them out. Walter resumed his place at the bar where he picked up his half full mug that had miraculously survived the melee. He finished the beer in a long series of gulps.

CHAPTER NINE

Anna Mae and David heard the sirens. Pushing a chair to the bedroom window, Anna Mae helped David up so that he could see the blue and white flashing lights. But, whatever was going on was so far away, there wasn't much to see.

David jumped down and scurried across the room to the bookshelf near his bed. "Horton," he said, shoving a book at Anna Mae. "Pweaseeee Annie! Read Horton Hatches the Egg!"

"Just one story," she said, taking the book from his small hands and ruffling his brown curls, "and then I have to study my spelling."

Monday's spelling test was important to her final grade. But she had the whole weekend to learn her words. She opened the book.

She read with comfortable ease, grateful as David cuddled against her. Although he couldn't read, he had heard the story so often that he practically knew it by heart. Pointing to the doleful Elephant balancing precariously on a bending tree branch in the middle of a thunderstorm, David wiggled and exclaimed, "Rain!"

"And he sat all day," Anna Mae read.

"He kept the egg warm!" David beamed.

"And he sat all night."

"Anna Mae!" Sarah called up the stairs. "David should have been in bed an hour ago."

David ran to the top of the stairs. "Annie is reading me a story."

"You go to bed!" Sarah ordered.

Grumbling, David went back to the bedroom. Anna Mae had already closed the book. "I'll read you the rest tomorrow."

Side by side, they knelt beside David's bed. Anna Mae had taught David to say his bedtime prayers. If it had been up to Sarah or Walter, he never would have learned. A few years back, when cleaning her aunt and uncles bedroom, she found a dusty box. In it was a Bible. Not long afterwards, Walter caught her reading the New Testament. He ripped it out of her hands and threw it across the room yelling, "Bullshit! All bullshit! I don't want you getting any goofy ideas reading that thing!"

If anything, that made Anna Mae even more eager to know what was on those pages. She hid the Bible in her closet behind her shoes and took it out when Walter wasn't around. The more she read, the stronger her faith grew and she began to take David to church almost every Sunday.

Now they knelt together side by side and she smiled as David blessed everyone from the mailman to the old woman down the street, who wore a winter coat when it wasn't cold. ". . . and God bless Anna Mae, and Stanley, and my mother, and...and...pweasee God, make Daddy not be mad when he gets home."

"Aaaa...men!"

*   *   *

It was after midnight when Walter left the bar. As his car swerved toward home, a picture of his father's face flashed through his head. And just as quickly, he was assaulted with a vivid image of his father attacking him with a shovel. Walter's meaty hands gripped the steering wheel as the car bounced up onto the curb and back down again only to veer over the white line. An oncoming car screeched to a stop. Walter, blinded by the car's headlights, swerved back into his own lane ignoring the curses that followed him.

Moments later, he pulled to the curb in front of his house, flipped the gearshift into park, and turned off the key. His muddled thoughts went back through time: the accident at the mill, hunting everywhere for Anna Mae, the hospital, the brawl at Mickey's, finding Anna Mae sitting in the church. Anna Mae. Anna Mae!

When he walked into the house, Sarah was sleeping in front of the new Dupont television. He walked upstairs. He stood in the doorway staring at Anna Mae who was sleeping with her spelling book open and her bedside lamp still lit. Anna Mae opened her eyes and saw him standing in the doorway.

* * *

The dream was always the same. She sat on a hard, black, shiny surface near a gigantic hole on top of a mountain. The pounding was deafening. Like a giant's footsteps somewhere behind her. It shook the ground. And there was fire. Fire above. Fire below. Out there everywhere—with the pounding. She covered her face with her arms. And although she couldn't see the flames, she knew they were receding. The pounding too, diminished. She was alone and terrified. Something that looked like a huge black umbrella without spokes, descended down from above. Down. Over her. Covering her. Smothering her. She pushed at the sides of the shiny material. It gave way to the pressure of her small hands.

But it didn't break. It just molded itself around her hands. And it was tightening, like a ghostly grip. She screamed.

Suddenly, she was floating on her back in the warm brown river. The current was slow, sluggish. The low water level revealed a five-foot mud bank. On top of the bank, vague shadow figures watched her. Anna Mae floated quietly, comfortably, at peace—in the warm brown water.

*   *   *

Four days later.

Anna Mae stood at the back of the schoolyard where a line of fall jackets were hanging haphazardly over the fence. Her classmates slowly came into focus as they ran around in the October sunlight. It had happened again. The last thing she remembered was Friday night, lying in bed studying her spelling.

Her friend, Debbie, out of breath and laughing, called to her. "Come on! Don't just stand there! Get in line!"

The slant of the sunlight told her school was just starting. She had learned to observe little details that went unnoticed by others. She had to be quick to hide her secret. It was scary. However, whatever caused her to black out was over now. It was Monday. Had she studied on the weekend? Of course she had. She always did her homework.

Debbie ran over to her and took her hand. "Come on!"

Shaking Debbie's hand away, Anna Mae joined the other students forming single lines to the school doors. She was just getting her bearings when Angelo Tamero approached. He was a head taller, with black curly hair, dimples, and dark brown eyes that sparkled when he looked at Anna Mae.

"Aren't you in the wrong line?" Debbie asked Angelo sarcastically.

"Naaaa!"

"Yes you are!"

A boy called from the fifth grade line. "Hey! Angelo! Get over here." Angelo grinned, yanked Anna Mae's ponytail, then laughing, ran to join his classmates. The bell rang.

Ten minutes later, Mrs. Wilson, a short, plump lady with gray braids rolled into a bun, called her third grade class to order. She then began passing out test papers. Anna Mae waited. Spelling was one of her best subjects. Surely, she had studied. Surely, she would remember her words. A few seconds later, the teacher handed her a test paper that was already completed. There were lots of mistakes and the paper was marked up with red pencil. There was a big 'D' in the top left corner.

Her name was at the top right corner. It was in her own handwriting. When had she taken this test? It must be a mistake. She looked at the day and date on the blackboard. Wednesday, October 5th. Wednesday? No. It can't be. Today is Monday. Is it Monday? She looked at the date under her name. Monday, October 3rd. She didn't remember taking the test. The blackboard said it was Wednesday.

Her chest hurt as she fought to hold back the tears. They streamed down her face anyway. Some of the other kids turned to look at her as she raised her hand.

"Anna Mae?" said Mrs. Wilson.

"Will you...can I talk to you after class?"

The teacher frowned. "Yes. Certainly."

A half an hour later, when the other students had left, Anna Mae stayed at her desk. She wanted to tell Mrs. Wilson the truth, that she didn't remember taking the test. She didn't remember Monday at all!

But did she dare? What would her teacher think? Would Mrs. Wilson tell the principal? Would they think she was crazy and put her in one of those places with bars on the windows?

"Anna Mae?"

"Never mind." She gathered her books and ran out of the room.

"Wait!" called the teacher.

Anna Mae didn't stop. She was afraid to tell. She would never tell anyone!

That night, when she was getting undressed she checked herself in the mirror. Her back was crisscrossed with angry red streaks. So that's what happened. She was almost relieved, for it seemed as though Walter's flare-ups came in cycles. It should be awhile now before she would lose another day.

CHAPTER TEN

Four years later
August 5, 1965

Sunlight pierced the morning mist that hung over Warrenvale like a shroud. Gone was the massive steel production of the 50's. The ear-splitting whistles, roars and hisses, were now reduced to an eerie hum or an occasional bang or clang. Two lone smokestacks poured pollution into the sky as the rest loomed like silent sentinels of the once prosperous town.

On this late summer Sunday morning, church bells resonated across town while inside St. Paul's, the stained glass windows reflected tinted beams down upon the gathering congregation.

Anna Mae McBride and David Lipinski were seated in a middle pew, waiting for the service to begin. Church was Anna Mae's lifeline; the one place where she found the strength to cope with her harsh family life and periodic blackouts. Earlier that morning she had spent a half an hour braiding her sun streaked blond hair and forced David to put on a white, starched shirt. Uncomfortable, he pulled at the collar and fidgeted in his seat.

She was about to reprimand him when four rows to the front of her, the Henderson family—mother, father,

Debbie, and her two younger brothers—stopped beside an empty pew. One by one, they inched their way across until there was enough room for everyone to sit down. Debbie Henderson, her silky chestnut hair held back by a wide yellow band, waved to Anna Mae.

Debbie was Anna Mae's best friend. In a few weeks they would be starting eighth grade together. Yet it was difficult for Anna Mae to manage a weak smile and she wished the family had seated themselves somewhere else.

If the Hendersons had been strangers, it would not have bothered her. However, she knew they were as devoted to each other as they appeared to be, and she was suddenly overwhelmed with jealousy. In the Lipinski house, only she and David went to church. Walter said it was a stupid waste of time. Sarah said she went to church every week for Friday night Bingo. Stanley accused Anna Mae of going to church because she thought she was better than everyone.

How could she be better than anyone when her own mother didn't want her? Not once in thirteen years had her mother, Becky McBride, tried to contact her: not a phone call, not a birthday card, nothing. Anna Mae felt the familiar sadness as Debbie turned around in her seat and waved again. With a twinge of guilt for being so envious, Anna Mae waved back.

How Anna Mae wished she could be as bubbly and outgoing as Debbie. But she couldn't let down her guard. If she allowed spontaneity into her life, she might be tempted to tell. She had to keep her blackouts a secret. And that kept her anxious and uptight.

She now knew Walter's beatings caused the lost time. No matter how hard she tried, she couldn't remember anything. Afterward she would try to hide her injuries. When they couldn't be hidden she lied, saying she had fallen or bumped into something.

From the back of the church, Father John's words filled the air. "We thank you, Lord, for bringing us together on this beautiful August morning. Be with us, Father..."

By the time Father John finished his opening prayer, Anna Mae's attention was centered on the service. She stood with the rest of the congregation and opened her hymnal. "Holy God we praise thy name..."

David stepped up on the kneeler to get a better view of the approaching procession. Anna Mae tugged at his shirt and told him to get down.

"Look, Annie!" David pointed. "There's Angelo!"

Angelo Tamero's white tunic barely reached below his knees. Carrying the tall wooden cross, he led the singing procession up the aisle towards the altar. Behind Angelo, two cherub-like little boys held candles. Despite double hemmed tunics, they still had to struggle along so they wouldn't trip.

As the three altar boys passed Anna Mae's pew, Angelo glanced at Anna Mae, his dimples betraying a suppressed smile. David giggled.

The procession moved forward. The singing grew louder. When they reached the altar, Angelo placed the cross in a holder beside the pulpit then joined the smaller boys, already sitting against the wall by the Bishop's chair.

With his dimples, high cheekbones, and black curly hair, Angelo Tamero was easily the most handsome boy in Warrenvale, and Anna Mae McBride's heart beat a little faster when she looked at him.

She put her hymnal down on the hard wooden bench, took the prayer book from the slot in front of her and opened it. Her cheeks felt hot. She was sorry she had looked at Angelo. It was wrong. Not because she looked at him, but because she liked looking at him, and especially in church.

Anna Mae struggled to concentrate. Her mind, like a squirrel leaping from tree to tree, would not be still. Angelo, the Hendersons, Debbie—so many conflicting emotions.

For the next twenty minutes, Anna Mae tried to look as though she was following the service. She kneeled when Father John led the congregation in prayer. She stood with her hymnal open when everyone sang. She sat with her hands folded when she was supposed to listen. But she wasn't listening.

She was sitting in her bed in the middle of the night, soaked with sweat as the same bad dream faded into the recesses of her mind. She was in the schoolyard standing alone by the fence trying to remember...

Father John was now standing in the pulpit. "The Holy Gospel of our Lord, Jesus Christ, according to St. Luke..."

I will not let my mind wander. I will not look at Angelo! I will not look at the Hendersons.

Five minutes later, Father John closed the Bible. Anna Mae let her gaze wander from the priest, to the wooden cross, to the choir in their blue robes, to the bench where Angelo sat with his hands folded. She frowned. If Angelo knew about her blackouts, he would think she was crazy and stay away forever!

The priest's voice again filled the room. She took a deep breath. She willed herself to listen to the sermon.

". . . and by his mercy, the lame walked and the blind received their sight."

And He even helped crazy people! He can help anyone. Even me. Please, God, help me to remember, to have no more blackouts—ever.

After the blessing, the dismissal came quickly. With Father John in the lead, the altar boys and the choir left the sanctuary through the side door.

David pulled her arm. "Com' on, Annie!"

She resisted his tug. She didn't want to mingle with the parishioners congregating outside the church. She didn't want to talk to Debbie or be polite to Mrs. Henderson. In this church, in this pew, she felt safe.

He pulled harder. "Annie! Come on! Let's go!"

By the time Anna Mae and David left, the only people outside were two old ladies, discussing the marigolds bordering the steps. Anna Mae looked up at the silky threads of cirrus clouds spanning the eastern sky. She made up her mind. She would make this a good day!

Anna Mae and David walked side by side over cracked and littered sidewalks. They passed the row houses with their windows streaked with soot. When they approached Vinko's Market, David ran ahead into the cluster of pigeons pecking at crumbs on the sidewalk. With a wave of his arms, he sent them fluttering up to the eaves of the three-story building. Avoiding a spatter of droppings on the sidewalk, Anna Mae took David by the hand and led him into the store. A ringing bell, the smell of sawdust and freshly baked bread, greeted them. A young man in a white apron, his arms full of cabbages, stepped out from behind the produce display. His face brightened when he saw Anna Mae.

"Hi, Joey," she said. "Working hard?"

He placed the cabbages into the bin. "I always work hard, Miss Anna Mae. I bet you and Davie went to church. Sometimes I go to church too."

Anna Mae smiled. Ever since she was a little girl, Joey Barns had made her feel good by showing a special interest in how she was doing. Anna Mae respected Vinko for employing Joey in spite of his limited intelligence. When Joey's mother died, Vinko and his wife set Joey up in a small apartment above the store.

Anna Mae picked up a loaf of warm, crusty, Italian bread and laid it on the counter. She then walked down the aisle to the dairy case in the back. Joey followed her, asking her how she was and how was school, and if everyone at home was okay. She never questioned his friendliness. She liked him. He was a nice person. There were times she felt she could confide in Joey, that he was the one person who would not judge her, would not think the blackouts meant she was crazy. However, she only saw him in the store and that certainly was not the place to tell secrets.

Ten minutes later, Vinko placed the bread, a half-gallon of milk, a pound of chipped ham and a dozen eggs into a big brown bag. Anna Mae put her money on the counter. Vinko had already rang it up when David held up a cherry popsicle. Before Anna Mae could protest, Joey handed Vinko fifteen cents.

David beamed. "Thanks, Joey!"

Back outside, the pigeons politely moved aside. David split the Popsicle with Anna Mae then ran ahead of her. She caught up to him. With her Aunt Sarah's white, embroidered handkerchief, she wiped the sugary red juice from his chin. To the rhythm of his steps and with the Popsicle now dripping sticky red syrup down his arm, David began reciting the names of his personal superstars, The Mercury Seven Astronauts. "Scott, (step) Carpenter, (step) John, (step) Glenn, (step) Gus (step) Grisom…"

In the middle of the block, in front of Jackson's Pool Hall, a group of teenage boys were gathered around a yellow Chevy convertible. She hoisted the bag of groceries onto her hip and began to cross the street. David didn't follow. "Come on!"

He sucked the last of the melted Popsicle off the stick. "That's a cool car. I wanna see it!"

"No!" She went back to the curb and took his hand.

"Ahhh crap!"

"What did you say?"

"Nothin.'"

When they reached the other side of the street, Anna Mae quickened her pace. She tried to ignore the catcalls and whistles aimed in her direction. She had just dragged David across another intersection when the squeal of tires and an explosion of engine power roared up behind them. To David's delight and Anna Mae's dismay, the yellow convertible pulled along the curb to a screeching stop. George Siminoski called out, "Want a lift?"

"No!"

"Annnieee!" David pulled his hand from her grip.

George grinned. "The kid wants a lift."

Anna Mae kept walking. A moment later, rumbling and bumping, the car lurched up and over the curb, the front end blocking their path.

"A pretty thing like you shouldn't have to carry that heavy bag all the way up the hill."

David swiped his sticky hand across the shiny, lemon colored fender.

"Hey, kid! Don't mess up my buggy!"

David stepped back.

George's sparse hair stuck out in scraggly wisps above his ears and his prescription sunglasses were as thick as the bottoms of Walter's beer bottles. The size of George's nose was even more evident, sticking out between the bottle bottoms. David covered his own little nose. "Honk! Honk!"

"David!" Anna Mae was about to apologize for David when George blatantly let his eyes wander down her body. She moved the grocery bag to cover herself. Taking David's hand, she stepped into the street, intending to walk around the back of the car. As they reached the rear bumper, George gunned the motor. It revved up so loudly she almost dropped the groceries and David's face turned chalk-white. Anna Mae quickly pulled David around the car. When they reached the curb, George flipped the gears into reverse and shot backward into the street.

Without looking back, Anna Mae and David fled up the street. At the bottom of Vickroy Street hill, they stopped to listen to the loud muffler fading into the distance. Determined not to let the incident ruin the day, she joked, "Maybe he'll drive off a bridge."

"And into the river," David added.

"And the Loch Ness Monster will eat him up."

"But not the car."

"Right!" She walked a few more steps. "Gus, (step) Grissom…"

David joined her. "Walter, (step) Shirra, (step) Junior! (step) Allan…"

CHAPTER ELEVEN

The following week, the temperature soared into the nineties. In town, brawny men in damp undershirts and middle-aged women in flimsy cotton dresses sat on the row house stoops, drinking cold beer or iced tea, too hot to even gossip with their neighbors. It wasn't any cooler in the Lipinski living room, where Stanley and his friend, JD, sat in front of a rattling fan.

Stanley didn't know what the initials JD stood for. JD, in his cut-off Levi's, sandals, tie-dyed tee shirt, long hair, fuzzy sideburns, a joint behind the ear, wouldn't tell anyone his last name or where he lived—just somewhere across the river. Stanley thought that was so cool. However, it pissed Stanley off that JD was tall, lean, blond and quick witted while he was short, dark, and paunchy. Worse yet, sometimes JD used words he didn't understand.

Stanley slid closer to the fan. "God, it's hot!"

"Where's everybody?"

"They'll be here pretty soon."

"Your parents?"

Stanley lit a reefer and took a deep drag, letting the smoke out with his words. "Hell no! Sarah took Davie to Bingo. My old man's working four to twelve."

"Where's your sister?"

"Let's get one thing straight," Stanley grumbled. "She's not my sister!"

"Okay, smart ass. Where's your cousin?"

"She's upstairs. And she's not my cousin either. She's not related to me at all!"

JD took the joint from Stanley's thick fingers and took a drag. "Since when?"

"Miss Anna Mae McBride was dumped on our doorstep," Stanley said. "She's Sarah's sister's kid. And Sarah's not my mother. She's my stepmother! So where's the connection?"

JD raised an eyebrow. "So she's fair game—even to you?"

"Yep! And she'll be fourteen in a few months. Have you noticed th' bod? I'll give her a year or so…"

*   *   *

From her bedroom, Anna Mae heard voices downstairs. Stanley had invited his hippie friends to celebrate his eighteenth birthday. She would spend the evening at Debbie's. But it was so hot outside, she put her usual modesty aside and dressed in her new blue and white shorts and matching halter.

She was sliding into her sandals when the beat of Jailhouse Rock shook the air. Below her window, the yellow convertible pulled to the curb. Four girls and six boys were crammed into the car. When they began climbing out, she grabbed her denim bag from her dresser and hurried into the hall. If she got downstairs soon enough, she could go through the kitchen and be out the back door before anyone saw her. But the crowd from the car was too fast. She reached the bottom of the hall steps just as they tumbled through the door.

"Whoa!" said George Siminoski blocking her path. Looking outlandish in his dashiki and leather headband, he held two cigarettes up to her face. "I got a couple joints. I'll share!"

She pushed the cigarettes aside. He grabbed her arm, squeezing so hard it hurt.

"Let go!"

He loosened his grip. "You stayin' for the party?"

"No! Get your hands off me."

When he released her arm, she pushed passed him. He grabbed her hair with one hand and slid the other beneath the back strap of her halter. She froze. He tugged at the strap. She elbowed him in the ribs and he pulled harder. "Stanleeee…"

*   *   *

In a fog of sweet-smelling blue smoke, George Siminoski sat dazed on the hallway floor; his right arm and shoulder pounding with pain. His left eye began to close where Stanley had punched him. He fumbled around the floor for his glasses. When he found them, the wire rims were bent, but the lenses were still intact. His hands trembled as he put them on. By the he couldn't see out of his left eye at all.

With Stanley and JD now out on the porch, George reclaimed his arrogance. He walked into the living room, where a skinny girl was draped across Walter's favorite chair, smoking a reefer. Since his own cigarettes were trampled in the scuffle, he snatched it from her. He would stay at the party. And that had nothing to do with Stanley's threat, *Step out that door and I'll kill you!*

Ignoring the crude remarks from those he felt beneath him, he retreated to a dim corner of the dining room where he leaned against the wall. The pain in his shoulder had subsided but the left side of his face was beginning to swell. He studied the smoking joint for a few moments, brought it to his lips, screwed up his face, dropped it onto the carpet and crushed it with his foot. He would wait until Stanley and JD smoked themselves brain dead—which wouldn't take long—then he'd leave. Next week he would be off to the university and out of this hellhole, away from this filthy mill town and its moron mentality. For all he cared, they could all drop dead. He was a far better breed.

*   *   *

On the porch, Stanley and JD were laughing so hard it was difficult to tell whether it was sweat or tears running down their faces.

"I can't believe it!" JD gasped. "Anna Mae never swears. She called him a four-eyed f...fu..."

"Fuckin' pervert!" shrieked Stanley, holding his side and stumbling back into the house.

JD tripped on the doorstep and fell flat out on the hall floor. "....and an idiot ass-hole."

"Stop!" begged Stanley who was doubled over from the pain in his side.

JD stood upright, staggered, then assumed a military posture. He turned to the bleary eyed teenagers sprawled about the living room and announced, "Let it be known by this esteemed assembly..."

"Man! Them's big words!" someone called out.

"As I was saying, this esteemed..."

"Speak English!" shouted another.

"Shut up, you imbeciles!" ordered JD, squaring his shoulders. "As I was about to announce to this esteemed assembly..."

"Esteeeemed asssem..." Another heckler.

"Damn it!" Stanley shouted. "Pay attention!"

With exception of an occasional spurt, the laughter subsided.

Walking back and forth imitating George's ridiculous swagger, JD continued, "I will now divulge that the virtuous and pure Miss Anna Mae Lipinski…"

"McBride," Stanley yelled. "Her name's McBride."

"The saintly Miss McBride has succumbed to Mr. Siminoski's low life plane of existence. Albeit a disappointment to those of us who admire her untainted goodness, Miss McBride blasted the little twerp with the wildest of wild harsh and evil words. And in her absence, we applaud her!"

Most of the kids didn't have the foggiest notion what JD had just said. Someone turned up the stereo and Elvis filled the room. "…and I can't help falling in love with you…"

*   *   *

Anna Mae's mouth was dry. She licked her lips and tasted soot. Her sweaty, bare legs stuck to the wooden pew. There were lights in the darkness. Little lights. Lots of little lights. And the familiar pungent scent of incense.

She breathed deep, gazing at the lights as they flickered like stars against a black sky. The black softened to gray. Images unfolded as a bank of votive candles bloomed before her.

Church? Okay. I'm in church. She looked to the Gothic windows. She turned around in her seat and looked toward the door. *Is it evening?* Traffic rumbled outside. Heavy traffic. The kind she would expect in early evening.

Wasn't I supposed to be at Debbie's? That's why I'm dressed this way. Stanley's party—I didn't want to be there so I was going to Debbie's.

She tilted her head thoughtfully. *And then what? Something about George.*

Frowning, she leaned back in the pew. *What was it?* She breathed deeply, stared at the candles, and waited. It was no use. She couldn't remember.

It was almost dark when Anna Mae hurried down the church steps. She paused beneath the streetlight in front of Vinko's Market, trying to decide which was the fastest way to Debbie's. Suddenly she was grabbed from behind. She lurched forward but could not break free.

"You little whore!" George Siminoski bellowed, scaring the pigeons into the street.

"What's wrong with you?" she yelled.

"Like you don't know!" he said, pushing her against the wall.

"You let me go," she threatened, "or I'll scream."

"Go ahead, bitch, scream!"

"Why are you doing this to me?" she wailed. "What did I ever do to you?"

"What did you do?" he asked tightening his grip as she winced in pain. "You're asking me? What did you do?"

Joey Barns stepped out of the shadows. "Let her go!"

George looked up. "Well! If it isn't the village idiot. Want something, stupid?"

"Let her go!" Joey seethed.

"Or what? Who's gonna' make me?"

The blow to George's head was as fast as it was unexpected. Before he could regain his balance, Joey had him in a chokehold, his leather headband down to his bloody nose and his thick glasses hanging precariously from his ears.

"Don't you ever touch her!" Joey shouted, hurling George to the sidewalk.

The frightened pigeons flew to the rooftops. Without taking his eyes from George, Joey put a protective arm around Anna Mae. She looked up with gratitude.

The side of George's face was throbbing in pain as he carefully adjusted his glasses. He then quickly got up and lunged toward Anna Mae. Joey blocked him with an outstretched hand, sending George stumbling off the curb. When he regained his balance, George moved backward toward the alley and his car. "I'm getting out of this filthy town," he shouted. "But I'll get you!" He pointed a shaky finger at Anna Mae. "If it takes the rest of my life, bitch! I'll get you!"

CHAPTER TWELVE

One and a half years have passed
March 20, 1966

The sky was overcast. The wind howled outside Anna Mae's bedroom window. With her freshman schoolbooks strewn across her bed, she snuggled back against the wall with *Biology One, Chapter Nine, Anatomy of a Frog,* open on her lap. However, she couldn't concentrate, because Stanley and JD had just gone up to the attic where she was sure they would get high. That was scary stuff.

Trying to dismiss her anxiety, she turned the page to a picture of a bisected frog with its vital organs color-coded. But she didn't look at it. Instead, she looked at the window where bare black branches slapped and scraped down the pane. It was starting to rain.

It worried her that David was at the Tamero's house, watching cartoons with Angelo's little brother, Johnny. Ever since Dobie Siminoski had been hurt at the mill, there were conflicting opinions as to how the ladle slipped. An investigation determined it was an accident. Nevertheless, Salvador Tamero insisted Walter had something to do with it. Walter said Salvador never set foot in the mill and couldn't possibly understand the complicated mechanics of ladling steel. Walter hated the entire Tamero family. More than once, he had threatened Anna Mae and David: *If I hear of either one of you going near that house, I'll wring your necks!*

Anna Mae hoped the rain wouldn't prevent David from getting home before Walter. She looked down at her book. *The frog has an external ear. Both eardrums, or tympanic membranes...*

BOOM! The thunder rolled like a freight train barreling across the sky. Lighting crackled as rain began falling in sheets. She picked up her book. *Tym -pan-ic membranes are exposed...*

Sarah went to Bingo last night and lost all the change in the coffee can. The money was set aside for extra groceries. And beer. Thank God she had four dollars from baby-sitting. Earlier that morning, she had told Sarah if she needed it, she could have it.

Anna Mae moved a foot that had fallen asleep. Blood rushed in with painful, prickly needles. She shifted her position and the pages of Biology One flipped to Mammals. As she rummaged around for the lost frog, she heard scuffling in the attic. Trying to ignore the disturbance above her, she found the frog and once again began reading. *There is only one bone in the frog's middle ear...*

"Rats!" She looked up. What the heck were they doing up there?

...and the body structure of a frog...body structure...

The mills were in trouble. Lately, all Walter did was fume about European imports and the steelworkers being laid off. He also paid more attention to the money in the coffee can.

Two weeks ago David won First Prize at the Regional Science Fair with his model Mercury Space Capsule. No other fourth grader had come close to matching David's entry. On that same night, Walter went to a meeting about the situation at the mill. Davie said he didn't care, but Anna Mae had seen the tears in his eyes when he stepped down from the podium.

...the body structure of a frog is very similar to the anatomy of a man. Both man and frog have the same kind of organs...

"Anna Mae!" Sarah called up the steps. "Anna Mae!"

"Yes, Aunt Sarah."

Her Aunt's voice was shrill and demanding. "You have to go to the store. We need bread."

"I'm coming!" She closed the book, took her baby-sitting money out of the dresser drawer and went downstairs where Sarah handed her a small grocery list saying, "And if you have enough money left, buy some Twinkies for Walter's lunch."

Anna Mae left the kitchen, hoping her four dollars would be sufficient. She wanted Sarah to appreciate her. But it seemed no matter what Anna Mae did, it was never enough.

"Take the umbrella," Sarah yelled from the kitchen. "I don't want the bread to get all soggy."

*   *   *

The air in the attic was thick and sweet. A bleary eyed Stanley sat cross-legged on his unmade bed. He had a patch of brown fuzz on his upper lip and his hair hung well below his hefty shoulders. JD, his dark glasses at the tip of his nose, crawled around on the hardwood floor, gathering pieces of David's model spacecraft. *Crunch!* He picked up the cracked tail fin. "Oh shit!"

Stanley looked at the pile of pieces. "You better hope Anna Mae doesn't find out you broke that!"

JD put the tail fin in the pile. "I thought Davie made the rocket."

Holding a reefer between his thumb and index finger, Stanley took a long, deep drag. For a few seconds he locked the smoke into his lungs, extracting as much intoxicant as he could. Without breathing he choked out the words, "Anna Mae looks after her baby brother."

"But you said..."

"I know! He ain't her brother. Don't start that bullshit."

JD laughed. "What is it with Anna Mae anyway? How come she can be so nice and then she's a royal bitch? It's like she's two different people."

Stanley slid down to the floor to sit across from JD. "You noticed?"

"Yeah. I noticed. What's with her anyway? Something wrong with her head?"

Stanley didn't want to tell anyone what went on under the Lipinski roof. He was ashamed of it. To the best of his knowledge, no one outside the family knew about Anna Mae's mood changes. Moreover, he wanted to keep it that way.

"Come on," JD urged. "You hiding something?"

"No!" Stanley answered too quickly.

"Just between buddies," JD coaxed.

"Nah. Not that much buddies."

JD reached into his shirt pocket. Palm up, he displayed a black capsule—speed—worth at least ten bucks. He stretched out his hand offering the pill to Stanley.

Stanley thought for a moment, took the pill, put it in his pocket and slid closer to JD. "You don't tell anyone! Never!"

"Who am I gonna tell? In a week, I'll be in boot camp. They'll probably send me to Vietnam."

"Okay," said Stanley. "Here it is. And don't laugh. You're right. Anna Mae is two people."

JD leaned back against the wall and blew smoke toward the ceiling. "This is gonna be good."

"The reason she is like she is, the best I can figure, is because my father hit her so hard and so much that he knocked her into two pieces."

"No shit!"

"When I was a little kid I used to sneak around and watch."

"No shit! Watch what?"

"Things."

"What things?"

"Just things."

"Come on, man." JD swung to hit Stanley but missed.

Stanley rubbed his forehead, thinking. "When she was little..."

"Your sister."

"My cousin."

"Okay, smart ass—your cousin. What happened to your cousin?"

"If you'll shut up, I'll tell you."

JD covered his mouth with his hand.

"When she was real little, my dad would beat her until she couldn't cry no more."

The hand dropped. "No shit!"

"And down the cellar we got a dirt floor. It's filthy down there. Nobody goes down there. Sarah don't want us goin' down there."

"Why?"

"Why what?"

"Why ain't you allowed down the cellar?"

"Because it's filthy, you idiot."

"What about Anna Mae?"

"That's what I'm tryin' ta tell ya." Then Stanley clamed up; just sat there with his hair hanging in his face.

"Tell me!"

"My dad hates Anna Mae because he got stuck raising her."

"No shit."

"A long time ago, I think I was seven or eight, I hid in the kitchen behind the cellar door. I could see through the crack. My dad was pullin' Anna Mae down the cellar. He had his hand over her mouth so she couldn't scream."

"Where was Sarah?"

"She wasn't home. But if she was, she wouldn't do nothin'. She couldn't do nothing.' She's afraid of my dad."

JD leaned forward. "Did Walter beat her?"

"Sarah?"

"No. That day you were lookin' through the crack. Did he beat Anna Mae?"

Stanley felt lightheaded. The room began to float around him. His whirling thoughts traveled backward, submerging him in horrible memories. He wished he had not accepted that Quaalude, that he had not agreed to tell. But most of all, he didn't want to remember. But it was too late. He was there. He could see it. And it was very, very bad.

"He pulled her down the cellar steps. She was so little. I saw him drag her across the dirt floor by her leg. The other leg got scraped. It was bleeding. There was soot smeared into the cuts. He got a wheelbarrow out of the coal bin and put it upside down on top of her."

JD jumped when Stanley yelled. "You little bitch!" It wasn't his own voice. It was Walter's.

"Please, Uncle Walter!" Now it was Anna Mae "I'll be good. Please! Let me out!"

"You stay there," Walter growled. "You stay there until I tell you to come out. And if you come out when

I'm not here, the monsters will get you. And they'll eat you alive!"

Stanley stopped talking. He shook his head to clear it. The room came into focus. JD sat like a statue, his dark glasses in his hand. Stanley looked straight into JD's wide eyes and whispered, "He did stuff like that all the time."

"Is he crazy?"

"I think so."

"How old was she?"

"Little. Maybe two or three."

"What did she do to make him so crazy?"

"I think she wet her pants."

CHAPTER THIRTEEN

With the grocery list in her pocket and the umbrella over her head, Anna Mae walked down the hill towards town. The rain had dwindled to a light drizzle, but the gutters were still gushing with dirty water. Anna Mae wished she had warned Stanley, because there was a union meeting at seven o'clock, Walter might come straight home after work. Not that she cared about Stanley. But anything that set Walter off could ricochet onto the whole family.

Anna Mae entered Vinko's Grocery. Water from her folded umbrella made a puddle on the floor. Joey rushed to mop it up, assuring her she wasn't the only one who had come in dripping.

With only four dollars, Anna Mae didn't want to embarrass herself by piling up more than she could pay for. She took out her list and was calculating the cost of the groceries when the mill's loud shrill whistle blasted the announcement of the end of the day shift. Three-thirty! Quitting time! The blood drained from her face. Were JD and Stanley still in the attic? Did Davie come home from Tamero's? Would Walter go straight home?

Joey leaned his mop against the wall near the door then approached Anna Mae. "Are you okay?"

She nodded as she placed a loaf of Town Talk bread on the counter. Maybe Walter would go to the bar and by the time he got home—no—Walter would want to go to that meeting sober.

Joey followed her to the nearby egg case where she studied the prices. "Anna Mae? What's wrong?"

"I'm a little nervous," she said leaning over to pick up a carton. "I guess sometimes I worry too much."

Joey smiled. "You sound just like your mother."

The hand holding the eggs stopped in mid-air. She stopped breathing. Had she heard right? Did he say what she thought he said? He did. He clearly said, 'You sound like your mother.'

With two hands, she carefully carried the eggs to the counter and placed them beside the bread. She willed herself to sound calm. "Oh?" She looked up at him. "Do you know my mother?"

Joey paled. "I have to go." He began walking away.

She grabbed his arm. "I asked you if you know my mother!"

"N...n—n—no. I don't. I don't know her." He tried to pull away. She tightened her grip, pulling him down the aisle and behind a pyramid of Cheerio boxes.

"Joey! You said I sounded like my mother. How do you know that I sound like my mother?"

He shrugged his shoulders, avoiding her eyes.

Panicked, she struggled to think of what to say next—to keep him talking. She would have to lie. "It's okay. I know that you and my mother are friends."

"We are," he said. "But she trusts me so I can't tell you nothin.'"

At the front of the store, the double doors banged open and six rowdy teenage boys pushed and shoved each other up to the counter. Joey hurried to the front of the store leaving Anna Mae standing behind the Cheerios, paralyzed with excitement—and fear. Fear of what?

Vinko and Joey sent three of the boys outside. Anna Mae fought to control the turbulence inside her. Nobody; not Sarah, not Olga, not Walter, especially not Walter, ever talked about her mother. And now Joey. He knows her mother.

She moved slowly up the aisle, picking up a can of baked beans and a package of Twinkies as she went. At the front counter, she placed the new items next to the eggs and bread. Joey was gone. She tried to figure out if she had enough money, but it was useless. Her head was spinning. She couldn't even count. Joey knew her mother! Finally, after fourteen years, she had something to go on. It was impossible to think of anything else.

She looked down the aisles and over the stacks of groceries. Joey was nowhere in sight. She walked past the meat counter to the doorway leading to the back room. There she saw a walk-in freezer, a crate of apples, cartons of cereal and a bushel of cabbage.

From behind her, Vinko asked, "Can I help you?"

"Where's Joey?"

"He went out back to help unload a truck."

"Oh." Disappointment weakened her knees. She followed Vinko to the cash register where she gave him her four dollars. Vinko packed her purchases in a brown bag, rang up the register, and handed back a dollar bill and some change.

Outside, under the worn and dripping awning, the pigeons pecked at a piece of wet bagel. *He knows my mother.* She wrapped her arms around the brown grocery bag then started walking. It had stopped raining. The day-shift mill workers created a tangle of heavy traffic. In the haze of exhaust fumes, tempers were short, horns honked and at the first intersection a driver rolled down his window to yell at another who gave him the finger. Anna Mae hugged the bag of groceries and looked down at the cracks in the sidewalk. At the second intersection and against a red light, she stepped into the street. Tires squealed, a horn blasted and someone yelled, "Girl! Look where you're going!"

He knows my mother.

A car clattered over the cobblestones close to the curb, splashing her with dirty water.

He knows my mother.

Despite the fact that her legs ached from the climb, she pressed herself to go faster.

Joey knows my mother.

Climbing the three steps to the porch, she could hear yelling inside. It seemed to be coming from the attic. She looked back to the street where she saw JD's car in Walter's spot. Walter's car was parked further up the street. She placed the groceries on the porch swing while wondering if she should go inside. The yelling seemed to be coming from the second floor.

Suddenly, David shot out from behind the swing. "Gotcha!"

She gasped. "Don't do that!" She reached out and touched his blue jacket. It was soaked and his shoes were muddy. "How long have you been hiding back there?"

He shrugged his shoulders and looked into the bag. "Can I have a Twinkie?"

"I only bought one. It's for your dad's lunch."

David crunched up his face, crossed his eyes, and stuck out his tongue.

"Don't do..."

A loud crash, combined with Walter's, "You junkie son-of-a-bitch!" and Sarah's, "Be careful! You'll hurt him," sent Anna Mae flying to the front door. She opened it a crack and saw JD half-falling, half-running down the second floor steps. He hurled himself towards the door. Before she could back away, he yanked it open, knocking her off balance and out of his way. He sprinted down the porch steps and into the street.

When Anna Mae regained her balance, she was looking straight into Walter's blue work shirt. A powerful hand grabbed her by the shoulder. That's the last thing she remembered.

CHAPTER FOURTEEN

Sunday morning

Anna Mae sat bolt upright in bed. The clock on the dresser said eleven fifteen. If she hurried, she could still make it to the last church service. Her back hurt and she felt as though she hadn't had much sleep. She eased herself out of bed and limped into the hall. Walter's snoring was loud enough to come through his closed bedroom door. If Walter was still sleeping, he more than likely had been drinking the night before. And if he had been drinking...

She went back to her room and pulled up the sleeve of her nightgown, checking for bruises. There were none. She looked around the room. Everything was in order. She looked in the mirror. Blue eyes underlined in puffy gray looked back at her. She tried to recall the previous night. It was useless. She picked up her hairbrush and began pulling it roughly through the blond tangles created by her restless sleep. Something bad had happened last night—like it always did when she didn't remember.

When her hair was tangle free, she pulled it into a pony-tail then crossed the room to sit on the edge of her bed, thinking that at least the family wouldn't be forced to listen to any of Walter's speeches today. Sometimes, if there was no Sunday football, Walter would herd Sarah, David, and Anna Mae—Stanley always managed to escape—into the living room where he would force them to listen to the ongoing problems that had plagued the steel industry from day one.

Anna Mae, David and Sarah would sit silently while Walter recapped recent events, then he raged on with detail after detail about how in the 30's the steelworkers had endured bloody battles when they tried to form a union. Despite her loathing for her uncle, Anna Mae found much of his ranting interesting. She knew Walter had the intelligence to be an asset to the union or to be promoted to an easier job. Instead he drank, swore, and lashed out at everyone around him.

There were times when she almost felt sorry for him, like when he talked about how, during a particularly violent protest, his father was ruthlessly beaten by the police. His eyes would glaze over and Anna Mae suspected that after it was all over, his father passed his own beating onto young Walter. Once she almost asked Uncle Walter if his father had beaten him. But she lost her nerve.

During these tirades, Walter would get furious if he felt one of them was not paying attention. Anna Mae always sat as close to David as possible. If Walter went on too long, David drifted off. She would wait until Walter wasn't looking then poke David in the ribs with her elbow.

About a month ago, her uncle was telling—for what seemed like the hundredth time—the story about how, under the leadership of the powerful John L. Lewis, workers finally got safer working conditions. As usual, Walter included details of the financial and legal disputes between union representatives and management. David didn't understand a word of it. He nodded off and almost fell over. Fortunately, Walter, so caught up in what he was saying, didn't see Anna Mae catch David before he hit the floor.

While David was bored to death, Sarah would pretend she understood. She'd nod when Walter was obviously stretching the truth—for instance that he, unlike his father who worked all the time—could stay home on Saturday and Sunday to rest, to go to church, to maybe have a beer or two. When did Walter ever go to church? Or have just two beers?

Six weeks ago, Walter was babbling on and on about accidents in the mill. He included gruesome details of men falling off beams or having arms or legs severed by the machines. That day, David was alert.

Last week, Walter had worked himself into a frenzy over increasing layoffs. Anna Mae had cringed at the filthy language.

"In nine goddamn years," he roared, "over a hundred thousand fuckin' steel workers have lost their jobs because of them stupid ass-hole union leaders! Not just here—all the mills! Pittsburgh! Youngstown! Aliquippa!

"The bastards aren't satisfied with anything. They want more fuckin' money, longer fuckin' vacations. Some big shot shit heads got thirteen weeks! They're gonna shut down all the mills! All of 'em! Cause' them stupid sons-a-bitches, I ain't gonna' have a job!"

Ringing church bells snapped her out of her reflections. She pulled her slippers out from under the bed. As she lifted her foot to put one on, her hands and leg stopped in mid-air. Did Walter get laid off? Is that why she couldn't remember what happened last night? She quickly put on the other slipper, stood up, and reached for her pink chenille robe that was draped over a nearby chair. After putting it on, she leaned over her bed and pulled the flowered comforter up. She then lovingly placed the aged and tattered Susie against a pillow. Now she would go downstairs and find out what happened last night.

Out in the hall, Walter's snoring was as loud as ever. She walked down the stairs carefully, each step accentuating the pain in her back.

The kitchen was dark and, she thought, *empty*. When she switched on the overhead light, she gasped. "Oh my God! What did he do to you?"

Sarah sat at the kitchen table, her faded flowered housecoat torn at the sleeve, the left side of her face a massive bruise, and her eye swollen shut. In the sudden glare of the ceiling light, her left hand flew up to cover the injured side of her face. There was a pint of Jack Daniel's and half a glass of whisky on the table. Her right hand trembled as she reached for it.

Anna Mae didn't know what to do. Aunt Sarah didn't drink. Or had the years of living with Walter changed that? It didn't matter now. She wanted to reach out, to comfort her aunt. But she couldn't. Sarah never responded to Anna Mae's attempts at physical affection.

Anna Mae watched as Sarah took a gulp of the whiskey. It sent her into a fit of coughing. She stood up, gasping for air. Rushing to the sink, Anna Mae filled a glass with cold water. Her aunt took the glass in both hands and drank small sips. Eventually the coughing stopped. Anna Mae took the glass and placed it on the counter as her compassion overcame her fear of rejection. She put her arms around her Aunt Sarah.

At first, Sarah was stiff and unyielding. Anna Mae held tighter. Several moments passed. Finally, her aunt's taut body relaxed and her voice quivered as she tried to speak. But the words came out as a series of whimpers. Anna Mae stroked the tangled brown hair. Sarah dropped her head onto Anna Mae's shoulder and began to cry.

"You need to go to the hospital," Anna Mae said.

"No!"

She held Sarah at arm's length. "Your face...have you looked in the mirror?"

Nodding, Sarah took a crumpled handkerchief from her pocket, dabbed the tears beneath her swollen eye and blew her nose.

"I'll go next door and get Olga," Anna Mae said. "Her husband will take us."

Sarah looked toward the kitchen doorway. "Shhhh, Walter will hear." She moved a few steps to a chair and sat down. "We can't tell Olga. We just can't."

Anna Mae knelt on the floor in front of Sarah. "We have to! Your eye—it might be really hurt." She began to get up. "I'm going to get Olga."

Sarah placed her hands on her niece's shoulders, but Anna Mae persisted. "Please! Let us take you. He's not going to wake up. You know he sleeps all day after a blow up."

Sarah leaned forward cupping Anna Mae's chin in her hand. "You're a good girl, Annie. We'll just make more trouble if we go."

Anna Mae desperately wanted to know what else had taken place the night before. She would have to choose her words carefully. In all these years she had managed to bluff her way through, keeping her lost time a secret, even from Sarah. She would have to risk asking something and decided upon: "Did Uncle Walter get laid off?"

"No," said Sarah. "Not that I know of."

So far so good. She tried again. "I really don't understand why Uncle Walter gets so upset about things like that."

"About the drugs?" said Sarah. "Walter caught Stanley red handed and—you heard him—he blamed me. He always blames me. I didn't even know that Stanley and his friend were in the attic."

So that was it. Anna Mae put her hand lightly across Sarah's lips. "Shhhh. Don't worry. It wasn't your fault."

Anna Mae rubbed her forehead. Could she have done something to prevent the blow-up? Probably not. If she had tried to break up Stanley and JD's little party, they would have laughed and sent her away. Or asked her to join them.

Anna Mae winced as a new wave of pain squeezed across her back.

She looked beyond her aunt to a chair that lay broken in the corner.

Sarah turned to look at the chair. "Is that what he hit you with?"

"I think so," Anna Mae said, aghast at the condition of the chair. "It all happened so fast."

David appeared in the kitchen doorway, his eyes wide with shock and anger. "I'll kill him!" He flew across the room and buried his face his mother's lap, sobbing, "I'll kill him! I'll kill him!"

Half an hour later, Sarah and Anna Mae sat at the kitchen table, their chairs pulled close together. The bottle and glass of whiskey were gone, and Sarah, despite the angry cut on her lip, was sipping a cup of hot tea. David sat at the far end of the table spooning circles in a bowl of Corn Flakes.

"Finish your cereal," said Anna Mae softly.

"I'm not hungry."

CHAPTER FIFTEEN

Later that afternoon, Anna Mae carried Biology One outside and sat on the porch swing. With the absence of weekday traffic, it was quiet on the hill. The rain and blustery winds had evolved into breezy kitten-soft sunshine, and the thermometer rested at a pleasant 66 degrees. Stanley and Walter were still sleeping. David had gone to Johnny Tamero's house and Sarah was inside napping on the couch in front of the TV.

Anna Mae braced the book against the arm of the swing. She reached back and undid the rubber band, letting her hair fall forward around her face. The sun's golden rays caught the wayward strands then reflected down on the book's glossy pages. She shifted the book to catch the shade and read the chapter title, 'The Anatomy of a Frog.'

I will learn this stuff if it kills me! Tracing the words with her index finger, she spent the next twenty minutes reading, occasionally pausing to memorize the spelling of a Latin term.

A faint sound broke her concentration. At the bottom of the porch steps, two robins were tapping their beaks and scratching on the small patch of mud and dead grass that was the Lipinski's front yard.

While watching the robins, she thought about Aunt Sarah. The morning's exchange warmed Anna Mae's heart. Despite the awful circumstances, it was the closest thing to mother-daughter time they had ever shared. She smiled at the robins. They reminded her of the pigeons in front of Vinko's. *Pigeons. Vinko's. Joey. Joey Barnes. Mother!*

She jumped up, dropped the book, rushed to the top of the steps, and placed her hand on the thin iron railing. As if in a dream, she descended the four steps to the sidewalk. Then she began to run.

Ten minutes later, perspiring and breathless, she burst into Vinko's Grocery. "Where's Joey?"

Vinko was arranging long loaves of freshly baked Italian bread. He turned to face her. "Good afternoon, young lady. Do you know you forgot your umbrella yesterday?"

She ignored the question and asked again, "Where's Joey?"

Now behind the counter, Vinko said, "I don't know. He's somewhere around here."

She quickly left the counter to make a frantic search of the store. When she didn't find Joey in the aisles or at the produce section, she rushed past the 'Employees Only' sign and into the back of the building where Joey Barns was sitting on a box of canned green beans. When he saw Anna Mae, he jumped to his feet. The blush on his face was not unusual. His averted eyes were.

"I'm sorry, Joey," she said. "I didn't mean to startle you."

He ran his huge strong hands down his soiled white apron and looked at the floor.

Vinko stood in the doorway. "Is everything okay back here?"

"It's okay, Mr. Vinko," said Anna Mae. "I just need to talk to Joey."

The grocer stood there for a few seconds, then left.

Anna Mae pushed a wooden stool close to the box of beans. Hesitantly, Joey resumed his seat.

"Joey," she began, "Yesterday you told me..."

He put his head down, avoiding her eyes.

She touched his hand. "It's okay, Joey. I'm not mad at you."

He studied his shoe. "I know."

"Are you upset because I asked about mother?"

"No."

"Then why won't you look at me?"

His eyes still downcast, he pushed his thinning hair off his forehead and shrugged his shoulders. She struggled to keep the desperation out of her voice. "Joey, I just want to know about my mother."

He glanced her way, swallowed hard, cleared his throat, and said softly, "Your mother will be mad if I tell."

"She won't be mad." Anna Mae sounded calm.

"I can't tell you. She made me promise."

Anna Mae's heart felt as though it would pound out of her chest. Joey clasped his long knobby fingers together with such pressure that they were turning white. Her need to know was greater than her concern for Joey's discomfort. However, she had to be careful. *Push him too hard and he might clam up.*

She took a deep breath. "Joey, if you tell me where my mother is, I'll tell her I tricked you into telling so she won't be mad at you."

He thoughtfully repeated, "She won't be mad."

"No. She won't be mad at you. I promise."

Joey wrung his hands and wiped them on his apron. His knees were shaking.

She tried again. "You can tell me about knowing my mother. Do you know where she is?"

"I-I-I don't know where s-s-she is. Sometimes she c-calls me. She wants to know if I seen you. If you come in the store and all—things like that she asks me."

Anna Mae was barely able to breathe. "Do you remember the last time she called?"

He nodded.

"And when was that?"

He looked at the ceiling.

"Was it last week?"

"No."

"Last month?"

"M-Maybe. She wanted to know if you was okay. I told her you was fine and that...that you're real pretty."

"And she didn't tell you where she is?"

"No. I think she don't want nobody to know. It's a secret."

Suddenly Vinko appeared in the doorway, holding Anna Mae's umbrella. "Joey, I need you out front."

Joey stood up and stepped toward the door.

"Please, Sir," Anna Mae begged. "Just a few more minutes."

Vinko looked at Joey who went back to sit on the box. Anna Mae knew that Vinko was wondering what a fifteen-year-old girl could possibly have to talk about with a slightly backward man of thirty-three. But he didn't ask. He placed the umbrella beside the bean box, touched Joey affectionately on the shoulder, said, "Take your time, kids," and left.

Joey seemed proud that his boss knew he was having an important conversation. He squared his shoulders, looked Anna Mae straight in the eyes, and said, "I don't know what it's okay to tell you."

"You can tell me anything, Joey. Anything at all." Fighting tears that were turning Joey's face into a blur, she pleaded, "You know what it's like, Joey...not having a mother."

"You have Miss Sarah."

"That's not the same. Please, Joey. I promise I won't get you into trouble. I just have to know. Don't you understand?" She was crying now. "Joey! Where is she? Where's my mother?"

He reached into his pocket and pulled out a clean, neatly pressed white handkerchief. "I don't know where she is. Honest!"

"If she calls you again," Anna Mae said taking the handkerchief, "will you tell her that I need her? Tell her—tell her I'm having some problems."

Joey's face glowed with compassion. Now the stronger of the two, he took her hand and said, "If there's anything I can do, I will do it. But I have to wait for her to call."

She wiped the tears from her face. "Joey? Can I ask you one more question?"

He nodded.

She twisted the damp handkerchief, trying to get up her nerve, afraid of an answer yet needing to ask anyway. "Do you know who my father is?"

"No. I don't know."

"It's not important," she said without emotion.

Anna Mae stood up, walked to the rear door, opened it a crack, and breathed in the fresh air. When she returned Joey said, "I think that maybe when you're eighteen—maybe then she might want to see you."

Anna Mae abruptly sat down on the stool. Her words were sharp, almost demanding. "Did she say that? Did my mother say that?"

He opened his mouth. Nothing came out. Anna Mae saw the fear on his face and regretted what must have seemed like an attack. "It's okay, Joey. I didn't mean to bite your head off."

"You—you didn't b-bite it off," he laughed. "It's still here."

She wanted to go on questioning him forever. On the other hand, she knew she had been lucky to learn as much as she did. She also knew how much Joey valued her friendship. She would never deliberately do anything to hurt him.

She placed her hands on his big shoulders and looked into his dark eyes. "You're my good friend, Joey. I am so grateful that you told me these things. And I promise," she crossed her heart. "I promise I will never, ever, tell anyone."

"Joey?" Vinko was standing in the doorway again.

Joey's eyes questioned Anna Mae. She nodded and they both stood up. Anna Mae wanted to give Joey a big hug, but she just smiled and said, "Thank you, Joey."

She was half way up the Vickroy street hill before she realized she had, once again, forgotten her umbrella.

CHAPTER SIXTEEN

Two years later
June 23, 1968

The huge amusement park sprawled colorfully amidst its gray and dismal surroundings. Since 1898, Kennywood Park had been an island of escape for steelworkers and their families; a place to abandon troubles in the back draft of a plunging roller coaster, or to relinquish all sense of balance in the huge, undulating Noah's Ark. It was the last weekend in June, the school picnic. Inside the park entrance, Anna Mae, with nine-year-old David in tow, waited for Debbie Henderson and Laura Smith.

Anna Mae gazed up at The Old Mill. The modern day reproduction of an outdated essential blended into boulders as old as the park itself. She looked to one side at a huge, simulated grinding wheel. It rotated under a flow of falling water, creating a current that escorted little boats through a winding channel.

Anna Mae was so impressed by the Mill that she failed to watch where she was going. As the couples were passing through the ticket line, she slammed right into Angelo. Laughing, he threw his arms around her. She suddenly realized that soon she would be sitting next to him on a slow ride through a dark tunnel. Her heart fluttered.

Clutching the string of her balloon, she tucked the Teddy Bear under her arm. Angelo helped her into the front seat of the wobbly boat that rocked even harder when Debbie and Jake climbed into the seat behind them. Laura and Tom would be in the next boat. Theirs would be held back for a few moments to insure the first couples an isolated journey.

Pulled by an underwater cable, the boat moved away from the boarding dock and glided slowly into the shadows. As they rounded the first bend, daylight surrendered to the dark. Anna Mae leaned closer to Angelo. He put his arm around her. On the Ferris Wheel, he had had his arm around her. But in this dark tunnel it was different: more intimate.

The little boat turned another bend and Anna Mae marveled at the beauty of a dim blue display of fairies sprinkling shimmering dust onto sleeping flowers. The blue lights evolved into sunshiny yellow, the blossoms opened and Angelo drew her closer. They floated back into the dark then out again to other amusing displays until they reached one long and very dark passageway, so dark she couldn't see Angelo's face. She felt his breath on her cheek and said softly, "You smell like hot dogs."

"Why are you whispering?" he murmured into her ear.

"Why are you whispering?" she countered.

"I asked you first."

"It's spooky in here!"

His arm tightened around her. She squeezed the bear against her chest. At home, even when she woke in the middle of the night, it wasn't this dark. There were always streetlights throwing shadows across her room. But this—this was an eerie solid black!

Suddenly, a flash of blinding white light illuminated the entire underground chamber. Startled, Anna Mae jerked away from Angelo. On a rock above her, shrouded in a web crawling with spiders, sat a hideous green faced witch. Anna Mae's eyes riveted on the terrifying figure.

In the back of the boat, Debbie and Jake were giggling. Anna Mae tried to assure herself. This is all fake! Her hands tingled. She fought to breathe.

This is not real. Not real! Breathe. That's it. Just breathe. And don't look at that witch. Close your eyes.

She could not close her eyes.

The boat moved too slowly. *Was it moving at all?* The bright light began to fade. Another cadaverous crone was alongside the boat. Its talons clawed the air. It cackled madly. She dropped the bear and let go of the balloon. It flew up into a canopy of spider webs.

Please, God! Get us out of here! Suddenly the gruesome display vanished into darkness and she leaned into the security of Angelo's arms. Her breathing was almost normal. Then the boat tilted.

"Sit Down!" Angelo yelled.

Jake was standing with one foot in the boat and the other stretched out onto a rock, groping blindly in the dark, trying to grab the string of Anna Mae's balloon.

"I almost have it!"

"You're gonna tip us over!"

Still trying to catch the string, Jake staggered to maintain his balance. But he couldn't do either. He landed on the back seat with enough force to lift the front of the boat. When it dropped back into the channel, water splashed everywhere and Jake couldn't stop laughing.

"That's not funny!" Debbie exclaimed.

Angelo mopped his wet face with the tail of his shirt as Anna Mae wiped hers with her hand. The balloon was

left behind along with the cackling witch and Anna
Mae's sense of safety.

"I'm so sorry," said Angelo turning to Anna Mae. "I
had no idea they changed so much stuff."

"I read it in the paper," Jake said from behind, "They
changed it to scare the girls so they'd come leaping into
our arms."

Angelo groaned and ran his fingers through his hair.
"I didn't know."

Anna Mae shuddered. Angelo put both arms around
her.

Jake laughed. "That'a boy! See, it worked!"

Anna Mae wondered if Jake was hugging Debbie.
She even managed to smile. That's when Angelo kissed
her. He just leaned down and kissed her right on the lips.
Just a little kiss. But enough to make her heart skip a
beat. "We'll be out of here soon," he said.

She heard something. "What's that pounding?"

"It sounds like a broken gear somewhere ahead of
us."

As the cable continued to pull the boat through the
channel, the pounding grew louder. Again, Anna Mae
moved away from Angelo. He reached out to her. She
shrugged him away.

Gears. He said it was a broken gear. Her body
tensed. It reminded her of what? What was it?

The air around her flickered with yellow light as
scattered bursts of simulated fire shot out of the
surrounding rocks. The pounding was now almost
deafening.

Was someone rocking the boat? No. It was bumping
from the bottom, bouncing her around on the seat. She
couldn't feel her hands.

Dear God, don't let this happen. Not here. Not now.

Angelo's strong arms tightened around her. She
pushed at his chest. "Let me go!"

134

His voice came from a distance. "Anna Mae! Don't look. Just put your head down. Please!"

The pounding grew louder. Her heart raced—her blood fearful in her veins. Then she saw it. Two spotlights streaked down from the stony roof and at the point where the rays came together, a charred body in smoking black rags pushed a wheelbarrow along the edge of the channel. Dangling over the side of the wheelbarrow was the arm of a skeleton. It was so near it brushed the side of the boat.

Please, God, get me out of here!

The pounding—a giant's footsteps. The earth was shaking. It shook the ground upon which she sat. And there was fire above, fire below. Out there everywhere—with the pounding.

Is that Angelo holding me? With every ounce of her strength, she pushed at the pressure that was smothering her—at the descending black umbrella. The shiny material gave way to the pressure. It molded itself around her. She couldn't breathe. Someone was screaming. *Who screamed? Did I scream?* She lunged forward, trying to get out of the boat.

"Hey! Be careful!" *Was that Jake?*

I have to get out of here! This is a bad place.
Someone was pulling her shirt. "Let me go!"

The boat rocked violently.

A loud, deep voice penetrated the darkness. "SIT DOWN IN THE BOAT! DO NOT ROCK THE BOAT! SIT DOWN IN THE BOAT! DO NOT ROCK THE BOAT!"

The pounding stopped. The flames vanished. Nothing was real. Where was she?

The shadow people. There they are. Up there—up on the bank—standing—watching—watching me in the brown river. So comfortable. So at peace. In the warm brown water. *It will be okay now. I'll be okay.* This was the place where nothing could hurt her. The place where, thirteen years ago, a terrified two-year-old had forged the path to a better reality.

*   *   *

Angelo's embrace completely encompassed the girl in his arms as the boat rounded two more curves and then shot out into the sunlight. Anna Mae, her face against his chest, was strangely quiet. She didn't seem to be frightened anymore. The ride supervisor, a burly man in a wet shirt, grabbed the side of the boat to stabilize it. He shook his head and grumbled, "That's the last time you kids get on this ride. Don't come back."

As soon as the supervisor tied the boat, Angelo helped Anna Mae onto the dock. He led her to the bench where they had been sitting before the ride. She sat down primly, smiling at him as he sat beside her.

"Well," said Jake, who stood nearby holding Debbie's hand, "she sure did get over that fast. What the hell happened in there?"

Before Angelo could respond, Tom said, "I always thought there was something weird about her."

Debbie shook loose of Jake's hand. "She's not weird! She has some problems at home. Big problems."

Laura began fussing with the mass of red curls that refused to stay on top of her head. "I know," she said in her most compassionate voice while struggling with a huge hair-clip. "I keep trying to help her come out of her shell. Sometimes it works. Sometimes she gets mad at me."

"What was she screaming about?" asked Tom.

"Beats me," said Jake. "Scared me half to death."

Laura gave up on her hair and let it fall carelessly to her shoulders as Debbie sat beside Anna Mae and handed her the now soiled Teddy Bear.

"Poor Teddy," Anna Mae said, "How'd he get so dirty?"

Debbie frowned. "He fell into the bottom of the boat."

Anna Mae turned the bear around in her hands. "Are you giving him to me?"

With a bewildered glance at Angelo, Debbie said to Anna Mae, "Don't you know he's yours?"

Anna Mae smiled at her friend, hugged the bear, and said, "Thank you."

Angelo frowned at Debbie and shook his head. "Leave it alone, Deb. She's just upset. She'll be okay. She just needs a few minutes to herself."

"But…"

"I said she's okay!"

"Really. I'm fine."

"But…"

"You go ahead," said Angelo. "I'll stay here with her."

"Are you sure?"

"I'm sure."

Debbie walked away to join the others who had wandered up the path.

She waited for her friends, she watched the groups of boisterous teenagers, smiled at the young couples holding hands, and wistfully gazed at entire families with grandparents and babies. Finally, Debbie and Laura emerged from the crowd. Like Anna Mae, they wore navy blue shorts and white T-shirts, with Warrenvale High displayed tied into a bright pile on top of her head. Anna Mae touched the long blond braid falling over her left shoulder, thinking the style was outdated. She wished she had let her hair hang loose. After a few excited giggles and some quick comments about the perfect weather, the girls walked three abreast down the wide walkway with David trailing behind.

David yanked the back of Anna Mae's shirt. "Annie! Look! Look, there's a merry-go-round. Can I ride it? Huh?"

Pulling her shirt out of his grip, she said, "Maybe later."

"But Annie..."

"No! Not now."

If she had been alone with David, she would have rode with him. But there were others to consider. Her sophisticated teenage girlfriends certainly wouldn't want to be seen riding around in circles on a bunch of wooden horses, so she ignored David's protests and continued walking. In a few minutes, the three friends reached the first roller coaster, The Racer, twin cars that ran on parallel tracks.

Laura squealed, "Let's ride!"

"I'll get sick," said Debbie.

"No you won't," Laura declared.

"Okay," said Debbie, "I'll go. But if I puke all over you, don't say a word."

As Laura and Debbie elbowed their way toward the ticket line, Anna Mae stayed behind. Laura turned and called out to Anna Mae, "Come on! Let's go!"

Anna Mae hated Laura's bossiness. She had good reason not to want to ride the coaster. It might frighten her and she didn't want to risk having a blackout at the school picnic. She stood in the walkway and didn't move an inch.

Debbie shouted from the ticket line. "Anna Mae! Where's David?"

Anna Mae looked around, then spun around, her eyes scanning the crowd. Panicked, she looked toward the boat pond benches across from the coaster. Not there. She stretched on her toes to look back up toward the park entrance. Nothing. She looked down the path toward the crowd standing at the Ferris Wheel. He wasn't there either.

Debbie ran to Anna Mae. "Do you see him?"

"No! He was here just a minute ago."

Obviously annoyed, Laura left her place in line. "What's wrong?"

"David's missing," said Debbie.

"He'll be back," Laura snapped. "Let's go!"

Anna Mae tried to sound calm. "You go ahead. I'll stay here and wait. He's probably just walking slow."

Laura put her hands on her hips and rolled her eyes. "Good grief, Anna Mae, the kid's old enough to take care of himself!"

Anna Mae was ready to snap back at Laura when Tom Nelson and Jake Tambellini emerged from the crowd. Tom was Laura's latest crush. Tall and arrogant, the first string quarterback for Warrenvale high was the only member of the team that wore his blue and gold football jersey to the picnic.

Next to Tom, short, hefty and wearing a plain white T-shirt, Jake's quiet and thoughtful demeanor contradicted the power he put into a tackle. Debbie adored him.

Anna Mae tried to hide her disappointment. Angelo Tamero, her hero running-back, wasn't with them. However, Jake caught her unspoken question and explained, "Angelo went somewhere. He just up and took off. He told us to wait for him," he glanced critically at Tom, "but big shot here couldn't be bothered."

"I think he wanted to ride the merry-go-round," Tom snickered. "At least he was heading that direction. He'll eventually find us."

Jake put his arm around Debbie. "You girls going on The Racer?"

Laura snuggled up to Tom. "Yes, we are."

139

They all looked at Anna Mae. "I'm okay," she said. "You go ahead. I'll wait here for Davie."

Laura pointed to Anna Mae. "She's afraid to go on The Racer."

"I am not!"

With her freckled nose in the air, Laura led Tom to the ticket line where she stood smugly beside him. Debbie and Jake lingered behind, but Anna Mae said, "Go on the ride. I'll be fine."

Two minutes later Anna Mae watched her friends walk up to the boarding platform and step into the coasters—Laura and Tom in one, Debbie and Jake in the other. As the racing cars began their slow crawl up the first incline, Anna Mae fought the familiar feeling of being left out. When the cars were out of sight, she walked toward the boat pond, where an elderly couple guided their small green craft through a scatter of floating popcorn.

I should have never given Davie his own riding tickets. Now what do I do? Should I stay here? Or go looking for him?

A blast of screams startled her, and she looked up at the racers now plunging downward behind the trees. *Thank God I didn't ride that thing!*

Again, she searched the small faces in the crowd. *Maybe Laura was right. Maybe Davie was old enough to take care of himself.* Calming herself with a few deep breaths, she sat down on the bench beside the boat pond.

*   *   *

Although he had asked them to wait, Angelo Tamero watched his buddies walk away. No big deal. He could catch up with them later. He was sure it was David he saw on the merry-go-round. And if David was on the merry-go-round, Anna Mae would be nearby.

The next time the carousel horses circled around, Angelo waved wildly to get David's attention. But David was too busy checking out the horse next to his that was bucking up and down. Finally, the ride stopped, and David scampered onto the bucking horse. Angelo leaped over the railing and mounted the stationary horse that David had been riding.

David laughed and wiggled on the saddle. "Hi, Angelo!"

"Hey, Davie! Race ya!"

"You can't race, silly. But I can go higher than you. Your horse can't go up and down."

A man with a huge white mustache and a green uniform walked between the riders collecting tickets. Angelo handed him one ticket for himself and another for David. The horses were again on the move. Angelo grinned. *How great to be a kid at Kennywood!*

As the horses circled, Angelo searched the spectators for Anna Mae. Was she still avoiding him? A month ago, he had taken her to see her favorite actress, Barbra Streisand, in Funny Girl. When they were leaving the theater, Anna Mae's Uncle Walter pulled his car to the curb and told her to get in. Anna Mae had looked a little nervous. When Angelo attempted to say something to Walter, he just rolled up his window, leaving Angelo standing in the bright light of the marquee. He feared Anna Mae didn't have her uncle's permission to go to the movie and hoped she wasn't in trouble.

The morning after the movie, Angelo had waited at the front of the school, hoping to see her. But she must have used another door. From that day on, each time Angelo spotted her, she would manage to disappear. It had been a month now since she talked to him. He wasn't going to let her get away this time.

Angelo, his head nodding up and down to follow the movement of David's bucking horse, yelled, "Where's Anna Mae?"

David shrugged his shoulders and looked very guilty.

"Is she here? With you?"

David shook his head.

"Well, where is she?"

David pointed down the main walkway and yelled, "She's with her girlfriends."

Angelo smiled to himself. He'd find her.

CHAPTER SEVENTEEN

On a small island in the middle of the boat pond, multicolored lights filtered through columns of water that shot forty feet into the air. A gust of cold mist enveloped Anna Mae and she shivered from the chill—or was it anxiety? Eventually, after what seemed like a long wait, her friends returned, arguing and laughing about who had won the neck and neck race.

She smiled up at the happy couples who were having such a good time. But when she turned her head to look down the pathway for David, her heart skipped a beat. Stanley and his Road Hog friends were walking straight towards her. She jumped to her feet, saying loudly, "Let's go!"

"Damn!" said Tom, "You look like you saw a ghost."

Anna Mae rushed up the path toward the park entrance.

"You're going the wrong way," shouted Laura.

Anna Mae walked faster.

The others hurried up behind her, circling around to block her path. "Did you see David?" Debbie asked.

"No," she said, breathing hard. Then, before she even turned around, she felt Stanley's presence.

"Well, well! What have we here?" In his high black boots, tight jeans, and soiled T-shirt with a pack of Luckies rolled into the sleeve, Stanley stood in front of his motorcycle buddies. He greeted her with a grin that bordered on a sneer.

Pete Maleski held his cycle helmet in his right hand and placed the other on Stanley's shoulder. Behind Pete, Spike O'Donald stood with his greasy hands on his hips, his black leather jacket open to display a white skull and crossbones on a black pullover. Since JD had disappeared into Vietnam, and George Siminoski dropped off the face of the earth, Stanley had hooked up with the local motorcycle gang, the Road Hogs. And he was meaner than ever.

"Where's my little brother?" Stanley asked.

Anna Mae's stomach turned over. She couldn't speak. The teenagers rallied around her and Debbie blurted out, "He's on the Rocket Ride!"

Stanley thought for a moment, his drug dilated pupils aimed in Debbie's direction. "Oh, really? By himself?"

Debbie took a step back. "Well, ah..."

The accusation was clear in Stanley's voice. "They just let him on? Little as he is? They let him ride all by himself?"

Anna Mae's fear mounted. What would Stanley do if he knew she had lost track of David? Laura stepped forward and said to Stanley, "Get lost, creep. We're here to have a good time. Go bother someone else."

Tom pulled Laura back. Jake, who was Stanley's height but more powerfully built, moved forward to challenge Stanley nose to nose. "You heard what she said. Get lost!"

"As soon as I know where..."

"Annie!"

Anna Mae's body went limp with relief as Angelo and David stepped out of the crowd. David's face was a mixture of excitement and guilt.

Stanley stepped around Jake and smiled down at David. "How was the Rocket Ride? They let you on all by yourself? A little shit like you?"

David caught the look in Anna Mae's eyes. He shot up on his tiptoes and stretched his neck, adding at least two inches to his height. "Sure! I'm not a baby, ya know!"

Angelo placed his hand on David's shoulder. "He was with me. You got a problem with that?"

Stanley turned to Anna Mae; "I wonder what my father will say about you hanging out with the Dago?"

In deference to his Italian friend, Jake's face turned red and his jaw clenched. "And who's gonna tell him?"

Stanley grinned broadly.

"You wouldn't dare!" said Debbie.

"Well now," Stanley sneered. "Who's gonna stop me?"

Pete shifted his helmet to his left hand and pulled Stanley away with his right. "Com' on Stan," he said. "That's the speed talkin.' Don't make trouble for the kids." He then gave Anna Mae a thumbs up.

"Don't worry, Honey," Spike added with a wink, "We'll kick his ass if he tells."

Stanley poked a finger at the white crossbones on Spike's black shirt. "You ain't bad enough to kick my ass."

Spike began to take off his leather jacket, but Stanley just spit on the ground and walked away. The teenagers breathed easier as they watched the Road Hogs walk toward the center of the park. When they were finally out of sight, Anna Mae swooped down and hugged David, who squealed, "Let go! You're squashing me!"

She looked up at Angelo. "Where did you find him?"

"He was on the merry-go-round. I didn't see you anywhere so we came looking for you."

Debbie frowned. "Do you think Stanley will tell?"

Anna Mae let go of David and stood up very straight. "I don't care if he does. Let him tell Walter. Today I'm going to have fun."

At Angelo's suggestion, they all walked to the picnic area where his family had a table. Angelo's mother, Maria, was a tiny woman in a flowered apron with black braids wrapped into a bun. She smiled warmly at the teenagers then continued laying out a feast. Angelo's father was a few yards away, playing catch with four boys David's age.

"Hey, Dad!" Angelo called out. "Do ya mind if Anna Mae's little brother hangs out with you?"

"Come on, David," bellowed Salvador Tamero. "We're gonna take this park by storm."

Anna Mae wasn't sure if she should let David go. Being with Angelo was bad enough. Now she had put David under the senior Tamero's supervision. Walter would go ballistic if he found out. But seeing the eager look on David's face, she got up her courage and told him it was okay. She was not going to let Stanley ruin her day, or David's either.

With David now in safe keeping, the couples walked back to the amusement area. As a group, they rode the Ferris Wheel, the Swan Ride, the Bumper Cars, and the Silver Plane that raised high into the air and flew around in circles. Then Laura decided they should all go on the Spinner.

Anna Mae looked up at the huge whirling cylinder where riders stood with their backs to a circular wall that spun faster and faster, building enough centrifugal force to stick the riders to the wall. Then the bottom dropped out!

Anna Mae clutched Angelo's arm so hard that her fingernails almost broke the skin. "I can't do that, Angelo. Please don't make me ride that thing."

Laura put her freckled nose in the air. "You have to get over being afraid, Anna Mae. It's part of growing up!"

Anna Mae was ready to snap back at Laura when Angelo dragged her away. As the rest of the group joined the Spinner ticket line, Angelo and Anna Mae headed for the arcade. Soon they were laughing, popping balloons with little darts, and shooting long rifles at hopping tin bunnies. When they left the arcade, Anna Mae proudly held a yellow helium balloon in one hand, and a big white Teddy Bear in the other.

When The Spinner ride was over, the two couples found Anna Mae and Angelo at the Hercules Pad. Laura's red hair looked as though it had been through a hurricane and it was now Anna Mae's turn to be smug. Angelo, his muscles flexed and wearing a jauntily tipped cowboy hat, slammed a gigantic mallet onto a pad that sent a red arrow flying 20 feet straight up. It whacked the target gong with a force that carried the sound half way across the park. Debbie looked at Angelo with total admiration. Laura's eyes turned two shades greener.

It was nearing four o'clock when they all converged upon the hot dog stand. While waiting for their orders to be filled, the boys dared the girls to take a ride in the Old Mill, generally known as the Tunnel of Love.

Laura giggled and shook her head. Anna Mae avoided Angelo's eyes. Debbie looked at Jake and said, "No way!"

With catsup, mustard and relish dripping from their hot dogs, they strolled in the direction of the Old Mill, found a bench across from it, sat down to finish their snacks, and then debate the issue.

The boys won.

CHAPTER EIGHTEEN

Angelo studied Anna Mae's face. She had a look in her eyes that wasn't there before, an expression so remote, so distant. She looked up at him. "What is it? Why are you looking at me like that?"

It seemed as though her voice had changed too. It was softer, more childlike. Or was it his imagination? Then she said something that sent shivers up his spine: "Wasn't it nice that Debbie gave me her Teddy Bear?"

He swallowed hard. She didn't remember that he had given her the Teddy Bear when he won it at the dart game. He took her hand. "Come on. Let's go over to the picnic area where there aren't so many people."

Hanging on to Angelo's hand and holding the bear by one foot, Anna Mae followed him like a docile child as he worked his way through the crowd. Now and then she would pause, look around at the people, the games, and the rides. At The Ferris Wheel, she stopped to look at the suspended baskets. He asked if she wanted to ride, but she shook her head and they moved on.

At last they reached the picnic area. He walked her past the table where his mother was gathering soiled paper plates. He led her to an isolated Oak tree at the edge of the grove. The earth smelled of newly cut grass. They sat on the ground under the tree. Anna Mae leaned back against the gnarled trunk and placed the bear on the ground beside her. He watched her eyes follow the sunbeams as they filtered down through the trees, scattering specks of light on the ground.

"Are you feeling better now?"

She didn't answer—just kept staring at the specks of light.

"Anna Mae? Anna Mae, what is it? What happened to you back there?"

She looked up into the cloudless sky where two wayward balloons floated in an ocean of blue. He put his hand on her chin and turned her head so she was facing him. "What in the world is going on?"

Her face was a blank.

"Talk to me!"

Nothing.

"Annie Mae, please! You're scaring me!"

Suddenly she shouted the word: Wheelbarrow! She seemed startled at the sound of her own voice.

"Wheelbarrow?"

"Yes, the wheelbarrow."

"What about it?"

"Oh, Angelo," she said, her voice strained, her face pale. "It's hard for me to explain." She paused and took a deep breath. "What did I do?"

He tried to hide his confusion. "You don't know what you did?"

"No, Angelo. I don't know."

"Why? How? I mean...you don't know?"

Tears were now flowing down her cheeks. They fell in huge droplets from her chin onto her lap. He reached into his hip pocket, pulled out a handkerchief and began to wipe them away. She took the handkerchief and did it herself.

"It's a long story," she said.

Angelo moved closer.

"I never told anyone. I'm afraid to tell."

"You can tell me anything," he said, removing his cowboy hat and placing it on the ground.

"It's always been my secret," she said, her voice fading. "Ever since I can remember I've had these...these...blackouts."

He could hardly hear her now. He leaned closer.

"I lose time," she whispered, seeming to be talking to herself. "Hours. Sometimes a day. Or more. I don't know where I was. Or what I did."

She paused and Angelo was afraid to speak, to do anything that would cause her to stop talking. Finally, her voice a bit louder, she continued. "It took me a long time to understand what it is and why it happens." She sat up straight, rigid. "Please don't tell anyone. Please!"

"Cross my heart."

She hung her head. "If you don't want to see me anymore, I'll understand. Just please, don't tell anyone."

"Anna Mae, if you tell me not to repeat something, I would never, ever do it. You can trust me. Don't you realize how important you are to me?"

She looked up. "What?"

"You're important to me. And nothing you tell me is going to change that. Anna Mae, I love you."

She looked at him with wide blue eyes as though she hadn't heard right. Then she looked away. "I guess...I think—I better tell you everything."

He tried to gather her close to comfort her. "Don't," she said, and pushed him away. "Just let me tell you."

He listened quietly while she talked. She told him about her blackouts, how she had become skilled at hiding her lost time, and that it was probably the result of Walter's beatings. She explained why she never dared to get too close to anyone. She was afraid they would find out and think she was crazy. By then, tears streamed down her face.

He didn't move a muscle. He sat mesmerized by every heartbreaking word. *This can't be that happy little girl with the long braids that I chased in the schoolyard—the same pretty girl I watched from my seat beside the Bishop's chair, hoping she was watching me too.*

She used his handkerchief to wipe the tears away. He marveled at how her long lashes made shadows on her cheeks. This beautiful girl has finally shared the truth of her life with someone she trusted. And he was that someone.

The lengthening shadows sent the sunbeams off in another direction, and the flecks of light that once sprinkled the ground were replaced by shadow. Angelo watched the haunted look in Anna Mae's eyes give way to a curious mixture of sadness and relief. All this time, all these years, she had been living on a tightrope, trying desperately not to lose her balance.

She touched his face. He took her into his arms and held her. She nestled her head on his shoulder. He ran his hand down her arm, petting her as though she were an injured kitten. He whispered, "Everything will be okay."

CHAPTER NINETEEN

The next day.

With the wall phone receiver cradled between her cheek and shoulder, Anna Mae took the last gulp of Pepsi, then tossed the bottle into the trash. "Nahhhh," she said into the receiver, "Davie never tells Walter anything...he might say that Stanley is lying...Debbie, it doesn't work that way in this house. You know how my uncle is. The rest of us have to look out for each other. Even Sarah...I know she's his wife, but—wait I hear someone coming."

Anna Mae put the receiver on the kitchen counter and went into the hallway. Whoever had come in had dirt on their shoes and the tracks went up the steps to the second floor. "Is that you, Davie?"

No answer.

Shrugging her shoulders, she went back to the kitchen and picked up the receiver. "I think Stanley came in...He might decide not to say anything...I know he's a troublemaker. Maybe he was just trying to impress his friends."

Although Anna Mae held the receiver an inch from her ear, she still heard Debbie's loud lecture. "...and you make sure Stanley never, ever, says anything to Walter about you and Angelo at the park. For God's sake, Anna Mae, stand up to him!"

Anna Mae wanted to ask her just how to do that but decided to leave it alone. Stanley wouldn't tell Walter. Yesterday, at the park, Stanley was high. He'd forget.

She glanced at the clock. "I have to go. Sarah told me to have the dishes done before she got back from the hospital...It's twelve o'clock...I think Mrs. Siminoski had a heart attack...I don't know. Dobie stays in the house all the time because of those awful burn scars. I heard they used the insurance money to help pay George's college tuition. That creep hasn't even come to see his sick mother. If Uncle Walter knew Aunt Sarah went to see Mrs. Siminoski he would have a fit...Debbie, I really have to go now."

Anna Mae hung the receiver on the wall mount, walked over to the sink full of dirty dishes, and pushed up the sleeves of her bulky gray sweatshirt. Now that school was out, she would be expected to take over most of the housework. In some ways, she didn't mind. She wanted Sarah's approval so much she would gladly clean the whole house to get it. Laura said that was an ungodly price to pay for a so-called mother.

Suddenly she realized that she wasn't alone. Before she could look around, Stanley said behind her, "Poor, poor Cinderella." He then turned toward the refrigerator, opened it, and swore. She supposed he was grumbling about the missing bottle of Pepsi. A few moments later she heard crackling as he tore open a bag of Ruffles. She placed a wet dish in the drainer. "There's some ginger ale in that box by the back door."

Stanley's mouth was full of chips. "Ansit warm as pith!"

"Ever heard of ice cubes?"

"Yeah! Get me a glass with some ice cubes, Cinderella!"

"Get it yourself." She picked up a frying pan caked with the remains of last night's meatballs. As she listened to Stanley chewing the Ruffles, she reminded herself that this was not a good time to antagonize him. She put the meatball pan into the dishwater to soak and dried her hands. She then went to the back door to get a can of ginger ale. She took a clean glass from the drainer, opened the freezer, and filled the glass with ice cubes. Stanley studied her as she walked to the table, poured the ginger ale over the ice, slid the glass in front of him, and sat down.

He looked at the glass. "What do you want?"

"Don't tell Walter."

He picked up the glass. "About you and the Dago?"

"About me and Angelo."

He smiled, took a long drink and refilled the glass.

She watched the ale foam over and onto Sarah's favorite tablecloth. A dark circle crawled into the yellow daisies. "Please don't make any trouble for me."

"I guess you don't want me to tell my father about Davie hanging out with that Johnny kid either."

She made an effort to sound nonchalant. "Davie only went on a few rides with Johnny. Look Stanley, if you tell Walter, me and Davie might not be the only ones who get hurt. You know how your father takes it out on everyone."

The glint in his eyes frightened her. "You mean he'd probably go after Sarah too? She went to see that Siminoski dame today, didn't she? My dad would kill her if he knew!"

How in the world did he know that Sarah was at the hospital? "Please, Stanley. You do things that Walter would have a fit about too."

Stanley looked down at his bare feet and wiggled his toes. Anna Mae now realized why she hadn't heard him come into the kitchen. "Com' on," she said. "What would you get out of it? Do you like it when he tears into the family?"

He stuck his bare feet back under the table. "Ain't much of a family. You got any money?"

"I have twenty dollars. Why?"

He lit a cigarette. "I need it."

"It's upstairs."

"Then go get it." He stood up, crossed the kitchen, and reached for the phone.

Anna Mae was upstairs moving things around in the bottom of her closet, looking for her hidden money when she heard Sarah downstairs. Not only was she letting herself be blackmailed, now Sarah would be on her because the dishes weren't done, the tablecloth was soiled, and there were dirty footprints on the hall rug.

"What'cha lookin' for?"

"David! Don't do that! I'm looking for the twenty dollars that was in my shoe. Did you see it?"

"I don't mess with your shoes," he said, kneeling down to help her look.

Sarah yelled up the steps. "Anna Mae! Why aren't these dishes done?"

Anna Mae yelled back, "I'll finish them later."

David held up a twenty-dollar bill. "Here it is."

She looked at the shoe in his hand. It was right where she had put it. "Davie," she said. "Go down and tell Stanley to come up here. And you stay downstairs." David looked at her like she had just told him to send up the living room couch. But he asked no questions. "And tell Aunt Sarah I'll be down in a minute."

Several minutes later, Stanley appeared at her bedroom door. Still on her knees straightening the shoes, Anna Mae reached up, trying to hand him the money. "Now promise you won't say anything to Walter!"

He pushed the money away. "No. I don't promise. Not yet. Now you got to go shopping for me. Go down to Jackson's Pool Hall. There'll be a guy—an older dude wearing a lot of gold. He's small. Sort of strange looking. Not Black. Not Spick. Just dark and weird. He wears a lot of gold chains. He might be in a big, blue Caddie. Or near it. Don't worry, he won't be inside the poolroom so you don't have to go in. I just talked to him. He's on his way to meet you."

Anna Mae looked up at Stanley in disbelief. He was telling her to buy drugs for him!

"Quit lookin' at me like that," said Stanley. "You know the score. You weren't born yesterday. Besides, he thinks they're for you—a new customer. He'll give you a good deal!"

She couldn't do it. She wouldn't do it! *You rotten piece of scum!* She stood up and threw the money at him. "No!"

Grinning, he picked up the twenty and began to walk away, commenting, "I wonder if my dad'll beat up Davie, or just you and Sarah."

Anna Mae lunged forward, grabbing at the long drab hair that hung in kinks down Stanley's back. He spun around holding the twenty-dollar bill in her face. She snatched it from his hand. He laughed. "That'a girl. Oh! Did I warn you to be careful? If you see the cops, go hang out at Vinko's for a minute."

Two minutes later she was on her way out the front door when Sarah called out to her. "Girl! You better get in here and finish these dishes."

"I'll finish them later," Anna Mae snapped, then slammed the door as hard as she could.

Anna Mae stopped at the bottom of the hill. Two blocks away, several young men loitered around

Jackson's Pool Hall. *I can't believe I'm doing this. What if I get caught?*

Images of Kennywood rapidly flashed across her mind: David running happily off with Johnny, Debbie and Jake ramming around in the bumper car, Angelo saying, *I love you.*

And then there was Stanley's comment: *I wonder if my dad'll beat up Davie, or just you and Sarah?*

She crossed the first intersection. *God, please forgive me. I don't have any choice. I can't let Stanley get us all in trouble. I just can't!*

At the next intersection she rushed to make the green light. That was when she saw it; the long, blue Cadillac parked in front of the pool hall. Before she could reach it, the big car pulled away from the curb. She stopped a building away from the pool hall. Maybe he won't come back. There was still time to change her mind. However, she willed herself to stay where she was, her feet cemented to the sidewalk. She waited.

He must have parked in the alley because he was walking, or rather strolling, straight towards her. He was small, with a yellowish brown face and a mahogany Afro. He wore a black suit and gold chains over a bright green turtleneck. Clamped between his teeth was a thin cigar.

Her hands shook as she fumbled to get the money out of the front pocket of her jeans.

He removed the cigar. "Well aren't you a pretty thang," he said in an accent Anna Mae could not identify. She handed him the twenty-dollar bill. He flashed an ivory grin, displaying one gold tooth, then took the money, sliding it up his sleeve in one smooth motion.

"Now, you gorgeous thang," he said. "You just walk with me a spell. I have something good for you. Very good."

Anna Mae wanted to run. *This guy is a freak!* With great effort she kept herself under control and walked beside him. After they had gone a short distance he reached for her hand. Her first instinct was to pull it away. But she quickly realized he was trying to slip her a small plastic package. She took it, holding it tightly in her sweaty fist. "Can I go now?"

"Of course you can, Darlin.' But you come back. I have some very good stuff."

Anna Mae turned abruptly and hurried away. When she reached the second intersection, she shoved the package into her hip pocket. Afraid someone had seen what she'd done, she walked faster. The loiterers, passersby and people in the cars that crawled along the city street all seemed indifferent. Nevertheless, she was convinced that someone would notice the suspicious bulge. She tugged at her gray sweatshirt, stretching it over her hip pocket. As she walked up the quieter, residential Vickroy Street Hill, she kept looking over her shoulder.

I'm just as bad as Stanley. Stanley! He forced me to do this! He doesn't care if I get caught.

During the short walk from the hilltop to her front steps, she felt the anxiety, the fear, as it twisted around in her chest. Then something inside her snapped, and the fear switched to fury. She charged into the house yelling, "Where is he? Where's Stanley?"

Sarah stood in the middle of the hall, holding the soiled tablecloth. "Who did this?"

"Stanley! Who else?" Anna Mae snapped. "Where is he?"

"Why aren't the dishes done? Where'd you run off to?"

"Where's Stanley?"

Sarah's cheeks turned red.

"I asked you where Stanley went!"

When Sarah didn't answer, Anna Mae pushed by her astonished aunt and charged up to the second floor.

"Stanley!" she yelled into the attic.

"Bring it up," he yelled back.

Slowly, deliberately, she climbed the steps to Stanley's attic room. She glanced at David's bed in the far corner and was relieved he wasn't there. Stanley, still in his bare feet, was sitting on an oversized pillow, his eyes never wavering from the small black and white TV screen. He held out his hand. "Give 'em here."

She slapped the package into his hand, turned away, and headed back toward the steps.

"What'd ya think of him?"

"That creep?"

"That cool dude from New York," he said to her back.

When she didn't answer, he jumped up, grabbed her by the arm, and spun her around. Holding the package of pills in her face, he asked, "Want one?"

"Let go!"

He twisted her arm behind her back, crushing her small breasts against his chest. She shoved at him with her free hand. With the pills still in his hand, he held her in a vise. Her struggle was ineffective until he laughed. Then suddenly, and with vicious determination, she brought up her knee. He released her quickly enough to jump aside. "You little bitch!"

With the swiftness of an attacking leopard, she lunged at him. He hurled her across the room. She slammed into the attic wall. The last thing she remembered was seeing the hardwood floor fly up at her.

CHAPTER TWENTY

Monday was Father John's day off. He stopped at the church to get some altar flowers for Mrs. Siminoski who was still in the hospital. As he walked into the sanctuary, he was dismayed to discover that the janitor had forgotten to turn on the lights. Even when it's sunny outside, the church tends to be a bit dark. And today was overcast. He had his hand on the light switch when he noticed someone sitting a few pews back from the candles. Not wanting to disturb the person, he abandoned the light switch.

On his way to get the vase of flowers at the far end of the altar, he recognized the person in the pew. It was Anna Mae McBride, the teenager who attended services almost every Sunday, along with the little tyke he knew to be her cousin. Occasionally, he would see her sitting alone in church during these odd hours. That concerned him.

Sixteen years before, Walter and Sarah Lipinski had sought his advice about whether or not they should keep Sarah's sister's baby. They had left his office, still unsure of what they were going to do. Through parish gossip, he heard that they had kept the baby.

He also heard that things were not good in the Lipinski household. But Sarah and Walter never came to church, and it was not his place to interfere.

Leaving the vase of flowers on the altar, he walked to where Anna Mae sat huddled in the pew. It was warm in the church and though she was wearing a sweatshirt, she seemed to be shivering. When he sat down beside her, she turned her head away.

"What's the trouble, young lady?" he asked.

She didn't respond.

"Anna Mae?"

She turned to face him, the shine of unshed tears in her eyes.

He touched her shoulder. "What's wrong, Anna Mae?"

She covered her face with her hands. He gently pulled them away. "What makes you so sad? Tell me."

She turned to him with a haunted look in her eyes.

"You can talk to me," he said. "I've been praying for you."

"Why?"

"I often see you sitting here alone. It's been worrying me."

Anna Mae studied him for a moment. "You've been praying for me?"

He nodded.

She turned her face back toward the candles. He waited patiently, hoping she would talk to him. But she just sat there staring straight ahead.

"Anna Mae," he spoke very softly, "I want to help you."

Tears began to run down her cheeks. He watched them drip off her chin; little diamonds in the candlelight. She reached into her sweatshirt pocket and took out a small embroidered handkerchief. She wiped her eyes roughly, as though they had betrayed her. He noticed the bruise on her left cheek and the scratches on her hand. "Did someone hurt you?"

She shrugged and blew her nose.

"What happened, Anna Mae?"

"I wish I knew," she said.

"You don't know what happened?"

"No. I don't know," she snapped. "I never know."

He was startled by the harshness in her voice and confused by her words. He studied her profile in the candlelight. How pretty she was. Then from those fragile features, he heard a voice filled with anguish: "All kinds of things happen. I do things. And I don't know that I did them. I don't remember."

"I don't understand."

"I know you don't. No one would understand. No one!"

"I'd like to try."

"You want to know? You really want to know?"

"Yes, I really want to know."

She wrapped her handkerchief around her hand, then unwrapped it.

Father John gently touched her face. "What happened to your cheek, Anna Mae? And those scratches on your hands? Who did that?"

"That's what I'm trying to tell you, Father John. I don't know. I don't know where they came from. I don't remember where I was before I was here. The last thing I remember is giving something to Stanley. I remember him asking me if I wanted some of what I gave him."

At another time, in different circumstances, Father John would have laughed at such an explanation. But this was serious. Anna Mae was serious. He repeated her words as statements rather than questions. "You don't remember where you were before you came here. You do remember giving something to Stanley. Do you remember what it was that you gave to Stanley?"

Anna Mae became defensive. "Yes, I know what I gave to Stanley."

"You don't have to be afraid, Anna Mae. Anything you tell me is totally confidential—just between you and me, and of course, God."

"God already knows!" she said, with a hint of a smile.

"You told Him?" He caught the humor.

"Not everything. But mostly everything."

He reached out and took her hand. "Anna Mae McBride, I like you. I truly want to be a good friend to you. And it so happens that I have all afternoon free."

Two hours later, after Anna Mae left the church, Father John pushed aside the pile of papers on his desk and plunked down the thick yellow phone book. Opening the top button of his black shirt he removed his white collar and tossed it carelessly onto the papers. He flipped through the phone book until he reached 'psychiatrists.' It took him a few moments to find Dr. Mikhail Rhukov's number and write it down.

This should never have happened. He looked at the chair where Walter Lipinski sat sixteen years ago. Walter didn't want to keep that baby and Sarah seemed afraid to speak up. Why hadn't he called to check? Why didn't he take the time to find a better solution? He thought back to his first year as priest in the Warrenvale parish. He had been young and inexperienced. It was a hard year; so much to learn, so many people to meet, so much to do.

The poor girl. He could still see the torment in her deep blue eyes. And all this time, she had told no one. *To carry such a terrible secret!*

He reached for the phone and dialed. The line was busy.

He tried desperately to force feelings of guilt out of his mind. He owed Anna Mae something. He owed her a lot. He dialed again. Busy.

Father, forgive me. If only I had realized. What can I do, Father? What can I do to help her?

He dialed again. "Hello? . . . May I speak to Mikhail...ah, I mean Dr. Rhukov...Hello Mikhail? It's John Falkowski..."

* * *

When Anna Mae walked out of the parish house, the air was thick with the rotten-egg stench of burning sulfur. She walked up the busy street, oblivious to the city noises that surrounded her. Father John had asked permission to call someone he knew: a psychiatrist. Father John said she wasn't crazy. That there was a condition, a mental condition...Dis-so-ci...Dissociative Amnesia. That's what he called it. He said 'Traumatic Amnesia' too. That was easier to pronounce.

She stopped in the midst of the pigeons that owned Vinko's sidewalk and peeked in the store window at the clock on the rear wall. It was only four thirty. She glanced up at the black smoke curling through the sky, wrinkled her nose, and then continued her walk home.

Now Father John and Angelo both knew about the blackouts. She couldn't decide if she felt relief or fear.

When Anna Mae got home, David was sitting on the couch with his knees pulled up, his feet on the cushions and Time Magazine spread across his knees. Anna Mae looked over his shoulder. The article on Surveyor Seven had to be too difficult for a boy in third grade. But David was smart and he traced the words across the page with his finger.

"How can you read with that television blasting?" she asked.

David looked up at her. "Dad wants to hear the five o'clock news."

She went to the kitchen where the air was thick with the aroma of Golumki, a stuffed cabbage dish Walter's mother had brought from the old country. Sarah stood in front of the stove mashing a pot of potatoes, perspiration running down her neck. Walter stood behind her impatiently, looking over her shoulder. Golumki was his favorite meal. Sarah set the masher on the stove and turned to her husband. "Tell David and Stanley that supper's almost ready."

When Walter left the kitchen, Anna Mae was afraid Sarah would scold her for her flippant behavior earlier that day. But, she didn't, and Anna Mae was relieved. It was dangerous to bring up their differences in front of Walter. The consequences were always a disaster.

Sarah scooped the now fluffy potatoes into a serving dish then removed a huge, steaming casserole from the oven. A few moments later, Sarah and Anna Mae carried platters of food into the dining room as Walter stomped up the second floor steps, yelling for Stanley.

"Turn that TV off," Sarah said to David.

"Wait!" he replied. "Come look at this."

Sarah and Anna Mae went into the living room to see what David found so interesting. From inside the Pittsburgh courthouse, a newscaster was concluding a report—something about New York. Sarah shrugged and went back to the kitchen. As David clicked off the TV, Anna Mae asked, "What was that about?"

"Bad drugs. Is dinner ready? I'm starved!"

The Golumki would stay hot, but the potatoes were beginning to cool. Sarah, Anna Mae, and David sat at the dining room table waiting for Walter and Stanley. Finally Sarah called out to her husband. He didn't reply. Then one set of footsteps came down from the attic. David looked at Anna Mae who looked at Sarah. Moments later the three of them turned to see Walter approaching them from the living room, his feet dragging, his face ghost white. He stood at the end of the table, his eyes staring blankly beyond them.

"He's dead," said Walter. "Stanley's dead."

CHAPTER TWENTY-ONE

Walter stood at the end of the table, his brutal announcement hanging in the air. Neither Sarah, nor David, nor Anna Mae moved or said a word. Maybe they didn't hear him right. Maybe Walter's sick sense of humor—it had to be a mistake.

It was not a mistake.

Sarah called Olga who called the police. Twenty minutes later, two uniformed officers arrived. The entire family followed them up to the third floor. David stopped at the top of the attic steps. Anna Mae and Sarah walked across the room to Stanley's bed. Holding each other tightly, they looked down at the body. Sarah gasped and covered her eyes. Anna Mae was transfixed. Stanley was lying across his urine soaked bed, eyes closed, mouth open, stiff, cold and white as ivory.

One of the officers said, "Looks like he's been dead for hours."

The other officer pulled Anna Mae and Sarah away from the body, saying, "I have to call the coroner."

Walter and David were the first to go downstairs. Sarah followed. Anna Mae, her knees weak, her legs unsteady, made her way down the two flights of steps to the first floor, all while holding onto the railing as though her life depended on it.

A half an hour later, Anna Mae sat on the living room couch with David huddling as close to her as he could get. Together they watched the coroner's technicians carry the black body bag down the steps, through the foyer, and out the door.

Two detectives took Sarah and Walter into the kitchen to ask questions. When they left, Sarah came to the living room. Still in shock, she calmly, as though nothing at all had happened, told Anna Mae and David to go to bed. Anna Mae wanted to do something to help Sarah, but she could hardly handle the tragedy herself.

Once upstairs, David would not go near the attic door. Anna Mae placed a thick quilt on her bedroom floor near the window where David curled up under his GI Joe blanket. Long after midnight, Anna Mae, still awake, lay on top of the covers. She stared at the ceiling, overwhelmed by the disturbing pictures that passed through her mind; red and blue strobe lights, bright badges on blue uniforms, the lifeless figure on Stanley's bed, the black body bag. Her stomach knotted into a hard pain as she wrestled with the crushing fear that the pills she had bought for Stanley caused his death.

Hours passed. Outside her window, the dark sky merged into morning's grayish yellow. She crawled under the covers and curled into a tight little ball. In her despair, she reached for her saving fantasy, the person she had convinced herself must be one step down from the angels. *Mother! Please help me. I'm scared. I don't know what to do. If I only knew where you were, I could go to you. You would know what to do.*

Tuesday morning, Anna Mae went downstairs into an uneasy silence. Walter had not gone to work. He sat at the kitchen table, staring at an empty coffee cup. David was in the living room leafing through an aviation magazine. He wasn't reading, just turning the pages. Sarah had gone next door. The police had said that today the coroner would do an autopsy to determine what caused Stanley's death. There should be an answer soon. Anna Mae went back upstairs to her room and waited.

At five o'clock, she heard loud knocking on the back door and went down to see who it was. As she entered the kitchen, Olga was handing Sarah a tuna casserole and hot, homemade bread. Anna Mae took the food from Sarah and put it on the stove. She then went to the living room where Walter was sleeping in his chair. A half-empty pint of Jim Beam sat on the end table. She turned on the TV and sat on the couch to watch the news.

"A tragedy hit a Warrenvale family last night when..."

Sarah flew into the room and turned up the volume.

With a pain in the pit of her stomach, Anna Mae watched the story unfold. She could not recall seeing the media trucks last night. But on the TV, in chilling black and white detail, police held back the crowd of curious neighbors while the coroner and two police officers lifted the long black body bag into the white coroner's wagon. Anna Mae felt the blood drain from her face. *God! Stanley's in that bag!*

"Walter, wake up," Sarah said shaking his shoulder. "Look, Walter, that's our house."

Walter opened his eyes, pushed her hand away, then went back to sleep. Anna Mae left the room. Was no one ever going to talk about it?

It was Wednesday, late afternoon, the second day after Stanley had been found dead. Anna Mae stood in the second floor hallway. She had just washed her hair and had a towel wrapped around her head. She was pushing a few wet tangles off her forehead when David emerged from her bedroom where he had slept on the floor the past two nights. Anna Mae had convinced David to back out of his "commitment" to play first base for a neighborhood team. However, he was still wearing his gray baseball shirt. They exchanged glances when they heard unfamiliar voices downstairs. Together they went to the landing to see who was there.

At the bottom of the steps, three men crowded into the hall. They were introducing themselves to Walter and Sarah. At the front of the group, Sergeant Edward Smith, slender and slightly under six feet, displayed his rank with a gold badge on the breast pocket of a white dress shirt. When Walter shook his hand, a heavy frown wrinkled the sergeant's young face.

Behind the sergeant and to the left, Officer Joe Murphy made a daunting appearance with his massive shoulders, intimidating blue uniform and glasses that had grown darker in the house. Anna Mae thought she remembered him from Monday night.

Behind the officers, Coroner Samuel Lessor stood with his back pressed against the front door and towered over his companions. He had thick brown hair, a basset hound face, and a piece of striped necktie hanging out of his jacket pocket.

When the three officials moved toward the living room, Anna Mae and David inched their way down the steps. It was then that Walter noticed them. He motioned them to leave, then followed the officials into the living room.

David, his face as gray as his shirt, huddled stubbornly behind Anna Mae. Earlier that day, he had told Anna Mae that death was something that happened to other people, old people, or bad guys on TV, even cartoon characters. Now he sat directly behind Anna Mae, pressing his face against the banister spindles, looking into the living room at the men investigating his half-brother's death.

"Sorry this has taken so long," said Sergeant Smith, "but we were waiting for the toxicology report."

While the coroner looked for a place to stand, where his height didn't block anyone's view, Officer Murphy politely removed his hat, saying, "So sorry for your loss."

Anna Mae and David scooted down a few more steps so they could see better. Walter, who had seated himself in his favorite chair, unsnapped a can of beer and took a long gulp. Sarah glanced at him sharply, then invited the officials to sit down.

Sergeant Smith sat on the couch. The coroner sat in an armchair across from the sergeant. Officer Murphy leaned against the dining room archway with his arms folded across his chest.

"Can I get you some coffee or something cold to drink?" Sarah asked.

Murphy was about to accept but was cut short by Coroner Lessor who said, "No thank you," and went straight to the point. "According to the blood tests, your son, Stanley, must have ingested the newest street drug, a homemade amphetamine three times stronger than the ones produced by pharmaceutical companies."

Officer Murphy placed his hands on his hips and in a voice that rumbled up from his gut, interrupted the coroner. "The street boys call' em 'fliers.' Your kid popped at least six. That's enough speed to kill an elephant!"

Anna Mae was hardly able to breathe as a hurricane of guilt whirled through her head. David leaned closer to Anna Mae and said in the thin high voice of a boy half his age, "Where do you think Stanley got those pills?"

Anna Mae stiffened. Did David know? No. He couldn't know. Nobody knew. It was just a question like all the other questions that he had been asking since the day he started talking. But her guilt was unrelenting.

In the living room, questions and conversation circled the gamut of Stanley's life. It soon became clear that

Sarah and Walter knew too little about their teenage son's friends and activities to be of much help. After a few more words of condolence, Sergeant Smith indicated the interview had ended by standing up and saying, "We'll catch whoever is selling the things. You can be certain of that!" Looking at his watch, he added, "I have to get back to the station. And Murphy here is already late for his afternoon shift."

The officers put on their hats as the coroner led the way to the front door. Walter usually became irritated if a person displayed authority, so Anna Mae was relieved when Walter respectfully shook Samuel Lessor's hand. She was also grateful that Walter did not make matters worse by asking stupid questions or worse yet, becoming belligerent.

When the small group entered the foyer, Officer Murphy looked up at Anna Mae and David. "Can we have a word with the kids?"

Walter moved to the base of the staircase and said, "They don't know nothing.'"

Sarah quickly added, "Anna Mae is a good girl. If she knew anything, she would have told us."

"Is that right?" Officer Murphy lowered his dark glasses and looked intently at Anna Mae. "Sometimes even good girls know things, but they don't say anything unless someone asks."

She stopped breathing—afraid she was going to faint.

"She don't know nothing,'" Walter repeated, his voice beginning to rise.

Sergeant Smith put a firm hand on Officer Murphy's shoulder. "Look, Murph," he said, "We don't need to upset the family any more than they already are."

"I was just tryin' to..."

"I know, I know," said the sergeant pulling Murphy away from the steps and turning him toward the door.

"If you feel, sometime in the future, that you should talk to these kids, you can come back. But check with me first."

When the door closed behind them, Anna Mae exhaled. This was only the beginning.

CHAPTER TWENTY-TWO

That night Anna Mae asked Walter to bring David's mattress down from the attic. "It's okay for now," Walter said when he placed the mattress by Anna Mae's bedroom window, "but David can't sleep in your room forever."

Anna Mae put clean sheets on the makeshift bed, then covered it with David's treasured GI Joe blanket. When he was comfortably under the covers, she climbed into her own bed. Exhausted, she began drifting off immediately. Suddenly, she was falling—falling into the dreaded nightmare. She tried to fight her way back, to wake up. Hanging on to the fragile edge of consciousness, the images, like ruthless vacuums pulled her back. It was the same deafening pounding, the same blistering flames. When her weakened hands futilely tried to hold back the sleek, black umbrella, it closed in to suffocate her.

Suddenly, she was floating, the warm brown river lapping at her sides. Up on the high riverbank the same people stood, looking down, watching—watching her float down the river. Then there was something new. A blurred human form stepped out of the crowd to the edge of the embankment. The figure began easing its way down the side, half-walking, half-sliding in the mud, all the while looking down at her. She could see its

eyes: reddish beams. Then it reached for her. *Stanley!*
She tried to scream. But there was no sound. Frantically,
she struggled in the water.

Her legs were tangled in the covers. Her constricted
vocal chords uttered a guttural cry. Someone grabbed
her shoulders and started shaking her. They were not the
same hands that had been reaching down from the
riverbank. They were not Stanley's hands. These hands
were trying to help her.

"Annie! Wake up! Are you awake? Annie!"

She bolted upright. With the hall light at his back, she
couldn't see his face. But she knew it was David. Thank
God! She was awake.

Saturated with sweat, her cotton nightgown stuck to
her body and yet she felt cold. It was still dark as death
outside, but when David turned his head, the light from
the hall was enough for her to see his face. It was as
white as the bed-sheet. She touched the hands that were
still on her shoulders and asked, "Did I wake you up?"

Nodding, he sat on the edge of the bed trying to catch
his breath.

"I was having that awful nightmare again," she said
wiping the perspiration from her face with the sheet.

"The same one?" he asked.

She nodded.

He looked at the floor and shook his head.

"Did I scream?"

"No. It wasn't exactly a scream."

"I thought I was screaming."

"I think you were trying to. But you couldn't." The
color was returning to David's face. "Are you okay
now?"

She hid her face in her hands, her tangled blond hair
hanging down as her head moved in a slight nod.

"Are you sure you're okay?"

"I'm sure," she mumbled into her hands then looked up. "Good grief, Davie! I must have scared you half to death."

"Just a little," he shrugged.

"Well," she said, "we better try to go back to sleep."

"I hope you don't have any more nightmares," David said crossing the room and dropping onto his mattress.

"I won't," she assured him. And she wouldn't. Because she would not allow herself to go back to sleep.

Anna Mae lay with her face to the wall, the trauma of the nightmare behind her. She needed to do some serious thinking. Maybe she should run away. Then she would never have to face up to her part in Stanley's death. Maybe if she had a fresh start, away from Walter, she wouldn't disappear into all those lost hours. She thought about Kennywood and Angelo kissing her. She pulled the blanket to her chin and curled into a tight warm ball savoring the memory.

The school picnic…that was only three days ago, three days since Stanley showed up with his motorcycle friends and tried to ruin everything. Two days since Stanley blackmailed her for twenty dollars by threatening to tell Walter about her and Angelo. Just two days. That's all.

She moved to the edge of the bed where her bare feet touched the cold floor. She could hear David's soft breathing and was glad he had been able to go back to sleep. Poor little kid! David had pulled his GI Joe blanket up and over his head so only a few blond curls were visible against the white pillow. *He isn't a baby anymore,* she thought. *But should I leave him? Will he be okay?*

She stood up, wandered across the room, and into the hall where she could hear Walter's muffled snoring. She would have to think things through; try to make some sense out of all the craziness. Glancing back into her room where a luminous clock sat on her dresser, she was surprised to see that it was after five—almost morning. When she looked away, her eyes settled on the attic door. It was shut tight. Locked. She shuddered.

Troubled thoughts went through her mind and she mentally talked to God. *You know, God, never in a million years would I have bought those drugs for Stanley. I was afraid—afraid that he would get us all into trouble. I couldn't let him do that.*

She moved to the top of the stairway and looked down into the dark foyer. *God, don't let those policemen come back. They'll put me in jail if they find out that I was the one who bought those pills.*

She went down the carpeted stairway. Her bare feet didn't make a sound, but her mind would not be quiet. Sarah went to see Mrs. Siminoski in the hospital. *That was good, God, wasn't it?* She shouldn't get beat up for doing that.

She stopped at the landing near the bottom of the steps, wiped her sweaty hands on her nightgown, and sat down with her back against the wall. *If I left, where would I go? I can't live like this anymore. I can't.*

She leaned sideways against the steps, rested her head on the soft carpet, and drifted into a kaleidoscope of sights, sounds, and voices: *Got any money? Look for the blue Cadillac. Traffic. A bright green turtleneck. Gold chains. Well, well, aren't you a pretty thang.* A dark hand reaching for her own. Drugs in her hip pocket...

She lifted her head from the step and listened. *Is that water running? What's that smell? Toast.*

Anna Mae slid on her rear to the edge of the landing. Someone was moving around in the kitchen. Was that Sarah packing Walter's lunch? No. Walter didn't have to go back to work until after Stanley's funeral. Walter and

Davie were still sleeping, so it had to be Sarah in the kitchen. This might be the opportunity she'd been waiting for. With Walter in a volatile mood, Sarah wouldn't dare tell him if Anna Mae were to bring up the forbidden subject: Becky McBride—her mother. And, if she could convince Sarah to tell her where her mother lived, she would have somewhere to go. That is, if her mother would have her. It was worth a try.

Anna Mae walked into the kitchen. The back door was open, sending the fragrance of lilacs to mingle with the smell of browning toast. Sarah was at the sink rinsing out the coffeepot.

"Good morning," said Sarah. "Why were you sleeping on the landing? I stepped right over you and you didn't move a muscle."

"I didn't mean to fall asleep," said Anna Mae, then quickly realized how dumb that sounded. She hadn't explained what she was doing on the landing in the first place. While Sarah prepared a fresh pot of coffee, Anna Mae told her about the nightmare and that she had no idea why she had come downstairs. However, she certainly had not intended to fall asleep.

By the time Anna Mae finished her explanation, the coffee was perking on the back burner and she and Sarah were sitting across from each other at the kitchen table with hot buttered toast and a jar of grape jelly between them. Sarah was wearing the housecoat with the ripped sleeve. She had sewn it a dozen times, but it was pulling apart again.

Anna Mae nodded at the sleeve. "Why don't you throw that old thing out?"

Sarah shrugged. "It's comfortable."

"It's falling apart! Don't you think you deserve something new once in a while?"

Sarah didn't respond. The rich aroma of coffee permeated the air. Anna Mae curled her bare toes on the cold linoleum, trying to tuck them into the hem of her nightgown. "Aunt Sarah, can I talk to you about something serious?"

Sarah walked to the cupboard, took out two coffee mugs, and set them on the counter. "Why sure," she said with a smile. "But first, would you like to have a cup of coffee? You're sixteen now. Not too young anymore."

Anna Mae was surprised to find her aunt in such good humor. Maybe it was an involuntary reaction to her stepson's death. Stanley had brought Aunt Sarah nothing but grief.

"Well?" Sarah asked while holding the coffeepot over the mugs. "Can I pour you some?" Anna Mae nodded. Sarah put both steaming cups on the table along with milk and sugar that Anna Mae used but Sarah did not.

Sarah watched as Anna Mae took her first uncertain sip, lowered the cup, and licked her lips. "It's good!" Anna Mae lied. She hated it. However, if drinking coffee made her older in Sarah's eyes, she would drink the whole darn pot.

"So what is it you want to talk about?" asked Sarah.

"Promise you won't get mad."

"I promise."

"I think I should be able to…to…" She took a deep breath. "I think I should go and live with my mother." *There! I said it!*

Sarah shifted in her chair but said nothing.

"Like you said," Anna Mae continued. "I'm not a little girl anymore. And anyway, what's so bad about my mother that nobody wants to tell me? What are you and Uncle Walter afraid of? Why did you have to take care of me? Where did my mother go? Why did she…"

"Why are you bringing this up now?" Sarah snapped. "Don't we have enough going on in this house?"

Anna Mae cut her short. "You promised you wouldn't get mad."

"I'm not mad. I just don't understand why now of all times..."

"Because now things will be different," said Anna Mae. "Walter's going to start drinking more than ever. And he'll resent me more than ever. Not only that, David won't sleep in the attic and neither will I. There won't be enough room with just two bedrooms."

"Wait a minute! What's that got..."

"Don't interrupt me!"

"I will interrupt! I'm not going to listen to anything about your mother now. Don't you think me and your uncle have enough to worry about?"

"Why does the world always have to revolve around you and Uncle Walter? I'm sixteen! I'm old enough to make my own decisions—to have some rights around this house. God knows I've earned them."

"You haven't earned anything." Sarah was beginning to raise her voice. "You're just lucky we took you when your grandmother died. You could have ended up in an orphanage."

"And maybe I would have been better off."

"How dare you," Sarah seethed getting up from her chair and looking down at Anna Mae. "How dare you...you...you ungrateful..."

Anna Mae jumped to her feet and leaned across the table, creating an eye-to-eye challenge. "You're the one who's ungrateful. I've been your slave ever since I was old enough to walk. I practically raised David. You were too busy worrying about Walter to even bother with your own baby."

"Why you...you..." Sarah sputtered.

"I wish you had put me in an orphanage. At least the people there would tell me what they know about my mother. At least I would have help finding her and if she wanted me, I could go stay with her."

Sarah practically fell into her chair. She looked up into Anna Mae's fiery eyes while suppressing a sob.

"What's the matter?" Anna Mae asked in a voice that was challenging rather than consoling.

Sarah pulled a Kleenex out of her pocket and wiped her eyes. "I didn't know you hated me so much."

Anna Mae sat down across from Sarah. She was not going to let herself be manipulated into feeling sorry for her aunt just so the subject of her mother would be forgotten. "I didn't say I hated you. So don't say that I did. I just want to live with my mother. Is that so wrong?"

Sarah's eyes filled with tears. "Your mother is my only sister. Did it ever occur to you that I would like to know where she is too? Your grandmother never told me anything, just that I should keep Becky's baby. And I did. I kept you even though Walter didn't want you."

Sarah's face paled as she realized what she had just said. But Anna Mae put her hand across the table, "I know that Aunt Sarah. Don't feel bad. You're not responsible for what Walter thinks."

The room went suddenly silent "Well, anyway," Sarah finally said, "about my sister—I really don't know where she is. And that's the truth."

CHAPTER TWENTY-THREE

Thursday, 10:45 AM

Anna Mae lay on her bed gazing at the ceiling while David sat on his mattress near the window, his arms wrapped around his legs, his chin resting on his knees. "I heard you arguing with my mom," he said. "Are you okay?"

"Why wouldn't I be okay?"

"I was just asking."

"Don't ask me anything. Leave me alone." Anna Mae pressed a pillow against the pain in her stomach, the pain that had plagued her since the evening of Stanley's overdose. Irritated by David's persistent gaze, she threw the pillow in his direction. It hit the curtains behind David's mattress. Relieved that she didn't break the window, she got up and walked to her dresser. She could see David's image in the mirror and she wanted to yell at him, to tell him to quit staring. Instead, she brushed her hair back, clipped it at the nape of her neck, and went to the closet. She took her blue cardigan off the hanger and put it on.

"Please don't leave," he pleaded. "Don't try to find your mother."

She walked toward the bedroom door. "You don't understand anything. Quit bugging me."

"Are you going somewhere?"

"What does it look like?"

"Where're you going?"

"Somewhere else!"

Anna Mae stood at the entrance of the sanctuary. Father John could have at least put some lights on. *Why did I come to the church anyway? To pray? What's the use? If God is so good, he would not have let Stanley die.*

"Anna Mae?" It was Father John.

"I can't talk now. I have to go."

"You just got here," he said. The priest was now close enough to touch. She knew he just wanted to help, but that made her even angrier. When Father John put his hand on her shoulder, she stiffened. "My goodness, Annie, you're as cold as ice."

She shrugged his hand away.

"I'm sure," Father John persisted, "that you're upset about what happened to your cousin. Would you like to talk about it?"

"I'm not upset about it. It was his own fault he died."

She expected Father John to be shocked. But he wasn't. "Come on Annie," he said putting his arm around her. He led her up the aisle, to the door leading out of the sanctuary. When they entered the hallway, he said, "I think we need to talk about this."

Unable to defy the priest who had been so helpful in the past, she allowed him to guide her down the hall and into his office. But, when he led her to the big, leather armchair, she refused to sit down.

"Annie," he said softly.

"Don't call me Annie!" she snapped. "Only David can call me Annie." As soon as the words were out, she wanted to apologize. However, she knew if she said another word she would burst into tears. She didn't want

194

to cry. She wanted to be strong, to deal with her frustration and guilt without relying on anyone. But, despite her best efforts, she dropped her head onto his chest and began to sob.

"I'm sorry," she said, looking at the spot where her tears darkened his black shirt. She made a clumsy attempt to wipe away the wet spot with the sleeve of her sweater. Then she dropped, limp as a puppet, into the armchair.

He pulled a straight-backed chair as close to her as he could, turned it around, and straddled it. When she looked up at him, his image was blurred. She wiped away the tears and Father John's face came back into focus.

"Now," he said. "You know you can trust me. I want you to tell me what's going on."

Anna Mae took a deep breath, trying to dispel the fear that screamed at her to keep her mouth shut. But she couldn't stop herself and the words gushed out like water from a broken dam.

An hour and a half later, Anna Mae and Father John sat in the Warrenvale police station's interrogation room. On the walls of the windowless room, the faded green paint had begun to peel. The oblong table was covered with scratches and cigarette burns. Sergeant Smith, his back to a one-way mirror, sat at one end, Father John and Anna Mae at the other. Under the table, Anna Mae's fingers were laced so tightly they burned. Father John removed his clerical collar and placed it on the table. They had been sitting in silence for a good three minutes.

The sergeant leaned his chair back, balancing on its rear legs. With his hands on the table, he began tapping his fingers. Finally he lowered the chair's front legs to the floor, stood up, turned around, and pulled down a shade to cover the mirror.

"Okay!" he said. "I'll make you a deal. Everything we say here will be completely confidential. If you're as innocent as you say you are, you won't be charged with anything. Now, tell me what you know."

Anna Mae's heart stopped. Sweat ran down from her armpits. Her voice sounded strange. "I didn't mean to. I mean he made me. He was going to tell Walter."

"Who was going to tell Walter?"

Lowering her head, she answered in a whisper.

"I didn't hear you," said the sergeant.

"Stanley."

The sergeant looked up at the clock above the door. It was 3:16. "It's okay Anna Mae. Just relax. Tell me what happened."

"I don't...ah...it's ah, a long story."

He glanced at the opaque window that was the upper half of the door to the hallway, frowned at the noise coming from the front desk, then looked back at Anna Mae. "I know you're afraid. But you have nothing to worry about. I want you to tell me everything you know."

Nothing to worry about? He doesn't know it was me who gave Stanley those pills. And now I have to tell him. Because if I don't tell him, someone else might die and that will be my fault too.

Sergeant Smith stood up and dragged his chair closer. He stood with his hand on the back of the chair looking down at Anna Mae. He waited.

"Stanley was going to tell Walter what we did at Kennywood. And about Sarah going to the hospital to see Mrs. Siminoski."

He slid his chair closer and sat down. "And what does that have to do with the drugs?"

She looked at Father John who remained as silent as a stone. *Why don't you help me? You know what happened. Don't just sit there saying nothing.* Unclasping her hands, she shifted uncomfortably, certain the perspiration was clear through her sweater. The commotion at the front desk was growing louder. *Maybe they caught that drug man and I won't have to tell Sergeant Smith anything.* She watched the door, hoping it would fly open and someone would come in and tell the sergeant that it was okay, that she could go home.

The sergeant looked at his watch. Anna Mae hadn't said a word for a full minute. The Sergeant stood up. With his hands on the table in front of Anna Mae, he leaned down, his face close to hers, "Look, young lady! If you're just going to waste my time..."

"He has a blue Cadillac!" Her own voice startled her.

"Stanley has a blue Cadillac?"

"No. Stanley told me about the Cadillac when I was looking for the money in the shoe."

"Whose money? What shoe?"

"Mine. I was going to give it to Stanley. But he wanted me to go."

"Go where?"

"To the pool room, to buy the...ah, I would have never gone, but..."

Sergeant Smith took his hands off the table and ran his fingers through his hair. His voice was low but firm. "Why don't you just start at the beginning? Go step by step. Don't leave anything out."

It took almost twenty-five minutes for him to drag a rational and convincing story from Anna Mae. Finally he said, "I need to know what this drug dealer looks like. I need a description."

She took a deep breath. "He's—he was, ah, not too tall. His face was sort of brown. Not really brown. Sort of yellow. Yellowish?"

She looked at Father John. He nodded.

"He had a big Afro. But it wasn't black like black people have. It was sort of, ah…not black…maybe like…it had red in it. Yeah. Red! And Black!" She shook her head. *That didn't make any sense.*

"You're doing fine," he said. "But you have to be more specific."

"Reddish-brown," she said. "That's it. He had a reddish-brown Afro."

The sergeant nodded and stood up. "Was he as tall as me?"

She shook her head.

He held his hand out level to his shoulder. "About that tall?"

"Yes," she said. "He wasn't much taller than me."

A burst of loud voices at the front desk broke Anna Mae's concentration. A man with a gravelly voice was yelling at someone. Anna Mae looked at the moving shadows behind the door-glass. A woman was shouting. The sergeant went to the door, opened it and yelled, "Keep it down!" Then he walked over to Anna Mae and placed his hand on her shoulder. "I'm not unfamiliar with Walter Lipinski's temper, so I understand completely. You're a brave girl, Anna Mae. And you've been a big help."

CHAPTER TWENTY-FOUR

Anna Mae had been at the police station for less than two hours. It seemed like ten. Was it just her imagination? Did the sergeant ask the same questions over and over again? Did he think she was lying?

Father John stood up and shook Sergeant Smith's hand. Smith turned to Anna Mae who was still sitting at the table. "I might need you to come back to pick the man you described out of the lineup."

Stunned, Anna Mae sprung to her feet. "You said no one would know. You promised!"

"I'll protect you," he said. "I keep my promises."

Father John snapped angrily, "She shouldn't have any further involvement. Anna Mae had the courage to come here..."

"And Anna Mae, legally, is an accessory. I cut her a generous deal. No one will know she talked to us and there will be no charges pressed."

Father John's cheeks turned red. He grabbed his collar from the table and shoved it in his pocket.

"I repeat," said the sergeant, his authority emphasized in the tone of his voice, "no one will know what transpired here. Anna Mae's a good kid who got herself sucked into a bad situation. But you have to understand that we have to get this piece of shit off the streets."

Father John grabbed Anna Mae's hand. "Come on! Let's get out of here!"

Anna Mae's knees threatened to buckle as he pulled her toward the door. She had never seen Father John so angry.

"Look, Father," said the sergeant. "This young lady is naive. She didn't realize the danger in what she was doing. I understand why she did it. She had good reason to be afraid of Walter Lipinski. He has a terrible temper and a bad reputation. It's a wonder someone didn't bash his brains in a long time ago. Anna Mae," he said, placing a hand against the door jam to block her path, "I promised you before and I'll promise you again, nothing is going to happen to you."

The reception area was packed with a strange assortment of people. Three busty females lingered around the raised front desk. One, in a red mini skirt had her foot on a chair and was straightening her fishnet stocking. The resulting view shocked Anna Mae and caused Father John to turn away. Another wore a lacy see-through blouse with nothing underneath. On a bench, a disheveled drunk sat next to an older, bearded man whose mismatched clothing was full of holes. Two officers were shoving a young, bald, black man in handcuffs toward a door with a sign, 'Keep Out, Police Personnel Only.'

Anna Mae looked around in amazement at a world she never knew existed. However, there was one person in that lobby that she did know existed. On the platform, seated behind a desk, his aviator glasses down on his nose, Officer Joe Murphy was watching her. She couldn't wait to leave.

Father John pushed the brass levers on the heavy double doors that led out of the station. "Com' on Annie. Let's get out of here."

She didn't move. He turned to see what was keeping her. She looked at Father John, then at Murphy. "Nothing. It's nothing," she mumbled.

Anna Mae gazed out her bedroom window, watching the twilight yield to the setting sun and the orange-yellow radiance of the Bessemer capture the western sky. It was hot and stuffy and she tugged at the old double hung window. For a moment, it seemed hopelessly stuck. Then it flew up with a bang. The rush of warm air quickly engulfed her in the conflicting smells of mill smoke and summer blossoms. She could hear the distant sound of rapid-blast fireworks, most likely set off by anxious youngsters who couldn't wait until next week's Fourth of July celebration.

She recalled last year when she had overheard Stanley and his motorcycle friends talking about how they had gone to Ohio to buy fireworks that were illegal in Pennsylvania. They had set some off in an alley close to a row of condemned houses. One of the houses caught fire, and three homeless men had to be rescued. A fireman had broken an ankle on a rotted stairwell. Two more had been taken to the hospital with smoke inhalation. She could still hear the sidesplitting laughter as Stanley and his friends watched the newscast covering the story.

Anna Mae knew, even then, that Stanley's repulsive behavior was rooted in a childhood as damaged as her own, a childhood of rejection and abuse. But whether it was his own fault, or hers, or the man who sold the lethal pills, Stanley didn't deserve to die so young.

She blamed herself. She was a coward. A stronger person would have refused to buy the pills in the first place. Father John had tried to convince her that Stanley's death was not her fault. That if she hadn't bought those pills, Stanley would have.

She thought about what they did when they left the police station. They had gone back to Father John's office. There he called his psychiatrist friend, Dr. Rhukov, to confirm the appointment he had made for her on Tuesday, July 2nd. She counted on her fingers. *Tomorrow's Friday. We'll have the viewing at the funeral home Saturday and the burial on Sunday. Then on Tuesday, July 2nd, at eleven o'clock—that's five days from now—I'll have to take the trolley to Pittsburgh.* The thought of traveling alone to Pittsburgh made her uneasy.

The warm breeze sent a wave of acrid smoke through the window and she covered her nose until it passed. She realized she no longer heard the distant fireworks and the sun had all but disappeared behind the hill across the river. Flaming orange clouds spanned the horizon and she suddenly felt peaceful. The angels of her childhood were still casting sparkles over the brown river water.

She heard a noise and turned around. "Supper's ready," Sarah said.

Anna Mae walked to the doorway. "I'm sorry. This thing about my mother makes me crazy sometimes. I had no right to take it out on you."

Sarah smiled. "You must be hungry."

"I'm not," said Anna Mae. "I'll get something later."

When Sarah left, Anna Mae went back to the window. She gazed at the distant sparkles. *The sergeant said I was an accessory. Father John said I had courage. He said that courage was being afraid and choosing to act anyway. Am I going to have the courage to go back to the station and pick out that man in a lineup?*

Maybe what I already told the sergeant was enough to help catch that creep. Maybe I'll never have to go back.

"Where did you go?"

"David! I've told you a million times not to sneak up on me."

"I didn't sneak up. I've been here for five hours."

"You have not!"

He walked to the window and she put her arm around him. "I owe you an apology, little guy. I know I've been a grouchy old witch."

Normally he would have pulled away. He was too old for hugs. But he didn't resist when she held him tighter.

"I'm sorry for being such a pest," he said.

"You're not a pest."

"Yes I am."

"No you're not!"

"I'm a pest. And you're a witch!"

She smiled down at him. "I'll buy that!"

CHAPTER TWENTY-FIVE

It was Friday, almost noon. Walter was watching TV in the living room. Anna Mae was at the kitchen table eating a bowl of Cheerios. Sarah had just hung up the kitchen phone, having completed the arrangements for the viewing that evening. Anna Mae was impressed with Sarah's efficiency.

The sound on the television suddenly got louder: "This is a Channel 11 Special News Bulletin. After a tip received by the Warrenvale police, a man from New York was arrested in McKees Rocks today in connection with several overdoses and one death linked to the street drug known as 'Flyers...'"

Sarah hurried into the living room, but Anna Mae went only as far as the hall doorway where she could barely see the screen.

"...Detective Robert Jenkins of Narcotics said that several bags of the drug and about $2,000 in cash were found in Armando Garcia's car, and that he was carrying a twenty-two-caliber handgun when he was apprehended. The suspect is now being held at the Allegheny County Jail."

Feeling as though she was stepping onto the edge of a knife, Anna Mae moved forward so she could see the screen better. There he was, with his hands cuffed behind his back and his gold chains swinging forward as he leaned over and turned his face away from the camera.

Walter stepped in front of the TV and turned it off.

"Why did you do that?" asked Sarah. "Don't you want to know what's going on?"

"I know what's going on!" he shot back. "Now shut up and leave me alone!"

"Walter," she said softly, "What can I do to help you feel better?"

"Nothing!"

When Walter walked toward the foyer, Anna Mae backed into the shadows under the steps and huddled against the wall.

Sarah called out to Walter, "Where are you going?"

Now at the front door, Walter mocked Sarah. "Where are you going? Where are you going? Damnit! Leave me alone!" He stormed out of the house, slamming the door behind him.

Anna Mae's mouth was so dry she couldn't swallow. Now what? Would she be called to pick the drug dealer out of a lineup like the sergeant had said? Or did the police already know enough without her? Tentatively, as though someone was watching her, she stepped out of the shadows. She then hurried upstairs to pull herself together.

An hour later, Anna Mae was busy in the kitchen where sympathetic neighbors were showing up with platters of food. Every time the phone rang, she shivered. Almost twenty-five minutes had passed before the dreaded call finally came. She lunged for the phone. "Hello?"

Sarah stood so close, Anna Mae could feel her breath on her neck. Anna Mae pressed the receiver as tight as she could against her ear in an effort to block the caller's voice. "Yes...Okay...No. That's okay. I'll walk...Bye."

"What was that about?" Sarah asked.

"Nothing. I have to go out. I'll be back later."

Anna Mae headed straight for the front door with Sarah at her heels, demanding to know where she was going.

"None of your business!"

Anna Mae half walked and half ran to Trinity Church. She arrived in time to hear Father John instructing his secretary to cancel all appointments for the rest of the day.

In the passenger seat of Father John's car, Anna Mae sat silently with her hands over her stomach. The pain had returned with a vengeance. They drove the fifteen miles through bumper-to-bumper traffic. It was after four when they arrived at the Pittsburgh Public Safety Building.

Father John led Anna Mae up the steps to the mezzanine where he had been instructed to meet with Detective Jenkins. Most city employees were gone for the day. Anna Mae thought the place looked more like an office building than a place where the police would bring a criminal.

A hefty man in a tight, black suit and striped tie appeared at the end of the hall. He walked toward them at a pace that was powerful, quick and almost military. After introducing himself, Detective Jenkins struggled out of his black jacket and draped it over his arm. He then led Anna Mae and Father John into a small, dark room where Jenkins asked her a few brief questions about her contact with the suspect. He then positioned her directly in front of a window that looked into a brightly-lit closet-like room.

A minute later an odd assortment of characters walked single file into the light and she felt as though her heart had stopped. The men stood well beyond the glass, holding cards with the numbers from one to five.

Anna Mae stumbled backward, her heart hammering so fiercely she could hear it in her ears.

"They can't see you," the detective assured her.

She knew that from crime shows she had seen on TV. However, from where she stood, it didn't seem possible that the men with the numbers couldn't see her. Detective Jenkins nudged her forward.

"That's him! Number three."

"You need to look at all of them. Number one," he said into a box on the wall, "step forward."

Anna Mae looked at the white man with oily black hair hanging to his shoulders. She shook her head.

"You can step back now," said the detective. "Number two."

A black man with a light complexion stepped forward with his head down. "Lift up your head!" Jenkins snapped into the box. The man lifted his head and Anna Mae saw the fear in his dark eyes.

"I said it was three!"

The detective was adamant. "You have to take a good look at all of them."

"I don't have to," she insisted staring at the yellowish-brown face in the middle of the line. "It's number three!" She buried her face in her hands and mumbled, "Get me out of here. Please!"

In the outer hall, Detective Jenkins struggled back into his jacket. As he straightened his tie, he assured her that she would have no further involvement as she was not the only witness. He told her he knew that Sergeant Smith promised not to implicate her. As far as the department was concerned, Anna Mae had rectified any wrong she had done. The only relief she felt was in her stomach. The pain was mercifully gone.

CHAPTER TWENTY-SIX

Stepik Brothers Funeral Home was plush but dignified. Anna Mae and Sarah stood in the archway entrance to Parlor Two. It had been awhile since Anna Mae had dressed up. After a lot of debating, she had finally chosen a sleeveless, navy blue cotton dress with an empire waist and pinpoint white blossoms. She had pulled back her hair with a silver barrette, letting it fall to the middle of her back.

In contrast, Sarah's choice in dress honored the old tradition. She wore a high-necked black dress that clung to the roll of fat around her waist and strained against her little round tummy. When she walked in her two-inch heels, she wobbled.

Anna Mae looked at Sarah, who was gazing across the room at the inexpensive brown casket. "It reminds me of my brother's funeral," Sarah said. "That was twenty years ago. But the lid was closed because of Joe's crushed head."

Anna Mae pushed the vision out of her mind. "What time is it?"

Sarah looked at her watch. "It's 6:45."

"Where's Uncle Walter?"

"At the bar with his brothers. I hope they don't stay too long."

"Or drink too much," added Anna Mae.

With the strong scent of flowers sweetening the air, they walked across the rose colored carpet to look at the floral arrangements. "When my brother died," said Sarah, "the flowers overflowed the room. And I swear that every single man who worked at the mill came to the funeral."

That said, Sarah wobbled off to find the funeral director and Anna Mae began to read the cards that accompanied the arrangements. The most elaborate was a four-foot tall flair of white lilies set in a mass of pincushion and fern. It was from the men at the mill. Beside it sat a small basket of yellow roses from Vinko. Next, mixed blossoms from Olga and Nick Nikovich. Near the foot of the casket, a tall vase held an elaborate spray of white chrysanthemums. Instead of reaching for the card, Anna Mae took a tentative step toward the casket.

She forced herself up the four broad, shallow steps to the landing where cushions had been placed so that people might kneel in comfort. She looked down at Stanley's hands, one placed on top of the other. Four days ago she had tried to put a twenty-dollar bill into those hands. But Stanley wouldn't take it. Later, in the attic, she had placed a small package of pills in those hands. Now his hands were so stiff and pale they didn't look real. She had done that. She killed him.

Struggling to accept the reality before her, she dropped to her knees on the soft cushion and closed her eyes. She remembered what Sergeant Smith had said. *The young lady is naive. She didn't realize. She was afraid—a good kid who got herself sucked into a bad situation.* And Father John: *It wasn't your fault.*

She opened her eyes and studied the cousin who had antagonized her for as far back as she could remember. Stanley's face was chalky, with an unnatural smile. His cheeks were a peculiar pink and his eyelashes dusty with powder. She wondered where the blue suit had come from. She had never seen it before. She hid her face in her hands. She wanted to pray. But she couldn't. Her mind was blank. So she just stayed there, kneeling in front of the casket with her face hidden.

"Annie? Don't cry, Annie."

She looked up. Through a blur of tears, she saw David who was all dressed up in a white shirt and necktie. David, who had recovered from the initial shock of Stanley's death, turned his back to the casket and sat on the kneeling cushion next to her. Pulling at his too tight tie, he said, "He really looks dead, doesn't he?"

Anna Mae retrieved a man sized handkerchief from her pocket and wiped away her tears, while asking, "How would you know what 'dead' looks like?"

"At Vinko's, once I saw a pigeon..."

Three whole days of anxiety and walking on eggshells had taken its toll. Something inside Anna Mae let go. She turned, looked at David, and said with a straight face, "You think Stanley looks like a dead pigeon?"

Unfortunately, despite their somber surroundings and the tragedy in the casket, Anna Mae and David broke into uncontrollable giggles.

Sarah instantly appeared with her hands on hips saying in a seething whisper, "You two are disgusting!" Then word-by-word her voice grew louder. "How. Can. You. Be. So. Disrespectful?" By the time she reached, "Go outside until you can act like decent human beings!" she was shouting.

From the middle of the room, the funeral director cleared his throat. He looked like a department store mannequin with his black suit and silver hair, except for the face that was an oblong portrait of disdain.

"Oh, I am so sorry," Sarah said as she waddled toward him, her tight, black dress inching its way up as the lace on her beige slip stayed put below her knees.

Anna Mae and David, who by then had lost control completely, fled toward the archway exit. As they rounded the bend into the lobby, Anna Mae crashed headlong into Nick Lipinski. David bounced off Walter and fell backward, landing hard against a bucket of green ferns. The bucket toppled, spilling the ferns and half bucket of smelly water across the rose colored carpet.

"Damnit!" Walter snapped. "What the hell..."

CHAPTER TWENTY-SEVEN

Pete Mileski and Spike O'Donnell were standing outside the funeral home, looking out of place in their boots, Levi's, and black tank tops. Each had the habitual cigarette tucked behind his ear and each carried a motorcycle helmet in the crook of his arm. Anna Mae turned to go back inside; however, Spike, smelling of axle grease and sweat, blocked her way. "Lookin' fer your boyfriend?"

"Tamero's down the street," added Pete.

"Forget that creep," said Spike. "Let's go fer a spin on m' bike."

"She can't," said Pete. "She's wearin' a dress."

Spike laughed. "She'll have to take it off."

Pete shoved Spike away from Anna Mae, saying, "Cut the shit! We're here to pay our respects."

As the Road Hogs walked into the funeral home, David pointed to Angelo's white Mazda parked half way down the block. Anna Mae began walking toward the car, but David, spotting a friend from school, headed in the opposite direction.

Moments later, Anna Mae stepped from the curb and climbed into the passenger side of the Mazda. Angelo turned to her, his left arm draped over the steering wheel, his right arm stretched across the top of the seat. He was wearing a tight tee shirt that made his arm muscles eye-catching. His dimpled smile displayed an even row of teeth that appeared all the whiter against his Mediterranean skin. His black hair curled down over his forehead and his dark eyes sparkled at the sight of her. "You look gorgeous!"

Anna Mae had not seen Angelo since the school picnic—before she bought those lethal pills—before Stanley died—before she went to Pittsburgh to pick Armando Garcia out of the lineup. Tenderly, she ran her fingers over the muscled arm that spanned the back of the seat. Her heart quickened. She hadn't felt this happy since they had been together at the park, under the oak tree, when he told her he loved her

"You've been through some real bad stuff," he said. She nodded.

"Why didn't you call me?"

"I wanted to."

"Then why didn't you?"

Some day she would tell him about her part in Stanley's death, but not now. "There was just too much going on," she said. "Besides, what would your mother think? Girls aren't supposed to call boys."

"Under the circumstances it would've been fine. And besides, my mother likes you."

"She doesn't even know me."

"She knows how I feel about you," he said. "Oh, yes. I almost forgot. My parents said to tell you they thought it best not to come to the funeral home on account of Walter. Mom sent some flowers. She said to tell you that you and your Aunt Sarah are in her prayers. She hopes what happened to Stanley won't make things worse for you."

Anna Mae stiffened. "What did you tell her about me?"

"Not much, only that you're a wonderful person and that Walter treats you terrible. That's all." He moved his arm from the back of the seat to pull her closer. She relaxed against him. He ran his fingers through the hair that hung down her back. "Do you know about Mrs. Siminoski?"

"She's in the hospital," said Anna Mae.

"She's out now. But the doctor has her on oxygen and she can't do anything. That idiot son of hers, George, never bothered to come and see her. He's going to Duquesne University. That's in Pittsburgh—only 10 miles from here. It's not like he's across the country. My mother went over to Simmie's to help out. My mother's like that. She helps people all the time. She said Simmie's house was really dirty and that it's hard to look at Dobie because his scars are so bad."

"Tell your mother that when the funeral is over I would like to help her at the Siminoski house."

"You don't have to."

"I know," she said. "But I want to."

"I'm afraid to call you at home," Angelo said. "I don't want to make Walter mad. My dad says Walter hates him. My dad doesn't like Walter either. My dad has something really bad against your uncle. That's for sure. Anyway. Forget about that. You just call the house anytime you want. My parents will understand."

She looked up into his dark eyes. "I'm so grateful to have you in my life."

He cradled the back of her head in his hand, gently pulling her forward, his warm lips touching hers. She leaned into his kiss until the full force of his passion enveloped her entire body. The arm that once rested on the steering wheel wrapped around her as his lips parted.

The thunder of motorcycles shattered the magic and Anna Mae pulled away from Angelo. In front of the car, Spike O'Donnell stopped his Harley, gunned his engine, and stared through the windshield. Pete Mileski maneuvered his cycle around to the driver's side, looked beyond Angelo and grinned at Anna Mae. "They're lookin' fer ya in the funeral home," he yelled. "Should I tell'em yer busy kissin' a dago?"

Spike, whose bike was blocking the car, added in a booming voice, "You better tell 'em, Pete. Stanley can't tell nobody nothin.'"

Anna Mae felt the blood rush to her face. Angelo reached for the door handle. As he began to open it, Pete Mileski, his heavy black boots stabilizing the bike, backed up, leaving room for Angelo to get out of the car.

Anna Mae gasped. "Don't!"

But Angelo jumped out in front of the cycle. For a horrifying second, Anna Mae feared that Pete would run him down. From the front of the car, Spike careened his bike around to Pete's side and shouted over the loud engines. "Let's go!"

Anna Mae jumped out of the passenger side and looked over the top of the car. Angelo was still facing Pete's cycle, his stance an unspoken challenge. She held her breath until finally Pete turned his front wheel toward the street. The bikes reared up and with a synchronized squeal of tires, the Road Hogs shot out into the street and were off.

When the noise and exhaust diminished, Anna Mae called out to Angelo. "I better go inside."

"Wait!"

"I'll call you. I promise," she said and hurried away.

Across the street from the funeral home, the Channel 11 News van pulled to the curb. A young man with red hair, wearing dark slacks, and a white shirt jumped out. He sprinted across the street trying to catch up to Anna Mae. She quickened her step and was through the double glass doors before he could reach her.

As she entered Parlor Two, she was surprised to see so many men from the mill. She wondered how long she had been gone. Spotting Sarah at the foot of the casket, she made her way through the crowd, thanking those who offered their condolences as she went. Finally, she reached Sarah who was standing next to the elaborate spray of white chrysanthemums. Anna Mae reached into the flowers and retrieved the card. It said: *May God be with you in your time of sorrow, Salvador & Marie Tamero & Family.* She slipped the card into her dress pocket. Though it was unlikely Walter would look at the cards, it wasn't worth taking a chance. Any mention of the Tamero family, especially Salvador, would cause Walter to explode.

"Excuse me," said a voice from behind.

She turned to see the man from the media van. She couldn't help but notice that his green eyes went well with his closely cropped red-hair. His shirt was unbuttoned at the collar, his media identification card clipped to his shirt pocket.

"Aren't you Anna Mae McBride?" he asked, "the deceased's cousin?"

He was too young to be anybody significant. But there was something about him that made him seem important. Furthermore, he not only knew her full name, he knew that Stanley was her cousin. Most people, if they didn't know the family well, knew neither.

"I know this probably isn't a good time," he said.

"Who are you?"

"I'm Bob McCarthy from Channel 11 News. "I'm sorry about your cousin. What a terrible tragedy for you and your family. Thank God the police arrested the man who..."

The white haired funeral director was suddenly at Robert McCarthy's side. "Out!" he ordered, pointing a long, stiff finger toward the door. "Right now! Out!"

"I was just..."

"Don't they teach you rookies any common courtesy?" he said, leading the reporter away by the elbow.

"Wait," said Sarah rushing toward them. "Anna Mae? Why don't you go outside and talk to the young man?"

As the funeral director and the reporter disappeared, Anna Mae turned to her Aunt Sarah, saying, "You're kidding."

"No," said Sarah. "I'm not kidding. You look so pretty in your good dress. I bet they have cameras outside. I bet if you talk to him he'll put you on TV."

Anna Mae glared at her. "That's ludicrous!"

As Sarah puzzled over the strange word, Anna Mae looked around the room for David. That's when she saw Officer Murphy. At first she wasn't sure it was him. He wasn't in uniform. But the darkened aviator glasses and the suit jacket that strained against his broad back left no question.

As Sarah continued to babble about going outside to talk to the press, Anna Mae wondered why Officer Murphy was at the funeral home. But on second thought, maybe it wasn't all that strange. Officers involved in this kind of thing probably try to pay their respects if they can. Also, from what she already knew of him, Anna Mae assumed that Office Murphy would relish the limelight waiting outside.

Making a mental note to avoid Murphy, she left Sarah, who had redirected her conversation to a neighbor from down the block. It was then that she saw Walter and his brothers standing at the far end of the room. And Officer Murphy was walking directly toward them. The men shook hands and began what seemed like a friendly conversation. She felt uneasy. Something was wrong. But she dismissed it. After all, today everything was wrong.

She turned away, relieved to see her friends, Debbie and Laura entering the room. She went to join them. This was going to be a long evening.

"I'm sorry," said David. He scooted around on the soggy carpet gathering the scattered ferns as Nick Lipinski up righted the black bucket. Anna Mae, picking pieces of fern off her dress, glanced at Andy Lipinski. His amused grin revealed a row of little yellow teeth beneath his huge gray mustache.

Walter pulled David by the back of his shirt, yanking him to his feet. "Get the fuck off the floor!"

"Easy, easy," Andy cautioned.

"Easy—shit!" Walter snarled, hurling his son across the lobby.

The wall stopped David from falling. Anna Mae looked at Walter. His eyes were glassy. Realizing he was drunk, she took David by the hand, dragged him out the double glass doors and into the warm air of early evening.

CHAPTER TWENTY-EIGHT

At Stepik Brothers Funeral Home, the people who had paid their respects were gone and the press had left an hour ago. Sarah was in the director's office clearing up a few details for tomorrow's burial while Walter paced the lobby. Anna Mae and David were outside.

Up to this point, supportive coworkers and neighbors had enabled Walter to avoid the reality of his son's death. However, the funeral home was now deserted. Walter stopped pacing and glanced into Parlor Two, at the brown casket that sat solemnly at the end of the room. His gaze then shifted to the place beside a cluster of flowers where Officer Murphy had pulled him aside to talk in private. Tight ropes of truth squeezed painfully around his chest and he couldn't catch his breath. He turned and looked out the double glass doors to where Anna Mae and David were sitting on a stone bench. He stared at Anna Mae for a long time. He lit a cigarette, went outside, walked right by the kids without saying a word, and went to his car that was parked at the front of the lot. He needed a drink. The family would have to walk home.

The bar at Mickey's Pub was almost empty. Walter crumpled his necktie into a ball, shoved it into his pocket but didn't bother to sit down. As he tossed down his first double bourbon, a fellow steelworker approached. Walter turned his back to the man. He didn't want to talk to anyone. He didn't want to be near anyone. Twenty minutes later, he finished his fourth and final double shot of bourbon. He wiped his mouth on his sleeve, bought two six packs of Iron City Beer and left.

When he got home he carelessly tossed his jacket in the direction of the banister. It fell on the stairs. He stumbled into the kitchen and put one six pack in the refrigerator. He brought the other to his chair in the living room where he sat in the dark, staring through the sheer curtains at the streetlight outside. His Chesterfields and Zippo lighter lay untouched on the end table.

Moving slowly, like a wounded animal, he finally snapped open a can of beer and took a small sip. He picked up the lighter and studied the etching of the naked lady. Years of use had worn away some the details, yet he could still make her out. He took a cigarette out of the pack and stuck it in his mouth. Then coiling his hands around the flame, he lit the cigarette.

Wisps of white hovered above him like miniature cirrus clouds at dusk. He ran his stubby fingers over the light brown stain on the dark end table. Long before he met Sarah, while he was still living with his first wife, and when Stanley was just a little boy, he had accidentally knocked over a glass of Jim Beam. The alcohol had left its scar. Walter put his empty can on top of the stain, opened another beer and held the cold metal against his forehead.

His gaze wandered around the room before settling on the floor. He frowned then leaned forward tilting his head. There were the sports magazines, all cut into pieces, scattered everywhere. He couldn't remember why he had become so angry with his son for cutting up those magazines.

He lifted his head and looked around the dark room. Stanley's teenage image flashed across his mind, with his long hair and that sorry imitation of a mustache. "He sure is a hellion, that kid," Walter said out loud. "Just like his old man."

A long ash fell from his cigarette. He lifted the fresh can of beer to his mouth and gulped voraciously until the can was empty. In a sudden burst of frustration, he hurled the empty can across the room. It hit the curtains and slid soundlessly to the carpet. He didn't bother to wipe away the beer that was dripping down his chin.

He never meant to call Stanley stupid. He knew that Stanley knew that he didn't really mean he was stupid—or an idiot. His son understood that sometimes fathers had to be hard on their children. Because they loved them. And Walter did love Stanley. As much as Walter could love. Walter wasn't aware of the tears mingled with beer dripping from his chin.

* * *

Sarah was still inside the funeral home. Anna Mae and David weren't surprised that Walter had left. They continued to wait on the bench so Sarah wouldn't have to walk home alone. It was after nine when she finally stepped out into the warm summer night.

As they began their walk home, the air was tainted with the usual odor of burning coke and sporadic whiffs of sulfur. Friday night partygoers were busy keeping the streets alive. Sarah seemed uneasy in the clamor of the small city at night. But David was captivated by the bright multicolored lights and the young people dressed in their trendy clothes. He stumbled along trying to look everywhere at once, not wanting to miss a thing. He asked Sarah if they could stop for a hamburger, but

Sarah didn't want to spend the money and was anxious to get home.

Despite all that had transpired in the past week, Anna Mae still struggled with the fact that Stanley was dead. Her memory of the black body bag as it was carried down from the attic was only a scene from a movie. However, the still figure in the casket, the pasty face, the powdery pink cheeks, the hands folded over a blue suit she had never seen before—that was certainly real. So why did she expect to hear Stanley roaring down the cobblestone streets with his motorcycle pals? Why did she look into the neon lit faces of the young toughs milling around the pool hall? What was that about?

As they neared the bottom of Vickroy Street, David, still grumbling about the hamburger, plodded along with his head down and his hands shoved into his pockets. By the time they reached the top of the hill, a cool breeze had almost blown away the putrid mill odors and Anna Mae threw back her head inhaling the refreshing scent of lilacs. A streetlight exposed the claw-like roots of the trees clinging to the hillside. They looked like giant cat legs. David picked up a few small stones and threw them up into the branches.

"Stop that!" said Sarah who was still trying to catch her breath after the climb.

David dropped the remaining stones. He pointed down the block to the old, blue Chevy parked in front of their house. "Is that Dad's car?"

"It is," said Anna Mae.

"I wonder if Nick and Andy are at the house," said Sarah.

"I don't see the truck," said David.

"How do you know they have a truck?" asked Anna Mae.

"Because I saw it," said David. "Me and my friends climbed up in the back of it. There was all kinds of broken bricks and stuff."

"You had no business in that truck," said Sarah halfheartedly.

Anna Mae wondered what Walter was doing home so early. He didn't have to go back to work until Monday. If he wanted to, he could have stayed at the bar all night. She followed Sarah up the wooden steps to the porch.

The three of them hesitated at the front door. Anna Mae looked at Sarah, and Sarah looked at David.

Anna Mae laughed nervously, then reached for the doorknob. As soon as she opened the door, she saw Walter's jacket on the steps. Anna Mae, Sarah, and David squeezed into the foyer just enough to shut the door behind them. Huddled together, they saw the smoke drifting like ghostly fingers from the living room. They exchanged glances, trying to decide who should go first. Sarah flicked on the hall light.

With Sarah's hand still on the light switch and David standing behind her, Anna Mae stepped forward and looked into the living room. Walter sat there with smoke leaking from his mouth and curling upward past his nose. He turned his head to look at her. His eyes were bloodshot slits between puffy lids and she felt the power behind his glare.

He knows, she thought. *He knows what I did.*

She wanted to run but she couldn't move.

Walter pushed himself up and out of the chair like a savage beast arising from slumber.

CHAPTER TWENTY-NINE

Two and a half weeks later

Anna Mae sat in the upholstered wing chair gazing through the big window at the neighboring building's tarred roof.

"Tell me again," Dr. Rhukov said.

She looked at the doctor. His thick black hair was cut short and sprinkled with gray. He had a high forehead, lively brown eyes set amid deep wrinkles, and a closely cropped gray beard. His soothing voice contained a trace of a Russian accent.

Anna Mae replied in a whisper. "I told you three times already."

The doctor's walnut desk was small and shiny, bare except for a Tiffany lamp on one corner and a tape recorder on the other. Anna Mae caught a whiff of lemon scented furniture polish.

"This will be the last time," the psychiatrist said.

Avoiding his penetrating gaze, she looked to the right where a long bookshelf sagged under thick volumes of medical books, stacks of dog-eared papers, file folders, and an occasional ornate knick-knack. The wall to her left was covered with framed awards and degrees: Psychiatric Medicine, Philosophy, Ethics, Abnormal Psychology and more. The degrees meant nothing to her, but there was something about him; the way he spoke to her with a voice so gentle, the way his friendly, intelligent brown eyes watched her over his rimless bifocals. He radiated an aura of kindness. She trusted him.

"I know this is difficult, Anna Mae," he said. "However, you must not avoid my question. I must be certain you have recalled everything possible."

"But that's all I remember, Doctor."

"So the last thing you remember is Walter getting up from his chair. Then you find yourself sitting on the back porch playing checkers with David. You are surprised to see his arm in a cast. The cast is dirty and covered with drawings and autographs. You realize you had been 'out' for a good while. Is that accurate, Anna Mae?"

She nodded.

"When you came in today, you said you were sorry you missed your appointment last week."

"I am. I'm sorry I missed that appointment. You must be very expensive, doctor. Father John told me not to worry about the money. But it wasn't right for me to not show up."

"You were here last week," he said.

"No, I wasn't."

"You were here. Think about it. If you were not here last week, how did you know to come today?"

"I found your card on my dresser with the appointment on it. Father John must have given it to me. Now that I think of it, why would the appointment be written on your card? Father John would write it on a piece of paper. I never even thought about that."

"You don't remember being here last week," he stated. "However, before we get into that, let me tell you that you are a very strong young lady to continue on with a normal life. My friend, John Falkowski, told me

234

that you make almost straight A's in school, that you go to church and..."

"I was here?"

"Yes."

"In this room?"

"Yes."

"And I talked to you?"

"Yes."

"What did I say?"

"We'll get to that in a moment," he said leaning forward on his elbows. "Are you absolutely sure you don't remember being here?"

"I'm sure!"

"Well then," he said, removing his glasses and rubbing his eyes. "I don't want you to be concerned. We already know that's why John, I mean Father Falkowski, wanted me to see you."

"I call him Father John."

"That's nice," he smiled. Then leaning thoughtfully back in his chair and making a temple with his fingers, he said, "Your Father John and I, we were boys together in Russia. My family was killed at the beginning of The Revolution. If it were not for John and his wonderful parents, I would have never been able to escape to America. Father John is my oldest and dearest friend. Do not worry about money. I do this for him, and for you, Anna Mae."

Anna Mae listened politely, waiting until she was sure he was finished, then asked, "Will you tell me what happened last week?"

"Ah, yes," he said. He put his glasses back on and was quiet for a few seconds. "I don't like to dive into these problems too quickly," he said. "You have already experienced so much pain, both physical and psychological. Your mind has protected you by blocking it out. Facing that is not easy. However, in my experience, it's the only way you can get better. To stop having these so-called blackouts."

"I want to get better, Dr. Rhukov. I'm afraid about what I did or said last week. But I want to know."

"You are not only a strong girl, Anna Mae, you are a brave girl too." He reached into the top desk drawer, pulled out a cassette tape and placed it into the recorder.

"You taped it?"

"With your permission. Are you sure you want to hear it?"

"Well, I guess so. I mean—yes. Yes! I would like to hear it."

"Before we do this," he said, "I want you to know that it might be very upsetting."

"Am I crazy?"

"No," he said with a hint of a smile. "You are not crazy. The mind is a delicate instrument. We have to be careful. If you find yourself becoming too upset, just tell me. We turn it off."

"Okay," she said softly.

He nodded and pushed the start button on the recorder. After a brief identification of time and date, Anna Mae said, on the tape, that it was okay to tape their conversation.

Anna Mae stared at the recorder as a few mundane questions were asked and answered. Suddenly she looked up. "That isn't me!"

Dr. Rhukov pushed the pause button. "It is you, Anna Mae. Most people are surprised at how they sound on a recording. You have to get used to it."

"Oh. Okay," she said.

Again, he pushed start. Her voice sounded detached and unemotional as she gave a detailed account of what happened to Stanley. She then talked about the funeral, giggling when relaying the story about David knocking over the ferns. She talked sweetly about Angelo, indignantly about the Road Hogs and compassionately about Sarah. When she got to the part about walking home after the viewing, her voice became shaky.

On the tape, Dr. Rhukov had assured her it was okay to stop whenever she wanted to. She said she wanted to continue.

She described how she, Sarah, and David were nervous about going into the house, how she was the one who opened the door and that Sarah switched on the light. The recorder went silent. Dr. Rhukov lifted his hand making a gesture that said, wait, there is more...

Walter, ah, he got up from his chair. He was looking at me with this insane, demented . . . I was so scared I couldn't move. He came after me. He called me a murderer and punched me so hard I fell backward and knocked Sarah down. Then he grabbed me by my hair and kept hitting and hitting. I could taste the blood in my mouth. Davie—I was really surprised—he ran to the dining room and came back with a chair. I was on the floor then. He swung the chair at Walter and hit him in the chest. It didn't even faze him. He grabbed the chair from Davie and threw it across the room and it almost hit the window. Then he grabbed Davie and twisted his arm. I heard it crack. God, it was awful. Davie let out this terrible scream. I was still on the floor. I tried to kick Walter's leg. He reached down and grabbed my foot. I bit his hand. He yelled and let go. I tried to roll away from him. He was on me like a wild animal. I thought, 'He's gonna kill me this time.

That's when the police came. They came right into the living room. I found out later that Olga—she's our next door neighbor—she called them. She called the police even though Sarah had told her a million times never to call the police. But she did.

Walter picked up the coffee table. Stuff fell all over the place—ashes and papers and stuff. He hit one of the policemen across the back with the end table. Another one pulled out a gun while two more wrestled Walter to the floor. It was horrible. Seeing a grown man go crazy like that. Crazier than he had ever been. Somehow they got his hands behind his back and put handcuffs on him. They took him to jail. They took me and Davie to the hospital because his arm was broke. Sarah too. She had a bad cut on her forehead. There was blood all over her face. I have no idea how that happened—how she got cut. In the ambulance, I asked her. But she wouldn't stop crying.

Anna Mae listened to the recorded account of her last beating with interest rather than emotion. She just didn't feel anything. Dr. Rhukov's gentle voice continued on the recorder: *And what about you, Anna Mae? How badly were you hurt?*

My lip was cut clean through. See? And see this? I still have these yellow marks on my arms. And you can see my eye. The bruises go away, but it will take a while. And two ribs are broken. They're all taped up...Walter...he's in jail. The next morning, early, before Stanley was buried, Sergeant Smith came to the house. He was so sorry about what happened. He said he was going to find out who told Walter that I gave Stanley those pills. He said Walter wasn't going to get out of jail for a long time. He'd see to that! I told him I was pretty sure it was Officer Murphy who told Walter. I told him about them talking at the funeral home and all. That Murphy cop had no right. Because of him, Walter was home—waiting for me.

There was a long silence. Then Anna Mae could hear herself on the tape crying—crying so hard that now, listening to herself, her eyes filled with tears.

That's good Anna Mae, the doctor said on the tape. *Just cry it out. It's good to cry. Do you want me to turn off the recorder?*

At that point, there was a rustling sound, a sharp click and then nothing.

Dr. Rhukov gave Anna Mae a tissue and she blew her nose. "That's it?" she asked, wiping her eyes.

"That's all that's on tape," he said, removing it from the recorder. He held it up, asking, "Do you want me to destroy it?"

"Oh, no. No!"

Dr. Rhukov put the cassette back in the drawer then placed his hands flat on the desk. He smiled. "I'm glad you said that. It shows me that you are serious about this therapy process. Now—I was watching you very closely while you listened to yourself on that tape. Do you know that?"

"Yes," she said.

"And do you know what I saw?"

"No."

"Nothing. No emotion. No reaction at all."

"But I cried!"

"Not until you heard yourself crying on the tape," he reminded her. "Before that, all the while you listened to that entire horrible episode, your face was as blank as a brick wall. Do you know what that tells me?"

"No."

"Think about it, Anna Mae. Make an effort to come up with some sort of an answer."

"I can't."

"Try."

Anna Mae lowered her head and studied her hands that were one on top of the other in her lap. Dr. Rhukov restated the question: "Why do you think you were not upset when you heard what you said last week?"

Her reply was barely audible. "I don't know."

"Yes. You do know. Now tell me why, when you heard yourself describe that beating…why you showed absolutely no emotion. You should have been horrified. Yes?"

"Yes. I should have. But I was trying to black it out. I didn't want to go back there, so my brain, I mean my feelings—they shut down."

Dr. Rhukov got up and walked around his desk to the back of her chair. He placed his hands firmly on her shoulders. "My very brave young lady," he said gently, "We can fix this."

CHAPTER THIRTY

Anna Mae stepped out into the July sunshine. The streets were bustling: university students with arms full of books, medical personnel with their white coats and green scrubs, and clerical types with nametags pinned to their blouses. Even the air was different than it was in the mill town: traffic exhaust mingled with cooking smells from scores of ethnic cafés and fast food restaurants. She walked to a busy corner. In less than two minutes, the bus stopped at the curb and she climbed aboard.

She took a seat by the window to watch the passing scenes of the big city. The memory of her voice on tape faded quickly. She did, however, think about the doctor. If she had a grandfather, or rather if she knew who her grandfather was, she would want him to be just like Dr. Rhukov. Leaning back and squaring her shoulders, she felt immensely satisfied about having made this trip all by herself. Ironically, she had made it before. However, since she didn't remember, it didn't count.

The ride home went quickly and before Anna Mae realized, she was in Warrenvale. She dropped her coins into the fare box and stepped down to the curb, into the familiar odor of smoke and soot. By the time she reached the top of Vickroy Street, she felt the fatigue of the day. She hadn't told Sarah about Dr. Rhukov. As she opened her front door, she hoped her long absence wouldn't be questioned.

Sarah's shrill voice greeted her. "Is that you, Anna Mae?"

She stopped inside the door. Someone was with Sarah in the living room.

"Anna Mae? Sweetheart?" Sarah's voice was gushing and artificial.

Cautiously, Anna Mae stepped forward. The hall was dim and in a flash of a frightening second, she thought Walter was waiting for her. Then just as quickly the illusion vanished, and Anna Mae continued into the sunlit living room.

Sarah was sitting at one end of the sofa and the Channel 11 News reporter, Bob McCarthy, was at the other. Sarah jumped up indicating that Anna Mae should sit next to the reporter. Anna Mae, still standing, looked at the man with the red hair and green eyes. Because of her two-week blackout, Anna Mae didn't know if she had seen the reporter since the funeral. Hesitantly, she sat down where Sarah had been sitting and asked, "What's going on here?"

"It's been two weeks since I've seen you…" he began.

Anna Mae thought, *well, that answers my first question.*

"…and I hope I'm not overstepping my boundaries, but I thought I would stop by and check on the family."

"We're fine," she said. "Is that all?"

Sarah's cheeks reddened. "Anna Mae! The nice young man just wants to know if we're okay."

Without taking her eyes from McCarthy, Anna Mae said, "The nice young man, Aunt Sarah, wants to put our family problems on the news."

Sarah looked at her in disbelief as Anna Mae wondered how much Sarah had already told the reporter.

Did she reveal the details of Stanley's death? And Walter's incarceration? Did she tell him enough to turn their tragedy into a sensational, two-minute news story? Before Anna Mae had a chance to ask, the front door flew open and banged shut.

"Five! Four! Three! Two! One! BLASTOFF!"

Roaring like rockets, David and Johnny Tamero bounded up the steps to the second floor. Anna Mae smiled. Since Walter had gone to jail, David's interest in aeronautics and the space program had skyrocketed. And his whole demeanor had changed. No longer tip-toeing around the house, David had become a normal, unrestrained and very annoying ten-year-old.

She wished it were as easy for her. Even now, she sometimes found herself listening for Walter's car or looking over her shoulder.

"I assure you," said Bob McCarthy, regaining Anna Mae's attention, "I am not here looking for a story. I just wanted to stop by and..."

Anna Mae shot him a look that stopped him cold. He began rubbing his hands together as though he weren't sure what to do with them. Then suddenly he clasped them together and stood up. "Well, I wanted to make sure you were all doing fine. And I see that you are," he said moving toward the foyer. "So I'll be going now."

Anna Mae didn't move from the sofa, but Sarah trailed after the reporter, fawning as she went, telling him he could drop by any time. When he was gone, she rushed back to the living room. "Anna Mae!" she said with great enthusiasm, "I think he likes you."

Anna Mae stood up and placed her hands on Sarah's shoulders. "I know you mean well," she said with affection, "but don't let that man in our house again."

Frowning, Sarah nodded dutifully. "I just said I think he likes you."

"That's not why he came here," said Anna Mae. "And besides he's too old for me."

The next day Sergeant Smith called Anna Mae at home. He apologized profusely over his inability to keep his promise to protect her. Though he couldn't change what happened in the past, he had done what he could to make up for it by cashing in on a favor. He had managed to get a court order. Walter would not make bail while awaiting trial. The call made Anna Mae feel better. It was nice to know somebody cared.

During the next two months the little family gradually adjusted to a peaceful but curiously empty home. Anna Mae kept all her appointments with Dr. Rhukov. Each session began with the doctor asking her if she wanted to listen to the tape again. No. She wanted to talk about present problems. One day she asked Dr. Rhukov, "Do I have to talk about the past? I know you want me to, but I hate the thought of going there."

"You will talk about it when you are ready," he told her. "Forcing the mind to give up its secrets too soon may cause great damage. So come and visit me each week and we will see how it goes."

On a sweltering afternoon in mid-August, Sarah and Anna Mae sat down at the dining room table to confront the mounting bills laid out before them. Sarah's rainy day savings were not going to last much longer. As she added and re-added the figures, Anna Mae kept wiping perspiration from her face with a kitchen towel. She had asked Angelo to ask his cousin if he needed help at The Pizza Parlor and she was waiting for his call.

"Listen to this!" David rushed into the room yelling. Nudging Sarah aside, he opened a newspaper on top of the bills. With his thick brown curls wet with sweat and hanging in his face, he all but crawled onto the table, leaning over the newspaper, and tracing the small print with his finger. "The interior of the moon has been found to be so lumpy that the resulting ir-reg-u-larity in the moon's gra-vi-ta-tional field may seriously com-com-pli-complicate efforts to land the astronauts at their des-ig-na-ted targets."

Sarah's face was a blank. Anna Mae rolled her eyes and looked at the ceiling.

"It says here," David enthusiastically continued, "The five circular seas under-lain by lumps of heavy material lie in the equa-tor-equatorial material region where the manned spacecraft Project Apollo are expected to operate."

Anna Mae put her hands on her hips. "Will you shut up and get that stupid paper off the table! Nobody cares about lumps on the moon."

He looked up at her. Despite the hurt in his eyes, Anna Mae reached for the newspaper, intending to remove it. But Sarah placed her hand firmly on the paper, saying, "It's okay, Davie. You can read it to me."

"You'll be sorry," David said to Anna Mae, "when the astronauts land on the moon and you don't know anything about it."

"I'll only be sorry that you won't be with them," she countered.

"So will I," he shot back.

"Stop it!" ordered Sarah.

His enthusiasm gone, David closed the newspaper, folded it carefully as though it were a precious document, then folded it again and tucked it under his arm. He looked at the papers on the table. "What's all this?"

"Bills!" Anna Mae snapped.

The phone rang and Anna Mae disappeared into the kitchen. Three minutes later, she was back in the dining room. "I got the job. I start tomorrow."

CHAPTER THIRTY-ONE

It was a chilly Saturday in early October. Cumulus clouds the color of wood-smoke drifted across the azure sky. Anna Mae, now a sophomore, and Angelo, a senior, sat together on Tamero's backyard swing. She was wearing a pink nylon jacket, Angelo, a blue Warrenvale High T-shirt. She wondered if he was cold. But she didn't ask him. She was more concerned about the conversation she knew was coming.

"I don't believe it," Angelo said, "You really don't remember the fireworks?"

She gazed at a clump of marigolds near the back fence. She was so tired of having to explain herself. By this time Angelo should know that Walter's attack back in July would have caused her a major blackout. When she didn't respond, Angelo leaned closer and laughed, "How could anyone forget fireworks?"

She put her head down and moved away from him. "That's not funny!"

"Sure it is," he said. And then he groaned. "Oh, I'm so sorry. I forgot. The fireworks—that came right after..."

"And I don't remember anything that happened for weeks!"

He reached out and cupped her chin, turning her face toward him. She saw the regret in his eyes. "I guess it is kinda funny," she said, not wanting him to feel worse.

He pulled her close. "No, Anna Mae, it isn't funny. No one should have to go through what you go through."

She pushed him away. "Your mother's watching."

Together they looked toward the back of his house, to the kitchen window. His mother was busy. She moved back and forth in front of the window. She wasn't looking out.

"She can't see us," he said.

"Well she might. And besides, you still haven't told me what your dad found out. I keep asking Sarah. She won't tell me. All she does is cry."

The swing jiggled as Angelo leaned back. He looked up into the brilliant orange and yellow leaves of the ancient oak that supported the swing. His face grew serious. "My dad said the reason there wasn't a trial was because your uncle's guilt was evident. Walter's lawyer told him it was better to plead guilty and make a deal. You know, like on television. That's when..."

"I know what a 'deal' is," she snapped.

Angelo held his hand up and methodically touched each finger with his thumb, counting the charges: "Two counts simple assault—that's for you and your Aunt Sarah. One count of aggravated assault—that's for David. The charge for Davie is worse. Aggravated assault usually means there was a weapon, but because of Davie being only ten years old...anyway, another charge for resisting arrest and another for assaulting an officer. My dad said Walter got off easy—he only got two to five years."

"Big deal," said Anna Mae.

"If it had gone to trial he probably would have gotten a whole lot more. Aggravated assault and assaulting an officer are bad news. Not only that, the charges could have been stacked."

"Stacked?"

"Yeah," he said, his voice taking on a know-it-all attitude. "In cop talk that means..."

She hit him playfully in the chest. "Don't give me that 'cop talk' crap. Just tell me what it means!"

"Cop talk?"

She stared at him, deadpan.

He quickly changed his attitude and his tone became serious. "As it is, the sentences run parallel. If they were stacked," he explained, "it would be one sentence after another. Walter would be in for a long, long time."

"I wish it had gone to trial," she said. "Two to five? I'll be eighteen—maybe twenty-one. Maybe I won't even be here. I hope I'm not here."

Angelo reached down and grabbed her bare foot. She tilted back in the swing as he removed her sandal and flung it across the yard. "You can't go anywhere without your shoes. Unless we elope. I would elope with you, shoes or no shoes," he said tickling her foot.

"Stop it!" she shrieked.

"Not until you say you'll stay for lunch."

"I'll stay! I'll stay," she giggled trying to kick him away.

He let go of her foot, then solemnly walked across the yard and picked her sandal out of the flowerbed. He brought it back, then dropped to his knees and slipped it onto her bare foot. "Y' know," he said looking up at her, "we're free now."

She reached down and ran her fingers through his thick, black hair. "I wish it were true. I don't think I'll ever be free of Walter."

"What does Dr. Rhukov say?"

She picked up a golden leaf and twirled it in her fingers. "Me and Dr. Rhukov, we go around and around and seem to go nowhere."

"You haven't had any more blackouts," he reminded her.

"That's because Walter's in jail."

"I bet he'll lose his temper and hurt someone in jail," Angelo said, "And then they'll keep him longer. Add on a few more years."

"Not likely," she said. She didn't want to talk about Walter anymore. Life was good now. She wanted to enjoy it.

Angelo's mother opened the back door, filling the brisk autumn air with the aroma of garlic, basil, and yeasty, hot homemade bread. "You kids come inside. Lunch is ready."

"Come on," he said pulling her up. "Let's go eat!"

The next morning, at the crack of dawn, Anna Mae and David went to the early church service. As soon as they came home, David ran upstairs to take off his good clothes. Anna Mae went to the kitchen to check on Sarah.

Slanted rays of morning sun brightened the table where Sarah sat with a half a cup of cold coffee. She held a crumpled handkerchief to her nose, her eyes were red and swollen.

Anna Mae sat down across from her. "Two to five years," she said, reaching across the table to touch Sarah's hand. "That's not such a long time."

"I miss Walter so much already," Sarah said. "He was the only one in the world who really loved me."

Anna Mae shook her head. Her Aunt was lost. Who would she now fawn over? Bend over backwards to please? Who would she wait for at the end of the day, hoping for a wee bit of recognition, a scrap of appreciation, or a crumb of affection? Anna Mae looked at the sleeve of Sarah's faded blue housecoat. It had been sewn together with yellow thread and was now pulling apart again. She wondered if Sarah knew the difference between love and abuse.

"He won't have a job when he gets out," Sarah said walking to the sink and dumping the cold coffee. "And after I pay the December bills, we won't have a dime left for Christmas." She thought for a moment then added, "Olga says she knows some people who are looking for a cleaning lady."

David, who had changed into worn-out jeans and a gray baseball shirt, said from the doorway, "I can get a paper route."

"No you can't!" Anna Mae snapped. "We get too many notes from your teacher as it is. Just do your homework. That's job enough for you."

David looked as though he had been punched in the stomach and Anna Mae was ashamed of herself. When had she changed from cherishing the little kid who was the brightest spot in the Lipinski household, to treating him like a pesky ten-year-old brother?

"I'm sorry," she said. "I know you're trying to help. If you want to get a paper-route, go ahead. I'll help you with your homework."

Paying no attention to Anna Mae's peace offering, David flopped himself onto a chair. "Just because you're almost seventeen, that doesn't give you the right to boss me around."

"I said I was sorry."

David ignored her. "I'm hungry."

"There's cornflakes in the cupboard," said Sarah.

"I'm sick of cornflakes," he said.

"Then eat some toast," said Anna Mae.

"I'm sick of toast."

"I have a good idea," said Anna Mae with feigned cheerfulness. "Why don't we all get dressed up and go out for breakfast?"

David jumped from his chair. "Can we? Huh?"

Sarah poured herself a fresh cup of coffee. "And where do you think we'll get the money?"

Anna Mae sighed and put her head in her hands. "I was only joking."

"Oh," said Sarah, trying to smile.

David, who wasn't smiling said, "Shit!"

Both Sarah and Anna Mae glared at David. Ignoring them, he went to the cupboard. With a look of disgust, he took out the box of cornflakes.

CHAPTER THIRTY-TWO

On the cold, dark, December evening, the future of Warrenvale looked bleak. When production at the mill had been high, the glare of the foundry fires painted the horizon with a yellow-orange glow. Now production was pitifully low, and only a few furnaces lit up the sky. Two smokestacks, however, could still emit enough smoke to taint the air at the top of Vickroy Street hill.

Anna Mae, bundled in her winter coat, sat on the front steps waiting for Angelo to drive her to work at The Pizza Parlor. With her hands shoved deep into her pockets, she thought about the mills. As much as people once hated the dirt and stench, the steel industry was what kept the valley alive. Now it was dying. Angelo's father, like thousands of others, had been laid off.

Anna Mae's family struggled along with the rest of the people in the valley. Sarah worked hard cleaning houses, earning only ten dollars a day. Anna Mae added to that from her pizza parlor job, keeping little for herself. Even Davie contributed a few fists-full of change from his paper route. Without Walter's paycheck, they did what they could to keep a roof over their heads. Many mill workers had lost their homes.

She gazed up into the starless sky. Everything in the world was all wrong.

Headlights climbed up and over the hill and she stood up. Holding the porch railing at the top of the steps, she stretched to see if it was Angelo's old white Mazda. But it was a bigger, darker car. She watched, curious as the car stopped in front of the house and the headlights went out. On the street side, the driver's door opened. It seemed as though someone was struggling to get out. When a male figure finally stood up, she could see his face over the car roof, but she didn't recognize him. She watched him make his way around the car. The man was on crutches. He seemed unsure of himself as he worked his way to the curb.

"JD!"

"In person!" he said smiling up at her from the sidewalk.

She was horrified. His left pant leg was pinned up above the knee. "Oh my God," she said hurrying down the steps. Now she was looking up at him. "What happened?"

"Gooks," he said. "They gave me my ticket home."

The white Mazda pulled up behind JD's car and Angelo got out. He looked back and forth between the two standing on the sidewalk.

"You remember JD," said Anna Mae.

"Yeah. I do—I think," said Angelo. "You were in Vietnam."

"Yeah," said JD shifting on his crutches.

Angelo looked at the pinned up pant leg. "I'm so sorry."

"Hey! It's the breaks. Could be dead, y' know."

"How long have you been back?" Anna Mae asked.

"A few weeks. I heard about Stanley. Tough break. How's your family doing?"

"We're managing," Anna Mae said. "Walter's in jail."

"So I heard." He suppressed a grin. "I'm glad you were out here. I wanted to tell you how sorry I am about Stanley. But I forgot about the steps. I'm not good with steps except for falling down them."

Anna Mae and Angelo exchanged anxious glances but JD just laughed. He hadn't lost his sense of humor. "Have you heard anything from George Siminoski?"

"Nothing," said Angelo. "The guy's a first class bastard!"

"A few times a week," said Anna Mae trying to hide the fact that she was freezing, "I help Angelo's mother at George's parents' home. Irene Siminoski's heart is so bad she can't do anything. And his father—those horrible scars! He just sits in his chair with the lights out watching television."

JD leaned against the car, taking his weight off the crutches. "Didn't he get some restitution from the mill? Something for facial reconstruction?"

"Yeah," said Angelo. "And Dobie put the money toward George's education. Personally, I think Dobie has gone a little crazy. George doesn't give a shit about his family. He never comes home."

"What a shame," said JD. "Some people just don't appreciate anything. They should send George to Vietnam and give him a taste of reality."

Anna Mae pulled her collar up, trying to warm her neck. "I have to go. I work at The Pizza Parlor," she said. "I'm sure Sarah would love to see you. Why don't you stop by tomorrow around two? We'll help you up the steps."

JD looked down at the space where his leg should have been.

"Okay," he said softly.

Angelo put his hand on JD's shoulder. "Hey, buddy. We're here if you need us."

JD nodded, then turned awkwardly on his crutches and maneuvered his way back to his car. Anna Mae watched him struggle. *It's true,* she thought. *Everything in the world is all wrong.*

CHAPTER THIRTY-THREE

July 16, 1969

Walter had been a resident at Pennsylvania's Western Penitentiary for almost eleven months now. Every Wednesday, Sarah went to visit him. On a busy corner in Warrenvale, she would wait for the bus with her head down, avoiding eye contact, convinced that everyone was looking at her—from store windows—from passing cars—as they walked by—looking at her, condemning her, pitying her because her husband was in prison. She was mortified, disgraced.

But she went anyway. She rode the bus into the sordid side of town and walked down a rutted concrete sidewalk into the ancient redbrick building. She passed through the metal detector in a line of people that, at first, made her so uneasy she was afraid to look at them. It had taken her months to accept the weekly insult of guards riffling through the personal items in her purse, and even longer to live with the occasional humiliation of being frisked. Now she was used to the whole process. The ordeal was routine.

It was a sweltering Wednesday in mid-July. Walter and Sarah were fortunate to have found a picnic table shaded by the tall brick watchtower at the corner of the prison yard. Many of the inmates had chosen to visit with their families in the recreation room. It wasn't any cooler inside, but at least it was out of the sun.

"So he didn't come," said Walter, taking a long drag on his cigarette and letting the smoke curl languidly upward.

Sarah shook her head. Walter was no longer the imposing figure that once dominated the Lipinski household. He seemed so much smaller against the backdrop of fellow inmates and uniformed guards. The lines in his face were more prominent and his hair was more gray than black.

Sarah had changed too. For almost a year, she had been in charge of her own life. She had acquired some self-confidence.

"You know that David's wrapped up in the space program," said Sarah. "And today they'll be launching a rocket to the moon. It won't land for days, but this is so important to David he can't pull himself away from the TV long enough to go to the bathroom."

"So he wets his pants," Walter said dryly.

Sarah frowned. She was getting tired of Walter's cutting remarks. Didn't he realize how hard it was for her to visit every week?

"And the bitch wouldn't come either?" Walter snapped. "She's watching that stupid rocket too? I thought she hated all that junk."

"Anna Mae is not a bitch! She's a very sweet young lady."

"So is the very sweet young lady glued to the boob-tube too?" he asked, his voice drenched in sarcasm.

"They're going to the moon, for God's sake." Sarah was beginning to raise her voice. "The whole world is watching!"

Walter glared at her as he wiped the sweat from his forehead. He then lit a second cigarette from the burning stub of the first.

"They still won't let you have your lighter?" she asked.

"How many times are you going to ask me that same stupid question? No lighters, Sarah. No lighters, no matches, no nail files, no knives, no forks, no guns, no shoehorns, no automatic weapons, no nothing. Understand? Don't ask me again!"

Sarah started to say that she was sorry. Walter cut her short. "This place is a shit-hole! You and those kids think it's some kind of picnic in here. I wrote David a letter, ya' know. I fuckin' apologized! And I wrote the bitch—the sweet young lady—a letter too. They can't be bothered to answer, much less visit. I don't care about Anna Mae. But I want to see my son. Do you hear me?!"

Sarah shifted on the bench. It was so hot her dress was sticking to her skin. She wanted to get up and pull it away from her body but she was too self-conscious.

A tall, black inmate with arms as big around as Sarah's thigh stopped by the table and took Walter's cigarette out of his hand without asking. Then he picked up Walter's pack of Chesterfields and took four more. He put three into his pocket. Using the cigarette that was already lit, he fired up the fourth, then handed the original back to Walter.

"This your old lady?" he asked, flashing a row of perfect white teeth.

Walter grunted. "Yes."

"You're lucky! That mother-fuckin' whore-o mine ain't been here fo' months."

Sarah cringed at the language as she watched the inmate swagger off. Then she turned back to Walter. "You just let him take your cigarettes? And you don't say anything?"

A vein pulsated on Walter's temple and his jaw muscles tightened. He said through clenched teeth,

"Shut up, woman! You just get the hell home and you tell David that if he ain't here next week I'll..."

"You'll what, Walter? You'll hit him? Is that what you think you can do? Beat him up again? In here?"

Walter's cigarette had burned down so far he singed his finger while lighting another. "Don't test me," he threatened.

Sarah stood up and pulled her sweaty dress away from her body. Slowly, she sat back down and looked her husband straight in the eyes. "Ya know what? Sooner or later there's going to be a parole hearing. And when there is, they'll want me to be there. And they'll probably ask me if I think you have changed. They'll want to know if I think you're still a threat to the family. They'll ask me, Walter. They'll want my opinion. They might even want David and Anna Mae to come."

Sarah saw the blood drain from her husband's face and for a split second she wondered if she had gone too far. She knew that if Walter became enraged he might just be crazy enough to attack her right there in the prison yard. She looked down at the table, wondering how she could reverse the effects of what she had just said.

"You're right, Sarah."

Sarah looked up.

Walter looked straight into her eyes. "I'm sorry."

She became wary.

"It's just that it's so hard to be here. I want to see my family."

She wondered if he was sincere.

"I want the chance to make things right." He leaned across the picnic table and kissed her on the cheek.

A whistle shrilled and a guard was on them in a flash. "Go near her again and you won't have any visitors for a year!"

266

Now almost everyone in the yard was looking at them. If they looked close enough, they would see that Sarah was smiling.

CHAPTER THIRTY-FOUR

July 20, 1969
Four days later.

Sunday was one of the busiest days at The Pizza Parlor. With all the ovens burning at full blast, the kitchen was as hot as Hades. Fortunately, Anna Mae was working out front in the air-conditioning.

"Two large with double cheese and pepperoni," said the scrawny teenage boy at the counter.

"And what would you like to drink?" Anna Mae asked, her eyes scanning a line of customers that almost reached to the door.

The boy who had just placed the order, looked across the room where the rest of his noisy group had crammed themselves into a booth. "You guys want Pepsi?" he called out.

The reply was in unison. "What?"

"Pepsi!" he shouted.

They all nodded.

Anna Mae slid the order slip through the slot into the kitchen, iced a row of glasses, filled them with Pepsi, and arranged the drinks on a tray. As she carried the tray to the counter, she saw Joey Barns elbowing his way to the front of the line, ignoring the threats of those who thought he was pushing to place an order.

He waved his arm, calling out to Anna Mae, "I have to talk to you!"

"Not now," she mouthed over the clamor of customers.

His face dropped in disappointment as he looked around for a place to sit. Finding none, he leaned against the wall, took a slip of paper out of his pocket, studied it, then put it back.

She looked at the clock. It was 3:42. Her replacement, Jenny, should have arrived twenty minutes ago. At 3:59, Jenny showed up stumbling over a barrage of excuses. Together they waited on the last of the customers.

Exhausted and irritated, Anna Mae rolled her apron into a ball, tossed it in the laundry bin, and walked over to Joey. A booth had emptied so they sat down.

Bursting with excitement, Joey held up the slip of paper. "I got it!"

Anna Mae felt her heart stop. She knew what was on that paper.

He held it up, waving it. "I came as soon as she gave it to me."

The heart that had stopped was now pounding. "You have my mother's phone number!"

Joey nodded so vigorously his hair flopped up and down. He held out the slip of paper. "I wrote it down," he said. "I was real careful. I didn't want to get the numbers wrong. I even asked her to say it again to make sure I didn't make a mistake. That was good, wasn't it?"

"That was very good." She took the paper from his hand, holding it like a rare gem. *My mother. My honest to God real mother. I'm sitting here holding my mother's phone number in my hand. This is it. This is what I've been waiting for all my life.*

Somebody was pushing at her shoulder. She stammered, "What? What?"

"Didn't you hear?" It was Angelo looking down at her. Angelo was working for his uncle's bricklaying company—hot, dirty work. He must have stopped at his house to shower because he smelled of soap and after-shave when he slid beside her into the booth. "It finally happened!"

"I know," Anna Mae said. "I have the number right here."

"What number?"

Before she could answer him, he threw his arms around her and exclaimed in a loud voice, "We did it! We landed on the moon!"

"I don't understand," she said. "What are you talking about?"

"Five minutes ago," he said looking at his watch. "I heard it on the car radio. At exactly 4:17, the United States of America landed on the moon!"

"Hot dog!" Joey exclaimed.

Word spread quickly and the place was in an uproar. Anna Mae was oblivious to the celebration going on around her. "Joey," she said. "I'm not eighteen. You told me my mother might contact me when I was eighteen."

"I told her about Walter being in jail and all. She got real happy. That's when she gave me the number."

Angelo got up and pulled at Anna Mae's arm. "We need to get to a television. They're gonna' get out of the space ship and walk on the moon. We gotta see that!"

She folded the precious piece of paper and put it in her shirt pocket. "Joey? Would it be all right if I called her from your place?"

"Sure."

"Come' on" she said to Angelo. "We're going to Joey's."

"Why?"

"I'll tell you in the car."

In the hot and stuffy apartment, Angelo and Joey sat quietly on the couch. Across the small room, sitting in a straight-back wooden chair, Anna Mae's hands trembled as she dialed the phone on the end table. She could feel Angelo and Joey watching her and suddenly, she wished the apartment were bigger so they didn't have to be in the same room. On the other hand, their nearness gave her courage. She listened to the phone ringing at the other end for what seemed forever. Then all too quickly, a woman's hesitant, high-pitched voice said, "Hello?"

Anna Mae opened her mouth. Nothing came out.

"Hello?" the woman said again.

Anna Mae froze.

"Hello? Is someone there? Is this Anna Mae?"

Surprised to hear her own name and now sure it was her mother on the other end of the line, Anna Mae's first reply was barely audible. Then quickly, and louder, she said, "Yes! This is Anna Mae. Are you Becky?"

In the ensuing silence, Anna Mae could hear the rickety hum of a fan in the background. The sound of it brought an intense realization that this was not an illusion—that her mother was actually somewhere out there and holding the phone to her ear. Anna Mae was trying to think of what to say next when the high pitched voice softened and asked, "Will you call me 'Mother?'"

The request took Anna Mae by surprise and she hesitated. Not wanting to do anything to push Becky away, she said, "Yes. I will." There was another long silence, so Anna Mae added, "I don't call Aunt Sarah 'mother.'"

The muffled sounds on the other end told Anna Mae that her mother was crying and suddenly her own eyes filled with tears. Neither of them said anything for a few seconds, and then her mother said softly, "I'm sorry. I am so, so sorry."

"It's okay…Mother."

"I know I don't deserve to be called Mother. I'm so sorry. I should have called you a long time ago. Does Sarah know you're calling me?"

"No."

"Are you at home?"

"No. I'm at Joey's place."

"Are you going to tell Sarah?"

"I don't know. I just finished work."

"Oh my. You're a big girl now. You have a job!"

Anna Mae couldn't make out the next few mumbled words. It sounded as though she was talking about Anna Mae when she was a baby, but she couldn't make sense of what her mother was saying.

"When can I see you?" Anna Mae asked.

"Oh my," said her mother. "I didn't think about that."

Anna Mae heard the clinking of what sounded like ice cubes in a glass. "Will you think about it?"

"I'll ah—I'll think about it. Oh my. I'm so sorry, Anna Mae. You were such a beautiful baby. I'm so, very, very sorry."

"But it would be okay for me to come to see you sometime, wouldn't it?"

"I said that I'll think—well, maybe we should wait a little."

"Wait?"

"For a while."

Anna Mae was devastated. Had she expected too much? Should she have been satisfied with just a phone call? "Do you live in Pittsburgh?"

"Oh my. I'm so sorry. You call me again, okay? Okay, Anna Mae?"

"I'll call again, Mother. I want to see you. I've waited so long. Mother? Mother?"

Anna Mae held the phone away from her ear and looked at it through a blur of tears. Angelo jumped up, took the phone from her hand and listened to a dial tone.

He placed the receiver in its cradle, then gathered Anna Mae into his arms. Joey went into his small kitchen to get her a cold drink.

Angelo picked up the slip of paper laying on the end table. He then retrieved a phone book from the lower shelf, and began flipping through the pages. "I can tell from this number that she lives in Pittsburgh. If her last name is still McBride, we might be able to get an address."

"And to think she was so close," said Anna Mae. "Why did I think she was somewhere across the country?"

Joey handed her a glass of ice water while offering an explanation. "You thought she was far away because you didn't know where she was."

"Here it is," said Angelo, "She lives on Foster Street, on the South Side. I know where that is."

Anna Mae looked over his shoulder at her mother's name and address. Suddenly the room was spinning. The hot, humid air in the small apartment was suffocating. She took a long drink of cool water then went to the open window to breathe. When her head cleared, she turned around and looked for a television set. There was none.

"Joey," she said, "would you like to come to my house to watch that moon thing?"

Anna Mae, Angelo, and Joey arrived at seven thirty and found David cemented in front of the television. He didn't look up. They went to the kitchen, stacked their paper plates with potato salad, kielbasa, and brownies and went back to the living room. Anna Mae sat on the couch between Joey and Angelo, who were almost as enthralled as David. Leaning forward, they watched the astronauts inside the Eagle, bobbing around in the moon's low gravity. Sarah brought them cans of Pepsi.

She then went back to the kitchen, got herself a plate of food, and joined them.

Anna Mae was looking at the screen but her mind was elsewhere. Sarah asked if something was bothering her. She told her aunt that The Pizza Parlor had been a madhouse, and she was just tired.

"Your Uncle Walter asked about you," Sarah said.

Anna Mae's reply was razor sharp. "Big deal!"

She recalled Joey telling her that Becky had only agreed to talk to her after she learned that Walter was in prison. Anna Mae wondered about that. She could still hear Becky's high-pitched voice. *Will you call me 'Mother? Oh my, you're a big girl now. You have a job!*

Hey!" David leaned over and nudged her. "Do you know what they call that place?"

"The moon," said Angelo, winking at Anna Mae.

David crossed his eyes. "The Sea of Tranquility, dummy!" He turned back to Anna Mae. "Remember the rocks? You said you didn't care about the rocks and now..."

"Don't bother Anna Mae," Sarah snapped. "She's tired."

Anna Mae remembered the precise tone in her mother's voice. *You were such a beautiful baby. I'm so very, very sorry.*

Angelo stood up, took the untouched plate of food from Anna Mae's lap, and placed it on the end table. Then taking her by the hand, he led her into the kitchen where he put his arms around her. "We'll go to see your mother as soon as we can."

She breathed his musky, man scent as she nodded into his chest. He unclipped her hair, letting it fall through his fingers while backing her against the sink. Their bodies melded together and his parted lips found hers. She could feel herself relaxing as Angelo tightened his embrace.

"Yuck!" said David from the doorway.

"Get out of here!" Anna Mae said.

"Mom," David yelled. "They're necking in the kitchen!"

"You mind your own business," said Sarah, pulling him away from the door and out of sight.

Anna Mae gave Angelo a quick kiss on the cheek then pushed him away. "We better go back with the others."

They returned to their seats on the couch where they watched the astronauts struggle into their space suits, hoist on their backpacks and depressurize the Eagle. Then Neil Armstrong, on his hands and knees, backed out of the spacecraft and onto a small platform. David's nose was five inches from the screen.

"Get out of the way!" said Anna Mae.

At 10:56, to the cheers of everyone in the Lipinski living room, Neil Armstrong descended the ladder—the first to put his feet solidly on the surface of the moon. David's jaw hung in awe. Joey's eyes were wide as saucers. Angelo squeezed Anna Mae's hand. Sarah kept eating.

"That's one small step for man; one giant leap for mankind."

Eighteen minutes later, Buzz Aldrin joined Neil Armstrong. Joey laughed like a little kid as the astronauts kangaroo-hopped around on the moon's surface.

"I told you so!" said David hopping around the room. "I told you they were going to walk on the moon and you said I was crazy. Do you think I'm crazy now?"

Anna Mae grabbed David by the shirt, pulling him down so she could kiss him on the cheek. "Just a little bit."

David wiped his cheek. "Yuck!"

CHAPTER THIRTY-FIVE

August 1969

July melted into August. Russia launched the spacecraft Zond 7. It circled the moon and took colored pictures. Thousands of Americans demonstrated against the war in Vietnam. Church attendance was at an all-time low and the steel valley lay in a pit of unemployment.

Anna Mae worked full time at The Pizza Parlor and a few hours a week, helping Angelo's mother care for Irene and Dobie Siminoski. Towards the end of the month, on a hot, humid afternoon, Angelo dropped Anna Mae off at the Siminoski's then went home to help his father with yard work. Anna Mae walked around to the back of the house, pushed open the ragged screen door and walked into the old fashion kitchen with its dented porcelain sink and worn yellow linoleum. Despite her cutoff jeans and tank top, Anna Mae could feel sweat trickle down her back.

Marie Tamero, holding a dust rag and a bottle of Pledge, walked into the kitchen. A single thick black braid hung down Maria's back. Her pretty face was etched with fine lines. But it was her eyes that Anna Mae always noticed first—large, dark, doe-like, and radiating kindness.

Without even saying hello, Maria gasped, "Mother of God! What did you do to your hair?"

Anna Mae ran her fingers through the short, uneven strands. On the right side, a big chunk was missing. "I cut it!"

"Why?"

Avoiding Maria's astonished stare, Anna Mae went to the table and began taking canned vegetables out of a brown grocery bag, then juggling an armful, she walked toward the cupboard, saying, "I guess I went a little nuts. How's Irene today?"

"Not much better. Why did you do that to your hair?"

At the far corner of the kitchen, Anna Mae opened the rusted metal cupboard and began arranging the cans on the bottom shelf.

"Did Angelo take you to Pittsburgh this morning?"

Anna Mae nodded, walked back to the table and picked up a box of rice. A picture of her mother flashed in her mind and the pain was almost physical. She stood motionless, holding the rice, fighting her tears.

"Sit down!" said Maria, more maternal than demanding. "This is the first time you actually saw your mother, isn't it?"

Anna Mae reached into another bag, but Maria put a firm hand on her arm. "Stop with the groceries!"

Anna Mae put the rice back on the table and sat down on a wobbly kitchen chair.

Maria sat beside her. "Tell me what happened."

"What about Irene?" asked Anna Mae.

"She's sleeping. She has her bell. She'll ring if she needs us. Now tell me."

Anna Mae traced a circle through the crumbs on the table. She felt Maria staring at the place where the chunk of hair had been lopped off. Next week she would talk to Dr. Rhukov about why she had done such a stupid thing. Today she had to live with it. She recalled gathering the golden strands from her bedroom floor, putting them into the wastebasket, and Angelo's reaction when she joined him on the porch. Once he had gotten over the shock, he said it looked cute. He was trying to be kind. He was lying.

Maria's voice interrupted her thoughts. "Do you want something cold to drink?"

"We got there about eleven," said Anna Mae, as though she had not heard the offer. "My mother lives in a really bad section of town. Her place is on the first floor. I don't think anyone lives upstairs. The houses are old and rundown. The one next door is condemned."

She could still see the squalor—the old newspapers piled on the couch, the stale smell of beer from the empty cans on the coffee table, the stench of rotting food in the kitchen.

"Was she glad to see you?" asked Maria.

"She was embarrassed about the house," said Anna Mae. "She started to run around picking things up. Angelo told her to sit down."

"He went in with you?"

"I asked him to."

"And?"

"She's only thirty-two. She looks fifty."

"You didn't tell her you were coming?"

"No," said Anna Mae. "Every time I called to ask if I could visit, she just kept putting me off. So I went anyway. She's not married. She has a little girl, Missy, about a year old."

Anna Mae didn't mention her mother's dirty blond hair and grease spotted blouse. She didn't tell Maria that her mother reeked of body odor and alcohol. Maria's brown eyes filled with compassion and Anna Mae knew that Maria knew there was more than what she was telling her.

"The baby was dirty and her diaper needed changed. I offered to do it, but Becky said no."

"You call her Becky?"

"Now I do."

"Why did you cut your hair?"

"When we got back from Pittsburgh I asked Angelo to take me home so I could change before we came over here. I don't know what got into me. I just grabbed the scissors and started cutting. Look at it," she said, pulling at the uneven ends.

Maria stood up and ran her fingers through Anna Mae's hair to check the damage. "It can be fixed. A little styling and it'll be fine."

The bell rang in the upstairs bedroom. Anna Mae said she would go. To get upstairs, she had to walk through the living room. It smelled of furniture polish and pipe tobacco. A single lamp in the corner cast a circle of light, leaving the room in semi-darkness except for the flickering of a twelve-inch black and white television. Dobie Siminoski sat in his easy chair in front of the television with his back to the stairway.

"Young lady," he said without turning around, "what's all the fuss about your hair?"

"I cut it, sir."

"Come over here. I want to see it."

Anna Mae walked across the room and stood by the side of the television. The right side of Mr. Siminoski's face was a mass of scar tissue reaching beyond where his hairline once was. His left ear consisted of a dab of flesh and his left eye, nearly blind, sagged into his cheekbone. When he looked up at Anna Mae, she didn't recoil. She was accustomed to the horrible disfigurement that had turned the former steelworker into a recluse. Anna Mae saw beyond the scars to find a thoughtful and kind old man.

He studied her for a moment. "It's nice! You look like a little girl."

She lowered her head, shaking it. "It's all crooked."

"Beauty is beauty," he said, waving a hand where the fingers were fused together, then quickly shoved his hand between the cushions of his chair. The bell upstairs rang again. "You better go see what that old biddy wants. Tell her to come down here. I need some company."

"I will," said Anna Mae and hurried up the steps.

Irene Siminoski was propped in her hospital bed. Her deep auburn hair flared out over the snow-white pillow. She wasn't a particularly pretty woman, her nose a bit too big and her eyes too close together. But people were drawn to her easy-going nature. Now in her early fifties, she was too young to be suffering with serious heart problems. Anna Mae admired how Irene had continued to take great care with her grooming despite her sunken eyes and sallow skin.

When Anna Mae entered the room, Irene's jaw dropped. However, before she could say anything, Anna Mae blurted out, "I cut it!"

Irene adjusted the nasal cannula that brought a constant supply of pure oxygen into her lungs. "Well, you could have been a little more careful."

"I was angry," explained Anna Mae. "I'll go to the beauty shop tomorrow and have it straightened out."

As Anna Mae helped her out of bed and to the bathroom, Irene chattered on about how many different hairstyles she had worn in her life.

Ten minutes later, she helped Irene back into bed. Anna Mae then said, "Mr. Siminoski would like you to come downstairs."

Irene reattached the oxygen line and adjusted herself against the pillows. "I'll go down later. Right now, I want to talk to you."

Anna Mae looked around for a place to sit. In the corner of the room was an overstuffed chair whose back and arms were draped with pieces of complex embroidery yellowed by the years. She sat down and waited.

"How long has Walter been in jail now?" Irene asked bluntly.

Anna Mae thought for a moment. "One year and one month."

"When's he getting out?"

"He won't have a parole hearing until a year from this October."

"Are you worried?"

"I try not to think about it."

"If it were up to me he'd never get out. They could gas him for all I care."

Anna Mae knew that Irene was a bit of a spitfire, yet she was surprised at how vengeful the sick woman's voice had become.

"I didn't know you knew my uncle."

"Oh, I know him all right! Walter is the most rotten, despicable, treacherous bastard that ever walked the earth."

Anna Mae became concerned about what all this anger could do to Irene's weakened heart.

"Please don't get upset," Anna Mae said getting up and going over to the bed. "Walter can't hurt anybody now. Can I bring you a dish of Jello?" she asked in a feeble attempt to change the subject.

"What a darling girl you are," said Irene, patting Anna Mae's hand. "Why don't you just help me downstairs and Dobie and I can have a snack together."

CHAPTER THIRTY-SIX

March 1970

Mrs. Reynolds, senior class history teacher, had a knack for calling on students who didn't know the answer. She also had a reputation for belittling remarks that reduced some students to tears. In a shrill, no nonsense voice, she addressed her class: "The Confederacy opened fire on a Union stronghold on April 12, 1861. Where did that battle take place?"

At the back of the classroom, Anna Mae, who hadn't studied, leaned behind the boy in front of her where Mrs. Reynolds couldn't see her. She ran her tongue over her dry lips and wiped her sweaty palms on her skirt.

Three nights a week at the Pizza Parlor and Saturday at the Siminoski's was enough work for any high school senior. Add to that, the workload she carried at home because Sarah cleaned other people's houses and not her own. Anna Mae hadn't the time or the energy, nor the incentive to keep up with her studies. And today she was completely exhausted.

"April 12, 1861—where did the Confederate army attack the Union forces? Does anyone know the answer?" Mrs. Reynolds's critical gaze scanned the classroom as she paced in front of the blackboard.

Anna Mae felt dizzy. Her heart began to palpitate. Suddenly, she was consumed by a fear, all out of proportion to her mere inability to answer a history question.

"Debbie Henderson, where did that battle take place?"

"Antietam," Debbie responded.

"Wrong! You should spend more time studying and less time flirting with the boys."

The teacher's tone of voice hurled a sting of harsh criticism, and Anna Mae thought she might be next. Fear gripped ice-cold in her veins, and overwhelmed her with a sense of immediate danger. It took all her strength to suppress the irrational terror that told her to get up and run.

She glanced around the room. The other students were all sitting at attention. Clearly, they didn't feel what she was feeling—an overpowering foreboding— that something was dreadfully wrong.

Mrs. Reynolds held up the history book, her sarcastic words incoherent as sweat dampened Anna Mae's under-arms and ran down her back. She lowered her head, trying to hide within herself—within the hysteria. Seconds ticked on. She lost all sense of time. For an alarming moment, she thought she was dying.

Then she remembered. She could almost hear Dr. Rhukov's comforting Russian accent: 'The fear is illogical. It feels like you will die, yes? In your mind, the chemicals get mixed up. They make a panic attack. You must tell yourself: This is not real. There is nothing to fear. And you must always come back to the breathing.'

Anna Mae willed herself to inhale deeply. Then exhale. Inhale. Exhale. Inhale. Exhale. *It's not real. There's nothing to fear. I'm not dying. I'm having a panic attack.* Her breathing slowly came back to normal.

From far away, sharp and insistent: "Anna Mae! Are you paying attention? Where did the Confederacy open fire?"

A boy next to her spoke up. "Fort Sumter."

"Did I ask you?" snapped Mrs. Reynolds. "Anna Mae, answer the question!"

With the terror now slipping away, Anna Mae looked to her left. Was anybody aware of what just happened? She looked to the right. Did it show?

Mrs. Reynolds was tapping a ruler on her desk. "Anna Mae McBride! If you don't start paying attention you will not be graduating."

* * *

On Saturday morning, Anna Mae told Maria Tamero she would not be able to help at the Siminoskis. She then took two busses to Oakland. Dr. Rhukov finished sorting his papers and placed them in a neat pile at the side of his desk. Anna Mae looked into the intense brown eyes behind the rimless bifocals. "It was the same thing, Dr. Rhukov."

"Another panic attack?"

She nodded. "Why am I having these now? I never had them before."

Dr. Rhukov placed the papers in a drawer, took a Kleenex from the box by the Tiffany lamp and wiped his glasses. "I think it has to do with meeting your mother," he said, returning the glasses to his nose. "Before you met her, you had hope for a better future, did you not?"

"What does that have to do with panic attacks?"

"Think about it. Think how meeting your mother has changed your life."

Anna Mae recalled last summer—the first time she met her mother, the first disappointment in a long succession of disappointments.

The Doctor was right. It had changed her. It had been a turning point; a circle completed that left the naiveté of her childhood behind. But what had that to do with the panic attacks? She looked at the doctor. "I don't get it."

"Listen closely," he said. "All your life you imagined your mother to be a fairy godmother. Yes? You convinced yourself that when you found her, she would make everything better. But now you know that's not going to happen."

The doctor waited for Anna Mae to respond, but she just sat there, looking at him.

"Someday we will uncover the abuse that has caused your basic instability. Psychic damage as severe as you suffer will not just go away. It's still there," he said tapping his head. "It's tucked into your deepest memory. And it's festering—it is the basis of all the problems: the mood swings, the panic attacks, the lost time."

"But since Walter went to jail, I haven't had a blackout. Whatever abuse there was, I should be over it. Shouldn't I?"

"No. You know that. As long as you had hope for the future—a belief that finding your mother was the answer to all your problems, the damage stayed put. However, now, as you say in America, 'there is no light bulb at the end of the tunnel.' I believe this has created subconscious havoc. And that havoc is emerging as panic attacks. Makes sense, yes?"

Anna Mae tried to think back to the time when she still lived with the illusion that her mother was going to rescue her. What the doctor said made sense. But it didn't solve the problem. She ran her fingers through the uneven hair that she had chopped when she was upset about her mother. It was now at the awful stage of being too short to tie back and too long to manage easily.

Dr. Rhukov asked, "Would you like to explore the theory?"

"The theory that if you cut your hair when you're angry it will grow back a mess?"

"Now don't try to jest your way out of this," he said, his lively brown eyes sparkling. "Answer my question. Would you like to talk about your mother and the effect she is having on your life?"

"No. Not now," said Anna Mae, then added, "My mother's going to Alcoholics Anonymous. I think she's slipping. But I don't want to talk about it."

"Okay. We won't talk about it."

"Did I tell you I asked her about my father?"

"No. When was that?"

"Last week. She told me some hair-brain story about a rock star who found her irresistible one night and then left town the next day. She didn't know his real name and she has no idea where he is now. Sarah said my mother had never been anywhere near a rock concert."

"Who do you believe? Your mother or your Aunt Sarah?"

"Aunt Sarah."

The doctor nodded and leaned forward on his elbows. "What about depression? Has that given you any problems lately?"

Anna Mae gazed beyond him to the big window. Charcoal clouds rolled across the April sky. She should have listened to Sarah and brought her umbrella.

"Don't drift away, young lady," the doctor said. "Talk to me about mood swings. How has that been since I last saw you?"

"On Monday and Tuesday I was totally depressed," she replied. "And then I got up on Wednesday and everything was okay. I felt great." She thought about that for a moment then said, "Angelo called. He's upset because I don't want to see him all the time. It's not that

I don't care for him. It's just that my senior year is a lot of pressure. Then there's the pizza parlor and helping Maria. She's trying to get Irene to get rid of some of her junk. Irene saves everything, every last scrap of paper. What can I do about the panic attacks, Dr. Rhukov?"

"You said the Librium makes you too lethargic. We could try a smaller dose," he said, opening a desk drawer to get some samples, "or another medication. Equanil sometimes helps."

"I don't want to take any more drugs."

"I'm reasonably sure," he said closing the drawer, "that the abuse started when you were a small child. To have established itself so deeply, something had to have happened when you were very, very young—under two years of age. You can't remember that far back. You remember when you were seven, maybe eight. If the abuse had started when you were eight years of age, most likely we would have broken through by now. However, this damage is so deep, so very hidden. Eventually we must reach it. Otherwise the depression, the panic attacks—I doubt very seriously if they will go away."

Anna Mae examined her pink fingernails then folded her hands in her lap. The doctor leaned forward on his elbows. "I think we need to attempt something more extreme to get at those memories."

With the toe of her right shoe, Anna Mae traced the intricate designs in the oriental carpet. Then she tucked both feet beneath her chair and looked at the doctor. "Extreme? What do you mean by extreme?"

"We could try sodium amytal. It is better known as the 'truth serum.' It will reduce your resistance..."

"Right now?" Anna Mae asked with enthusiasm.

Dr. Rhukov smiled. "My, you're eager. But no. Under the circumstances, with the severity of your problem, we must be in a controlled environment.

Somewhere if your reaction is too upsetting, there will be help available."

"The hospital?"

He nodded.

"A mental hospital?"

"Yes. You will be graduating in a few months. You will have time. And don't worry about the cost."

"Dr. Rhukov," she said firmly, "I'm not going into any mental hospital. I'm not crazy!" She paused for a moment, then added, "Am I?"

"No, no, no! I tell you again and again. You are not crazy. And you must stop using the word 'crazy.' I don't like that word."

"Am I mentally ill?"

"That depends on what you mean by mentally ill," he said.

"You're the shrink," she said. "What do you say it means?"

"Most mental problems are caused by chemical imbalance in the brain. The question is, did the imbalance cause the condition? Or did the condition cause the imbalance? In your case, I am convinced the condition—the abuse, caused the imbalance. If it were the other way around, I might be able to give you a drug to even it out—to make it normal.

"I have told you many times before, the blackouts, the panic attacks, the mood swings are the result of both physical and psychic trauma. This is essentially the same thing that happens to some of our soldiers coming back from Vietnam. Post-Traumatic Stress Syndrome is what they call it."

"Is that what you call it?"

"No. I call the blackouts, Traumatic Amnesia."

Anna Mae sat silent, thinking. Finally, she said, "I think I understand. But what can I do about it?"

"Just what we're doing," he replied. "It is not an easy process. Sometimes drugs help. Sometimes not. I believe we must get you to remember what has happened to you. And that will take as long as it takes." Suddenly a roll of thunder rattled the windows. Lightning crackled and the Tiffany lamp flickered. Doctor Rhukov reached into his pocket for his wallet, then held out a twenty-dollar bill. "You take a Taxi Cab. It's going to be a big storm."

CHAPTER THIRTY-SEVEN

1970

A cold and blustery March gave way to April's warm showers. May produced a zillion flowers, then June arrived and Anna Mae graduated. It was a disheartening ceremony. She should have been near the top of her class. She wasn't. Her grades were only average. She was devastated.

She spent the summer working at The Pizza Parlor, helping at Siminoski's, and occasionally dating Angelo. Her mood swings continued; however, the panic attacks had begun to subside. Sometimes she would wake up in the middle of the night to find the bedclothes soaked with sweat. Dr. Rhukov wanted her to sign herself into Western Psychiatric Hospital so he could use medication to help her to remember what happened during those blackouts.

She wouldn't go.

David's interest in the space program was insatiable. He had moved into the attic, and by mid-summer the walls were obliterated by newspaper articles, magazine pictures of the space program, and colorful posters of Star Trek characters.

In August, Irene Siminoski's failing heart stopped and she died in her sleep. The funeral was as tragic as it was brief. Dobie's disfigurement kept him in the shadows and as far as Anna Mae knew, his only son, George, was not there to comfort him. Soon afterwards, Maria Tamero began helping Dobie with the heart-wrenching task of going through his late wife's belongings. Maria would drop off Irene's clothing at the Salvation Army. She gave Irene's saved letters for Dobie to read as he sat alone at night.

By the end of summer, Walter had completed his mandatory two years in prison. With ever-increasing concern, Anna Mae watched the calendar, counting the months, then the days. A long time ago, Angelo had told her that if Walter's behavior was not good he would not be released. Only last month Angelo said that prisoners are rarely let go at the first parole hearing. Nevertheless, by the end of September her concern had become a deep anxiety and her panic attacks returned.

She struggled, she prayed, she fought to contain her fear as she counted the days to Walter's first parole hearing in mid-October.

*   *   *

October 13, 1970 – Tuesday

The guards at Western Penitentiary led Walter through the myriad of iron gates, down a narrow hallway and into an ancient but newly painted room for his parole hearing. Having been coached by his fellow inmates, he respectfully admitted his crimes to the row of sour faced men on the Parole Board. He assured them he was very, very sorry. This, combined with two years and four months of good behavior and his devoted wife by his side, made the appropriate impression. Parole was granted. Walter was a free man.

Despite the good news, Walter smoldered as he walked back to his cell to collect his personal belongings. Sarah hadn't had the sense to bring enough money for a cab and he was damned if he'd take a bus home. He told Sarah to call Olga. The Nikovich's had a car. They could pick him up.

In the brisk autumn air, Walter, wearing only a thin summer shirt, paced the cracked sidewalk outside the prison. "Why the fuck didn't you bring me a jacket?"

"I'm sorry," said Sarah as she began to remove her light cotton coat. "You can put this around your shoulders."

"Keep it," he snapped. *The woman hasn't changed a bit,* he thought. *Just as dumb as ever.*

They waited for over an hour, most of which was made more annoying by Sarah's endless, cheerful chatter. By the time the old green Ford pulled to the curb, Walter was fuming. However, once he and Sarah were in the back seat, he made a valiant effort to be civil to Olga and Pete Nikovich. After all, they had driven all the way to Pittsburgh to pick up a man they didn't even like.

During the long ride home, Walter tried to make small talk with Pete.

But the brawny old Russian kept his eyes on the heavy traffic and replied only enough to let Walter know he had nothing to say. Olga and Sarah, who usually talked non-stop, remained quiet in the uneasy silence.

An hour later, Pete parked the car in the back alley and he and Olga went down the weedy path to their own back door. Sarah tried to take Walter's hand as they walked toward the rear of their house. He pushed it away. A moment later he inhaled the unmistakable aroma of hot Gulumki. It was then that the reality of his release hit him. He was out! He was home! He smiled at his wife and took her hand. Sarah looked up at him like a new bride.

* * *

Anna Mae was upstairs when they came in. She could hear David downstairs talking. There was some laughter and the clatter of dishes. Then she heard Walter's voice. It was strange—eerie—a voice out of a bad dream. How could she do this? How could she live under the same roof with him? She would have to leave. But what about David? And Sarah? Who would be here for them?

She checked herself in the mirror trying to convince herself she did not look as unglued as she felt, then headed downstairs. She stopped in the kitchen doorway, hoping David's presence would give her courage. But David was nowhere in sight. Sarah stood by the stove, mashing a huge pot of potatoes. Walter was sitting at the table with his back to Anna Mae and holding a can of beer. His dark hair was streaked with gray and he looked pitifully small compared to the oversized brute she remembered.

She tried to keep the quiver out of her voice. "Hello, Uncle Walter."

He turned and looked up at her. She thought she saw a spark of anger in his eyes. He took a sip of beer, wiped his mouth on his sleeve and said, "You're thinner."

Anna Mae tried to step forward into the kitchen, but her feet were cemented to the spot. For lack of anything better to say, she asked, "Where's Davie?"

Sarah turned from the potato pot. "He went upstairs to get something. Will you set the dining room table? We're having a celebration."

Anna Mae didn't remember passing David in the hall. Was she that out of it? There was a pile of Sarah's good dishes neatly stacked on the Formica counter. She willed herself to walk across the kitchen and pick them up. She had just started toward the doorway when David raced into the kitchen, almost knocking the dishes out of her hands.

"Look out!" she shrieked.

"Sorry," said David waving a newspaper.

"You never look where you're going!"

"You weren't looking. You bumped into me."

"I did not!"

*   *   *

Walter listened to the exchange with disdain. *Damnit! Sarah and the kids had taken over. Well, that was going to change.* While he was in prison, Sarah told him that Anna Mae got her driver's license and a cheap used car. Anna Mae hadn't even had the decency to visit. She could have brought David. Or was he too busy with his space shit?

David spread the newspaper across the table. "Look Dad! It's about Apollo 13. It tells you how they had to redesign the oxygen tank."

Walter pushed the paper out of his way. *Space rocket gibberish! The kid should be playing football. These women have turned my son into a sissy. I'll put an end to that, and a lot of other bullshit too!*

CHAPTER THIRTY-EIGHT

The next day Sarah went to one of her cleaning jobs. David was in school. Walter was sleeping late. Anna Mae's mother, Becky, had been making progress in AA, and Anna Mae was feeling good about their developing relationship. Not wanting to be alone with Walter on his first day home, she would go to Becky's house. At ten o'clock, in a gesture of reconciliation, she left her car keys on the kitchen table with a note to Walter, saying he could use her car if he wanted to go somewhere.

Before she took the bus to Pittsburgh, she stopped at Trinity Church. The sanctuary was dim and quiet with a hint of incense in the air. She walked to the candle bank and sat down. As she unbuttoned her jacket and slid forward onto her knees, the familiar comfort of safety engulfed her. How many times had she sought refuge in these pews? She looked beyond a single burning candle to the tall wooden cross. It had been five years since she watched Angelo in his short white tunic, placing the cross in its holder. She remembered how her heart beat a little faster when she looked at him. She also recalled what a terrible time in her life that had been. She was so young, so helpless, so utterly confused.

But worst of all, she thought she was crazy. Thank God for Doctor Rhukov. She hadn't had a blackout for over two years.

Now Walter was home.

She took two dollars from her purse and squeezed them through the narrow slot next to the candle bank. Holding the long lighter wick, she touched one flame to light another. Bowing her head, she prayed silently for strength—for herself, for Sarah, for David. She thought she should pray for Walter, pray that he was happy to be home, pray that he would appreciate his family, pray that he would no longer be violent. But she couldn't. In her heart there was no charity, no sincerity. She was still afraid of him.

The bus arrived in Pittsburgh before noon. In the brisk October air, the sun was bright and warm. She enjoyed the short walk to her mother's house. Becky had told her it wasn't necessary to knock so she walked right in and was immediately met by the aroma of something good baking in the oven.

Little Missy toddled toward her squealing with delight. Gathering her half-sister into her arms, she noticed that the toddler didn't smell like urine and was wearing clean overalls. Carrying Missy, Anna Mae walked through the tidy living room to the kitchen. Becky stood by the stove with a sheet of hot, chocolate chip cookies in one hand and a spatula in the other. She swooped the spatula through the air. "Look! The house is clean. The laundry's done. And I have a pot of coffee perking."

Anna Mae put the little girl in her highchair, then pulled up a chair and sat down.

"Surprised?" Becky asked, looking around.

"The house looks great," said Anna Mae. Except for baking things, the kitchen was spotless.

"I haven't had a drink in four weeks," said her mother while scooping the cookies onto a platter. She then gave Missy a sippy cup filled with milk and a warm cookie. While the baby was busy squeezing the melted chocolate chips through her pudgy little fingers, Becky poured two cups of steaming coffee.

Anna Mae watched her mother closely. Becky's dark blond hair was neatly clipped behind her ears and she was wearing light pink lipstick.

Her mother placed the coffee and the plate of cookies on the table, then sat down across from her. It was then that Anna Mae saw the Alcoholics Anonymous guidebook, The Twelve-Step Program, on the table. Becky picked it up and held it in both hands.

"Anna Mae," she said, "this book is my bible. When a person has been drinking as long as I have, well, we make a lot of mistakes. Sometimes we hurt people without meaning to."

Anna Mae still didn't like coffee but she sipped it politely as her mother ran her hand over the book's cover. "There is so much I need to say to you. So much to make up for."

"No you don't," said Anna Mae putting down her cup and reaching for a cookie. "I'm just happy that you're doing so well."

"But that's not enough," said Becky. "I've got to repair some of the damage I've done."

Anna Mae took a bite of the cookie, savoring the chocolate as it melted in her mouth. Anna Mae wished her mother would save the serious conversation for another time.

But Becky was determined. She opened the book and ran her finger down one of the pages. "Here it is," she said. "Step Eight: Make a list of all the persons I have harmed and be willing to make amends."

Holding her finger on that exact spot, Becky looked up at her daughter. "You're the main one," she said. "You're the one I've hurt the most. All those times when I called Joey Barns...I was drunk. I never called when I was sober. I wanted to stay out of your life so I wouldn't ruin it. After a few drinks, I would pick up the phone—not all the time, but too often. That had to really upset you."

"It did," said Anna Mae, washing the cookie down with the coffee. "Poor Joey. I wish I had a dollar for all the times I accused him of knowing where you were and not telling me."

"And that's my fault too," said Becky. "I'll never be able to make that up to you." She lowered her voice to almost a whisper. "I don't expect you to forgive me."

Evidently, Becky had been doing a lot of soul searching since their last visit. Anna Mae had never thought about whether or not she would forgive her mother.

"You don't have to say anything," said Becky. "I just need to tell you that I'm facing the bad things I've done. And that I am so sorry."

Anna Mae felt nothing. For all Anna Mae had been through, it seemed like a shallow apology. Becky didn't know about her blackouts or that she was seeing a psychiatrist or that Walter was an abusive drunk. However, this was not the time to tell her. Her mother was trying to fix her own life and she was feeling enough guilt. No need to add more to the mix. She had learned that from Dr. Rhukov. One small step at a time. That's how you fix things. You don't try to do it all at once.

Becky invaded her thoughts. "I need to tell you why I left when you were a baby. I didn't want to hurt Sarah..."

Missy was nodding off and Anna Mae used that as an excuse get away from her mother. "I'll put Missy in her crib." She flipped up the highchair tray and carried the toddler to the tiny room that Becky shared with her young daughter.

"You were a beautiful baby," Becky said from the doorway.

After all the years of yearning to know what had happened when she was a baby, Anna Mae did not want to hear it now. Dealing with Walter's release from prison would take all her energy.

Anna Mae gently placed Missy in her crib, found a baby wipe in a nearby box and cleaned the melted chocolate from the little fingers, saying, "Could we talk about this some other time?"

"I wanted to keep you so bad," Becky persisted. "But I thought I had disgraced my family. I was so young. I thought it was my fault. If I stayed, I would have to depend on everyone and God only knows how often my shame would be thrown in my face. But most of all, I was afraid that in a moment of weakness I would tell everyone the truth. I knew it would kill Sarah if she ever found out."

Exasperated, Anna Mae turned to face Becky and snapped, "Found out what?"

"Your father was not a singer in a rock band."

"I didn't think so," said Anna Mae, sidestepping her mother and walking back to the kitchen. "So who is my father?"

"I'm sorry," said Becky following her. "I shouldn't have brought this up."

"Well, you already did," Anna Mae said harshly. "So tell me!"

"Sit down," said Becky.

Anna Mae plunked herself down in a kitchen chair. Becky's hands were trembling as she too sat down.

"Only Grandma McBride knew. She made me promise I would never tell so Sarah wouldn't be hurt. You won't tell Sarah, will you?"

"What? Tell Sarah what? For God's sake, Becky, what are you trying to say?"

"When I was fifteen," said Becky, reaching for the Twelve-Step book and hugging it to her chest as though it could give her strength. "When I was fifteen, Walter raped me."

Anna Mae froze. In a voice barely above a whisper, she said, "Say that again?"

Becky squeezed the book tighter. "I said...when I was fifteen, Walter raped me. Walter is your father."

Anna Mae felt the blood drain from her face. She saw her mother's mouth moving but didn't hear a word she was saying. The room became a blur. Anna Mae stood up and moved towards the door. First slowly, and then faster and faster until she was running. She ran out the door, down the city sidewalk, past the condemned house, the junk strewn lot, then across two busy intersections where the bus seemed to be waiting for her.

Her knees threatened to buckle as she climbed up the three steps and found a seat near the front of the bus. The streets leading out of Pittsburgh could have been on another planet. As she rode past the unfamiliar buildings, she lost all sense of time. Then suddenly she was in Warrenvale. She got off the bus, forgetting to pay her fare. The driver called her back. Without bothering to count it, she threw a pocket full of change into the coin box.

CHAPTER THIRTY-NINE

October 16, 1970 – Friday

Iron bars threw long shadows across the concrete floor into a space no bigger than a large closet, seven by ten feet to be exact. The wake up buzzer in the women's section of Allegheny County Jail was loud and long and harsh. Anna Mae sat up quickly and scrambled into the corner of the cot. With her back against the cinder block wall, she pulled her knees to her chest, clinging to a raggedy army blanket that scraped her skin. Her head ached. Her surroundings were a blur.

When her vision cleared, a man in a green uniform appeared at the other side of the bars. The iron door flew open with a bang. "Get up, McBride!"

She pushed herself tight against the wall, confused and terrified.

"Com' on! I ain't got all day."

She looked at the opposite wall: a seatless commode, a metal mirror, and a small rusted sink. The damp air smelled of disinfectant. She ran a hand over her clothing. She was wearing a faded-orange cotton top, drawstring pants, her own tennis shoes, no laces, and no socks. She was in jail.

There had been some kind of mistake. The man in the green uniform was going to take her somewhere. She would find out what happened. They would let her go.

"Com' on, McBride. You're wanted in court."

She whimpered, "I have to go to the bathroom."

"Well, hurry up."

She looked at the exposed toilet. "In there?"

"We frown against people peeing on the floor."

"I don't have to go," she said, crawling out of the corner and standing up.

"Your hands," said the guard, dangling cuffs in her face.

She held out her hands and he slapped them on. He got down on one knee and clamped her ankles with leg-irons. He then led her through a series of barred doors that were opened by an unseen sentry pressing a release buzzer, then closed with a loud metal against metal bang. She stumbled along, dragging the chain connecting her ankles. The handcuffs pinched at the slightest move.

With lockup behind them, they were joined by a deputy sheriff with a silver star on his tan uniform. Together the men escorted her across a sandstone overpass to the second floor of the Allegheny County Courthouse. They led her to the holding room where the sheriff instructed her to sit down. The guard left. The sheriff stood by the door.

From where she sat, she could see the outer corridor—men in suits carrying briefcases, scurrying about while an assortment of people in more casual clothing leaned against the walls or sat on the wide window ledges, looking down into the courtyard.

At the far end of the hall, in front of Courtroom 300, two police officers were engaged in a hand waving discussion. A man carrying a thick file folder flew out of the courtroom and passed between them without missing a step. He was tall and slender with broad shoulders. When he hurried down the hall toward the holding room, his pinstripe jacket flapped behind him. Skidding to a stop at the doorway, he brushed his thick, black hair away from his forehead. His intense brown eyes settled on Anna Mae.

"Ah! There you are!" he said, stepping inside the small room. He flipped open a folding chair, sat down in front of her and opened the folder. "I'm Ivan Hammerstein. I'll be your attorney for now." He extended a bony wrist to look at his watch. "We don't have time to go over this." He looked at the sheriff. "Can you take off the iron?"

"No!"

"Okay. Well, let's go. Don't say anything," he instructed Anna Mae.

The deputy sheriff grabbed Anna Mae by the arm, lifted her to her feet and roughly guided her down the hall. On her other side, the tall attorney rattled on about the impending arraignment. "You just let me do the talking. We'll plead 'not guilty' for now. I was just stuck with this case. I mean, assigned. I don't know much about it. McBride. Good Irish name! You just leave everything to me."

Courtroom 300 was crowded. The sheriff stopped in the doorway, letting the tall attorney take Anna Mae to the defendant's side of the courtroom where they stood behind a bare table. To her right, standing in front of another table, a short, slim man with thick auburn hair and wearing a tailored black suit, placed his brief case on the table then turned to look at her.

Hammerstein leaned down and whispered into Anna Mae's ear. "Oh shit. That district attorney—Tom Simon—he's a lizard. Don't look at him."

Judge Wittier was a small, worried looking man with thinning white hair and thick half glasses, perched on the top of his head. He cracked the gavel and the room fell silent.

"Docket number 5390," the bailiff announced. "The Commonwealth of Pennsylvania versus Anna Mae McBride. Murder in the first degree."

What? No! This isn't real. Murder? I'm dreaming. Oh my God, what's going on here? I can't breathe.

After a quick glance at Anna Mae, the judge lowered his glasses to look at the papers the bailiff set before him. "Miss McBride, to the charge of murdering Walter Lipinski, how do you plead?"

Anna Mae gripped the edge of the table. The room was spinning.

"How do you plead, Miss McBride?" the judge repeated.

Walter? My God! I don't remem...did I blackout? Her knees began to give way.

"Not guilty," Hammerstein almost shouted. "She pleads 'not guilty.'" He grabbed her by the elbow. "Your Honor. May the defendant sit down? I think she's going to pass out."

"Have a seat, Miss McBride," said the judge.

"Thank you, Your Honor," said Ivan Hammerstein as he helped Anna Mae into a chair. When he returned to his position behind the bare table, he cleared his throat, brushed a few strands of black hair from his forehead and said, "Judge Wittier, Your Honor, we request the defendant be freed on her own recognizance."

"That's outrageous," said the DA.

"It would seem so," said the judge.

Ivan Hammerstein glared at the DA but addressed the Judge. "With all due respect, Your Honor, Assistant District Attorney—Tom Simon, knows nothing about my client."

"And neither do you," snapped Tom Simon. "Mr. Hammerstein was handed this case only ten minutes ago. The Commonwealth requests Miss McBride be remanded without bail."

"That's unwarranted," said Hammerstein. "Miss McBride is not a flight risk."

"I beg to differ, Your Honor," said the DA. "The murder of which the defendant is accused is of the most egregious nature. For God's sake! She nearly butchered the man."

"Objection!"

"You don't need to object, counselor," said Judge Wittier. "This is not a trial."

"My objection is," said Hammerstein, "that the prosecution's statement presupposes guilt. My client has pleaded 'not guilty.' Unless this court proves otherwise, the prosecution better keep his big mouth shut!"

Judge Wittier motioned the bailiff to the bench and leaned toward him to ask a question. The bailiff replied. The judge nodded then turned back to the courtroom. "Mr. Hammerstein. In the short period of time you have been assigned to this defendant, you cannot make an accurate assessment as to whether or not Miss McBride is a flight risk. Therefore, Miss McBride is remanded until you can give the court a convincing reason to grant bail. Next case!"

Anna Mae looked at Assistant District Attorney Tom Simon. He returned her gaze, smiling. But the smile wasn't reaching his eyes.

*   *   *

Sitting in the back of the courtroom, Angelo Tamero felt his heart sink as he watched Ivan Hammerstein and the deputy sheriff help Anna Mae out of her chair. Restrained as though she were a dangerous criminal, Anna Mae was led out of the courtroom. *This is all wrong,* Angelo thought. *Anna Mae is incapable of hurting anyone. What I saw on yesterday's news was a bunch of overzealous policemen trying to prove to the public, regardless of who they hurt, that they were crackerjack cops. Walter was murdered all right. And whoever killed him is still out there. Because it certainly wasn't Anna Mae!*

CHAPTER FORTY

Anna Mae sat up and stretched her arms. How long had she had been sleeping? Someone had slid a food tray under the bars. She wasn't hungry. She looked at the metal toilet and recalled using it when she came back from court. No one was around at the time, but it was still humiliating.

Murder! They said I killed Walter. And that tall lawyer...he said he would talk to me later. How long ago had that been?

A guard appeared on the other side of the bars. "McBride, your attorney is here." He opened the cell, placed the tray of uneaten food on her cot and cuffed her hands behind her back. He led her down the tier through the barred doors that buzzed open and banged shut. Holding her roughly by the elbow, he escorted her to a windowless room where Ivan Hammerstein waited at a long table. The guard removed the handcuffs and left.

Anna Mae rubbed her wrists while looking at the sheaf of papers spread in front of the lawyer. She took a seat across from him.

He brushed a few wayward strands of thick, black hair from his forehead. "Before we get started, I have to know if you want me to represent you. Or do you have someone else in mind."

Anna Mae gazed at the bony hands resting on the papers. *What was he talking about? Why did she have to hire a lawyer? Who would pay for it? Who would pay for this one?*

Ivan Hammerstein waited a few seconds then asked, "Is your family going to obtain counsel?"

"No. I mean...I don't know. I don't think so. We don't have much money."

"I've been appointed by the court to represent you. Is that the way you want to go?"

"I don't have any money to pay you."

"You don't need any. My firm, Ruben, Ruben and Smith, do ten percent pro bono."

"Pro bono?"

"Free. No cost."

"But why would you..."

"Just because. Now let's get down to business. As I think you already know, my name is Ivan Hammerstein. You can call me Ivan. I'm only an associate in the firm, but don't let that bother you. I'm damn good. You couldn't do better if you paid. And I've been up against that red-wigged lizard before."

For the first time since she had been catapulted into this horrible mess, she smiled. "I think his hair is auburn."

"Well, that's more like it," he said approvingly. "You really do need to smile more. Open up. I didn't think you noticed anyone in that courtroom. Auburn, huh?"

She nodded. "Will you help me?"

"Sure, Honey. You don't mind if once in a while I call you 'Honey.' It's a bad habit of mine. I get myself into trouble with women's libbers. But sometimes it just slips out. I might be an incurable male chauvinist but you won't find anyone who will work harder to win a case. So I'm on?" he said reaching over the papers to shake her hand.

Anna Mae didn't move the hands that were locked together under the table. "Why do they think I killed Walter? What did I do?"

Ivan retracted his hand. "Why don't you tell me?"

"I don't remember what I did to make them put me in here."

The lawyer leaned back, squinted, and lifted an eyebrow.

She raised her voice. "Honest! I don't remember."

"Miss McBride," he said leaning forward on his elbows, "you have to do better than that."

"I can't," she said. "Maybe you should talk to my doctor first."

"Your doctor. And who might that be?"

"Dr. Rhukov."

"Mikhail Rhukov? That shrink?"

"Yes. What day is this?"

Ivan's face went deadpan. He swallowed hard. In clipped words he said, "Today is Friday, October 16th, 1970. Do you know that you're in the Allegheny County Jail?"

"Yes."

"And unless a miracle happens you're going to trial?"

"Why?"

"You know why! The police report says that yesterday you murdered your uncle, Walter Lipinski." He looked down at the top page and added, "With an ax."

She stared at him. "I killed my Uncle Walter with an ax?"

"Did you?" asked the lawyer. "Did you kill your uncle?"

"No! Yesterday? Yesterday—I think it was yesterday, I was in Pittsburgh at my mother's house."

"You remember that?"

"Yes. And that's all I remember about yesterday. Why do the police say I killed Walter?"

"You don't know?" He shook his head. Without bothering to put the papers in order, he shoved them into his badly worn briefcase and snapped it shut. "I need to talk to Dr. Rhukov. I'll see you when I get back."

CHAPTER FORTY-ONE

In the Nikovich living room, Olga and Pete sat across from Sarah. "We don't mind you stay here," said Olga. "But that's you house and some time you will haf to go back. Maybe now is good. My husband will go vith us."

Five minutes later, Olga, Pete, and Sarah stood in front of the Lipinski back door that led directly into the kitchen. Pete opened the door and stepped inside. Olga and Sarah followed. On the kitchen table, next to Anna Mae's car keys, Thursday's newspaper fluttered to life. A stench of decay permeated the dim and soundless kitchen. Olga brought a handkerchief to her nose as the two women stopped a few steps away from a pool of blood.

"My God," whispered Sarah.

Pete switched on the light, exposing the full horror of yesterday's violence. Blood was splattered from floor to ceiling. A dried-up ham sandwich lay on the Formica counter. In the sink, slivers of ceramic and bits of browning lettuce surrounded a broken mug. In the middle of the floor, a toppled chair rested where it had fallen.

"We haf to clean it up," said Olga, walking to the sink. She began putting the shattered pieces of ceramic into what was left of the broken mug. She told Pete to get the mop and bucket at the top of the cellar stairs.

Sarah picked up the fallen chair, dragged it into a corner, and sat down. When Olga saw the glazed look in Sarah's eyes, she took her by the hand and led her out of the kitchen. They had just entered the living room when they heard footsteps on the front porch. Olga went to the door and opened it.

"Are you Sarah?" asked a tiny woman with warm brown eyes and dark hair braided down her back.

"I'm the neighbor," said Olga, noticing the stranger's black cashmere jacket with its white mink collar. "Sarah's in the living room."

"May I come in?"

Olga stayed in the doorway, blocking it.

"I'm sorry," said the woman. "I'm Maria Tamero—Angelo's mother. David's been staying at my house. Oh, this is such a terrible tragedy."

Olga stepped aside, letting Maria walk into the living room where she took off her coat and tossed it on the couch. Sarah, her face white and her eyes vacant, was sitting on a straight-backed chair near the window.

"Oh, you poor woman," Maria said rushing across the living room and grasping Sarah's hand. "We've been praying for Anna Mae—and you. I don't believe for one moment that Anna Mae...that Anna Mae..."

"Killed Walter," Sarah finished the sentence.

"That's what I say," Olga agreed. "Annie is a good girl. She wouldn't do such a thing."

The phone in the kitchen rang and Olga went to answer it.

"It's you sister, Becky," Olga called from the kitchen. "Do you want to talk to her?"

Olga knew that Sarah had refused to speak to Becky during the entire time Anna Mae was building a relationship with her. She also knew that her niece had been to see Becky yesterday. Maybe Anna Mae was still at her mother's in the afternoon when Walter was killed.

If Becky would tell that to the police, they would have to let Anna Mae out of jail.

Sarah walked into the kitchen and took the phone from her neighbor's hand. Olga went back into the living room. Maria was standing by the window and wringing her hands. "Is there anything I can do to help, Sarah?"

"Me and my husband live just next door," said Olga. "Before I thought that maybe Sarah would feel better if she vas home. But the kitchen—you should see it! Looks like the devil himself vas there. My husband is just now cleaning it. But I think David should stay at your house."

The conversation suddenly stopped as both women looked toward the kitchen where Sarah was yelling hysterically. "You told her what? Walter? You liar! You goddamn liar!"

Olga rushed to the kitchen and yanked the phone out of Sarah's hand as Sarah broke into sobs. "What's going on here?" Olga barked into the phone. "Why are you saying bad things to Sarah who already is upset? Don't give me no excuses...you don't call this house no more," Olga said and slammed the phone on the receiver.

Olga then turned to Sarah who collapsed into her arms, gasping between sobs. "Becky said...Walter...Walter is...is...Anna Mae's...father!"

Olga helped Sarah back to the living room. Together they sat on the edge of the couch. Olga kept her arm around Sarah, saying, "Why would you sister say such a thing?"

"What did she say?" asked Maria, who was now sitting in the straight back chair.

Olga didn't answer Maria's question, but she did say, "That voman—that Becky has brought nothing but trouble to Sarah. She dumped her own baby so she don't have to take care of her. Dat baby vas Anna Mae. She never calls to see if her baby is dead or what. Now she wants to be Annie's mama."

Without waiting for a response from Maria, Olga went to the kitchen and came back with a small striped dishtowel. Sarah used it to wipe her face and blow her nose. Olga then returned to her place on the couch next to Sarah. Maria had her head down. She appeared to be praying.

At last Sarah stopped crying. Maria looked at her watch and said she should be going. Olga jumped up to get the coat. She ran her fingers through the soft fur collar and rubbed the cashmere against her wrinkled cheek.

CHAPTER FORTY-TWO

"You have a visitor," the guard said as he cuffed Anna Mae. He then led her by the elbow, down the hall to the iron door leading out of the cellblock. In a long enclosure, inmates were sitting in small partitioned areas, talking on telephones through wire-embedded glass. He guided her into an empty cubicle where she sat on a metal stool that was bolted to the floor. "Visiting hours are almost over," the guard told her. "You'll have to make it quick. Tell your friend to come earlier next time."

On the other side of the glass, Angelo, his face ashen, held a receiver and stared at her through the glass. She felt a mixture of relief and humiliation. With the handcuffs in full view, she pushed her oily, shoulder length hair out of her face—the face that she hadn't washed since she woke up in this god-forsaken hellhole. She didn't have to wonder how terrible she looked. Angelo's distraught expression said it all. She wanted to curl up and die.

Angelo motioned at her to pick up the receiver that was lying on her side of a counter. Struggling with the handcuffs, she pressed it tightly against her ear. Angelo was saying something but she couldn't hear him.

On Anna Mae's left, a thin woman with short dark hair, leaned back so she could see around the partition.

"I'll be finished with this jerk in a second, honey. You can use my phone. That one don't work."

When the woman disappeared behind the partition, the man she was talking to slammed his receiver on the counter, swore, and left. After the woman left, Angelo and Anna Mae moved to the next enclosure and picked up the phones. Angelo spoke first. "Can you hear me now?"

Anna Mae wilted at the sound of his voice. She was devastated that he had to sit on the other side of the glass with wires crisscrossing his face—the first familiar face in a maze of hostile strangers. She struggled to find her voice, and when she did, it sounded more like a plea than a statement. "I can hear you. Angelo! They say I killed Walter. I don't remember anything."

"You don't remember being arrested?"

"No."

"Do you remember being under the steps next to the kitchen when the police came?"

"No!"

"You were screaming so loud the neighbors heard you. And the blood—it was all over you. You don't remember Olga trying to get you to stop screaming?"

She stiffened. *Blood? Screaming? What was he telling her?* When she replied her voice was shaky: "No, I don't remember being home at all. The last thing I remember is going to see my mother. I remember sitting in her kitchen talking." She closed her eyes and rubbed her forehead. "And when I woke up I was in here. Someone made a mistake."

After a brief silence, he asked, "How are you doing? Are you okay?"

She raised her voice. "No! I'm not okay! Would you be okay if they did this to you?"

The shadow of a guard loomed over her. "Keep it down."

"I'm sorry," she said, tears now flowing down her face. She lifted the tail of her orange pullover to wipe them away.

"My father says he can get you a good lawyer," said Angelo.

"I have a lawyer," she snapped.

"The court gave you one?"

"Yes."

"That's not good enough. You need a good lawyer." What did Angelo know about lawyers, anyway? And why was she getting so irritated? "I think he's a good lawyer," she said trying to calm herself. "His name is Hammerstein. Ivan Hammerstein."

"You need my uncle Michello's lawyer. He's Italian."

Oh, yes! The Italian thing again. She could barely control her annoyance. "Angelo, I don't want your uncle's lawyer. I can't pay him and I don't want him. I just want to get out of here."

"You really need to try to remember where you were—what you were doing when Walter was killed. That's the only way they're going to let you out. You have to tell the detectives why they found you under the steps."

Ever since she woke up her emotions had been bouncing all over the map. Now anger boiled up from her feet. "Remember? What are you talking about? You know I won't remember. All these years, Angelo. Not once…not once—never…ever…could I remember. Think of something else, Einstein!"

Angelo looked as though he'd been punched in the face. Anna Mae immediately regretted her unwarranted sarcasm. A buzzer obliterated Angelo's reply. The guard announced that time was up. Before the phones went dead, Angelo said, "I left something for you."

As Anna Mae stood to go, she smiled weakly and mouthed the words, 'I'm sorry.' She then followed the other inmates as they were led, in single file, out of the phone room. Half way down the corridor, the guard informed Anna Mae that she had been moved to 'A Range.'

An overweight, tall and masculine female guard, whose nametag identified her as Officer Harriet Clauson, escorted her toward a short flight of iron steps. At the top of the steps there were two doors. The one on the left was made of wood. A sign said 'Employees Only.' The other consisted of big, black bars. Anna Mae and Officer Clauson, were buzzed into the barred area where over a dozen women were standing around in small groups.

A-Range smelled of mildew and body odor. Near the matron's empty metal desk, Clauson roughly removed Anna Mae's handcuffs. She then led her past a series of open cells to the last one in the row. Clauson nudged her into it, indicating that this was where she would stay. It looked much like her previous cell except for the bare mattress and rolled up bedding. "If you have any problems," the officer said as she was leaving, "tell the matron or one of us officers."

Anna Mae stood in the middle of the cell, bewildered. An emaciated black girl with huge, wide-set, brown eyes looked into the cell. "They call me Chocolate," she said. "What'cha in for?"

"None of your business," snapped Officer Clauson, who had returned and was holding a brown bag. Pushing Chocolate aside, she said to Anna Mae, "Your boyfriend left this for you."

By this time a group of women were milling around Anna Mae's cell and staring curiously at the girl who looked as out of place as a ballerina in a men's locker room. As soon as Officer Clauson left, a tall white woman with bad teeth stepped inside the cell and grabbed the bag from her hand. She skipped out, laughing and holding it above her head. "What'll you give me for this?" she jeered.

Anna Mae was petrified.

"Give her the bag, bitch!" said the girl who called herself Chocolate.

"Make me!" said the other. She took a Bible out of the bag and waved it over her head.

Chocolate lunged for the Bible. Suddenly someone yelled, "Here she comes!"

The woman with bad teeth dropped the bag and threw the Bible into the cell. It landed open on the mattress.

Clauson stuck her head into the cell. "You okay?"

Without waiting for an answer, the guard ran after the woman who had thrown the Bible.

"I gotta see this," said Chocolate and took off after the guard.

Anna Mae sat down on the bare mattress. She couldn't stop trembling. It was a nightmare. Only she wasn't dreaming. It was all terrifyingly real.

She picked up the open Bible. It was her Bible—the one she had found a long time ago when she was cleaning Sarah's bedroom. She ran her hand over the open pages. Soon the words came into focus.

"The Lord is my shepherd, I shall not want..."

Maria blushed. "My husband gave it to me for our 25th wedding anniversary. I don't like to wear it with the valley's hard times and so many people out of work. But his feelings are hurt if I don't wear it."

"A husband like that, every woman should have," said Olga smiling.

"Uh hum," said Pete stepping into the room holding a mop and wearing soap bubbles on his arms.

Olga handed Maria the coat, went over and kissed her husband on the cheek and said, "Mine Peter is better than a thousand of dose coats."

Sarah started to cry again.

CHAPTER FORTY-THREE

January 17, 1971

Anna Mae's once glowing complexion had faded into what was referred to as the jailhouse pallor. She had lost weight and dark circles around her eyes gave her a gaunt appearance. Her dull blond hair was pulled back and secured with a rubber band, and there was a hardness about her—a stony, resolute force in the set of her jaw.

After a cold, tasteless lunch, she sat on her cot and opened a letter from Angelo's mother. For the past three months Maria's letters were a cherished connection to the life Anna Mae once knew.

Dear Anna Mae,
Christmas was a sad time without you here. Sarah and David came to our house for supper. We invited Olga and Pete but they wanted to stay home. I think they celebrate Russian Orthodox Christmas.

The construction business is always slow during the winter months so Angelo has been working with his Uncle Tony, putting up drywall. I guess he told you all about that when he visited.

Dobie has not been doing well. Ever since he went through Irene's old letters, he has been going downhill. He just sits in the living room staring at the TV. Even when it's on! We do what we can, but he misses his wife so badly. I don't think he will ever be the same again. We haven't told him about Walter or what happened to you. It would only add to his depression.

Everyone here in the valley knows you are innocent. I don't know what the DA thinks he can accomplish by sending detectives to talk to all your friends. I called Becky the other day. She didn't seem to want to talk to me so I didn't stay on the phone. I know she doesn't go to see you or anything. I don't know what her problem is, but don't you worry about it. Sarah loves you like a daughter. You don't need to bother yourself about Becky.

Angelo says it's cold in that old jail in the winter. I bought you some flannel pajamas and a sweatshirt. Angelo will bring them when he comes. It's hard to believe that they can keep you there until the trial. Sarah says that after the Grand Jury met, Mr. Hammerstein tried to get you out on bail again. Where do they think you will go? Next month, when you are finally proven innocent, I hope you will get some kind of compensation for what you have been through.

'Chocolate' sounds like a good friend. Sometimes when young women get on drugs, they do terrible things to buy what they need. It's too bad Chocolate doesn't have anyone. When she gets out, maybe we can do something to help her.

Angelo just came home and says to tell you he loves you and will see you Saturday. We are all praying for you. You're a good girl, Anna Mae. Read your Bible and stay strong.

Love,
Maria

Anna Mae lowered the letter to her lap and looked across the cell at the calendar taped to the cinder block wall. When she stood up, Maria's letter fluttered to the floor. Ignoring the letter, she lifted the January page and stared at the thick black circle surrounding February 8th. Twenty-two days to go. She had been in jail for ninety-five days and felt like she had aged ten years.

She let the calendar page settle back to January, picked up Maria's letter, folded it, and placed it in the neat little pile of letters under her cot. Feeling the unrelenting chill of the ancient building, she hugged her arms around her bulky, blue sweater and walked over to the open cell door. She looked out into the area where inmates could gather as long as there were no problems. Chocolate was walking slowly in her direction. Yesterday she had been in a fight with another prisoner and now the guards had her full of dope—the county's idea of inmate control.

'A Range' was a section for women who were accused of violent crimes and for those who were mentally unbalanced. Chocolate, whose real name was Tanisha Jones, was awaiting trial for stabbing her pimp. He didn't die. However, he was permanently scarred and had to have part of his intestines removed. When Tanisha was thirteen, the pimp had given her enough drugs to develop an addiction. When she was fifteen, he named her Chocolate and put her out on the street. If she didn't earn enough money, he'd beat her. Anna Mae felt deep compassion for the pretty black girl who, at the age of twenty-one, was facing serious prison time.

Anna Mae leaned against the wall and watched Chocolate drag her feet in the aptly named Thorazine shuffle. When Chocolate finally reached her, Anna Mae put her arm around her lethargic friend's slumped shoulders.

"Are you okay?" Anna Mae asked.

Chocolate nodded and mumbled something.

"I can't hear you," said Anna Mae.

"Not important," said Chocolate.

Anna Mae saw the goose bumps on her brown arms. She took off her sweater and helped her friend put it on.

"Thank you," said Chocolate.

"I see my shrink today," said Anna Mae as they leaned side by side against the wall.

"That's right." Chocolate's voice was dry, monotone.

"He's gonna hypnotize me to see if he can get me to remember."

Chocolate looked at Anna Mae with bleary eyes. "Ain't you 'fraid?"

"A little."

"What if you 'member you did it?"

"Then I'll be on trial for murder."

"Ain't you already?"

"Well, yes...but they don't have any proof."

"If you did it, jes don't tell."

"I don't know," said Anna Mae shaking her head. "I think my lawyer will argue not guilty by reason of insanity."

Chocolate thought about that for a few seconds and then said, "You ain't crazy, Annie. Walter was crazy. Not you. You don't belong here."

"Neither do you," said Anna Mae.

"Yes, I do," said Chocolate looking at the floor. "I ain't no good. Just a common street whore..."

"Don't say that," said Anna Mae. "When you get out of here..."

"I ain't gettin' out."

Officer Clauson was walking toward them. Anna Mae reached out and tenderly buttoned the blue sweater. "Get some sleep," she said. "Let that crap they gave you wear off."

CHAPTER FORTY-FOUR

Dr. Rhukov took off his heavy, winter coat and laid it on the table. He then removed his black Cossack hat and smoothed down the hair that was sticking up in the back. Someone had brought a recliner into the conference room and Anna Mae was sitting on its edge with her hands folded. The doctor pulled a chair beside her and sat down. His forehead was pink from the frigid January weather and his gray beard was fuller than Anna Mae remembered. However, his lively brown eyes were as captivating as always.

"How have you been?" he asked.

"Okay." Her voice was soft and noncommittal.

"I don't think you have been okay," he said. "You must be terribly stressed. You've had panic attacks? Yes?"

"No, surprisingly, I haven't."

"Has Father John been to see you?"

"A few times," she said. "Can we get on with this?"

"Of course. If you feel you are ready."

"I'm ready as I'll ever be," she said, sliding back into the soft cushions.

After a few more minutes of casual conversation, it was time to begin. "Now as we work together," said the doctor, "I want you to hold onto this thought. No matter what comes into your mind you will be aware that it is not happening now…that it is only a memory—nothing you remember can hurt you."

"What if I remember that I killed Walter?"

"If that is so, then we will handle it. Remember that we want the truth. Your best defense is the truth, no matter what the truth is. Yes?"

"Yes."

"Now I want you to try to relax. Take a few deep breaths. That's right. Close your eyes and breathe deeply."

After talking her through a toe to head relaxation technique, Dr. Rhukov's mellow voice began leading Anna Mae inward, into the farthest reaches of her mind. She could still hear the sounds of the jail in the distance: muffled voices, iron doors banging shut, an occasional yell. She made an effort to concentrate on Dr. Rhukov's monotonous, soothing voice and soon the sounds began to fade and she grew increasingly unaware of the passing of time. A picture began forming in her mind.

"…and everything is peaceful now," he was saying. "The field of flowers wave in the soft summer breeze and their sweet scent fills the air. You breathe in the sweet smell of summer flowers. You breathe in…and out…in…and out. And you are going deeper…deeper into the flowers. And at the count of ten you will be asleep.

"Deeper…deeper…deeper…one.

"Down…down…down…two..."

She could feel herself floating downward, softly, like a feather on the breeze she went down…deeper...Dr. Rhukov's voice became fainter, farther away. And the flowers began to blend into a Van Gogh painting as she grew more peaceful, calm, and serene.

"Deeper…deeper…deeper…nine.

"Down…down…down…ten.

"You are now in an altered state of consciousness. You can hear my voice clearly and you will answer my questions. You will remember the things that were once hidden. And you will tell me what you recall. But you will always be aware that whatever comes into your mind is not happening now—that it is only a memory. Nothing more. Nobody...nothing can hurt you."

Anna Mae felt as though she could drift in the peacefulness forever. Dr. Rhukov then asked her to go back to Wednesday, October 14, 1970. She shifted uneasily when he asked: "It's early morning. Where are you?"

"In my bedroom."

"What are you doing?"

"I'm getting dressed."

"Where is the rest of the family?"

"Sarah had to go to one of her cleaning jobs. David is in school."

Dr. Rhukov said nothing for a few moments as he let the images solidify in Anna Mae's mind. He then asked, "How are you feeling?"

"I'm nervous...uneasy. I don't want to be home alone with Walter. I'm going to Pittsburgh to visit my mother."

"Good," said the doctor. "It is now ten-thirty. Where are you?"

"I'm in church."

"Describe the church."

"There's a red carpet leading to the altar. The sun is shining through the stained glass windows. I can smell incense. There's only one candle burning in the candle bank. Usually there's more." She lifted her head and looked up.

"What do you see?"

"The cross. The tall wooden cross."

"Does the cross have any significance?"

"It reminds me of Angelo. He used to carry it when he was an altar boy. That cross always made me feel safe. Maybe because it's in the church where I feel safe anyway."

"Do you feel safe anywhere else?"

"No."

"Tell me about Angelo."

For several minutes Anna Mae talked about Angelo, about how he was her best friend and how she could confide in him. When she was finished, she was smiling.

"Now move ahead a few moments and tell me how you feel."

"I feel peaceful. I'm lighting candles. I pray for all of us; Sarah, David and myself. But not Walter."

"How does that make you feel? Not praying for Walter."

"Like maybe I don't have enough faith. I'm still afraid of him."

"Do you feel guilty?"

"No."

"It is now eleven o'clock. Where are you?"

"On the bus going to Pittsburgh."

Having successfully cemented Anna Mae in the past, the doctor began moving her along faster. She went with ease into the forgotten time of that day. She talked about arriving at her mother's spotless house, about the aroma of baking cookies, Missy in her highchair and her mother's sobriety.

Suddenly Anna Mae's voice became a bit shrill and her words were more clipped, more deliberate, "Here it is," she said, pointing to something in front of her. "Step Eight," she nodded. "Make a list of all the persons I harmed, and become willing to make amends to them."

"Who is that?" asked the doctor. "Is that you talking?"

Anna Mae moved restlessly. Her hands gripped the arms of the recliner and the muscles in her jaw twitched. "Relax," said the doctor. "Take a few deep breaths. That's right. Relax your hands, Anna Mae. That's good. Everything is peaceful. You will not be disturbed by anything you remember. You will stay calm and serene as though you are watching a movie. What you see in the movie is happening to the characters on the screen. What's happening now?"

"I need to tell you why I left when you were a baby," she said in the same high-pitched voice. "I didn't want to hurt Sarah. You were a beautiful baby..."

"Who said, 'you were a beautiful baby?'"

Anna Mae took a deep breath and replied, "It's the older woman. She's telling that to the girl."

"Excellent," encouraged the doctor. "You are doing fine..."

"The woman tells the girl that her father was not a singer in a rock band. She's trying to explain something to the girl, but the girl doesn't want to hear it." Abruptly Anna Mae stopped talking. Her body stiffened.

"This is only a movie," the doctor reminded her. "You are sitting in a theater looking up at the screen. There are other people around you. You are safe."

Anna Mae nodded. "The woman was raped. She is telling the girl..." Anna Mae's voice trailed away, her breathing quick and shallow as her hands gripped the armrests.

"Easy, now," said the doctor. "Remember. You are safe. What you are seeing and hearing—it is all happening to the people in the movie. It will not upset you." He waited until Anna Mae's breathing returned to normal, then asked: "Who did the man rape?"

"The older woman."

"The woman told that to the girl? She told the girl that a man raped her?"

"Yes."

"Very good," said the doctor. "You are still very relaxed. You smell the flowers as you watch the movie. It's an interesting movie but it doesn't affect you in any way."

"The girl is very upset," said Anna Mae without emotion. "She's asking the woman to repeat what she said. And the woman is saying that when she was fifteen, a man named Walter raped her. She tells the girl that Walter is her father—the girl's father."

Dr. Rhukov felt a surge of outrage and had to struggle to keep the trembling out of his voice. "You're doing fine, Anna Mae..."

"The girl is hysterical." Anna Mae's face turned white.

With skilled pacing of his words, Dr. Rhukov quickly pulled Anna Mae out of the scene, sending her back to the field of flowers. When she appeared to be relaxed again, he guided her back to the movie and asked her to continue.

"The girl's running out of the house." A pink blush returned to Anna Mae's face. "She's running to the bus stop. She's crying. The bus comes right away. Now she's wiping her eyes so the people on the bus won't see her crying. She's found a seat in the middle of the bus. She's thinking about what that woman said. She's looking at the other people. She wonders if they can tell how upset she is."

Not wanting to tire Anna Mae or have her slip back into first person, Dr. Rhukov talked her back into the soft summer breeze and the sweet scent of flowers. He studied the features of the girl he had come to care about almost as a daughter. The days, the weeks, the months in jail had washed the color out of her once glowing complexion. The luster that once shone in her golden hair had dissolved into a dull dirty blond. And the sadness he once saw in her had given way to defeat.

He looked at his watch. It was time to move her forward, back to the movie strategy that kept her strong emotions at bay. He guided 'the girl' back to the bus. Anna Mae told Dr. Rhukov that when the girl got off the bus she forgot to pay her fare and the driver called her back. Then the girl in the movie was walking through town, past the pool hall where someone named JD called out to her. But the girl was too upset to stop and talk. The doctor listened intently as Anna Mae described how the girl hurried up Vickroy Street Hill, went into the house. She was disappointed when she saw the man named Walter sleeping on the couch. She went upstairs to her bedroom.

Anna Mae began making the motions of brushing her hair and then dropped the imaginary brush, saying; "The girl hears something banging downstairs. She's nervous but that doesn't stop her. She's going to confront that Walter person. She's going to ask him if what the woman said was true—that he is her father.

"She's going down the steps." At this point Anna Mae laughed a little. "Her knees are like rubber so she's hanging onto the banister." She stopped talking and seemed to be listening.

Dr. Rhukov was hesitant to interrupt Anna Mae's thought process. But Anna Mae appeared to be frozen in time so he risked the question. "What's happening?"

"It sounds as though a glass broke," she said, her voice shaky. "The girl's wondering if Walter is drunk again. But she doesn't care. If he dares touch her she's going to go after him. He beats her, ya' know. But if he's drunk enough she thinks she can get the best of him."

Again she stopped talking and Dr. Rhukov gave her a gentle reminder that it was all just a movie.

Anna Mae nodded. "A movie. A movie..."

"Yes," he assured her. "It's just a movie."

"A movie," she repeated. Suddenly her whole body tensed. She shrieked, "No! No it's not! It's not! It's real! My God. Oh my God," she gasped and leaped from the recliner. Frantically she scrambled around the edges of the small room until she reached a corner where she fell into a crouch, covered her eyes and began screaming.

The doctor shouted, "What do you see, Anna Mae?" Guards rushed into the room. "Leave her alone!" the doctor shrieked. "Don't touch her!"

Without taking his eyes from Anna Mae, the doctor pushed one of the guards away from the form that huddled in the corner. "Anna Mae! Tell me! Why are you screaming? What do you see? Tell me, Anna Mae!"

Like a wild animal, Anna Mae tried to crawl up the wall as the guards pushed the doctor aside and lunged at her flailing arms. Finally, one cuff locked shut.

Dr. Rhukov crawled on his knees until he was next to her. "Tell me," he pleaded, "Anna Mae! What do you see?"

The doctor winced as the guard yanked her arms backward, snapped on the second cuff and yanked her to her feet. Dr. Rhukov, out of breath, leaned back into the corner. He reached into his pocket and pulled out a hypodermic needle. "She needs a sedative," he said, removing the cap. He struggled to stand as quickly as his arthritic knees would allow. The guards pushed Anna Mae down on the edge of the recliner. Dr. Rhukov looked into Anna Mae's tear streaked face.

"I didn't remember," she whimpered.

"No," he said, gently pushing up her sleeve and inserting the needle, "You didn't remember."

CHAPTER FORTY-FIVE

February 8, 1971 – Monday

"All rise!" The bailiff's voice boomed across the packed courtroom: "This court is now in session. The honorable Allen B. Wittier presiding. The Commonwealth of Pennsylvania versus Anna Mae McBride. Case number 5390: Murder in the First Degree."

Anna Mae sat at the defense table, her head down and barely breathing.

"Keep your head up," Ivan whispered.

Anna Mae struggled to straighten her back and lift her head. She wore a plain beige dress and her hair was loosely pulled back by a wide beige band. She had waited forever for this crucial moment when the trial would begin. Last Friday's jury selection had taken all day, and included a grade school teacher—tiny and straight laced, a steel worker with skin the color of oatmeal, a cold, unsmiling business man in a black suit, and a homemaker that Ivan said reminded him of a Bavarian bar maid. Anna Mae had watched as each was selected—these strangers who held her life in their hands. Back in her cell she had prayed every night that they would believe that she honestly didn't remember anything.

That morning, Ivan told her that he finally succeeded in getting the judge to throw out the crime scene photos as evidence, deeming them unnecessarily inflammatory. She had grown to have confidence in the lanky man whose brown eyes sparkled when he got excited. She looked at the table where Ivan's hands rested on a sheaf of papers, and for the first time noticed his long fingers and Harvard ring. She thought herself lucky to have him.

"Ladies and gentleman of the jury..."

Anna Mae took a deep breath as Assistant District Attorney Tom Simon began his opening statement.

"...my name is Thomas G. Simon. I'm the Assistant District Attorney representing the Commonwealth, which means, good people, that I represent you, the people of Pennsylvania."

Short, trim, pompous, and wearing the obvious auburn wig, ADA Tom Simon strutted before the jury like a courting peacock. Ivan Hammerstein silently drummed the fingers of his Harvard hand on the defense table while Anna Mae listened in stunned disbelief as the district attorney walked the jury through his version of what happened on that life-changing day of Wednesday, October 14th, 1970.

"...and that day, at her mother's house, when she was told the shocking news that Walter Lipinski...the man who she thought was her uncle...the man who had given her a home and his heart...the man who had labored untiringly to support her with back breaking work in the unforgiving heat of the mill...the man she blamed for every disturbing detail of her miserable life and the man she absolutely hated—was, in fact, her father. And that same day last October, she went home in a fit of rage, took an ax and hacked him to death."

Ivan placed a supporting hand on Anna Mae's ice-cold arm. "Keep your head up."

"And you will hear testimony from good citizens of this valley community, Anna Mae McBride's own friends, and even Sarah Lipinski, the defendant's aunt and Walter's grieving widow—the woman who raised Anna Mae McBride, that the defendant, McBride, is indeed capable of this despicable crime. The prosecution contends that Anna Mae McBride does indeed remember every last lethal swing of that bloody ax!

"Ladies and gentlemen of the jury, good and honest citizens of this state, you will recognize Anna Mae McBride for what she really is—an absolute liar! And you will find her guilty of premeditated murder. That is murder in the first degree!"

As Thomas G. Simon walked with arrogant casualness back to the prosecution table, Anna Mae could feel the accusation in the eyes of the jury. When she glanced in their direction, she saw the steelworker, arms folded across his chest, glaring at her.

"Don't look at them," Ivan snapped. "Keep your head up. Look straight ahead. Good. Now stay like that until I get back!"

Ivan Hammerstein swooped out of his chair and in a second he was standing before the jury where he waited until all eyes were on him.

"She didn't do it. And you," he said with a sweeping wave of his hand, indicating the twelve people who leaned forward to hear what the defense attorney had to say, "...ladies and gentlemen of the jury, all through this trial, you remember—the defendant, Anna Mae McBride, did not do it! Don't let any paid psychiatrist convince you that she remembers anything. Because she doesn't. She saw something. More than likely she saw the person who murdered her uncle. But Anna Mae McBride does not remember what she saw. Psychiatrists call it Traumatic Amnesia. Remember those words: Traumatic Amnesia. Walter Lipinski was savagely attacked and bludgeoned to death with an ax. And this young, sweet and innocent girl," he turned to look at Anna Mae who was still facing forward exactly as instructed, "this unworldly and church going young woman witnessed that attack. And there is not a psychiatrist alive, at least not a good one, who wouldn't agree that it is within the range of normal human behavior to repress—to block out…such a shocking and bloody crime.

"The term is Traumatic Amnesia. Anna Mae saw something horrible and she does not remember what she saw. Furthermore, any shoddy evidence the prosecution presents will reek of reasonable doubt. There were no witnesses. There is no murder weapon. When the police investigated this crime they jumped to a conclusion and stayed with it, blatantly ignoring any suggestion to pursue another avenue. And so I urge you, throughout this trial, remember—Anna Mae McBride did not kill the man she knew as her uncle. She did not murder Walter Lipinski."

Defense Attorney Ivan Hammerstein paused just long enough to let his last words sink in. "Thank you," he said, then he returned to the defense table to resume his seat beside Anna Mae.

"Present your case, Counselor," said the judge.

Assistant District Attorney, Thomas G. Simon called his first witness and Becky McBride walked from the back of the courtroom to be sworn in. Her dark blond hair was neatly trimmed and she wore a navy blue suit with a white blouse. Anna Mae, although forewarned, was heartsick that her mother was testifying for the prosecution. "State your full name, please."

"Rebecca Sadie McBride. They call me Becky."

"May I call you Becky?"

"Yes."

"Thank you," said Simon. And then turning to the judge, "Let the record show that Miss McBride is a hostile witness."

Anna Mae whispered to Ivan, "What's that mean?"

He whispered back, "She doesn't want to testify for Simon."

"Miss McBride, do you see your daughter sitting in the courtroom?"

"Yes."

"Please point her out to the jury."

For the next eight minutes, Tom Simon asked Anna Mae's mother a series of questions that brought her to the moment when she told her daughter that Walter was her father. "And how did she react when you told her?"

"She was shocked."

"Would you say she was angry?"

"No."

"But she walked out, didn't she? She stormed out of the house, didn't she? She was furious, wasn't she?"

Ivan leaped to his feet. "Objection!"

"Sustained. Careful Simon," admonished Judge Wittier. "The witness already said that the defendant was shocked, not angry. The jury will disregard the questions."

"Is it normal," asked Simon as though he had not been reprimanded, "for your daughter to just walk out of your house without as much as a goodbye?"

"No."

"Then she was upset."

"I guess."

"Would you say she had good reason to be upset?"

"Yes."

"And she was probably angry wasn't she..."

Ivan stopped midway between sitting and standing as Judge Wittier issued another warning.

"No more questions," said Simon in a sarcastic tone.

"Redirect?" asked the judge.

Ivan stood up. "What was your daughter's demeanor when she left your house on October 14th?"

"She was shocked," said Becky.

"Thank you!" Ivan sat down.

CHAPTER FORTY-SIX

The next morning the courtroom was packed. Tom Simon had gone to a great deal of trouble to make himself look good. He wore a blue suit and his maroon silk tie, contrasted nicely with his tan shirt. Ivan, on the other hand, dressed in his usual gray pinstripe, his jacket hanging loosely from his broad shoulders and the sleeves a smidgen too short.

The jury stumbled around each other in an effort to claim the same seats they had occupied the previous day. The court officer told them that from now on they were to form an appropriate line so that their entrance into the courtroom would be more orderly.

Anna Mae's beige dress was wrinkled and she had dark circles under her eyes. Back in her cell, a kindly matron had attempted to cover them with makeup. It helped some, but not enough. With her trembling hands clutched under the table she looked at District Attorney Tom Simon. The judge told him to call his first witness.

Jake Jeffrey, a large man with big teeth and no neck, walked to the stand. His tweed jacket, at least one size too small, pulled tightly across his back and wouldn't button in front. As he was sworn in, he stood as erect as his beer belly would allow and pursed his lips in a self-important smirk that caused Tom Simon to cringe and Ivan Hammerstein to gloat.

After Jeffrey was sworn in and seated, he answered the usual preliminaries, including the fact that he was a bus driver for the Pittsburgh Port Authority.

"Do you remember the defendant boarding your bus last October 14th at approximately 1:05 P.M.?"

"Yes."

"And what, if anything, did you notice about the defendant?"

"She seemed mad."

"Mad as in 'angry?'" Simon looked at the jury.

"Yes."

"And who did she seem to be mad at?" Simon asked, still looking at the jury.

"Objection," said Hammerstein. "The witness is stating the defendant's mood as though it were a fact. Unless he had a definite way of knowing how she felt, this testimony is bogus."

"The witness, "Simon countered, "said Anna Mae appeared to be mad. He didn't say it was a certainty."

"I'll allow it," said the judge, then looked hard at Simon. "But make sure your witness understands he is only to testify to what he knows, not what he thinks he knows."

Simon turned back to his witness. "So what made you think she was angry?"

Jake Jeffery shrugged his massive shoulders.

"Excuse me?"

Jeffery looked at his shoes.

"Answer the question," said the judge.

He looked up and said, "I don't know."

"What don't you know?" asked Simon.

"What you said. I mean that she was mad," said Jeffery shifting his enormous bulk in the witness chair.

"Was her face red?"

"No."

"Did she say something to one of the other passengers? Could you hear it in her voice?"

"I ah—no."

"But when she boarded the bus she was angry."

"Yes."

"So whatever made her angry had to have happened before she got on your bus."

"Yes."

"You were sure she was angry because you could see it on her face?"

"Objection! This 'angry' crap is becoming redundant!"

"Sustained," Judge Wittier snapped. "Get on with it!"

"What happened when Anna Mae McBride got off the bus?" Simon asked.

Jeffery frowned, "Who?"

Laughter erupted in the courtroom. Wittier slammed his gavel and Simon rephrased the question. "What happened when the defendant," Simon indicated Anna Mae with a wave of his hand. "What happened when she got off the bus?"

Jeffery leaned into the microphone. "She forgot to pay."

"Do you know why she forgot to pay?"

"Objection!" said Ivan standing. "This witness could not possibly know if the defendant was angry and he sure as hell couldn't know why she forgot to pay."

"Sustained," said the judge. "And watch your language."

"What was Anna Mae's—the defendant's attitude when you called her back to pay. You did call her back, didn't you?"

"Yes, I did, sir. The Port Authority can't afford to..."

"Just answer the question," Simon snapped. And before Jeffrey could forget the question, Simon asked it again. "What was the defendant's attitude when you called her back to pay?"

"She seemed angry about something."

Ivan Hammerstein dropped his head on the defense table as though he had passed out. Tom Simon said, "Thank you! No more questions," and walked back to the prosecution table.

Hammerstein, his head still on the defense table, looked at Anna Mae and said, "Watch this." He then stood up and walked over to the witness who fidgeted nervously. Ivan, thoughtfully massaging the bridge of his nose with his thumb and forefinger, said, "You stated that when Anna Mae McBride boarded your bus she appeared angry?"

"Yes." Jeffery's self-important smirk had dissolved into perspiration.

"When was that?"

"Excuse me?"

"When did Anna Mae McBride get on your bus?"

The bus driver looked desperately at Tom Simon.

"You don't know the exact day?"

"I can't remember the exact day."

"But you do remember that she seemed angry."

"Yes."

"How many people who get on your bus seem angry?"

Jeffery shrugged his shoulders.

"How many?"

Jeffery was silent.

"Answer the question," said Judge Wittier.

"I don't know how many people are angry when they get on the bus!" Jeffery stared at the lock of black hair hanging over the tall defense attorney's forehead. "I have to watch the traffic! A good bus driver always keeps his eyes on the road!"

"That's very commendable," said Ivan, then waited until Jeffery squared his shoulders and smiled at the jury. "How many people forget to pay their fare?"

Jeffery looked back at Ivan. "I don't know."

"How many people who forget to pay their fare are just thinking about something else, maybe even something pleasant?"

"I don't know."

"Do you mean that you don't know what they're thinking about?"

"No. I mean. I don't know."

"So you really don't know what they're feeling. Is that correct?"

"Objection," shouted Simon. "He's trying to confuse the witness."

"Overruled," said Wittier with a slight smile.

"You are an intelligent man, Mr. Jeffery," Ivan said. "You have to take some pretty difficult tests in order to qualify for a position with the Port Authority, don't you?"

"Yes."

"And it is possible that the defendant forgot to pay her fare because she was in deep thought, isn't it?"

"Yes. It's possible," said Jeffery.

Hammerstein brushed the hair off his forehead. "No more questions."

CHAPTER FORTY-SEVEN

It was noon. Judge Wittier called for a lunch break. Forty-five minutes later the jury filed back into the courtroom in an orderly manner. The next witness was sworn in.

"Please state your name," said the bailiff.

"JD."

"Your full name."

"Jeremiah Dakin Jones."

The bailiff held out the Bible. "Do you swear to tell the truth, the whole truth, and nothing but the truth, so help you God?"

"I do."

"You may be seated."

In one sweep, JD propped his crutches against the Judge's bench and swiveled himself into the witness chair. Tom Simon approached him.

"Jeremiah Dakin," said Simon, smiling. "An unusual name."

JD didn't answer. He looked around for the black District Attorney, Lester Young, who had talked to him a month before. Young had been easy to talk to and JD had talked freely, feeling he could rely on Lester Young not to twist what he said. JD looked at Tom Simon. He saw coldness, and malice in those eyes.

"Jeremiah," Simon began, "may I call you JD?"

"Mr. Jones," said JD.

"Pardon me?"

"I said, call me Mr. Jones."

Simon bristled. "Mr. Jones. What is your relationship to the defendant?"

"We're friends," said JD.

"Before we get into the friendship, I'd like to ask you a few questions about yourself."

"Shoot!"

"If I'm not being too personal, Mr. Jones, would you tell the jury how you acquired your tragic disability?"

"Some crazy doctor cut off my leg."

"Isn't it true, Mr. Jones that you were fighting for our country in Vietnam when you stepped on a land mine?"

"I sure as hell stepped on something."

There was laughter in the courtroom and Tom Simon waited patiently until it was quiet.

"Isn't it true," said Simon, "that you, in fact, crossed the 17th parallel and were running along a rice paddy south of Dong Hoi to rescue a fallen comrade?"

"Is that where I was? Shit! I thought I was in Georgia."

More laughter.

"Mr. Jones," said Judge Wittier, "Stop trying to be cute and just answer the questions."

"Yes, Your Honor." JD, aware that the district attorney was trying to evoke the jury's sympathies, was determined to hinder his efforts any way he could.

"Isn't it true," said Simon, "that you have been awarded a Bronze Star for your bravery?"

"Yes," said JD. He hadn't mentioned the medal to Lester. Simon had done his homework.

"I think it's marvelous that a young man like yourself would volunteer to fight for his country," said Simon.

JD looked at Hammerstein. Why was he just sitting there? Isn't he going to stop this line of questioning?

Hammerstein made no move to object. JD looked back at Simon and his self-assured, smug demeanor. JD knew that look. It reminded him of someone—someone he didn't like.

"I was drafted," said JD, willing to bet that the prosecutor already knew that and was stupid enough to think that JD would try to enhance his image by agreeing that he volunteered.

But Simon wouldn't let the hero thing go. "And to think you actually risked your own life to save another soldier."

JD stared hard at the district attorney's hair. Something was odd about that color and it was way too thick.

"Mr. Jones, you said that you and Anna Mae McBride were friends."

"We are."

"Were you always friends?"

"No."

"How long have you known the defendant?"

"About eight years."

"And eight years ago you were friends with her cousin, Stanley Lipinski, were you not?"

"I was."

"And was the defendant, Anna Mae McBride, living in the same house as her cousin, Stanley Lipinski?"

"Yes."

"And the murder victim, Walter Lipinski, was Stanley's father, was he not?"

"Yes."

Simon continued the questions until the Lipinski household members were clearly placed under the same roof. Then he said, "Now think back, Mr. Jones, to Friday, August 11, 1965—to Stanley's sixteenth birthday party."

JD frowned, exaggerating deep, deep thought. "Got it!"

Judge Wittier lifted his half-glasses to his white hair and turned to look down at JD, disapproval clear on his face. Tom Simon loosened his silk tie, walked back to the prosecution's table to check his notes, then asked from a distance, "Who was at that party?"

"Excuse me?"

"I asked you," Simon said in a louder voice, "Who was at Stanley's sixteenth birthday party?"

JD shrugged. "Miscellaneous entities."

"That's enough!" roared the judge. "Mr. Jones, if you cannot control your urge to make a mockery of this most serious murder trial, you'll be cited for contempt of court. Is that clear?"

"Yes, Your Honor."

"Now answer the question!"

"There were a lot of different people at that party," said JD.

"Could you name a few?" asked Tom Simon.

"Objection," said Ivan Hammerstein, standing. "Relevance?"

"Counselor," said the judge to Simon, "Just where are you going with this?"

"I intend to demonstrate to this jury, Your Honor, that Miss McBride is not the sweet, soft spoken girl the defense will claim she is."

"Well get on with it," snapped the judge.

"What about my objection?" asked Hammerstein.

"Overruled. Sit down."

"There was an incident between the defendant and someone at that party, was there not, Mr. Jones?"

"Yes."

"Will you please tell the jury what happened?"

"Well...there was this nerd that tried to put the make on Anna Mae and she cussed him out." JD saw a blush in Tom Simon's cheeks that wasn't there before. "Stanley kicked the shit out of him. That's all that happened."

"All?" said Simon dryly. "Didn't the defendant, Anna Mae McBride, fly into a rage? Didn't she use every swear word in the book? Wasn't she totally out of control? Didn't she..."

"Objection!"

"Sustained."

"I apologize Your Honor," said Simon with fake humility. "If the jury will please excuse the profanity," Simon continued, "didn't she call this young man, George Siminoski—who happened to wear glasses. Didn't the defendant, Anna Mae McBride, call him, among other repulsive names—a four-eyed fuckin' pervert?"

"Yes." said JD. He studied district attorney; the weird way he walked when he paced back and forth, the way he frowned, the way his forced smile wasn't reflected in the cold animosity in his eyes. Who was this guy? And what did Tom Simon have against him?

"Answer the question," said the judge.

"What question?"

"Ask it again, counselor," said Judge Wittier.

The district attorney sounded as though he was making an effort to keep his voice even and businesslike. "Didn't Anna Mae McBride call George Siminoski..." JD saw Simon gulp. "...an idiot ass-hole?"

"Yes. She did call him that. The guy was a creep. She was just a kid. Thirteen, I think. And that geek cornered her in the hallway and tried to feel her up."

At this point JD was blatantly staring at Tom Simon's face. The district attorney averted his eyes then turned and walked back to the prosecution's table. After taking a few deep breaths he turned back to the witness, calmly asking, "On a scale of one to ten, how angry was the defendant? Ten being the angriest."

JD did not want to answer that question.

"Remember, you are under oath," said Simon.

JD looked over at the trembling girl in the beige dress. She stared back at him—a vacant look in her eyes.

"Answer the question," said the judge. "On a scale of one..."

"No one could blame her," JD said softly. "She was a ten."

The judge then stated that it was getting late and that the examination of Jeremiah Dakin Jones would continue the next day at nine o'clock. JD manned his crutches and hopped down from the witness stand. He passed the sheriff whose automatic pistol rode high on his hip, then paused at the prosecution's table where he took one last long look at District Attorney Tom Simon and said under his breath, "Oh, my God!"

CHAPTER FORTY-EIGHT

Anna Mae pushed the phone tight against her ear and looked through the wire embedded glass at JD. "You've gotta be kidding!"

"I'm dead serious," he said. "I think the DA...Tom Simon is really George Siminoski. Didn't you see Simon's face when I said George was a nerd?"

"No..."

"And that weird little walk—didn't you notice that?"

"No," she said. "Didn't George go to Duquesne University's Law School?"

"He did. Have you seen him since he left the valley eight years ago?"

"I haven't seen him since the night of the party after I left—when he attacked me in front of Vinko's."

"He did what?"

"He hid his car in the alley behind Vinko's then jumped out at me when I walked by. He said that someday he was going to 'get me.' I haven't seen him since. He wasn't even at his mother's funeral. At least not while I was there."

"So it could be him," said JD as he winced and rubbed the thigh of his amputated leg. "Damn thing still hurts!"

Anna Mae, too involved in her own problems to appreciate JD's pain, said, "But he can't do this trial if he knows me, can he?"

"I think he can," said JD. "But he threatened you, and that's prejudicial. But let's not jump the gun. After he's through with me on the witness stand, I'll do some investigating. Meanwhile, don't say anything to Hammerstein. If it is George, and things are going bad for you, I think Ivan can call a mistrial. But if we're winning, well, the hell with it. Did anyone hear George threaten you?"

"Joey Barns did. He was right there."

"Well, if that DA is George, he's not going to be able to think as clearly as an objective lawyer would, especially since he can't have had that much experience. He might be his own worst enemy."

Anna Mae thought about that for a few moments and then said, "I'm sorry about your leg. I didn't know it still hurts."

"It doesn't hurt all the time. It's the damn weather. It's freezing out there."

"It's cold in here too. This jail has to be over a hundred years old."

"I better go," said JD, "Angelo's waiting to talk to you. I like him. He's a great guy."

When JD got up to leave, a fat woman in a scraggly, brown fur coat moved over and grabbed the phone.

"She's not done," said JD balancing on his crutches. "She has another visitor."

The lady looked at Anna Mae and said, "Shit!"

*   *   *

Wednesday 2:30 AM

In the dark, on the cot in her cold and lonely cell, Anna Mae lay unable to sleep. Where was her mother? Why didn't she come to visit? Why was she not in the courtroom? Was she drinking again?

She turned on her side, curling herself into a ball, pulling the scratchy blanket over her cold nose. David was such a support. He had been to see her at least once a week and told her if she wanted to call home, he would pay for the collect call with his paper route money. When Sarah answered the phone Anna Mae never knew what to say. Most of the time, before Sarah was put in the position to accept or reject the call, Anna Mae hung up.

Sarah was grieving. She had waited so long for her husband to get out of jail. And now this. Sarah was at the trial every day. But she always sat near the back of the courtroom. She never came to visit.

Does she hate me? Does she think I killed Walter? Lord, why did you let this happen? What did I ever do to deserve this? Why don't you help me?

What kind of a God are you? I'm sick of praying— tired of begging. Maybe I should go to the devil for help. Maybe he'll care. Because you don't. You just don't care!

Father John had been to see her on Sunday. He said that God is good and that she should trust Him. But she told Father John—came right out and said it: God isn't good! A loving God, a God who really cared, wouldn't let bad things happen to good people. Father John said God wasn't responsible for what happened, that we all live in a fallen world—out of Eden was the way he put it. Anna Mae wouldn't buy it. She was mad at God. She no longer trusted Him.

That night, when Anna Mae was asleep, she spent her dream staring at the pieces of the broken cross. She didn't want to fix it. It was just a pile of big sticks. That's all. A pile of big, dirty sticks!

*   *   *

After the lunch break, Olga Nikovich took the stand. Her pulled back hair was now silvery white, and she wore a stylish, maroon, two piece dress. When she hoisted her short body into the witness chair, her feet dangled an inch from the floor. She folded her pudgy hands in her lap and looked Tom Simon directly in the eyes.

Olga was not the least bit intimidated by the prosecutor's aggressive approach as he hurried her through her relationship with the Lipinskis in general and Anna Mae in specific. In her broken English, she blocked his every effort to twist her words. "She is good girl, Annie is. She don't hurt nobody and to me she is always a sweetheart."

Simon grunted as though Olga's last comment was ludicrous. He then said, "Now let's go back to Tuesday, October 14th. Where were you that afternoon around two o'clock?"

"In my kitchen I was, making strudels."

Simon stepped aside so the jury had full view of the witness. "Now tell the court what you heard and what you did that day."

Olga glanced at the jury. The schoolteacher, her head slightly tilted, listened intently. The mill worker leaned forward, a look of empathy in his eyes. Olga looked back to the little man who stood before her. His puffed-up posture reminded her of a picture she once saw of the czar.

"Answer the question," said the judge.

Olga's attention slipped back to the present. She looked straight ahead, beyond Simon to the packed courtroom. So many people!

Tom Simon opened his mouth, but before he could speak she straightened her shoulders and began to talk. "I was stretching the strudel dough across mine kitchen table when this horrible screamink—I heard it. My hands, they went," she demonstrated a quick flip of her wrists. "A big hole in the dough, I made it. But I didn't know about that hole. I yelled, 'Pete! Peter! We haf to go and see what is somethink bad happens next door.' Peter, my husband, he shouldn't hear so well maybe the screamink, so he hollered at me, 'Don't you go get into someone's business!'

"But, I call him again. 'Peter Nikovich you come here right now!' But he didn't, so I tink—the hell vith you, and by myself I go next door. Poor Annie! She was screamink so loud and I go through the back door and I was going to find Annie and I almost tripped—he was right there, down on the kitchen floor—that was Walter, but Annie was screamink. So I went around Walter on the floor and poor Annie under the steps. I tried to get hold of her. She was pushing and pushing me—like this." Another demonstration.

"And screamink! Like…like…like…I don't know. And she don't stop. She hides in the hall, under the steps, so I was there. 'Annie! Stop screamink,' I said it. Then she was crying and the police came right in the house. And that is what happened and what I saw."

Simon waited a few seconds, then asked, "Was the back door open or closed when you reached the house?"

"I don't remember," said Olga, shaken by having to recall the scene.

"There are two doors at the back of the house, are there not? A storm door and the main door, correct?"

Olga mumbled something as she rummaged through her purse for her embroidered handkerchief, which she used to wipe her eyes. Simon, too wrapped up in what he was trying to accomplish, asked a bit louder, "At the back of the Lipinski house, there is a storm door and the main door, correct?"

Olga ran her wrinkled fingers over the lace on the edge of the handkerchief. "One door that in the summer it had the screen, and the other one."

"The door that used to have the screen, you had to pull that open, didn't you?"

Olga nodded.

The judge gently reminded her, "Answer 'yes' or 'no,' so that the court reporter can write it down."

Olga looked at the court reporter whose fingers had been flying over some keys, but she was not writing anything. Frowning, Olga said, "Yes, I pull it open."

"And the other door, it was closed tight, wasn't it?"

"I don't remember."

"Now think hard." Simon emphasized every word. "Was the main back door closed? Not the one that used to have the screen—the other one—the main door. Did you have to open it when you were going to see what all the screamink...screaming was about?"

"That door, I told you, I don't remember anythink about it. You can ask me fifty times about that door and I don't remember."

Simon walked back to the prosecution table to check his notes and then gathering a few, walked back to the witness.

"What was the condition of the kitchen when you entered the Lipinski house?" Simon asked.

"Walter was on the floor."

"And the rest of the kitchen? How did it look?"

"I don't remember."

"Was there blood?"

Tom Simon impatiently waited for a reply that didn't come. "You said that you saw Walter on the floor," he pressed on. "Did you, at that time, know he was dead?"

Olga straightened her shoulders and replied, "I thought he vas drunk."

A snicker from the courtroom quickly came and went.

"Did you, at that time, see any blood?" he asked again.

"I don't look for blood. Poor Annie vas screamink!"

"Did you notice that Anna Mae's clothes were soaked with blood?"

"Objection! Leading!"

"Sustained. Rephrase that question, counselor."

"Was there anything on Anna Mae's clothes?"

"Blood."

"Do you remember seeing blood on her hands?"

Olga wiped her eyes with her handkerchief. "No. Only on da clothes."

Simon looked thoughtfully at the jury. Olga looked to see what he was looking at. She saw compassion in the steelworker's eyes. The schoolteacher was glaring at Tom Simon.

"Your Honor, I have no more questions at this time. However, I would like to reserve the right to recall this witness at a later date."

"Noted," said Judge Wittier. "Mr. Hammerstein?"

Ivan Hammerstein approached Olga Nikovich while buttoning his pinstripe jacket. He looked warmly at the witness as he asked, "Are you absolutely sure you do not remember that the back door was wide open?"

"Objection! He's leading the witness!"

"Sustained," said the judge. "The jury will disregard that question." And then to Hammerstein, "You know better than that! Rephrase the question."

"Was the door wide open?"

Olga sighed. "I said it. I don't remember!"

"That's fine, Mrs. Nikovich. I have one more question for you."

Olga waited.

"Did the strudel turn out good?"

"It had a big hole. I trew that dough away."

CHAPTER FORTY-NINE

Olga wriggled forward out of the witness chair until her feet touched the floor. She then stood up, hooked her purse in the crook of her arm, and marched up the aisle to the middle of the courtroom where Peter was sitting. A young man in a sport coat got up so Olga could sit next to her husband.

At that same moment, the doors at the back of the courtroom flew open. Officer Joe Murphy walked down the aisle in full dress uniform with his shoulders back, his head held high, and his hat tucked under his arm. At the front of the courtroom, his hand on the Bible and standing as stiff as The Castle Guard, he swore to tell the truth. After checking to assure his tie was straight, he sat down.

Simon quickly led his new witness through the necessary preliminaries. He then took him to the day of the murder: "Tell the court what happened when you were on duty on October 14, 1970."

"Officer Zacowitz and I had just completed an accident call. Actually, it was only a fender bender. Some people make such a big deal of these things," he said, absently running his fingers over the silver emblem on his cap. "Anyway, we had just returned to the squad car when we got a call over the radio that there was a disturbance at 927 Vickroy Street. I recognized the address immediately. That was the Lipinski house at the top of the hill. I also remembered that Walter Lipinski had just gotten out of prison. I knew we better get going fast. I snapped on the siren and we took off."

"What did you see as you approached the house?"

"There were several neighbors standing around outside."

"Now describe what happened when you entered the house."

"I went in first," said Murphy. "Someone was screaming like a wild woman. Someone else was telling her to calm down. From the front door, I could see up the steps to the second floor and down the hall to the kitchen. Olga Nikovich was standing in the hallway near the back of the steps. I approached her. That's when I saw the young woman on the floor behind the steps acting all hysterical."

"Is the person you saw in the courtroom?"

Murphy pointed to Anna Mae. "She's right over there."

"Let the notes show that the witness has pointed to the defendant."

Anna Mae shuddered, afraid that what the officer was about to describe would throw her back into shocking memories and she would go berserk in court. *And what if she did kill Walter and it came out in front of all these people? In front of Sarah!* She tried not to listen to Officer Murphy's description of Walter's bludgeoned body as it lay face down in a pool of blood, feet pointing in the direction of the hallway.

When the district attorney displayed an evidence bag containing blood-splattered clothing, Anna Mae asked her attorney, "Are those mine?"

"Be quiet!" snapped Hammerstein.

Her lawyer's harsh reproof destroyed what little comfort she felt by his presence and she closed her eyes, wanting to disappear, wanting to die. As Officer Murphy continued his testimony, Anna Mae was assailed with a fear she had not felt while listening to the other witnesses. Maybe it was because he was the first person on the stand that was not a hostile witness and that he seemed to revel in this limelight. In addition, she felt that for whatever reason, he disliked her intensely. The pain in her abdomen returned and she wished she had accepted the anti-acid offered by the guard, Harriet Clauson. She closed her eyes and placed her hand on her stomach.

Ivan jabbed her with his bony elbow. "Open your eyes! Lift up your head! Pay attention!"

She forced herself to do as she was told.

"...so I put in a call to homicide."

"Where was your partner, Officer Zacowitz, when all this was going on?"

"He was a few minutes behind me. I think he tripped on the front step and hurt his ankle. Anyway, when he finally did get into the house, he looked after the old lady—I mean Mrs. Nako...Nako..."

"Nikovich," said Simon.

"That's right. Mrs. Nikovich."

"Officer Murphy," said Simon in a tone that indicated a change of direction. "Was there another time in your career when you encountered the defendant, Anna Mae McBride?"

"Yes, when she gave her cousin, Stanley, the drugs that killed him."

"OBJECTION!" Hammerstein flew across the twelve feet to the bench and skidded to a halt in front of Simon. "What the hell are you talking about?"

"Like you didn't know!" barked Simon.

The air was now charged with tension. Judge Wittier glared at the two attorneys and said something that Anna Mae couldn't hear. She felt the jury's accusing gaze as she watched the animated discussion before the bench. She took deep breaths, trying to stop her stomach from hurting and her head from spinning.

"My chambers!" snapped Judge Wittier. He then made it clear to the jury that they were to completely disregard Officer Murphy's last remark. After that the judge checked his watch and adjourned for the day. Ivan told Anna Mae to go with the sheriff. Then he walked away, leaving her to struggle with the fear that weakened her knees and caused her heart to pound. She was grateful to the sheriff who allowed her to lean on his arm as she left the courtroom.

*   *   *

Judge Wittier took his seat behind his huge mahogany desk. On the other side of the desk, seated in a straight back chair, Ivan Hammerstein felt as though he'd been hit in the head by a two by four. A few feet away, in two comfortable upholstered chairs, Tom Simon sat next to Officer Murphy. Ivan Hammerstein glared at them. What the hell had Murphy been talking about? What did that cop know that he should have known?

Judge Wittier looked at Hammerstein. "You didn't know about this?"

"No!"

"It's not in the police file," said Simon.

Hammerstein could barely contain his fury. "How in the hell can he say that in court when there's nothing to substantiate his claim? And even if it's true, which I seriously doubt—it's outrageously inadmissible!"

Ignoring Hammerstein's outburst, Simon addressed the judge: "I intend to use it to establish the defendant's psychotic tendencies."

"My client has a clean record. There is nothing..."

Simon interrupted: "It may not be on record. But I can prove..."

Hammerstein stood up, towered over Simon and shouted, "What you proved is that you're an ass-hole and this is good cause for a mistrial."

"He's right—about the mistrial," said the Judge. Then looking up at Hammerstein, "Is that what you want, counselor? A mistrial?"

Ivan was beside himself with frustration. He paced before the desk. "If you will tell the jury," he said to the Judge, "that there was no basis for Officer Murphy's remark and that he has incurred a hefty fine for his misleading and slanderous remark, I'll agree to continue with this trial."

"Done!" said the judge. "And as for you, Simon, if you allow one more witness to speak so appallingly out of turn, I'll throw you both in jail!"

Ivan Hammerstein was not completely appeased; however, to stop the trial at this point may be more than Anna Mae could cope with. In addition, the jury may be so outraged by Murphy's erroneous testimony and the DA's part in it, Tom Simon's credibility might go down the drain.

He decided not to pursue it further with Anna Mae. The kid was on the verge of falling apart and she didn't need her own attorney questioning her past. He had personally checked her record and there was nothing in any police report. That was good enough for Ivan Hammerstein.

$$* \quad * \quad *$$

Wednesday, 6:45 P.M.

Anna Mae looked through the wire embedded glass, seeing, but not seeing Angelo. She was tired, angry, and horribly discouraged. Ivan had talked to her at length about Officer Murphy's shocking remarks, but even though Ivan had made his best effort, it had taken a great deal of time to settle her down—somewhat.

Now Angelo was rattling on about the disputed Lipinski back door. The issue as to whether Olga found it open or closed was pertinent to the case. Anna Mae heard nothing he said. She was thinking about Chocolate, who had just been sentenced to three to five years in the State Penitentiary. Anna Mae would miss the young, black woman. More than once Chocolate had stuck her neck out to protect Anna Mae. In addition, if it hadn't been for Chocolate's constant coaching, Anna Mae would have been an easy mark for the numerous perverted and violent inmates. Now Chocolate was gone.

"Are you listening?" Angelo barked into the phone.

"What!" Anna Mae shot back.

"I've been telling you that Ivan thinks Olga couldn't have heard you screaming if the back door was closed. Ivan thinks he can prove that the back door was left open by whoever killed Walter. They're going to the house tonight to test it out."

"Good for them," said Anna Mae dryly.

"Anna Mae—sweetheart," pleaded Angelo, "If Ivan can prove the back door was open, that paves the way for another suspect." When she didn't respond he added, "I love you so much, Anna Mae. This will all be over soon. I promise."

At last, Anna Mae really looked at Angelo. She ached to reach out and touch the curls that tumbled onto his forehead, to kiss his slightly full and sensuous lips. Angelo placed his hand on the glass. She matched her own hand with his, feeling the cold surface that kept them apart.

"Anna Mae?"

"Yes?"

"Everything is going to be all right," he said softly. "Why don't we pray together?"

She jerked back, pulling her hand away. "Pray?" she snapped. "To who? God? Just pray and do the right thing and everything will be all right. Angelo! That's bullshit!"

Angelo lowered his hand and tried to say something, but she talked over him. "All my life, Angelo, I've tried to do the right thing. But all Sarah ever cared about was Walter—Walter, Walter, Walter! My whole life is screwed up because of that bastard!'"

Angelo cringed at the language Anna Mae heard every day. He wondered if she realized how much of it was slipping into her own vocabulary. He hated the change in her. His sweet, soft-spoken Anna Mae was becoming more crass every day. As he watched her through the wire embedded glass, her blue eyes were as hard as crystal.

"...and...and...and you know the blackouts?" she fumed, "I knew, way back...way, way, way back, why I had those blackouts. I knew Walter was beating me. Even when I was too young to know, I knew. It just took me a long time to face it. And still I tried to do the right thing. I stuck by Sarah when Walter was in prison. I got a job to help with bills. I went to school and made decent grades..."

As Anna Mae rattled on, it occurred to Angelo that all during their long relationship he had never heard her complain. Never before had she expressed resentment over the rotten cards she had been dealt in her life. He held up his hands, palms forward. "Whoa! Settle down, Anna Mae."

But she didn't stop, and tears began pouring down her face. "I could have been on the honor roll. But no! I had everybody else's shit to deal with. And that son-of-a-bitch..."

He sighed and shook his head at the profanity.

"...that son-of-a-bitch gets out of prison...he comes home, and I even leave him my keys so he can use my car and I take a goddamn bus to Becky's house and when I get there I find out that—that bastard!...that fuckin' bastard is my father..."

Angelo held the phone inches from his ear, but she didn't seem to notice, or care.

"But that wasn't enough! I go home and I'm gonna' confront him, but he's sleeping. God, I'm so damn considerate. I don't want to bother him. He's lied to me and beat me all my life and Miss Idiot here...I just let him sleep.

"I go upstairs, wait until I hear him get up and I go downstairs to confront him. I want that bastard to finally admit the truth. And suddenly I'm in here!" she sobbed. "And you want me to pray?" she added, wiping her forearm across her nose. "Where the hell is God? Where is He?"

"Anna Mae...don't..."

"I want to go home. I don't want to be here, Angelo," she seethed, unable to see him through a blur of tears. "I just want to go home!"

Angelo was silent as he watched her cry. Eventually she looked up at him. He didn't know how to comfort her. Finally, he said, "I'm so sorry you have to go through all this."

By morning, Anna Mae had convinced herself that she was not a murderess. At 9:00 A.M., she took her seat at the defense table with new determination. She would beat this thing. She had a good lawyer and more than ten witnesses ready to testify on her behalf. Dr. Rhukov would convince the jury that she truly didn't remember what she saw on the day Walter was killed. And Ivan would prove that the real killer ran out the back door.

The jury had not yet entered. Anna Mae looked around for David, who had told Angelo he would skip school to be in court today. She didn't see David. However, Bob McCarthy was in his usual seat at the back. He was looking straight at her. He smiled and gave her a thumbs-up. She quickly turned away. A minute later, the jury filed into the courtroom and soon afterwards, Tom Simon called his first witness of the day.

Homicide Detective Nancy Miller, sharp featured, short and rail thin, described the murder scene pretty much as the other witnesses had. Then Ivan Hammerstein's cross established that no murder weapon had been found. His precise question was, "Detective Miller, I find it odd that the district attorney has thus far not produced a murder weapon. Can you shed any light on this issue?"

"We looked everywhere. We did not find a murder weapon," she replied.

"And in the absence of a weapon at the scene of the crime—considering that the defendant was discovered at the scene, did you pursue another avenue of investigation?"

"The house, the yard, even the surrounding area was thoroughly searched. But no weapon was found."

"Let me repeat the question," said Hammerstein, "Did you pursue another avenue of investigation?"

"No."

"Why not?"

Detective Miller's voice was soaked in sarcasm. "The defendant was found crouched under the hall steps and screaming hysterically minutes after the murder."

"So that means she did it?" snapped Hammerstein. "You just jumped to the first conclusion and let it go at that!"

"Objection!"

"Sustained."

"I'm finished with this witness," said Hammerstein and walked back to the defense table shaking his head.

CHAPTER FIFTY

Hammerstein drummed his fingers on the defense table as District Attorney Tom Simon directed the bailiff to set up a tripod. The tripod would be used to display poster-board sketches of the body's position and wounds. Moments later the tall, somewhat unkempt, multi-degreed forensic pathologist, Dr. Philip Houston, was sworn in. Before beginning his questioning, Tom Simon repeatedly slapped a pointer in his hand while strutting before the jury, as though he were somehow responsible for the scientific expertise about to be presented.

Hammerstein's theory was that someone had entered through the back door, killed Walter, and then left the same way he had come in. The prosecution claimed that no such someone existed. Simon claimed that Anna Mae had gone downstairs, murder weapon in hand, killed Walter, and disposed of the weapon. She then went back into the hallway and deliberately positioned herself under the second floor steps. There she began screaming as though she had just arrived and had seen the murderer, or at least the bloody body. When the police came, she claimed that she didn't remember anything.

If Tom Simon could prove that the killer had entered the kitchen from the inside hallway door, that would add credibility to his circumstantial evidence case.

As the questioning moved ahead, Hammerstein began scribbling notes on his yellow legal pad. At first he wasn't impressed with Houston's testimony. It didn't take a genius to determine that it was the blow to Walter's head, the one that cracked his skull, which finally killed him. Then Dr. Houston got up from the witness chair. He towered over Tom Simon as he took the pointer from his hand and used it to indicate how, in his opinion, the murderer was in the kitchen-to-hall doorway when the fatal blow was struck.

Hammerstein was drawing a stick figure replica on display, when Anna Mae doubled over in pain. He glanced at her. "You okay?"

She nodded.

Ivan was becoming increasingly concerned about his client's health. He considered asking for a recess, but continued scrawling arrows this way and that around the stick figure. Fifteen minutes later, when Philip Houston concluded his testimony, Hammerstein, legal pad in hand, approached the witness.

"How long, Dr. Houston, have you been the forensic pathologist for Allegheny County?"

"One year, eight months," said Houston.

"And during that time, how many cases similar to this one have you worked on?"

"No two cases are exactly alike," the witness said.

"I didn't ask you if you worked on a case that was 'the same as.' I asked how many 'similar cases.'"

"I would have to go through my files to answer that."

"You mean that in one year and eight months you can't remember if you worked on a case where the victim was axed to death?"

"Objection."

"Sustained."

The pathologist straightened his back to display his full height, which, if he were standing, would have been markedly taller than the tall defense attorney. "I assume that is not a question."

Hammerstein paused, looked at the jury, and tossed the legal pad on the defense table. He then turned to Houston. "In this particular case, you could be wrong, couldn't you?"

"If there was a possibility of my being wrong, I would have said so."

Hammerstein glanced at Anna Mae who appeared to be struggling with her stomach pain. Again he considered asking for a recess, but he decided not to stop the momentum. Hammerstein led Houston to admit that he had stated in court that a woman's fatal blow to the head had been the result of falling down fifteen concrete steps. Two days after Houston had testified, the woman's husband confessed that he had hit his wife with the corner of a brass trophy, then dragged her to the pool area and threw her down the steps. The woman was dead before the fall.

"So," said Hammerstein, "Can we presume that the final blow to Walter's head possibly…possibly could have been inflicted by someone who had entered through the back door?"

With his face expressionless, but his eyes alive with anger, Houston said through clenched teeth, "I suppose it's possible."

"Could you please speak a little louder," said Hammerstein.

"I suppose it's possible!"

Hammerstein glanced at Simon, whose face was white, "Thank you. I have no more questions, Dr. Houston." An elaborate emphasis on the word, 'doctor.'

*   *   *

In the conference room, during lunch break, Hammerstein brought Anna Mae a Zantac to quiet her raging stomach. Although she felt better, she pushed away the ham sandwich delivered from the deli, content to sip on the vanilla milkshake. Eventually, she asked Ivan to ask Olga if she could find something else for her to wear. The simple beige dress the matron was kind enough to press each evening was dirty, and Anna Mae had lost five more pounds, causing it to hang like a sack. Ivan said it looked fine. But what do men know.

At 1:30, Anna Mae took her seat at the defense table. It seemed as though the trial was dragging on forever. It had started on Monday morning and it was now only Thursday afternoon. Ivan had said that it was moving along quickly for a murder trial. The prosecution had two more witnesses and they would testify today. Tomorrow, Friday, the defense would begin.

Anna Mae watched the jury file in. The homemaker looked tired. The teacher was chatting with the businessman as though they were at a cocktail party rather than a murder trial. The steelworker, who had seemed bored all morning, now sat with his eyes closed and his head nodding.

Under the defense table, Anna Mae squeezed her hands together so tightly they burned. She hoped she was wrong, thinking that the jury, those twelve people who would soon determine how she would spend the rest of her life, looked bored.

"The Commonwealth calls Dr. Henry C. Connely."

Anna Mae studied the court psychiatrist as he was being sworn in. He was in his early fifties, very short and very thin, and wearing a perfectly fitted dark brown suit and rimless glasses. He had a full head of coal black hair—not one strand out of place. Having sworn to tell the truth, he sat in the witness chair, squared his shoulders, stretched his undersized body to the maximum, and primly folded his hands on his lap.

Tom Simon approached the witness with his usual actor's flair. Anna Mae suppressed a smile as she recalled Hammerstein's pet name for the prosecutor—the little red lizard. Then she remembered what JD had told her.

Could it be…

As Dr. Connely recited his impressive list of medical and psychiatric degrees, Anna Mae watched Tom Simon. He did display something in his strut that reminded her of George Siminoski. However, that's where the similarity ended.

Was JD wrong? What had happened to the fat little boy with the thick glasses? The smartest kid in school? Where was the pimply teenager with the big nose? Why had no one seen him in the valley since he left for the university? Could he have so totally altered his appearance that he was now unrecognizable?

In front of her, the questions and testimony continued to drone on as Anna Mae's thoughts went back to that stifling Friday night in 1965, the night of Stanley's sixteenth birthday party. Vague memories of the obnoxious George Siminoski cornering her under the hall steps drifted through her mind. She remembered that she had a brief blackout then awakened in church. She remembered leaving the church and passing Vinko's market, and George hiding in the alley, waiting for her.

Joey was there. Joey actually hit George! And then—oh yes—George shouted at her. 'I'm getting out of this filthy town. But I'll get you!' He had pointed his fat finger at her, threatening, 'If it takes the rest of my life I'll get you!'

Anna Mae's disturbing memories quickly vanished when she heard Hammerstein mumble under his breath, "son-of-a-bitch!"

She glanced at Dr. Connely, who was saying, "…and not only is it my professional opinion that the defendant is lying, Anna Mae McBride clearly exhibits sociopathic tendencies."

Simon, facing the jury with his usual self-assured demeanor, let the statement sink in. He then said to the doctor, "Would you please explain 'sociopath' in layman's terms."

"Anna Mae is a borderline sociopath," replied the doctor straightening his already perfect tie. "By that I mean she has antisocial tendencies. She doesn't relate well to others and doesn't quite fit in. Also, there's a matter of conscience. A sociopath makes no distinction between right and wrong. Therefore, if she tells a lie, she can be quite convincing. She does not react to her own dishonesty as a normal person would. I suspect she could pass a lie detector test even if she's guilty."

"Objection!" Hammerstein was on his feet.

"Dr. Connely! You know better than that," scowled the judge. "Strike that last remark."

"I apologize, Your Honor," said the doctor. "I only meant the comment rhetorically."

"Bullshit!" said Hammerstein.

Judge Wittier's face was scarlet. "Use that language in my courtroom again," he said to Hammerstein, "and you'll be trying this case from a jail cell." He then addressed the prosecutor, "And one more outlandish remark from any of your witnesses and I'll throw out the entire testimony."

Judge Wittier then cleared his throat, shuffled some papers, and checked to see if his half-glasses were still perched on top of his head. When his face finally returned to its normal flesh tone, he said to Simon, "Do you have any more questions for this witness?"

Tom Simon thought for a moment "No Sir, Your Honor." He then walked to the prosecution table and sat down.

"You can step down," said the judge to the doctor.

"Your Honor?" said Hammerstein stepping forward.

"Oh! Yes. I'm sorry. Stay where you are!"

For a few seconds Dr. Connely didn't know whether he should sit or stand. At last he lowered himself back into the witness chair and adjusted his glasses.

"Counselor?" said the judge.

"I only have three questions," said Hammerstein.

"Proceed."

"Did you get paid for your performance? Ah...I mean testimony?"

Simon jumped up but before he could object, Judge Wittier waved him down.

"Yes," said the court's psychiatrist.

"And how much time did you spend with the defendant?"

The doctor brushed an invisible strand of black hair from his forehead and said, "About three hours."

"Good!" said Hammerstein. "And did you get paid for your three hour examination of the defendant?"

"Yes. I did."

"That's good. I'm glad to hear that," said Hammerstein. "I have no more questions for this witness."

When Hammerstein returned to the defense table, Anna Mae whispered frantically, "Is that it? Aren't you gonna do something about what he said?"

"Shhhh. Trust me."

Next, Sarah Lipinski was sworn in. Anna Mae tried not to look at her aunt. But it was impossible. Sarah seemed as though she had aged ten years. Her drab brown hair was teased into an outdated, fifties hairstyle.

She had gained weight and her heavily rouged cheeks were plump above her fleshy, double chin. She was wearing her coffee colored pants suit. It had once fit perfectly, but was now so snug that the shoulder pads lifted every time she moved her arms. Anna Mae's heart went out to this woman who had been like a mother to her.

Sarah shifted nervously as Tom Simon approached. "Mrs. Lipinski, what was your relationship to the victim?"

Sarah looked at Anna Mae, her eyes narrowed with unbridled anger. She leaned into the microphone and said harshly, "He…Walter is my—Walter was my husband."

Anna Mae cringed. All through these torturous months she had wondered about Sarah's feelings. Her aunt never visited her at the jail. She hadn't even sent a note of encouragement. Ivan always avoided the subject and none of Anna Mae's visitors—not Angelo, not David, not Father John, not one person would tell her anything about Sarah's emotional state, nor would they say whether or not Sarah thought she was guilty. But now she knew. The one person she desperately wanted to believe in her innocence did not believe her. Her Aunt Sarah believed she had killed Walter.

For the next twenty minutes, Anna Mae struggled to remain composed as she listened to Sarah's shocking testimony—a fabricated, yet heart-wrenching story of how she and Walter had lovingly taken baby Anna Mae into their home when her promiscuous mother, Becky McBride, had practically left her on their doorstep.

Ivan scribbled on his legal pad and slid it in front of Anna Mae. *Don't worry. I'll deal with this.*

When Sarah finished painting the outrageous picture of the Lipinski's loving parenting, Simon went to the prosecution table to review his notes. While walking back to his witness, he paused before the jury to enlist their support for what was to come. Then, facing Sarah, he asked, "Would you say that the defendant, Anna Mae McBride, is a nice young lady?"

"Not all the time," said Sarah.

"And would you tell the court of a time when she wasn't so nice?"

"I couldn't believe it!" she replied, sounding as though she were reading a script. "But then again, I shouldn't have been surprised. My niece, Anna Mae, at her cousin Stanley's funeral—she was laughing! She stood right next to Stanley's casket and laughed like she was at some kind of party. It was horrible. The director had to ask her to leave!"

Sarah's response was obviously well rehearsed, a tribute to Simon's ability to coach his witness into presenting a callous defendant, while tiptoeing through the inadmissible subject of Stanley's untimely death.

Ivan exhaled noisily as Anna Mae saw the disdain in the jury's eyes. She felt a lump in her throat and the sting of unshed tears. Her breathing became quick and shallow. It took all of her willpower to keep from bursting into sobs.

"Be strong," Ivan whispered.

"I'm trying."

"Your aunt is so gullible. I can reverse this on cross."

"I hope so."

Bang! "Mr. Hammerstein!" The Judge's loud voice carried across the courtroom. "Save your conversations for recess."

"I'm sorry, Your Honor."

"Don't be sorry. Just be quiet! Continue counselor."

Simon looked at Ivan and Anna Mae with a slight smile on his lips and a glint of malice in his eyes. Still looking at Anna Mae, he continued, "Mrs. Lipinski, tell me about the relationship between your niece and your late husband."

"Everybody thinks Walter was such a bad man," said Sarah with tears running down her face. "But you should have heard Anna Mae talk back to him. He would be telling her something and she would mouth off to him."

"And how was her language?"

She wiped the tears with the back of her hand. Her voice quivered. "Sometimes she swore. It was awful. She would yell at him—terrible language. Maybe Walter was wrong to hit her, but if she had just kept her mouth shut, things would have been a lot better."

Anna Mae stifled a smile. *I talked back? Good for me!*

"Did you ever tell Anna Mae not to talk back to Walter?"

"Lots of times."

"And did she listen?"

"She would say she didn't remember doing it."

Anna Mae recalled how, eons ago, before Walter went to prison, Sarah would scold her for talking back. So many times, she had tried to explain to Sarah that she didn't remember. But Sarah never believed her.

Tom Simon faced the jury. "So she has been using the 'I don't remember excuse all along.'"

"Objection!"

"Sustained."

"What about mood swings? Didn't you say at the deposition that Anna Mae had severe mood swings and that she would change from this nice sweet girl to a holy terror?"

"Something like that," said Sarah, looking at Anna Mae with cold eyes.

Anna Mae looked back at Sarah. *How can you do this? Why are you saying these things?*

"When Anna Mae was being a holy terror," continued Simon, "Did it ever appear that she didn't know what she was doing?"

"No. She knew."

"At any time did you think Anna Mae had a mental problem that resulted in her not remembering her own actions?"

"Objection."

"Overruled."

"Mrs. Lipinski, you had the opportunity to observe the defendant more than anyone. Did you ever see anything in her behavior indicating she was 'out of it?'"

"Objection."

"Overruled."

Anna Mae, stifling her frustration, looked straight ahead. Her face was bland but her mind was racing. How could she and Sarah have lived in the same house for nineteen years and Sarah not even question whether or not she was telling the truth when she said she didn't remember? Was Sarah that dense? Unobservant? Oblivious to what had to be obvious at least a few times?

Sarah, who had been concentrating on the prosecutor, now looked at the jury. "No. Anna Mae was never 'out of it.' She always knew what she was doing."

"No more questions."

Anna Mae cried her way through a half-hour recess, and then Ivan Hammerstein escorted her back to the courtroom to begin his cross.

His first questions took Sarah back to 1951 when she had told Father Falkowski that Walter did not want them to keep her sister's baby.

"So Walter didn't want Anna Mae from the beginning...isn't that true?"

"He did want her," Sarah lied. "But you know how men are."

"How are they? Do they come home drunk and beat young children? Do they beat their wives? Do they land in prison for assault?"

"Objection!"

"Sustained."

Anna Mae only half listened as Ivan tried to bend Sarah's testimony back to the truth, to make it obvious to the jury that Sarah's account of Anna Mae's behavior was shaky at best. But Anna Mae's heart was broken. All her life she had wanted Sarah's love and approval. When Walter was in jail, the relationship between her and Sarah was as near to mother/daughter as Anna Mae could ever hope for. And now this! Anna Mae didn't think she would survive the pain.

"Do you consider yourself an expert on mental illnesses?" asked Hammerstein.

"No!" Sarah was now defensive.

"Isn't it possible that your niece, Anna Mae, was suffering from memory losses that you were not aware of?"

"She lived in my house. I saw her every day."

"I didn't ask you that. I asked if it were possible that you were not able to discern a problem right in front of you?"

"I beg your pardon?"

"Discern—notice—be aware."

"I didn't notice anything. Anna Mae didn't have any problems with her memory."

"Inasmuch as you are not an expert in the psychiatric field, in the area of Traumatic Amnesia to be exact, and because you were so close, maybe you couldn't see the forest for the trees. Isn't it possible that you just weren't smart enough to see the problem?"

Sarah's face reddened. "I am smart enough to know that Anna Mae caused all the problems in the house and that she probably killed my husband!"

The blood drained from Hammerstein's face. "I want that stricken from the record!"

"Calm down, Counselor," said Judge Wittier. He then glared down thorough his half-glasses at Sarah. "Mrs. Lipinski! You are not in this court to pass judgment. That's for the jury to decide. Another remark like that one and I'll punish you with a serious fine. Is that clear?" He then addressed the court stenographer: "Strike that!" Then the jury: "Disregard that statement! You did not hear it. It will not be brought up in deliberation."

Satisfied that the judge had done all he could, but knowing the damage had been done, Hammerstein continued his questioning. "Mrs. Lipinski, in the nineteen years that the defendant has lived with you, considering that children are sometimes mischievous, did Anna Mae ever take any change from your purse, or perhaps some money that was just lying around?"

"No. I don't think so."

"Not counting the memory issue, has Anna Mae ever lied to you?"

Sarah shifted in the witness chair, and eyed the defense attorney defiantly.

"Answer the question," Hammerstein demanded. "Has Anna Mae ever lied to you?"

"I don't know."

Hammerstein hurried to the defense table and picked up a yellow legal pad. "In your deposition, Mrs. Lipinski, you said, and these are your exact words, 'Anna Mae never lied to me. That's one thing I was always thankful for. She wasn't like some of the other teenagers who lied to their parents. She was a very honest girl.' Isn't that what you told me during the deposition?"

"I don't remember saying that," said Sarah.

"Seems you don't remember a lot of things," said Hammerstein as he slapped the legal pad on the defense table and sat down. "Your Honor, I have no more questions at this time, but I reserve the right to recall this witness."

"Granted."

Tom Simon stood up. "Redirect, Your Honor."

"Go ahead," said Wittier.

Simon strutted over to Sarah and said, "Mrs. Lipinski, do you love Anna Mae?"

"I do...I mean I did."

"So you wouldn't deliberately get up here and say things that would hurt her if they were not true."

"No, I wouldn't."

CHAPTER FIFTY-ONE

Thursday Evening

Wrapped tightly in the rough woolen blanket, Anna Mae sat on the edge of her cot shivering. It was below zero outside and no more than fifty-five degrees in her cell. But the cold was nothing compared to Sarah's betrayal—that was more than Anna Mae could endure.

She had refused supper and twice the matron had told her she had visitors: Angelo and Olga. She declined both visits. Nothing, not even the sympathy and support of those who cared could change what Sarah had said on that witness stand.

She placed her hard pillow against the cinder-block wall and leaned back, wishing she could cry. It might alleviate some of the pain that was actually physical. But tears would not come. She thought about the Bible that lay on the floor in the far corner, under a pile of books and magazines. She wondered if God, too, would turn against her. She had given Him reason enough.

The blanket fell from her shoulders as she slid off the cot and onto the floor. She pulled the Bible from under the pile, letting the rest of the reading material tumble away. She sat on the cement floor with her back against the cot, opened the Bible at random, and began to read: *Hold not thy peace, O God of my praise. For the mouth of the wicked and the mouth of the deceitful are opened against me; they have spoken against me with a lying tongue; they compassed me with words of hatred; and fought against me without cause and they have rewarded me evil for good and hatred for my love.*

She sat there staring at the words, astonished that once again she had opened her Bible to exactly the right place. *God does speak to me! He is here, in this jail, in this cell.* "God, please don't be mad at me," she whispered.

"Did you say something?" the matron asked through the bars.

"I was talking to God."

"I hope He hears you!"

Anna Mae couldn't tell if the matron was being sarcastic or not, but she didn't care. With the Bible in her hand, she stood up then sat on the cot. *God, I am so sorry.* She lay down, pulled the blanket over herself and curled on her side to be as warm as possible, cradling the Bible in her arms as if it were a baby.

Time passed. She felt warmer, almost comfortable. Before the warden rang the 'lights out' bell, Anna Mae was asleep.

Something was pounding like a giant's footsteps. She was sitting on the hard, vibrating ground overlooking the raging brown river. Ivan was standing beside her but she ignored him and looked into the distance.

Suddenly, a faceless entity, the embodiment of evil appeared. It was suspended in mid-air, looming over the river and effortlessly breaking a wooden cross into smaller and smaller pieces. In her dream, she stood up, unafraid, and with nothing but empty air under her feet she walked toward it. The evil entity receded farther and farther back into darkness, leaving the pieces of broken wood at Anna Mae's feet.

Ivan was shouting at her to get back, and that it was dangerous where she stood over the broken cross—that she would fall into the powerful current and drown. But she willed him to be silent.

Suspended over the river, she gathered some of the pieces, wondering if she could ever fix it. She sensed a presence and looked up into a light. A shimmering bright beam flowed from the light, embracing her in perfect peace. An angelic figure, clothed in a radiant white robe, stepped out of the light and took her by the hand. The angel wanted her to follow. With complete trust, Anna Mae let herself be led. Together they floated into the brilliant white mist. Ivan called frantically. "No! Anna Mae! Don't do it. Don't go there. You're going to drown!"

There was the witness chair. The angel motioned her to sit.

"No!" Ivan screamed.

Anna Mae willed him silent. She sat in the witness chair.

*   *   *

"That's crazy!"

Ivan Hammerstein took off his jacket and threw it on the conference table. Trying not to raise his voice, he explained. "No defense attorney in his right mind would let you take the witness stand. That's nuts! I'm telling you, Anna Mae! No! You'll screw up everything."

"But, in the dream..."

He smacked himself on his forehead with his palm. "Good God, girl! You don't win murder trials in your dreams."

"I have a right to testify if I want to," she said, pacing with determined steps on the other side of the conference table.

"You've been talkin' to those jail-house lawyers again," Ivan accused. "For Christ sake! You'll end up with the death penalty."

Anna Mae put her hands on the table and leaned over to face her attorney. "I want to testify today," she said. "It's my right!"

"Now listen to me, Anna Mae. Dr. Rhukov is going to open our defense this morning. Then Father John will back up his testimony by repeating what you told him about the memory losses. Angelo will back him up. Even David..."

"I never told David."

"He knows!" Ivan shouted, then lowering his voice, "He told me he suspected for a long time. So he's gonna' stretch the truth a bit. Who cares? It's the truth, isn't it? You have memory losses. I can prove it. For God's sake, Anna Mae, we're walking a shaky tightrope as it is."

"I want to testify, Ivan. Today!"

"Look...I plan to put JD back on the stand. There was that incident where Walter clobbered him. The Lipinski brothers will also recount some of Walter's violent episodes. They will testify that a lot of people hated Walter. Reasonable doubt. That is all we have to prove: memory loss, reasonable doubt."

"I want to testify. Today!"

Ivan Hammerstein collapsed into a chair, his thick, black hair in as much disarray as the thoughts flying through his mind. For once, he didn't bother to brush it back. Leaning forward with his head down, almost between his knees, as if he were trying to prevent himself from fainting, he said, "Today, huh?"

"Today!"

He massaged the bridge of his nose with thumb and forefinger. "How about next week?"

She walked over, pulled up a chair and sat down facing him. "Ivan! This is my life. My trial. My right to testify if I want to. And I want to testify today."

He shook his head. He had never seen her like this before. She was always so compliant, so timid. But now! The girl was so damn sure of herself. If he put her on the stand, what in the hell would he ask her? 'Will you please tell the jury what you didn't see? Will you tell the jury about your memory? Or rather lack of it? How was your relationship with your uncle? Bad enough to kill him?'

"This is insane! You do not want to go up against that sleazy, red-haired lizard!" he said.

"Today, Ivan!"

He leaned back in his chair, brushed the hair off his forehead, felt the blood drain from his face and waited for his head to clear. With resignation he said, "Wait here." He got up and walked out the door.

Ten minutes later, he was back. "I just bought us thirty minutes. Who knows? Maybe the mere audacity of it will work in our favor. Now here's what I want you to do..."

Anna Mae listened carefully to the instructions: answer each question with as few words as possible, don't add anything, and for God's sake, stay cool when Tom Simon cross-examines you.

He went over the probable pressures and accusations the district attorney would use to attack her. "You got that?"

"Yes."

They sat in silence for a few moments. She waiting. He thinking. Finally, taking her by the hand, he said, "Just do this one thing. Let me start with Dr. Rhukov.

That will lay a good foundation for who you are. Will you do that?"

"All right," she said.

The conference room door opened and the bailiff told them they had thirty seconds to get into the courtroom. Anna Mae handed Ivan his jacket and smiled. "It will be okay," she said.

"I certainly hope so," he shot back.

CHAPTER FIFTY-TWO

From his seat at the defense table, Ivan Hammerstein watched the guard escort Anna Mae into the courtroom. There was a positive aura about her that Ivan had never seen before. She held her head higher, her back straighter, and her steps were surer. The jurors were watching her too, and Hammerstein hoped that Anna Mae's new demeanor would not work against her. For the past week, she had presented an austere appearance that easily could have evoked jury sympathy. Now, at the defense table, she sat next to him with her shoulders squared and her head up. She looked too sure of herself—not a good thing.

The bailiff's strong voice broke the silence. "The defense calls Doctor Mikhail Rhukov."

The jurors' gaze turned from Anna Mae to Dr. Rhukov, who walked down the aisle in a well-worn navy blue suit. His thick, black hair was neatly trimmed and sprinkled with more gray than Anna Mae remembered. His closely cropped beard gave him an air of distinction. After he was sworn in and seated, he reached into his breast pocket to retrieve his bifocals. When he put them on, he looked toward the jury with his lively, intelligent brown eyes. Ivan breathed a little easier, thinking that surely the jury would notice the difference between the strained, obsessively neat, court appointed Dr. Connely, and Dr. Rhukov's relaxed, informal, yet confident manner.

As Hammerstein led the doctor through his educational history, he felt as though Dr. Rhukov's Russian accent made his witness sound more like a bona fide psychiatrist. From the corner of his eye, Hammerstein saw the schoolteacher smiling. Good. The doctor was likable.

After Rhukov's numerous degrees and accomplishments had been presented, Ivan asked, "Have you been paid for your appearance in court today?"

"No."

"What is your normal fee, Dr. Rhukov? Say for an ordinary, one hour office visit?"

"Around a hundred or so."

"When Anna Mae became your patient, how much did you charge her for a one hour session?"

"Anna Mae's parish priest, Father John Falkowski, is a very good friend of mine," the doctor explained as he removed his glasses. "I took Anna Mae's case as a favor to John. Now that I know the young lady, I prefer to treat her without charge. Anna Mae McBride is a fine young woman."

Hammerstein let the doctor's last statement sink in, then said, "Before we get into the details of her condition, Dr. Rhukov, would you tell the court how many hours you have spent with the defendant?"

"I have been seeing Anna Mae since July of '68. That's about two and a half years."

"Have you ever counted the hours?"

The doctor shook his head. "No. But I saw Anna Mae, I would guess, on an overall average of twice a month."

"Let's see," Hammerstein said going back to the defense table to do the math. "That comes to about sixty-two hours. Does that sound about right?"

"Yes."

"And having spent sixty-two hours with the defendant, Anna Mae McBride, what is your diagnosis?"

"In my professional opinion, Miss McBride suffers with the condition called Traumatic Amnesia. Some call it Dissociative Amnesia. In her case, in times of severe stress she slips into a fugue. When the condition subsides, she does not remember anything that happened."

"For us lay people, Doctor, explain 'fugue.'"

"A fugue is a disturbed state of consciousness in which the one affected functions as though conscious, but upon recovery has no recollection."

"How long do these fugues—Anna Mae calls them blackouts—last?"

"It varies. Could be an hour, even a day. When she first came to see me, she had just recovered from a two week time loss."

"That's a considerable amount of time," said Hammerstein buttoning his jacket. "Tell me doctor, during these fugue states—blackouts—might she display conduct contradictory to her basic character?"

"Only to a degree. This condition does not produce the extreme fluctuation as demonstrated in MPD—multiple personality disorder. In a fugue state the individual, in this case Anna Mae, would not behave beyond the perimeters of her normal moral or ethical boundaries."

After a brief pause, Hammerstein looked at the jury. "Dr. Rhukov, do you think that another doctor can make a diagnosis of Traumatic Amnesia, or maybe Schizophrenia, or even Borderline Sociopath, in three hours?"

Tom Simon stood up. "Objection! Speculative. Dr. Rhukov can't determine what another doctor can or cannot do."

"Since when?" said Hammerstein.

"Overruled," said Judge Wittier.

Tom Simon would not sit down.

"Counselor," said the Judge to Simon, "your objection has been overruled!"

Hammerstein stared at Tom Simon until he sat down, then turned back to the doctor. "Let me put that question another way. Can a psychiatrist rule out a diagnosis of Traumatic Amnesia after spending three hours with a patient?"

"He could rule out anything he wanted to rule out, but that would not make it so. A good psychiatrist does not jump to conclusions. Psychiatry is not like other medical fields. For instance, an orthopedic surgeon might look at a patient's arm and know immediately it is broken. A lung specialist can see a lesion on an x-ray. However, the human brain is tremendously complex. A doctor of psychiatry must spend a considerable amount of time with his patients."

Hammerstein nodded and said, "More than three hours, wouldn't you say?"

"Yes. A great deal more," said Dr. Rhukov.

"Now let's switch to another area," said Hammerstein, glancing at the jury and noting that they were paying close attention. "Dr. Rhukov, when did the defendant's memory losses start?"

"When she was a very small child. And about the age of nine she realized her memory losses were directly linked to Walter Lipinski's abuse."

"Objection!"

"Grounds?"

Tom Simon stood up. "How could the defendant know there was abuse if she was in a—ah, fugue?"

"Overruled."

The doctor replaced his glasses while looking up at the judge. "So I may reply?"

"Go ahead, Doctor."

Directing his words straight to the jury, the doctor said, "Miss McBride had revealed to me on numerous occasions that when Walter Lipinski would go out at night and drink a considerable amount of alcohol, she invariably woke up the next morning with cuts and bruises. Though she did not remember, the connection was obvious."

"Objection," said Simon getting up from his seat. "For one thing, that's hearsay and another—the girl was only guessing."

"Your objection is overruled, counselor," said Wittier. "This testimony comes from a highly regarded psychiatrist's knowledge about the defendant. Sit down."

"But..."

"Sit down!"

"Yes, your honor," Simon grumbled.

Hammerstein, in his best serious tone addressed the doctor, "In-as-much as the defendant knew—realized...her so called uncle was responsible for her injuries. Now, in your professional opinion, considering Anna Mae's basic character, would you say she is capable of such a vicious crime?"

"No," said the doctor glancing tenderly at Anna Mae. "She is not capable."

Simon was again on his feet. "Objection! Calls for an opinion."

Thinking he might not have heard right, Hammerstein turned and looked at the prosecutor.

"I do believe," said Judge Wittier sarcastically, "the reason for putting any expert in the witness chair is to obtain an opinion."

Red faced and without replying, Tom Simon walked back to his table and plopped into his chair.

"And also," Hammerstein continued as though nothing unusual had happened, "in your professional opinion, Dr. Rhukov, does the defendant, Anna Mae McBride remember what she saw the day Walter Lipinski was murdered?"

"No," Rhukov said emphatically. "When I tried to get Anna Mae to remember what she saw that day by means of hypnosis, it was evident that whatever she saw was so horrifying that the shock—and this is not at all unusual even in a mentally healthy person—the shock of what she saw completely blocked the memory. It is also true that this kind of amnesia is usually accompanied by a memory loss well before and after the incident."

"So what you're saying, Doctor, is that even though the defendant had previously suffered from Traumatic Amnesia—in this particular incident her memory loss is completely normal."

The doctor looked at Anna Mae, the compassion clear on his face. "That is exactly what I am saying."

"Thank you, Dr. Rhukov," said Hammerstein. He then walked back to the defense table and sat down next to Anna Mae.

The judge asked Simon if he was ready to cross. To Hammerstein's surprise, Tom Simon had no questions for Dr. Rhukov.

CHAPTER FIFTY-THREE

Ivan Hammerstein watched the jury file into the courtroom six seconds shy of the fifteen-minute break. The courtroom was called to order.

"Call your next witness."

"The defense calls Anna Mae McBride."

Anna Mae stood up and brushed the wrinkles from her dress. Her blond hair was pulled severely back by a rubber band, revealing her face that was a bit pale. However, she held her head high and looked straight ahead as she walked to the witness stand. The courtroom was silent. Dead silent.

Judge Wittier put down his gavel and threw an incredulous look at Ivan Hammerstein. Tom Simon leaned forward in his chair and dropped his pen. It bounced from the table to the floor. He didn't bother to pick it up.

At the front of the courtroom, Hammerstein stood beneath the American flag, rubbing his neck. He decided it would be best not to state that Anna Mae was testifying against his advice. It might destroy her credibility. In addition, if the jury found her guilty, Ivan planned to insist she appeal on the grounds of inadequate counsel. But that was a problem for another time. Now he had to focus on the job at hand.

"Do you swear to tell the truth, the whole truth, and nothing but the truth, so help you God?"

"I do."

Anna Mae was looking at something behind Ivan and he turned to see Tom Simon baring his perfect, white teeth in a malevolent grin. Although this was Simon's first murder trial, Ivan knew that Simon was smart enough to realize that putting Anna Mae on the stand was incredibly stupid. Moreover, Ivan Hammerstein would bet a thousand dollars that the prosecutor was already imagining how he could chop Anna Mae into pieces.

Ivan frowned, cleared his throat and moved in front of Anna Mae to block her view of Simon. She had been instructed to always keep her eyes on her attorney. She looked up at him, apology written on her face. He nodded his acceptance.

Brushing the hair from his forehead, Ivan began to lead Anna Mae through a series of questions about her childhood, her school years, her grades and her religious beliefs. In the jury box, the businessman, arms folded across his chest, alternating his critical gaze from Hammerstein to Anna Mae and back. The homemaker, who reminded Ivan of a barmaid, shot the businessman a skeptical glance. Despite Anna Mae's account of a run-of-the-mill, good-girl history, Ivan was becoming uneasy about the jury.

"Now tell us, Anna Mae, about your Uncle Walter. What kind of person was he?"

"He was not a nice man," she said. "He drank a lot and was abusive."

"Objection!" Simon shouted not bothering to stand up. "She's trying to slander the victim."

"Overruled."

"Did you hate him?" Ivan asked

"No," she said. "He would upset me sometimes, especially when he drank or picked on David or Aunt Sarah. But I didn't hate him. Sometimes I even felt sorry for him. Aunt Sarah said he had a terrible childhood."

"Objection," said Simon. "Hearsay."

"I'll allow it. Be careful, counselor," said Judge Wittier.

Ivan made a feeble effort to straighten his lopsided tie, then said to his client, "Without going into too much detail, what did your Aunt Sarah tell you?"

"Aunt Sarah told me that Walter's father used to beat him because he blamed him for his mother's death..."

Tom Simon was now on his feet. "Objection. Hearsay."

"I said, I'll allow it."

Simon scowled and sat down.

Not wanting to test Judge Wittier's patience, Ivan moved ahead. "And so your uncle grew up to be a violent and hard drinking man."

"Objection. Leading."

Judge Wittier leaned forward and looked at Hammerstein, his face reflecting his frustration. "Please rephrase the question, counselor."

The defense attorney realized that Simon was using a rapid-fire series of objections to frustrate Anna Mae and confuse the jury. Gritting his teeth he continued, "Did Walter hit you? Or more specifically, did he beat you?"

On his feet again, Simon persisted, "Objection. Leading."

"Overruled! Crack your law books prosecutor and read what it says under 'Leading.'"

Ivan waited for the murmured laughter to subside then asked again, "Did Walter hit you or actually beat you?"

"I think he beat me."

Hammerstein was impressed that Anna Mae was able to maintain her concentration. "You think?" he asked. "Don't you know?"

"I was never consciously aware...I mean it was during the blackouts. Dr. Rhukov calls it Traumatic Amnesia—the doctor said it was the beatings that caused the amnesia..."

"Objection. Hearsay."

Finally, Judge Wittier called both attorneys to the bench. He warned Simon: "If you continue to impede the defense with your irrelevant objections, I'll hold you in contempt. Is that understood?"

"Yes, Your Honor."

The prosecutor's cheeks flushed. As the two lawyers walked away from the judge's bench, Simon's eyes shot bolts of anger in Hammerstein's direction.

Ignoring Simon, Hammerstein continued: "As you were saying, Anna Mae—the doctor thought it was the beatings that caused the amnesia?"

"Actually, I figured that out myself when I was about nine. I would wake up in the morning with bruises and I couldn't remember what had happened the night before. But it was always after Walter had come home drunk."

"Is that why you finally went to see Dr. Rhukov?"

"Yes. When I was sixteen, there was an episode at Kennywood..."

"We'll get to that later," said Hammerstein. "Anna Mae, when was the first time you were aware of lost time?"

Anna Mae lowered her head. She looked at her hands that were clasped in her lap. Ivan had touched on this in the conference room. There hadn't been enough time to go into detail. But he had assured her that nothing should present a problem as long as she told the truth.

"When was the first time?" he asked again.

"Susie," she said. "My doll, Susie, was all torn up."
Anna Mae's hands were trembling. She still had not
looked up.

"Take your time," Ivan said.

"I must have been around three or four years old."
Her voice was soft but could still be heard. "It was late. I
was in bed when Aunt Sarah brought me my doll. Her
clothes, Susie's nightie, it was torn. Her face was
cracked. I couldn't remember how it happened. Aunt
Sarah wasn't worried about my doll. She made a big
fuss over me, like I was hurt. I didn't know I was hurt. I
was just concerned about my baby doll."

Anna Mae looked up and scanned the courtroom.
Ivan followed her gaze as it led to the rear of the
courtroom and rested on Sarah. He cleared his throat and
Anna Mae looked back at him. Her eyes glistened with
tears.

"How old did you say you were?"

"I don't know. Maybe three? Three and a half?"

Suddenly Anna Mae's face brightened and she
laughed to herself.

"What's funny?" Ivan asked.

"Stanley—that same night," she smiled as the tears
dripped over her lower lashes. "His feet were sticking
out from under his bed," she said wiping them from her
cheeks. "I guess," she said, taking a deep breath. "I
guess now that I think of it…it wasn't really funny. Poor
kid. He was probably terrified."

"At that time, where was Walter?"

"I don't know where he was then. But it was because
of him that Stanley was hiding under the bed. I know it
was. I mean Walter had to have been on one of his
rampages..."

"Objection. Speculative," said Simon without getting
up.

"That's ridiculous," said Hammerstein. "The witness is only recounting what she thought as a child."

"And that's not speculation?" shot Simon. "Where did you go to law school?"

The gavel hit the maple bench so hard that Hammerstein jumped. "That's enough," snapped the judge. "The jury is to disregard the witness's opinion as to why Stanley's feet were sticking out from under the bed. Proceed counselor."

"And so, Anna Mae, the night your baby doll was damaged you did not remember how it happened. Is that correct?"

"Yes, that's correct."

Ivan walked to the defense table and picked up a legal pad. He looked at it for a second, put it down, then asked his client, "Was there another incident when you didn't remember a period of time?"

"There were lots of them."

"Can you tell us of another time?"

"I was in third grade," she said. She seemed to be bracing herself for an onslaught of emotion that didn't come. "There was an accident at the mill. When the sirens went off, the classroom became a madhouse. It scared me half to death. I know I had a blackout because when I woke up, I was in church. I woke up in church a lot."

"Woke up?"

"Yes. I would go there—to the church I mean, because that was the only place where I felt safe. And then I would wake up—in church."

"What do you mean by, 'wake up?' Explain that."

"Well, that's what I kinda call it. But I'm not in bed. It's not that kind of waking up. I like, suddenly become aware that I'm not where I was a minute ago. Only it wasn't a minute. It's hours, sometimes days. And then I remember the last thing that happened before I blacked out. Well, most of the time anyway. Sometimes it takes me a little while to figure out where I was and what was happening when I blacked out. When I wake up, I know time has passed. Then I have to figure out how much time. It was so hard because I didn't want anyone to know."

Hammerstein glanced at the jury to see if they showed any compassion. They did. He continued, "Why? Why didn't you want anyone to know?"

Anna Mae shifted uneasily, gripping the arms of the chair.

He asked again, "Why didn't you want anyone to know?"

"Answer the question," said Judge Wittier.

She spoke in a whisper. "I was afraid I was crazy."

"I didn't hear you," said Hammerstein. "Can you speak a little louder?"

"I was afraid I was crazy and that they would put me in a mental hospital. So I didn't tell anyone."

"Objection!"

Hammerstein turned and looked at Simon.

"On what grounds?" asked the judge.

"Relevance?" said Simon.

"Sit down," said the judge.

Ivan shot a snide glance at his adversary, whose inexperience had caught up with him.

Following Ivan's lead, Anna Mae continued her explanation of other times she had blacked out and some of the ways she had bluffed her way through them. She was doing a good job. If Ivan was reading the jury correctly, they believed her.

When she gave a brief account of the Kennywood incident, the schoolteacher was nodding, and the businessman was leaning forward, his hands folded, his elbows on his knees. However, the steelworker remained ramrod straight, eyes narrowed, sizing up Anna Mae. Hammerstein turned back to his witness.

"Now, let's go to the day Walter Lipinski was murdered. Would you please describe to the jury, as you remember them, the events of October 14, 1970?"

Anna Mae stiffened, her breathing became shallow. "I got up at around nine o'clock—maybe nine thirty..."

Simon jumped up. "Your Honor! Does the witness know what time it was or not?"

"What's your objection?" asked the judge.

"He doesn't have an objection," said Hammerstein. "He's harassing the witness."

"I'll repeat the question, Anna Mae," Hammerstein said. "Will you tell the jury what you did on Tuesday, October 14th 1970?"

"I got up around nine-fifteen," she said, then waited a few seconds for the objection that didn't come. She then talked about not wanting to be alone with her uncle, about leaving the car keys on the table, about taking the bus to her mother's house in Pittsburgh. "It was so nice for a change," she said with a slight smile. "Becky, I mean my mother, had stopped drinking. Her house was clean. So was little Missy. And my mother was making cookies."

Suddenly Anna Mae stopped talking. She let go of the arms of the chair and covered her face. Ivan saw a slight tremble in her hands. He gave her a moment to regroup. When she took her hands away from her face, he said, "So the house was clean and your mother was making cookies. Anything else, Anna Mae?"

"We sat at the table and had coffee. She had this book." Anna Mae looked at her attorney, her eyes begging him not to make her continue. Then lowering her gaze, she took a deep breath. "It was because of that book that she told me…she told me that…that he was— that Walter was ..."

"You'll have to speak a little louder," said
Hammerstein. "What did your mother tell you? What
was that last word?"

"My Father! She told me that Walter Lipinski was
my father."

The jury shifted in their seats. There was a loud
murmur in the courtroom. Anna Mae's face was flushed.
She was visibly shaking. Ivan waited until the noise
subsided. Hoping she would not break down, he pushed
forward. "Do you know, Anna Mae, why in all these
years it was kept a secret? Do you know why you or
anyone else in the family was not told that Walter
Lipinski was your father?"

No answer.

Ivan paced in front of his client, trying to find a
suitable way to ask his next question. He could think of
nothing that would spare Anna Mae, so he simply said,
"I know this is painful for you. It had to be a terrible
shock. But we need to know. Did your mother, Becky
McBride, tell you that Walter raped her?"

Simon jumped up. "Objection! Leading."

"Overruled."

Anna Mae looked at the floor and mumbled. Judge
Wittier leaned down from his seat, saying gently,
"Young lady, you'll have to speak a little louder. Now
tell the jury what your mother said to you that day."

Anna Mae took a deep breath and looked directly at
Ivan, who had not missed the empathy in the judge's
voice.

"Becky—my mother…she told me that when she was
fifteen, that Walter raped her. The man I thought was
my uncle was really my father."

The room was silent as Hammerstein reiterated his
client's last statement. "So at the age of nineteen you
finally learned that, not only was Walter Lipinski your

father, but when your mother was only fifteen, he had raped her."

"Yes. And now the police think..." Her face reddened. Tears welled up, spilling over her cheeks. Struggling to stay in control, she choked out the words, "I didn't—I couldn't have—I would never..."

Hammerstein handed her a handkerchief, then looked at his watch. It was eleven forty-five. He wanted Anna Mae's testimony to continue until the end of the day. That way it would stay with the jury throughout the weekend. The last thing he needed was for Tom Simon to attack her on a Friday, leaving the jury two full days to digest the damage. He could request a recess but the judge would know he was stalling. He had to make a move. He had to prolong Anna Mae's testimony.

He waited for a few moments while Anna Mae wiped her eyes and blew her nose. When she appeared to be somewhat composed, he tried to signal her with a look to indicate that she should request a recess. But she didn't understand.

Finally he relented: "Your Honor, if it please the court, may Miss McBride take a break?"

Anna Mae roughly wiped away the remaining tears. "I don't need a break."

Ivan gritted his teeth. *Damn it, girl! Don't you get it?* But how could she? What did she know about courtroom strategy and the propensities of juries? Now, with a recess clearly out of the question, Ivan continued, "And so, when your mother, Becky McBride, finally told you the truth about your father, what did you do?"

"I left."

"And where did you go when you left your mother's house?"

For a moment, Anna Mae just stared at the floor. When she finally looked up, she was calm—too calm—too composed. It was as though she was outside of herself, watching, totally detached and unemotional as she recounted her trip home. Hammerstein hoped the jury would not misjudge its meaning.

It took her a good five minutes to arrive at the crucial moment. Then her entire demeanor changed. She grew pale, ashen, forcefully twisting Ivan's handkerchief with both hands. Her voice raised an octave higher, bordering on hysteria as she continued, "...and then I heard a loud noise. I went downstairs thinking Uncle Walter was awake."

She had a distant look in her eyes and seemed to have stopped breathing.

"And then what happened?" Hammerstein prompted, hoping she wouldn't break. "What did you see when you went downstairs?"

Anna Mae looked up and said calmly, "I don't remember what I saw. A few weeks ago Dr. Rhukov hypnotized me, trying to help me remember. I went into hysterics. They had to pin me down and give me a sedative. I didn't remember then and I still can't remember. I'm sorry."

She looked at the judge, at her lawyer, and finally at the jury. Then with heartfelt sincerity, she added, "I wish to God I could remember."

CHAPTER FIFTY-FOUR

Ivan's words echoed in Anna Mae's mind as she walked back to the witness stand: *Don't let him get to you. Just answer yes or no. Don't volunteer anything. His jawbone isn't connected to his brain.*

She hadn't been able to eat lunch and felt weak as she lowered herself into the heavy, straight-back chair. At the prosecution table, Tom Simon was making an elaborate display of organizing his notes. She looked across the room at Ivan. He gave her a thumbs up.

"Counselor," said Judge Wittier nodding at Tom Simon. "Your witness."

Simon remained in his seat, his notes now in a neat little stack. He looked at Anna Mae and asked, "How many times have you gone over it?"

"Excuse me?"

"That story...what was it? Oh yes—memory loss. How many times have you gone over that story?"

"You mean about the day Walter was...was..."

"Murdered," he said. "How many times?"

"Never," said Anna Mae.

Tom Simon stood up, straightened his tie, and walked to the other side of the prosecution's table. He leaned against it and folded his arms. "Do you mean to tell me that you never went over your story with your lawyer?"

"No."

"Excuse my ignorance," said Simon, unfolding his arms and stepping forward, "but it's customary for an attorney to review—go over—rehearse…his witness's testimony."

"Is that a question?" asked Anna Mae.

Laughter rippled through the courtroom, "Do you mean to tell me that you and Mr. Hammerstein did not go over what you were going to say when you took the witness stand?"

"No, we didn't," she said. "There wasn't time."

"Are you telling me that from October 14, 1970 until now, there wasn't time to rehearse an alibi?"

"Objection!"

"Sustained. Would you care to re-word that Simon?"

"How many times in the past four months have you gone over your testimony?"

"None."

Simon took a deep breath. "You did not go over your testimony with your lawyer?"

"You heard what she said," snapped the judge. "Now get on with it."

Simon walked around in a little circle shaking his head, then stopped to study Anna Mae with narrowed eyes. "In your testimony," he asked, "you said that when you were about three years old, your cousin Stanley was sleeping under the bed. Is that correct?"

"Yes."

"Did that little boy grow up to be the same young man who died from the pills you gave him?"

Anna Mae felt the blood rush to her face as Hammerstein flew out of his chair. In three seconds, both lawyers were standing before the bench. As the jurors murmured among themselves, Anna Mae's stomach twisted itself into a painful knot. Ivan was furious, but Anna Mae couldn't hear the combative whispers between the judge and the two lawyers. The heated discussion seemed to go on forever. Anna Mae jumped when a loud bang of the gavel marked its conclusion.

Ivan Hammerstein, somewhat appeased, took long strides back to the defense table, where he pushed back his unbuttoned jacket and stood with his hands on his hips. Tom Simon removed a handkerchief from his pocket and wiped his forehead. Clearly agitated, Simon said to the judge, "Your Honor, will you please ask Mr. Hammerstein to sit down."

Hammerstein didn't budge.

"Your Honor!" Simon repeated, "Tell him to sit down!"

"Sit down," said the judge.

Hammerstein took his time settling into his chair behind the defense table.

Judge Wittier gave lengthy instructions to the jury to completely disregard the prosecutor's last question. He then said to Simon, "Are you ready to proceed?"

Simon turned his back to Hammerstein's glare, cleared his throat, and looked at Anna Mae. "Did you hate your Uncle Walter?"

"No," said Anna Mae.

"Do you mean to tell me, after having testified that as far back as you can remember, the man you knew as your uncle was knocking you around…do you want this jury to believe that you liked him?"

Ivan had warned her, answer simply and honestly. Don't let Simon twist your words. "No, I didn't like him," she said. "But I didn't hate him either."

Shaking his head, Simon flaunted exasperation. When he was confident that the jury caught his demonstration, he said, "Let's go back to June 28, 1968. There was a funeral was there not?"

The pain returned to Anna Mae's stomach. Was that Stanley's funeral he was talking about? Is he going back there again?

"I repeat," said Simon an octave higher, "Do you remember the funeral of a family member back in sixty-eight?"

"Yes," said Anna Mae, wiping her sweaty hands on her dress. She looked hard at Tom Simon, studying him—his eyes—the way he moved. Something about the prosecutor was familiar. Or was it her imagination?

"And after the funeral," Simon continued, "can you tell the court what happened."

"My Uncle Walter—that was when I still thought he was my uncle. He was drunk again. He attacked the whole family."

"And who do you mean by the family?"

"Aunt Sarah, David and me."

"And what do you mean by attacked?"

"He beat us up. He broke David's arm."

"You remember that, do you?"

"Yes."

"Excuse me," said Simon glancing at the jury, "I didn't quite hear your answer. Did you say you remembered it?"

"Yes."

The prosecutor stood perfectly still, a hint of a smile at the corner of his lips, centering his attention on the now wary schoolteacher. "Didn't you tell this court that you never remembered when Walter was drunk and abusive?"

Hammerstein slid down in his seat and groaned.

"I didn't actually remember it..."

"But you just said you did. Isn't that what you said?"

"What I meant was..."

"You just said Walter attacked the whole family— that you remember it."

446

"It was two weeks..."

"And David had a broken arm?"

"Yes, but I..."

"And you remember that happening..."

"Yes. I mean no! It was two weeks..."

"And you remember Walter being arrested..."

"Objection!" Hammerstein jumped up and sprinted halfway to the bench. "He's badgering the witness! He won't let her finish a sentence."

"Sustained. Mr. Simon, let the witness answer the questions."

Ivan Hammerstein went back to his seat. He had warned her not to let Simon confuse her. Why had she said she remembered? Why didn't she think before she answered?

Simon stepped closer, blocking her view of the defense table. "You remembered that after the funeral Walter attacked his wife, Sarah, his son, David and you. Was he was arrested for that?"

"Objection. He's leading the witness!"

"Overruled," said the judge who looked over his half glasses at Anna Mae, the skepticism evident on his face.

Anna Mae breathed deeply. Then without a question having been asked she said in a loud voice, "It was two weeks later that I found out what happened that night."

"But that's not what you said two minutes ago," Simon snapped. "Will the court stenographer please go back and find Anna Mae's first answer to that same question."

The stenographer ran the roll of shorthand paper through her fingers until she found the question.

Witness: "He beat us up. David had a broken arm."

Prosecutor: "You remember that, do you?"

Witness: "Yes."

Tom Simon strolled over to the jury and leaned an elbow on the railing. Singling out the steelworker, he asked, "The defendant said she remembered, didn't she?"

"Objection!" said Hammerstein.

"Sustained," said Judge Wittier. "Mr. Simon, address your questions to the witness, not the jury."

Simon nodded and walked away from the jury box. "Now which is it?" he asked, his hands spread theatrically. "Miss McBride, do you, or do you not remember? Can you keep your story straight?"

"Objection!"

"Sustained."

"You're trying to confuse me," Anna Mae blurted out. "I didn't remember the actual beating. When I woke up two weeks later..."

"We don't need any explanation," interrupted Simon. "Just answer yes or no. Did you remember?"

"Objection!"

"Overruled."

"NO!"

"But you said you did!"

Anna Mae leaned forward in the witness chair. "I didn't know what Walter did that night until two weeks later. Two weeks! Two weeks went by before I learned what had happened. I didn't remember it! David and Aunt Sarah told me what happened."

Simon ignored her reply and quickly switched his focus. "Isn't it true that you hated your uncle—your father—Walter Lipinski. The victim in this brutal murder?"

Hammerstein was on his feet. "Objection. That question was already asked and answered."

"Sustained."

Anna Mae barely heard Ivan or the judge. Her breathing had become shallow. She felt smothered, pressured, backed into a corner, and the familiar fear of an oncoming panic attack. *Please God, don't let it happen. Not here. Not now.*

"Miss McBride," Simon asked, "Was there any affection at all between you and the victim—the man you believed to be your uncle?"

She tried to focus but couldn't see him clearly.

"Will you please answer my question?"

The scene before her was shifting. Simon's image was now in shadow. She saw a light behind Simon—a figure? *Is that you? From my dream? Are you here to help me?* The figure began to radiate. Anna Mae scanned the courtroom. No one else sees her! She breathed deeply and grew calmer.

The prosecutor's voice shattered the vision. "Miss McBride! Are you listening? Was there any..."

Anna Mae looked directly into Tom Simon's eyes. But she didn't reply.

He quickly switched his line of questioning. "Do you remember going to your mother's house last October 14th?"

"Yes."

"Do you remember your mother telling you that Walter Lipinski was your father?"

"Yes."

"You were enraged, weren't you?"

"No."

"You weren't? Were you happy to hear that Walter was your father?"

"No."

"Of course you weren't happy. You were furious, weren't you?"

"No. I wasn't furious."

"But didn't discovering that the man who had been abusing you since you were a toddler—didn't that make you so furious that you walked out without even saying goodbye?"

"No, I..."

"You didn't walk out?"

"I was not! I was..."

"Weren't you so preoccupied with what you were going to do that you forgot to pay your bus fare?"

"Yes. But..."

"Didn't the bus driver have to call..."

"Objection! Badgering!"

"Sustained."

Anna Mae watched Simon walk back and forth in increasingly agitated strides, stopping finally with his back to the jury. "After you learned that Walter was your father, weren't you so immersed in planning your revenge that you failed to hear your friend, Jeremiah, call you from across a very narrow street? Isn't that true?"

"No."

"Oh? You heard him? You heard Jeremiah, or JD as you call him. Aare you saying you did hear him?"

"No, I didn't hear him, but it wasn't because..."

"You were upset, weren't you?"

"Yes."

"Isn't it true that you were so upset by what you just learned that you didn't even hear..."

"Objection!" Hammerstein was on his feet. "She answered the question!" He turned to Simon, "Damn you! Quit badgering my client."

"The objection is sustained," said Judge Wittier. "However, this is my courtroom and if a litigant is to be reprimanded, I'll be the one to do it. Mr. Simon, stop badgering the witness."

Tom Simon stepped closer to Anna Mae, unbuttoned his jacket, put his hands into his pockets, and rocked back on his heels. In a low, sinister voice, he said, "Last October 14th, after you left your mother's house, just what did you intend to do when you got home?"

"I don't know," said Anna Mae, feeling her breathing quicken.

"You planned to go home and kill Walter, didn't you?"

"Objection! Move to strike!"

"Overruled."

"Isn't it true that in the time it took you to get from your mother's house in Pittsburgh, to your own house in the valley...isn't it true that you made up your mind that you would get the ax from the shed and go after your uncle? And weren't you depending on him being so drunk you could..."

"Objection! Your Honor," shouted Hammerstein, "The prosecutor's writing his own scenario."

"Sustained," bellowed the Judge to a bang of his gavel. "Be careful, counselor."

"Can I finish the question?"

"No!"

Simon, eyes glinting with malice said, "You hated Walter Lipinski enough to kill him, didn't you?"

"No," she said. The viciousness in Simon's voice caused Anna Mae to shudder.

"Where did you hide the ax?" he hissed.

Anna Mae frowned and leaned forward in the witness chair. *That voice. There's something about that voice!*

"Where did you hide the ax?" he repeated.

She had heard it before—that voice. She knew that voice. And now she remembered where she had heard it.

I'll get you! If it takes me the rest of my life, bitch! I'll get you!

"Answer the question!" Simon demanded. "Where is the ax?"

Suddenly her memory broke open and the whole thing came flooding back. Anna Mae's heart was pounding. "I didn't kill Walter."

"Didn't you go to the kitchen intending to..."

"I only wanted to talk to him."

"Is that why your clothes were covered with blood? Because you were talking to him?"

The courtroom was becoming a blur and Anna Mae's hands were growing numb. "I didn't kill Walter," she repeated.

"Where's the ax now, Anna Mae?"

"I saw it..."

"You saw the ax?"

"Yes."

Simon moved closer, glowering at his witness. "You lied to the police, didn't you?"

"I didn't lie to anybody."

"Didn't you tell the police that you didn't remember what you did?"

"I didn't do anything," she said slowly rising to her feet. "But you!" she pointed an accusing finger into the prosecutor's face. "Why didn't you come home and take care of your father?"

"Excuse me?"

"George!" she seethed. "George Siminoski! If you had only come home and taken care of your father. If you hadn't left him alone and in misery. He needed you. But no! All you cared about was the money he got from the accident. The mill—that ladle—it wasn't an accident, George. Walter did it! Walter rigged that ladle so it poured off-center. And somehow your father found out. My God—that pitiful old man!"

From a distance, Anna Mae heard the judge's admonishments, but the words continued to tumble from her lips.

"Your father killed him, George! That poor, damaged, lonely, crazed old man! He had the ax, George. Walter was already on the floor when I got there. Blood everywhere! I heard what your father was saying. 'You! It was you!' your father kept repeating..."

Dr. Rhukov dashed to the front of the courtroom. Angelo leaped over the rail almost knocking Ivan over.

"...your father was out of his mind, crazy..."

The bailiff grabbed Angelo by the arm, pulling him back to the defense table. Ivan just stood there, stunned.

"...I saw him hitting Walter with the ax. It was your father, George! I remember! I saw it and I remember!"

Anna Mae ignored the turmoil in the courtroom and Judge Wittier banged the gavel.

"Go home, George!" she yelled. "Go home and talk to your father! He'll tell you where the ax is. He'll tell you why he killed Walter. Ask him to tell you how my uncle—how my father—how Walter Lipinski rigged that ladle of hot steel because he wanted your father's job. Go home and ask him, George. He'll tell you where to find the ax."

Tom Simon's face was white. He stumbled backward, collided with the prosecution table then collapsed into his chair.

The courtroom was in a frenzy. Angelo and Ivan guided a trembling Anna Mae to the defense table. Dr. Rhukov took her hand as she sat down beside him. "God bless you," he said over the chaos, "You did it!"

"Order! This courtroom is called to order! Sit down!" Judge Wittier addressed no one in particular and whacked his gavel one final time. "This court will take a one hour recess."

The bailiff led the jury out, but only a few spectators left the courtroom. JD leaned over the railing. "I was right, wasn't I? A nose job, a weight loss, contacts, that terrible wig, the son-of-a-bitch almost pulled it off."

"Dr. Rhukov," said Anna Mae as tears ran down her face, "I remembered!" She said it over and over and the doctor kept nodding, "Yes, yes, yes! You remembered. Do you know what this means? You will get better now."

She looked up at Joey Barn's whose unrestrained joy made her smile. "Will you get out of jail? Will you? Huh?"

A woman's voice came from behind her. "You didn't do it! My God! I didn't believe you. I am so sorry."

Anna Mae turned and saw Sarah standing on the other side of the rail. Her face was ashen and streaked with tears. Anna Mae stood up, reached over the railing and pulled her aunt into an embrace. Sarah wept in Anna Mae's arms. "It's over now," said Anna Mae. "The nightmare is over."

A few feet away Ivan Hammerstein watched the happy chaos. Then he turned to look at Tom Simon who was standing by the defense table dazed and disorientated. Hesitantly, Ivan stepped closer. Simon looked up; perspiration ran down his face, his tie was undone and his jacket hung lopsided from his shoulders. He was holding his briefcase with papers sticking out haphazardly.

Thomas G. Simon—George Thomas Siminoski, was no longer the pompous, self-serving man he had been twenty minutes before. He was utterly destroyed.

Defense Attorney Ivan Hammerstein walked over to State Prosecutor Tom Simon and gently led him by the elbow out of the courtroom.

CHAPTER FIFTY-FIVE

February 14, 1971
Sunday

The icy winter sun streamed through Anna Mae's bedroom window, creating golden highlights in her hair as it spilled over the pillow. The barely perceptible rise and fall of the flowered comforter confirmed the soundness of her slumber.

"I bet she sleeps for five days," said David peeking into the room.

Sarah had to look up at David for he had grown so tall. "Poor thing," she said, stepping into the room and tucking the comforter around her niece. "How could I have..."

"Forget it, Mom," David said gently. "It's over. She doesn't blame you."

David followed his mother downstairs to the kitchen. A breakfast of bacon, eggs, toast, and pancakes sat untouched and cooling on the stove. "You don't care if I eat some of this, do you?" said David, heaping the food onto a plate.

Sarah smiled at her son. "May as well. But when you're finished, get some of those fresh oranges out of the refrigerator and squeeze them. Anna Mae loves fresh squeezed orange juice."

Sarah was placing the food into the oven to keep warm when the doorbell rang. Moments later, out in the foyer, Angelo removed his snowy shoes and walked into the kitchen. He waved the Sunday newspaper. "She made the front page," he said draping his heavy woolen jacket over the back of a kitchen chair and spreading the paper on top of David's breakfast.

David stuck his head under the newspaper and kept eating.

"McBride is Innocent," Angelo read aloud. "On Friday, in Judge Wittier's courtroom, Anna Mae McBride, in an explosion of memory, identified the man who bludgeoned Walter Lipinski to death..."

Sarah poured Angelo a mug of steaming coffee then sat at the table to listen.

"...the police found Dobie Siminoski at home. The housekeeper, Maria Tamero said Mr. Siminoski had been deeply depressed for months. and that she had tried to get him to see a doctor but he had refused. When the police told Siminoski he was under arrest for murder, he submitted without protest.

"Cooperating fully, Dobie Siminoski led the arresting officers to the shed where they retrieved the murder weapon. The ax was coated with dried blood. Officer Smith told the reporters that Siminoski asked what had taken them so long to arrest him. He appeared to have been waiting for them.

"Maria Tamero said that Dobie had not watched television since his wife died in August of 1970. She said that she believed if Mr. Siminoski had known Anna Mae McBride was on trial for the Lipinski murder, he would have come forward. Siminoski did not appear to realize the amount of time that had elapsed between the murder and his arrest.

"It was later discovered..."

Anna Mae appeared in the doorway and Angelo stopped reading. With her eyes puffy from sleep, and her long hair hanging in tangles, she clutched her pink chenille robe together at the neck. "What time is it?"

Angelo reached out, pulled her onto his lap and happily locked both arms around her. "Time for you to get up, sleepy head."

She kissed his forehead. "Please! Put that newspaper away. I don't want to hear another word about that trial. I just want to be home."

Angelo removed the paper from David's head, folded it and placed it under his chair.

With a gust of frigid air, Olga Nikovich burst through the back door. "Oh! Mine Annie! Mine Annie is home!" she squealed. "Let me look at you!" She shrugged out of a coat that was made for Siberian winters, colliding with David's chair in the process. David leaned over to recover a forkful of pancakes from the floor. The doorbell rang again.

"Good grief!" said Sarah heading down the hallway. "It's not even eleven o'clock yet!"

The press reporter, Robert McCarthy, stamped his snowy feet on the foyer floor and blew into his hands to warm them. Sarah hung his wet coat on the banister. "Don't worry about your feet. It's only cold water. The rug will dry."

Anna Mae suddenly felt self-conscious. All these people and here she is in her bathrobe and her hair, looking like a Halloween wig. She slid from Angelo's lap, hurried by McCarthy and ran up the second floor steps. When she reached the top landing, she stopped to listen to the reporter: "Angelo's mother found a pile of papers in Dobie's room. They were old letters and stuff, dating back to the winter of sixty-one. Apparently, shortly after the accident, the men at the mill approached Irene with their suspicions that the tipped ladle was not an accident. They were convinced that Walter Lipinski had done something to cause it. There was a written description of how they thought Walter had rigged the ladle and a list of signatures—fellow steelworkers who wanted to dispute the expert's findings and formally accuse Walter. But they would need Dobie's cooperation."

Anna Mae was now sitting on the top step listening intently.

"In an effort to protect her husband from further trauma, Irene Siminoski had asked the mill workers not to pursue their suspicions. Dobie was still going through an agonizing healing process. But almost worse than that was the severe emotional pain. All he had to look forward to were months of rehabilitation and permanent scars. Irene felt it would serve no good purpose for her husband to learn that Walter, who Dobie considered a friend, deliberately rigged that ladle intending to hurt him, simply because he was next in line for that job. So she asked the mill workers not to pursue it and hid the papers.

"After his wife died, it took Dobie months to gather up the courage to go through her things. That was when he discovered the pile of papers that revealed everything. Dobie remembered that he had seen Walter just before the accident. And Walter was definitely at the wrong place at the wrong time. Dobie was convinced that it was Walter Lipinski who ruined his life. Already unstable, that drove Dobie right over the edge."

Not wanting to hear more, Anna Mae went to her room. She dressed slowly, pinning her jeans that were an inch too big at the waist. Standing in front of the mirror, she pulled a baggy gray sweat shirt over her head. The jail shampoo had dried her hair so badly she could hardly comb through the knots. When her hair was finally tangle free, she applied a pale shade of pink lipstick.

She stood staring into the mirror. She was different now—a different person completely. Dr. Rhukov said that her memory returning on the witness stand was a giant step toward her recovery. Now, with no effort at all, she could recall the tragic events of the day Walter was murdered. But, she pushed them out of her mind. There would be plenty time for that when she went back to therapy.

The long, lonely howl of a train whistled echoed across the valley. She walked over to the window and opened it to let in a cold breeze. She gazed into the distance, at the silent, snow covered mills. The sky was icy clear, with no ugly black pollution spewing out of the smokestacks that stood like silent sentries across the horizon. Corporate greed and foreign imports had finally wiped out the heart blood of the valley's steel industry. Her eyes traveled to the river beyond. She smiled. Her angels were, again, casting sparkles over the water.

"Anna Mae! Annie!" David called from the bottom of the stairs. "Are you okay?"

"I'll be right down," she said.

"You better hurry," yelled Angelo from the kitchen. "He's drinking your orange juice!"

She heard someone climbing the steps. Then Sarah was standing in the doorway. Anna Mae walked over and put her arms around Sarah. They stood there holding each other for a moment, and then together they turned and went downstairs.

Other books by Mary Ann:

Into the Mind of Mary Ann Gouze

Made in the USA
Middletown, DE
07 February 2017